KISSING THE DRAGON

He stroked her lips open with his thumb. "I have a boon or two of my own I'd like ye to agree upon before I take ye as my lady wife."

Akira remained compliant.

"Ye will allow me to kiss ye every morn . . ." He kissed her bottom lip. "And every eve . . ." He kissed her top lip. "And anytime I feel the need to press your sweet lips to mine." With this request, he tilted his head and flicked his tongue in her mouth. She jerked, but he held her firmly until she returned his kiss with equal abandon.

He forced himself away, but lingered on the pulse in her neck still beating wildly against his lips. "Will ye agree to my conditions as I have agreed to yours?" he whispered in her ear, waiting for her to catch her breath.

"'Tis all ye ask of me?"

"For the nonce."

"Do I have to return your kisses?"

"Aye." Calin nearly laughed.

"I'll do my best to honor your boon, m'laird . . ."

Books by Kimberly Killion

HER ONE DESIRE

HIGHLAND DRAGON

Published by Kensington Publishing Corporation

HIGHLAND DRAGON

KIMBERLY KILLION

ZEBRA BOOKS
Kensington Publishing Corp.
http://www.kensingtonbooks.com

ZEBRA BOOKS are published by

Kensington Publishing Corp.
119 West 40th Street
New York, NY 10018

All Kensington titles, imprints, and distributed lines are available at special quantity discounts for bulk purchases for sales promotion, premiums, fund-raising, educational, or institutional use.

Special book excerpts or customized printings can also be created to fit specific needs. For details, write or phone the office of the Kensington Special Sales Manager: Attn. Special Sales Department. Kensington Publishing Corp., 119 West 40th Street, New York, NY 10018. Phone: 1-800-221-2647.

Zebra and the Z logo Reg. U.S. Pat. & TM Off.

ISBN-13: 978-1-4201-0441-7
ISBN-10: 1-4201-0441-1

First Printing: October 2009
10 9 8 7 6 5 4 3 2

Printed in the United States of America

For Myah and Hayden:

Dream big,
aspire to greatness,
and make good decisions

Acknowledgments

I would like to extend special thanks to some of the people who have walked beside me on my writing journey:

To my family, for eating cereal for supper and wearing mismatched socks. Your sacrifices allowed me the chance to follow a dream.

To Mom and Dad, for your fortitude. Thank you for always encouraging me to be creative even when that creativity came in the form of striped eye shadow.

To my sister, Jill, for inspiring me to be strong, determined, and rebellious.

To Sug, for being my first reader, and Wanda, for recognizing my sense of artistry early on. Through your example, you both have taught me the importance of family.

To my friend, Jeff, for being the first man to read my story and for taking care of me when my mind is elsewhere. Emily is a lucky woman.

To the women of MORWA, for the camaraderie and unwavering support. I will treasure the friendships forever.

To the readers, remember to fall in love every day.

And finally, thank you to Hilary Sares, for taking a chance on me. You will be greatly missed.

Prologue

Hidden behind a false panel, ten-year-old Calin MacLeod covered his ears with sweaty palms. The screams echoing throughout Brycen Castle were loud enough to loosen his teeth.

Lena Kinnon cried for mercy with every gut-wrenching contraction, but didn't receive the slightest morsel of compassion from the many men present. Her position held no dignity, sprawled atop the council table like a sacrificial lamb. The wool of her soiled sark draped between her raised knees and provided her little privacy. No one wiped her brow or offered soothing words of comfort.

A woman was supposed to suffer during childbirth to pay for the sins of Eve. Even at his young age, Calin knew the laws of the church. He also knew Lena had already suffered more than any woman in Clan Kinnon. The bruises speckling her pale skin were evidence of the constant torture she endured at the hands of her ruthless husband.

The sliver of space between the wooden planks where Calin hid was no wider than the trunk of a sapling, but provided a view of Da, Laird MacLeod, who stood against a stone pilaster opposite Laird Kinnon. Da's dark hair had grayed at the temples over the recent months, and his face sagged in weariness, but his rigid stance displayed his contained rage. With his eyes narrowed, Da stroked the golden bull's head engraved into the signet ring he wore and glared at his enemy.

Two pairs of MacLeod warriors flanked each side of Da, while four Kinnon warriors surrounded Laird Baen Kinnon. All were unarmed as was previously agreed upon by both lairds.

"Ye keep screamin', wife. It'll cleanse your black English soul." Laird Kinnon paced the council chamber, a sneer twisting his pitted face.

Calin hated the chieftain of his neighboring clan as much as Da did. Laird Kinnon was a cold-hearted demon. Anyone who would beat his lady wife during her childbearing time walked upon this earth with the devil's black blood flowing through his veins.

"Ye bear me another bitch and it will be your last."

"Please, Baen, have ye no mercy? Send for the midwife, please." Lena gripped the sides of her belly and arched her back.

Laird Kinnon slapped her across the face with an open palm. Sweat sprayed over the tabletop. "Still your tongue, wife, or I'll cut it out." He spread his arms wide, gesturing to the many warriors present. "There be plenty o' eager hands awaitin' to catch my male bairn as soon as ye free him from your spoiled womb."

Calin bit his tongue to avoid cursing the man as venomously as Da always did. Calin had lived his whole life without a mam to kiss his cheek or offer him praise. Over the past few months, Lena had been like a mother to him. She was kind and gentle and Laird Kinnon should burn in the deepest pit of Hell for the way he abused his lady wife. Calin didn't have to be an aged warrior to know this was wrong. Lena's child was nothing more to Laird Kinnon than a binding contract.

A contract that affected Calin's future. Which was precisely why he'd disobeyed Da's direct order not to follow him to the Kinnon keep when word of Lena's lying-in arrived. If Lena bore a daughter, the babe would become his betrothed.

Calin and his friend, Kendrick Neish of Clan Kinnon, had discovered the secluded compartment just two months past after stumbling into the pitch-black caverns beneath the castle. Since then, they had become privy to every council meeting between their clans. They knew of war and how the English wanted to reign over Scotland. Both had heard the gruesome tales of entire villages being slaughtered. Neither he nor Kendrick wanted their clans to suffer such a fate. Calin knew they were supposed to be enemies, but they wanted the same thing—an alliance.

For five hours, Calin had hugged his twisted limbs in the narrow space while Lena labored in the corner. His arse tingled, and his toes had gone numb hours before inside his leather brogues. The dank odor of moldy floor rushes drifted into his hiding place. A prayer floated into his ear.

"*Fàilte dhut a Mhoire, tha thu lan de na gràsan . . .*" In the Gaelic tongue, Father Harrald prayed to the Blessed Mother while he paced the edge of the chamber. The granite beads of his rosary clattered with his every movement. The young priest had been summoned to perform the baptism or to administer Last Rites in the event this child didn't survive—as Lena's previous three babes had not.

Lena pushed and Calin sucked in air.

He exhaled when she did. Her whole body convulsed, his shivered. Wet ropes of black hair clung to her face and neck. Propped on her elbows, her head fell back. Her mouth opened, and she screamed in agony.

One of the warriors caught the babe just as it slid from Lena's body.

Calin held his breath awaiting the outcome.

"A lass, Laird Kinnon," the old man announced grimly while he held the babe by the ankles and slapped her rump. He then laid her atop Lena's quivering abdomen.

Lena pulled the crying child to her breast and stroked her newborn skin. Relief washed over her face and tears spilled over her cheeks when she smiled at Da. All would be well now.

"Seal off the hall and bring me the other child." The cord still attached his infant daughter to his wife when Laird Kinnon commanded his seneschal. Dark eyes blazed with contempt as he stared directly at Da. "Ye will ne'er hold claim to my land. Nor will ye e'er touch my wife again."

"I have ne'er wanted your land." Da stepped closer to Lena.

"But ye dinnae deny touching my wife."

Da glanced at Lena.

A dozen broad-shouldered men materialized from the darkened recesses of Brycen Castle. Their weapons flickered beneath golden wall torches. A raw-boned nursemaid, escorted by another warrior, entered the chamber, her fear evident in sunken wide eyes. In her arms, she held another babe swaddled in striped wool, its fists swatted the air. With trembling hands, she placed the babe in the crook of Laird Kinnon's arm.

Confused, Calin studied the exchange. Laird Kinnon had agreed to unite their clans if Lena bore a daughter.

Laird Kinnon turned to his warriors. "Send their miserable souls to the devil. All of them." His tone was devoid of mercy. Of compassion. Of any emotion except contempt.

He stepped out of the keep onto the stone rampart. "I have a son!" he shouted.

The villagers of Dalkirth roared their approval while the words echoed in Calin's ears.

Nay! 'Tis a lie! He gawked in horror as the shadowed knights charged his clansmen. Da's devoted seneschal used a flaming pitch-pine torch to defend the attack. His efforts were futile. With one swing of a halberd, a Kinnon warrior beheaded him. Another fiend slashed one of the MacLeod warriors from gullet to navel. Fists clutched enemy plaid as he fell to his knees.

Calin's heart tripped. His hands flattened against the panel. His nose pressed into the crack. *Oh saints, help them!*

The saints could no more help his kinsmen than the bits of wood they used as shield and sword. The Kinnon warriors buried the steel of their weapons into the MacLeods' flesh, spreading pools of dark blood over their crossbarred plaids. Slaughtered before his eyes were Da's most loyal kinsmen. Calin's stomach convulsed and saliva grew thick in his mouth. He wanted to run and hide his eyes from the nightmare.

Standing amid the four fallen men, Da was trapped. His hand slid to the empty scabbard at his hip. There was no weapon. No claymore to defend himself against this preplanned attack. Six Kinnons surrounded Da. He turned toward Lena.

Calin froze. Unshed tears scalded his eyes. *Run, Da!* he screamed in his head, but instead, Da fell upon Lena. He brushed the tears from her cheeks then pressed his lips to hers.

A single warrior cast a shadow over Da like a demon cloaked in black mist. Leather-clad hands gripped the hilt of a battle-axe and raised the lethal weapon over his head. In one thrust, he buried the steel between Da's shoulders.

Lena screamed as his body slid off her and crumpled to the floor.

Calin choked on the knot in his throat as the bloody massacre branded an image in his mind. His pulse pounded in his neck, making his cries hard to swallow. Terrified they would find him, he splayed his violently shaking fingers over his eyes, all the while chastising himself for cowardice. His world went black, along with his mind, his heart, his soul.

The dying groans of suffering drummed through his ears,

but the scream slicing through the air brought sight back to his eyes.

Lena.

Shame flooded Calin as he watched the same warrior unsheathe a black dirk from his stocking. He held Lena's chin while he slashed the sharp *sgian dubh* across her throat. With her infant daughter nuzzling at her breast, Lena's head fell to the side, giving Calin one last look into crystal-blue eyes before the terror in her face vanished along with her spirit.

The warrior's leathered hand hovered over the nape of the babe. His other hand held the weapon that would end her short life. The coppery taste of blood pooled on Calin's tongue from where he bit the inside of his cheek.

Father Harrald dropped to his knees at the warrior's feet. "Save your soul and cease. Please, cease. I beg of ye. The others had been baptized. She must be baptized."

The Kinnon warrior hoisted the priest up by the hood of his habit and pointed his dirk at one of the other warriors. "Confess." The clansmen gave their confessions one by one, binding Father Harrald to clerical secrecy. After the last warrior reconciled his sins, he shoved the priest toward Lena. "Ye may proceed with the rites. Someone will return to collect the babe."

The men vanished into the shadows from whence they came.

The violent turn of events had Calin near to retching. He gripped his churning gut with clenched fingers and stared at the babe still nestled atop her dead mother's bosom—daughter to the demon who murdered his father, but also his betrothed. He didn't know whether to hate her or protect her. He had nary a doubt her brief life would tragically end in much the same way as Lena's first three daughters.

The fire's reflection flickered off the blade Father Harrald used to sever the cord binding the babe to her mother. The priest washed the remnants of birth from her skin and laid her in a pile of linens next to Lena. His voice quavered with the administration of blessed sacraments. "*An tAthair, An Mac, An Spiorad Naomh.*" Signing the cross over the babe, he blew breath upon her, and baptized her with holy oils.

Calin crawled from his hiding place, wiping the wetness from his cheeks. He raked the patch of brown hair falling loosely over his brow, while stepping over the blood and carnage. Unable to tear his gaze from Da's body, he let the sickly sweet stench of death fill his nostrils and revive his spirit with the promise of vengeance. The metallic acid thickened in his throat, but he swallowed his fear, his grief, his newfound hate. He had but one purpose now—avenge his father's death. And to do so, he needed the babe.

Father Harrald flinched. "Young Calin, ye must not be here."

Ignoring the priest, Calin knelt at Da's side. He brushed a lock of graying hair from Da's damp brow and willed him to stand, but his skin paled as a pool of blood welled beneath him. Calin bent to his ear. "Blood of my blood. I'll not fail ye, Da. I vow it."

Father Harrald's hand rested on Calin's shoulder. "They'll murder ye, just as sure as they will the babe. Ye must go."

"Father Harrald, ye will see that Da and these men are returned to MacLeod soil. Get word to Uncle Kerk. Tell him I am weel, and I'll be home soon." Calin wished his voice didn't falter. He needed to be a man, a warrior. He swallowed hard then pulled the signet ring from Da's limp hand and set the engraved crest against a glowing ember in the hearth.

Calin couldn't meet the priest's eyes. "An eye for an eye. She's the key to the alliance, and she belongs to me." He spoke with defiance as he handled the squirming babe. He carried her to the hearth and set her atop a wooden basin. Using a strip of heavy wool to retrieve the signet ring from a hot coal, he rolled her onto her side and branded her bottom with the

MacLeod crest. She let out a shrill scream, followed by shuddering sobs. He wrapped the babe in linens, then secured her in Lena's striped *arisaid*, fastening the wool with her family brooch. He held her close and attempted to coo her into submission. One day he would tell her about her mam and how kind Lena had been to him.

So many questions stirred in Calin's troubled mind, but one in particular needed answering. "I know ye heard Da's confession a sennight past. I also know ye are bound by the seal o' the confessional, so I'll understand if ye cannae answer my question."

"What's your question, my son?" Father Harrald scanned the entrance to the chamber.

"Da loved Lena." Calin paused with his gaze fixed on the newborn bundle. "Is this babe of my own blood?"

"Nay. Lena was swollen with her fourth child before she ever met your da. Rest assured, your young bride is not your sister. Now ye must go, quickly."

Retrieving a torch from a wall bracket, Calin reentered the nook. The babe whimpered against his chest. A tiny hand swatted his chin. She was warm and smelled of innocence. He glanced over his shoulder at Da's body, his eyes lowered. He should have done something. At least tried to stop them. He was weak, spineless. A coward.

Calin's eyes found Father Harrald, his skin gray with worry. "What will ye tell them when they return for the babe?"

"I'll tell them a warrior took her. 'Twill not be a lie."

Chapter One

August 1502

How can Hell be so cold?

Akira Neish inhaled gulps of icy air as she struggled to keep pace with the guard's strides. She clutched the rope binding her to the warrior in an effort to ease the pain pulsing around her bruised wrists. As she stumbled down a stone stairwell behind him, she prayed her weak legs wouldn't collapse beneath her. She felt certain this passageway must lead straight to Satan's realm.

They reached the end of the tunnel where a single pitch-pine torch illuminated a door. The rock walls glistened with seepage, and the smell of soot burned the flesh in her throat.

Her guard stopped abruptly. Akira caught herself just before she might have crashed into his back. The screech of scraping iron sent a jolt of dread up her spine as he slid the crossbar to release the door. Akira swallowed hard, fearing the fate that awaited her on the other side. The warrior ducked beneath the doorjamb and pulled her into a room lit by firelight.

Whispers flitted through the air.

Akira's breath hitched when she saw the women. They were

everywhere—old and young, chained to the floor, huddled in groups. Their haunted eyes glowed in the torchlight, and all wore yellow shifts, thin enough to see through. Who were they? What was this place?

Before she could study them further, the guard roughly hauled her up beside him. Her black hair webbed over her face with the abrupt movement.

He bent to her ear. "Think ye the MacLeods who brought ye here are evil? Wait til ye meet the MacLeods of the outer isles." He licked her cheek. His vile odor made bile rise in her throat, but she refused to let him see her fear. His dark brows rose and his lips curled into an ugly snarl. "Now 'tis time ye pay for kicking me in the bollocks, lass."

Placing his booted foot atop a barrel, he forced her to bend over his leg. She had to stand on her toes to lessen the crushing of her ribs against his thigh. His fingers wrapped around the back of her neck, holding her in place. Akira knew what was about to happen and braced herself for the humiliation.

"I advise all o' ye to keep a distance from her. She's a witch," he hollered to the captives. The mockery in his voice brought familiar tears to her eyes. She'd been dragged across the outer isles behind her captor's foul-smelling horses only to be tormented by her secret.

Cold air crept up her thighs as he raised the skirt of her kirtle, exposing the mark on her backside for all to see. The devil's mark. Gasps echoed through the cavern, warning Akira she would find no pity here, nor friends or allies.

Shame heated her skin, and an age-old anger erupted within her just as it had when the children of her clan had cast their stones and taunts. She refused to be displayed like an animal, regardless of what it might cost her. She pulled back, opened her mouth wide, and bit the heathen's thigh so hard her jaw pinched.

"Ach! Ye bitch!" Grabbing a fistful of her hair, he jerked

her upright. The tip of his dagger made a painful dent in the base of her throat. "Fortunate for ye, 'tis against the code to mark the captives."

He led her toward the darkest nook in the cavern. Her struggles were futile against his warrior strength. He clasped an iron shackle to her ankle and chained her to a spike in the stone floor, then held her chin between his filthy fingers. "Mayhap I'll return to dress ye instead of Auld Nattie."

He was vermin. A blood-sucking leech. She sorely wanted to bite him again or, better yet, gut him with his own dagger, but he turned on his heel and swaggered to the door. The bar clanked, and his fading footsteps left her in welcomed silence.

Her body ached from days of being bound, and the stone floor offered no comfort. She cupped her cold hands to her mouth and blew into her palms. Akira didn't have to scan the cavern to feel the women's accusations. This wasn't the first time she'd been treated like a leper, nor would it be the last, she suspected.

Why was this happening to her? Why had the MacLeods taken her from her clan's homelands? She bowed her head and prayed Kendrick would come to her aid. But in the three days it took her and her captors to make the journey, she hadn't once seen any sign of her brother. Akira's only solace was that the men from her neighboring clan hadn't delivered her sister into the hands of these demons. Isobel would have never survived the journey across MacLeod soil.

Kendrick would come. He had to.

Calin studied his childhood friend's size from the thick foliage of late summer. The wee runt grew up brawny.

It would take a man of great force to take Kendrick Neish down—over six feet of raw muscle covered with tufts of dark red hair. Kendrick outweighed him by two stone as a lad, but Calin now matched his height and weight. He could take him.

Calin emerged and cinched a forearm around his old friend's bearded neck.

Kendrick jerked, but quickly checked his initial shock and clutched his hands behind Calin's head. Blue sky and green pine branches filled Calin's vision as he found himself somersaulted over Kendrick's back and into the thin trunk of a birch tree. It snapped. At least he won the battle against the tree, but he'd sorely misjudged his old friend's strength.

He jumped to his feet and swiveled. Kendrick's attention diverted to his sisters frolicking beneath the pelting sprays of a thunderous waterfall. As soon as Kendrick conceded defeat, Calin would figure out which one of the lassies was his bride.

He drove a clenched fist into Kendrick's gut, doubling him over with a grunt. Before Calin could act again, his feet were hauled out from under him, sending him sprawling to the ground on his backside. The air whooshed from his lungs. His eyes flew open in time to see Kendrick lunge for him. Calin dodged, rolled over the forest debris and regained his position. Just once, he wanted to win a brawl against Kendrick. But Calin battled in play and his bride's brother fought to protect his sisters. According to her missives, there were six sisters in all.

Kendrick's color turned red, his nostrils flared, and his pose took on the stance of an angered warrior. Calin suspected he would lose this battle just as Kendrick dove at him. Calin held one hand out as a shield, but Kendrick twisted that arm behind him. Within a blink, Kendrick cradled Calin's head in the crook of his arm, constricting the air in his throat.

"Ye be on Kinnon soil, mon, and it would take verra little to snap your wee neck between my brawny arms."

His comment was delivered with such force Calin couldn't help but laugh at the man.

Kendrick leaned to the side to study him. "Are ye addlebrained, mon? Mayhap a wee bit light in the head?" Kendrick released him with a forceful shove into a bed of prickly pine needles.

From a squatting position, Calin offered him a crooked, ornery grin. "Ye wound me, Kendrick. Ye'd forget the face of an auld friend?"

"I'll rot in Hell afore I claim a mon who attacks me from behind as a friend." Kendrick's burr lifted with his agitation while his arms crossed stubbornly over his broad chest.

Brushing pine needles from his bare thighs, Calin stood, wrinkled his nose, and sniffed the air in jest. "Ye reek like two-day-old haggis, but not rotten yet."

Kendrick eyed him warily. His jaw tilted.

Calin couldn't stop the smug grin from lifting his lips while he waited for Kendrick to recognize him. After all, a decade had passed since last they'd seen each other.

Only seconds later, Kendrick pummeled him to the ground in a roar of merriment. "Ye randy, pigheaded, arrogant, wee *bastaird*, ye, Calin MacLeod."

Calin wrestled with the giant in a heap of fists and feet. He took three blows. One to his nose, the other two connected with his ribs. Eight and twenty was too old for such frivolous horseplay, especially on his wedding day.

Kendrick pinned him. "Ye concede, mon?" he asked an instant before Calin straddled him.

"Nay. 'Tis my turn to win."

But Kendrick didn't accept defeat. They rolled in a tangle of limbs, both bleeding from the nose, knuckles maimed and raw, and bare knees in much the same state. Sprawled on his back, Calin clutched his bruised ribs, now suffering from his laughter.

"'Tis been too long, MacLeod," Kendrick said with a bit of resentment in his voice. "Far too long."

"I could've gone another decade without seeing your ugly

puss." Flashing a smile, Calin struggled to his feet then extended a hand to his friend.

"'Tis time?" Kendrick asked.

"Aye. I met with the Donalds on the Sabbath. They're in agreement. Laird Kinnon's throng of thieving warriors has stolen the last of my chattel. Laird Kinnon has made many enemies over the years. No one will aid him in protecting these borders if the English invade our coastal waters."

"Then we gather the Isle's council and Laird Kinnon will reign nay more. And Clan Kinnon will be cleansed of his bloodied hands. I'll send a spit-boy to ride with the torch at twilight and gather the rebels. When do ye wish to meet?"

"Soon, Kendrick. Soon your laird will pay for his crimes against both of us." Calin clapped Kendrick on the back, grateful he remained dedicated to their cause. So many years had passed since they'd stumbled into each other in the pitch-black caverns beneath Brycen Castle. They'd bonded in secrecy knowing they were supposed to be enemies, but they had wanted the same thing—an alliance.

Pulling back a pine branch, Calin peeked at the bevy of beauties skipping around the waterfall. In their gaiety, they twirled and danced, dragging the hems of their kirtles through the water. He couldn't contain his enthusiasm. Eighteen years had passed since he'd entrusted Kendrick with his wee bride, and by dusk he had every intention of taking the lass back to Cànwyck Castle and making her his wife. He prayed he could look upon her face and just see a woman, and not the daughter of the man who murdered his father. Regardless of how he saw her, he had a vow to fulfill and a clan to protect.

A clan that was currently preparing for his wedding.

When he'd left MacLeod land earlier today, the bailey was abuzz. The clan's matrons spent early morning filling the chapel with fresh-cut bluebells, yellow saxifrage, and wild primroses. MacLeods had been trickling in for two days to attend the festivities. A handful of brutes had been warming whisky and ogling the village maidens. An onslaught of babes was sure to arrive in nine months, and he hoped one might belong to him and his new bride.

Haunches of wild boar, venison, and mutton sputtered and hissed over the spits and filled the halls of Cànwyck Castle with a savory smell. All the while, Father Harrald worked feverishly on writing the personal blessing he would deliver following the evening ceremony.

The only thing missing was the bride. His bride. Akira Neish.

Calin had intended to retrieve her a day or two in advance, but he'd assured himself she would be compliant. To date, there hadn't been a woman to refuse him, and he held confident that his bride would melt beneath his charm. Mayhap there would be time on their way back to Cànwyck Castle to woo her a wee bit before making her his lady wife.

"Which of the lassies is she?" Calin scanned the beauties cavorting around the pool of water. "Please, tell me that"—he pointed—"is not her. She looks to be a healthy eater."

Kendrick's wrinkled forehead expressed confusion, but he answered. "*That*"—he pointed at the plump redhead—"is Maggie, and she and her husband, Logan Donald, are expectin' late autumn."

"Then how about the tall beauty?" Calin raised both eyebrows, hoping he chose correctly.

"That's Neala. She's wife to the smith's brother. Did Akira send—"

"Ach!" Out of nowhere came a blast of icy water to Calin's backside. He sucked in air. The warmth of August had done little to take the frigid sting from the water. He spun on his heel to capture the assailant. The roar of the waterfall may have drowned out their footsteps, but the shrieking nymphs holding two empty pails behind him didn't stand a chance of escape. Kendrick held one girl by the wrist, while Calin grabbed the other around the waist. The girls slithered free of their captors, collapsing against each other in a fit of giggles.

Calin shook his muddled head. They were identical in every way—from their strawberry-blond ringlets, to their slender noses, and moss-green eyes. If he'd the time to count, he suspected he might find the same number of freckles atop their noses. He faintly recalled Akira mentioning the twins in her missives, but at least eight years separated those memories. He never knew why she stopped writing to him.

"And this pair o' lassies would be Riona and Fiona," Kendrick introduced the twosome. "Everyone just calls them Iona, cause ye cannae tell one from the other."

"'Tis a pleasure to meet such a bonnie fine pair of lassies." Calin bowed with grace before brushing chaste kisses across their petite knuckles. Their giggles increased and they blushed simultaneously. When he returned his attention to the waterfall, his eyes landed on the innocent young woman sitting beneath the protective foliage of an old ash tree, both ankles tucked neatly under her kirtle, and a book held just beneath her chin.

He motioned at her. "That's her. I knew my bride would be the bonnie smart one."

Kendrick's smile faded, his stature stiffened. "Enough, MacLeod! Girls, fetch up your sisters. We head back at once." Kendrick's tone turned ferocious. "Why are ye here, MacLeod?"

Calin speculated on Kendrick's change of mood. He thought his missive had been very clear. "I wrote a month ago to inform ye I was coming for Akira."

"And ye wrote a year ago statin' the same thing. I started forming the rebellion when ye sent the first query, and Laird Kinnon's suspicions o' betrayal have only mounted during your delay. Do ye know what 'tis like trainin' alongside that bastard? Where in all o' Scots have ye been for the past year?"

Calin had spent his first year as chieftain in regret. He broke eye contact with Kendrick as he recalled the deceptive woman who had deluded him and prevented him from coming sooner. Bitterness held thick on his tongue. "I was detained, but I am here now and ready to form our alliance as promised." Gesturing once again at the girl beneath the tree, he asked with more persistence, "Is that Akira?"

"Nay. Her name is Isobel, and she is not your precious bride either and ye weel know it. Why do ye toy with us, MacLeod?"

Calin tried to understand Kendrick's sudden spike in mood. "I know 'tis been a long time, auld friend, but—"

"Enough games!" Kendrick cut off his words, eyeing Calin cautiously. "Two MacLeods came here a sennight ago. I was tendin' the herd while the girls went to pick berries. Your men were proddin' at Isobel when Akira jumped onto one o' their backs. The girls said she beat your mon with a switch like a wild animal. The one MacLeod grabbed at her waist and ripped the wool o' her kirtle. When they caught sight o' the birthmark on her backside, they called her a witch, and then hauled her over the back o' their mount onto her belly. One o' them told Isobel to inform me that 'twas time." Kendrick's tone grew bitter. "Ye could've at least made a place for her kin at the weddin'."

This revelation enraged Calin. The flesh beneath his eye began to pulse. None too gently, he pushed Kendrick into a sticky pine branch. "Ye dunderheid. There has been nay wedding. I dinnae send for her. Hell and damnation!"

Kendrick's eyes narrowed and his head cocked. He shoved Calin back, hard enough to set him off balance. "They were MacLeods. If ye dinnae send them, then who took her and where?"

"The MacLeod warriors are loyal to me. They wouldnae

betray me, nor would any of them steal my bride." Calin defended his kinsmen, but he trusted Kendrick as one of his own. What would any MacLeod gain by taking her? He struggled with the question, but he had neither the answer, nor the time to contemplate the issue. A sennight fell between him and Akira's captors, making any trail impossible to track. A sickly sensation attacked his gut when he thought of the place they might have taken her. How the hell would he ever find her there? He wouldn't know Akira if he saw her.

Calin made a gesture in the air with the quick jerk of his wrist. Three of his warriors emerged from the grove on horseback. Sirius came to a halt at his side, just as the black stallion had been trained to do. "We must ride at once. Can your sisters see themselves home?" he asked and mounted the warhorse.

"Nay. They cannae." Kendrick tossed a sideways glance at the girls gathered around Isobel. The eldest held the reins to a chestnut-colored roan and waited.

"If I've been informed correctly, the cot-house ye moved into is not far from here. They look plenty able to see themselves home."

Kendrick turned to walk away.

Irritation mounting, Calin wondered how Kendrick could be so apathetic about the sister he'd fostered since birth. "Have ye nay interest in the welfare of your *other* sister, or is she of nay concern to ye now?"

Kendrick rounded hastily and shot him a look of disdain. "I am nay an idiot! Ye dinnae care about Akira's welfare. Your first concern is the alliance and we cannae unite the clans without her. So ye can quit the play-actin' and just admit it. Ye wouldnae know the lass if she bit ye on the arse."

Calin ignored his statement, though it galled him to acknowledge Kendrick spoke the truth. He steadied Sirius. The beast must have sensed his exasperation.

"I intend to ride with ye only because I know Akira, and she'll not go with ye of her own free will."

Why the hell not? He'd provided for her over the years and sent private monies to the Abbot at Beauly Priory for her education. He'd seen the secret of her lineage protected. Besides Uncle Kerk and Aunt Wanda, only Kendrick and Akira's foster mother knew Laird Kinnon had sired her. He had hoped Akira would enter their union without protest. Arguing these facts with Kendrick now seemed a moot point. "We've nay time to tarry. We ride at once."

Kendrick's face reddened and his fingers curled into fists. "Though Akira's safety concerns me, I've five more to care for first. Isobel cannae walk. She's been crippled most of her life. Since Da passed, there is nay one strong enough to carry her except myself, now that Akira's gone."

Calin felt like a complete arse. Now he understood why Isobel wasn't up skipping around the loch with her sisters. "Ye tend to your kin. I have to return to the keep and petition the council for monies. We'll meet at dusk where our soil borders the Donalds'. Come alone. She is on MacLeod soil."

Kendrick's harsh features softened. "Do ye know where they've taken her then?" he asked, his tone hopeful.

"Aye. If what ye say is true, there's only one place a MacLeod would take a woman believed to be a witch—*Tigh Diabhail*." Calin kicked his stallion into a full-blown gallop and prayed silently he wouldn't be too late. *Tigh Diabhail* was Hell's den and appropriately named the Devil's House. He'd been there only once before, but the conduct of his brothers-in-arms repulsed him to the point he never wanted to return. Formerly, the isolated port had served as a weaponry exchange for King James' predecessors, but now they only bartered female captives.

And what they did to the virgins was horrific beyond imagination.

Chapter Two

"How many men do ye think I killed in Drumchatt, cousin?"

"I dinnae know, Jaime. But I'm certain ye believe 'twas more than I." Calin rolled his eyes beneath his lids. After listening to the tenth battle story, he regretted bringing his cousin along to rescue his bride.

Although Jaime was like a brother to Calin, he'd always been undisciplined. Though three years younger, Jaime constantly strived to best him. If Calin killed a red deer with six points, then Jaime set out to kill one with ten. The desire to surpass Calin made Jaime a determined warrior, and Calin admitted to being proud of that quality in his cousin.

"Think ye the number was greater than fifty?" Jaime asked, continuing his exaggerated tale of valor as Calin crested the rise.

Morning's blue mist blanketed the small island of Bania. Scores of MacLeod men littered the landscape below, but this breed of MacLeods weren't brethren Calin cared to call kin. He reigned in his warhorse, every muscle in his body ached from the three-day journey. Not conditioned to the wider saddle, his arse had long since gone numb. The three MacLeod warriors along with Kendrick cantered up beside Calin and paused to look down at the tented pavilions.

"I'd bet my hind teeth the number was closer to a hundred," Jaime said, oblivious of the fact that they'd reached their destination. "Think ye the number—"

"Jaime," Kendrick interrupted, agitation pinching his brows tight. "Ye speak another word, and I'll remove those hind teeth ye just wagered."

Calin grinned, causing Jaime to frown, after which they spent the final leg over the knoll in blissful silence.

Calin had little trouble gaining admittance. His gold proved all the encouragement the bastards needed to permit him, his three kinsmen, and Kendrick beneath the canvas with the rest of the swine.

By late afternoon, attendants shuffled in and out of the main tent. Most wore the heavy Highland plaid, but some were clad in dress fashionable in France and Germany. Surcoats embroidered with their country's crests identified the nationality of each man not wearing a plaid. Trimmed in gold braids, their heavy tunics hung loosely over snug-fitting trews.

Though the year was well into summer, the salty gales from the sea crept beneath the walls like icy splinters. The bystanders shivered from time to time while they bartered for one woman after another on the auction block, but Calin's skin didn't even pebble. The depravity surrounding him heated his blood and sent waves of fury through his very soul.

The bidding ceased at dusk at which point the wastrels spent their coin on hearty amounts of ale and told stories of battle. Their lies grew bigger with every barrel rolled onto the dais. Calin would've given anything to be back astride his steed with his bride safely in tow, listening to one of Jaime's tales. Instead, he was buried within a crowd of rancid-smelling Highlanders, wondering if their stench had seeped into his pores.

At dawn, the auctioneer took up his gavel and began the day anew. After a grouping of olive-skinned women were sold, a blond child was hauled onto the wooden platform. She was easily the youngest maid brought to the dais since they'd arrived. The girl hadn't even grown into her overbite and, as clearly seen through the thin gauze of her shift, she hadn't developed. She couldn't be more than ten years of age. Her hands were bound loosely in front of her, and her head bowed in obedience while tears of humiliation rolled down her cheeks. Calin couldn't bear it. He would find a place for her at Cànwyck Castle. Mayhap with the laundress. He motioned to his man in the back to prepare the funds.

The baritone hum within the pavilion dwindled when the shrilling cadence of the auctioneer began. "How much am I offered for such a prize? Now, my good men. What a sight the lass will be in your beds. How much am I offered? Speak quickly, for she will surely sell." Standing behind a scaffold, the auctioneer slicked graying strands over his balding head while awaiting the bids.

"Is she a virgin?" one of the bystanders asked in a surly voice.

"Lass, answer the mon's question," the auctioneer ordered.

The color rose in her cheeks, and Calin damned each and every one of these men to the fiery pits of Hell.

"Nay." Her answer was barely audible.

Disappointed moans filled the air, which disgusted Calin further. Half these men weren't here to purchase brides or servants, but to witness the entertainment *Tigh Diabhail* provided.

Calin assumed the girl lied, as most of the bystanders did, but the bylaws stated that each captive must answer the same question prior to purchase.

A man sobbed at Calin's left, catching his attention; his

wrinkled face shone wet with tears. He clutched a satchel in one fist and stared glassy-eyed at the girl.

The auctioneer slurred over a string of numbers, guiding three men through their bids. The man at Calin's side only managed to enter a small bid early on.

"Is she your kin?" Calin asked without looking at him.

"My daughter," he finally answered after a long pause.

"Bid what ye must. I will cover the remainder."

"I cannae repay ye."

"Ye will owe me nothing."

Within seconds the bidding ended and the man successfully purchased the girl for thirty groats, twenty of which Calin gladly supplied.

"Bless ye, sir," the man offered then pushed his way to the front. The guards tossed the girl from the dais with no regard for her safety, and Calin wanted nothing more than to see them hang from the tallest tree in the Highlands. The thought of Akira manhandled by these foul heathens made his jaw lock and his palms sweat. Desperation clawed at him, making his fingers pulse.

What if she'd already been sold? What if she'd never even been brought here?

Just as the questions entered his mind, the untamed hiss of the next captive pierced through the drone of bidders. Hair black as midnight framed her porcelain face—a face twisted into a ferocious expression of revulsion. Oaths spewed from her mouth in English, French, Gaelic, and another language Calin didn't recognize. Two sentries in black hooded robes restrained her, and unlike the other women, her hands were bound tightly behind her.

"Christ, that's Akira," Kendrick announced in a loud whisper then started for the dais.

"Nay." Calin placed a firm hand on Kendrick's chest. "Dinnae draw attention to us or our interest in her." Calin spoke calmly enough, but his insides were erupting. If the guards dared to strike her, he was fully prepared to start a war.

She lunged at the men confining her to the platform. The woman certainly didn't lack for spit and fire. She was a fighter. Though relieved he'd found her safe, Calin worried over their initial meeting. Introducing himself to his bride under these circumstances might prove to be an awkward task.

When she drove a knee into the groin of one of her guards, Calin recoiled and instinctively cupped his bollocks. The injured sentry grabbed a mass of her hair, twisted her sideways, and forced her to her knees. Her eyes bled desperation just as she hollered out. The high-pitch note of pain bounced off the canvas walls.

Calin's hands fisted into tight knots. Had he been permitted to keep a weapon, these men would be skewered over the end of his broadsword. He gestured to his clansmen dispersed amongst the crowd. With the silent order, the three men exited posthaste. "Remove your hood," he commanded Kendrick. "If possible, I want her to see ye. Mayhap 'twill calm her spirits."

"Did I happen to mention Akira has a bit of a temper?"

"A bit?" Calin eyed him warily, but he had no time for banter now. "We will retrieve Akira by any means necessary. When we leave, she will ride with me, and I will deal with her *temper*."

The same gruff voice sounded out of the crowd. "Is she a virgin?"

He hoped she possessed the wit to reply the same as all the others. His breath caught in his throat, waiting for her answer. *Say nay. Say ye are not a virgin.* He willed her to answer accordingly.

The guards tightened their hold on her, giving her encouragement to answer the question. Her eyes narrowed into dark slits. She tilted her dainty chin and stared at the barbarian who asked the question. "Aye, I am a virgin. And I intend to stay that way."

Calin's gut plunged to his knees.

Silence fell over the assembly. A silence so absolute the breaking waves could be heard over the cliff behind the pavilion.

The hush lasted two heartbeats, then cheers resounded, and a bawl of bedlam rumbled. Every man's eyes brimmed with lust.

Damn foolish wench! Could she not have told a wee white lie? How dim of wit could the lass be not to answer the same as the rest? The siller he'd sent for her rearing had not been spent wisely. Rolling his neck until it popped several times, he tried to control his frustrations.

The auctioneer stiffened his grip on his gavel. He flashed a wicked smile at a woman standing behind him. "Nattie, fetch the oils."

The crude spectators roared even louder and, though it seemed impossible, the narrow space of the tent tripled in attendance, as if the bastards outside could smell a virgin. The shrill sound of heckling amplified with every passing second. Two more guards wormed their way through the crowd collecting added compensation.

A flush of uneasiness crept over Kendrick's face. "What's amiss?"

"These men pay extra to witness the sale of a virgin. The coin goes to the chieftain who turns a blind eye to such an atrocity. I fear my bride is not only going to cost me far more than I intended to pay, but she's to provide the entertainment as weel." The dark tone of his voice matched the outrage of his thoughts. "I suspect your sister has nay idea what her pride is about to cost her."

Calin offered a silent prayer for Saint Boniface to aid him, then hollered, "Twenty groats."

"Twenty groats I am offered," cried the auctioneer. "Who'll offer more?"

"Thirty-fi'," proffered another, tripping over a foreign language.

"Fifty."

"Seventy-five."

The bids escalated at a startling pace, quickly reaching three hundred. Calin intended to win, even if it cost him every coin he'd brought. The fires of Hades would be doused before he let another man touch his woman. He'd waited far too long to secure the alliance and avenge his father's blood.

"I bid five hundred groats," Calin hollered.

Curious whispers hissed through the crowd as hundreds of eyes studied him. The bid shocked the crowd and Kendrick as well. "Have ye that much siller with ye, mon?"

"Aye," Calin answered briefly then awaited any challenge, his heart hammering in his chest. He'd never been one to flaunt or squander the MacLeod coin, but the survival of Clan MacLeod depended on his retrieval of this woman. *His woman.*

"Who'll give me more than five hundred groats?" the auctioneer shouted, but no response came. The smack of his gavel ended the bidding. "Sold!"

Calin's men waited with the haversacks of siller. With the dip of his chin, he ordered his seneschal to complete the bill of sale with the bailiff. He parted the crowd to stand at the edge of the raised dais as all the other buyers before him had done, but instead of tossing Akira over his shoulder, the guards backed her to the furthest edge of the platform.

A blue-flame of energy surged within him—a possessive desire to protect, to claim, to kill. Fingers balled into fists primed for battle.

"Bring out the bed. Bring out the bed," the crowd chanted.

The auctioneer gave orders for preparations to begin. The guards pulled back moth-eaten drapes revealing a rusty frame holding a straw-filled mattress. The woman, whom the auctioneer referred to as Nattie, reappeared with a steaming pail of oil.

Calin held the auctioneer's stare as he spoke with contempt. "My seneschal has finalized the sale. I demand ye relinquish this woman unto me!"

"She'll be delivered accordingly, but as clearly defined in the precepts of your bill of sale, nay woman leaves *Tigh Diabhail* with her maidenhead intact."

Akira inhaled sharply, drawing Calin's attention. The hot color of fury drained from her face and was replaced with pale-white terror. She wavered slightly before she closed her mouth and regained enough wit to glare at him. Although he didn't feel he deserved such a fierce look, Calin held eye contact with her as they pulled him to the dais.

Her guards doubled in number to hold her limbs immobile while Nattie reached beneath Akira's flimsy shift with a small sponge to wipe oils between her legs. With her hands still bound behind her back, Akira was defenseless against the bawdy woman's boldness.

Two more henchmen carried the bed to the platform's center. Despite Akira's resistance, the guards placed her on the mattress. She tried to bolt, but they flung her back atop the soiled tick and tightened a leather strap over her ribs.

Calin's muscles clenched. He wanted to kill every one of these bastards. He could reveal who he was, but his status as laird held no esteem amongst these swine. He would only be inviting trouble. Knowing he had little choice other than to proceed with the deed, Calin held his arms outstretched and allowed the guards to divest him of his plaid and *léine* shirt. Much to the old crone's apparent disappointment, he declined Nattie's administration of oils and accepted a white cloth as he approached the bed.

He crawled atop Akira on all fours, covering her from head to toe. Mocking their privacy, the guards lowered a gauze canopy—caging them like breeding animals on public display.

She violently thrashed her head side to side, whipping a black web of hair to veil her features.

"*Imigh sa diabhal, bastún,*" Akira cursed at him in Gaelic. And then in French. "*Focal leat! Retournez à la pute qui t'a accouchée!*"

"I am nay a bastard, and my mother wasnae a whore." Calin calmly corrected her expletives. Her obscene vocabulary both shocked and impressed him.

"To the devil with your black blood. May ye rot alongside the *bitseach* that birthed ye."

"Nor was my mother a bitch." Although Calin knew little about the woman who died giving birth to him, he felt a sense of honor to protect his mother from such heinous names. He exhaled dramatically, shook his head, and tsked. "How can such a vulgar tongue be placed betwixt the lips of such a bonnie fine mouth?"

In response, Akira spat on him. She then thrust forward, ramming her forehead into the bridge of his nose. The impact against his skull reverberated clear to his back teeth.

Hell and damnation, his bride was a hoyden! Shaking his head, his eyes refocused to find her completely unaffected by the blow.

"Ye are an ox, and if ye've any intention of touching me, ye will live to regret it. Does it give ye a sense of power to have your way with me, knowing ye are twice my size and probably weigh over twenty stones? I know men like ye. Satan's men. My benefactor will see ye punished and send ye back to your father in Hell!" Akira continued her threats in Gaelic, her profanity becoming more colorful with every blast of condemnation.

She was hysterical. He needed to do something to gain the slightest trust from her, but she screamed as if possessed.

"Akira!" he shouted her given name.

She froze. Her eyes twitched and scanned his face as

if searching for some sign of familiarity. "How do ye know my name?"

Gently, Calin brushed the wild black wisps of hair from her petrified expression. The howling pandemonium of the spectators grew distant as he took in the remarkable beauty of his bride. Her eyes were a piercing blue that shone like polished sapphires beneath a thick fan of sooty lashes. Her rose-colored lips were full and pouty, and her chin held strong with an unbreakable pride. She was a mirror image of Lena. Calin admitted a certain amount of relief. Nonetheless, he would have married Akira with hairy moles and a third eye. The safety of his clan depended on their union.

Her skirmish seemed to cease, because he pinned her legs beneath him, but her entire body trembled. He leaned into the side of her face and inhaled a salty-sweat scent dusted with a feminine lure. "Your name is Akira Neish of Clan Kinnon. Your kin are Neala, Maggie, Isobel, Riona and Fiona. Ye are daughter to Murrdock and Vanora Neish. I am here with your brother, Kendrick, to take ye home. I'll not harm ye, nor will I steal your virginity. There is nay reason for ye to trust me, but I've nay time to beg ye to do as I say. Do ye understand what they expect me to do to ye?"

Akira nodded, terror licked her wide eyes. "Do I know ye?"

"Nay. But ye will." Calin cocked a half grin and wished he had the time to kiss her quivering lips and reassure her all would be well. His knees straddled her legs now, and his gaze lowered to the generous curve of her breasts threatening to unravel the bowed ribbons of her shift from her struggle.

The guards stood no further than three arm lengths away. Calin knew he needed to solicit more cooperation from her to make their audience believers of their union. "I need for ye to part your legs."

She blanched. "I will not. I dinnae care how much ye know about me, I'll not do as ye ask."

The look of rebellion on her face told Calin she had no intention of obeying him. "By the saints, woman. Ye will part your legs or they will do it for ye." He glanced at the guards who seemed anxious to come to his aid.

Akira wished she were prone to swooning like her sisters. But try as she did, her mind refused to aid her. She squeezed her eyes tight, bit her lower lip, and then did as the heathen asked. He repositioned himself then slid his hand between their bodies. She instantly regretted trusting him. Certain he'd touch her in an inappropriate manner, she bucked beneath him.

"If ye dinnae cease your movements, my body will ignore my chivalrous intention to protect your virtue."

The back of his hand brushed against her feminine curls, and piercing fear sliced through Akira's abdomen. Was this how she would lose her virginity? To a beast who bid the highest coin? Would her benefactor still have her if she came to him spoiled?

The crowd's obscene chants drummed in her ears at the same deafening beat of her pounding heart. She prayed silently for God to save her, but was convinced, now more than ever, the devil had branded her.

She *was* cursed.

The man scanned his surroundings before flicking a small blade out of a leather wristband. "I am going to spread blood over your legs," he offered coolly, as if he performed the act daily.

Was he going to cut himself? Was he going to cut her? "Nay! Please." The vise of her knees clamped tightly against his hips, giving him little space to work. Humiliation crawled up her chest and burned her ears as the pagan manipulated his hand intimately between their bodies. In hushed tones, she prayed for penance.

He winced, sucking air through his nose, and proceeded to

rub slick blood between her thighs. The prickling sting of tears blinded her. A muffled cough smothered the fear rising in her throat. Her chest convulsed with the beginnings of a sob.

She turned away.

The man spoke her name, but his actions repelled her to the point she couldn't open her eyes.

"Look at me," he urged.

She finally did. The amber eyes staring back at her rimmed with fatigue and trapped a thousand morsels of regret.

"Cry out, lass," he demanded, then cursed the saints in a harsh whisper. "Holler loud enough for the bastards to hear ye."

This request was not difficult to fulfill. Akira opened her mouth and screamed. The high-octave note caused the brute's eyes to squint. He brushed the cloth across her thigh, after which he vaulted off her, holding the blood-spattered linen high for all to see. Proof of the vile deed.

He quickly dressed, after which he caught a woolen plaid tossed at him from the crowd. Akira lifted her head enough to see her brother smile at her. The brief moment of relief was stolen from her when the man freed her from her bindings, wrapped her in a checked wool, and then tossed her over his shoulder.

The ineffectual scissoring of her feet did little to improve her situation, so she drove her fists into his hard flanks. "Put me down, ye overgrown ox!"

From her awkward angle, Akira could see his clansmen trailing close behind as they charged out of the pavilion. He hoisted her onto his saddled steed before mounting behind her, then stormed across the moor, leaving *Tigh Diabhail* in their wake.

Though she relished the idea of being free of the devil's house, Akira feared the man gripping her possessively around the waist.

Who in all o' Scots was he?

Chapter Three

Akira poked an elbow into the ox's rib cage. He grunted but ignored her. They'd been riding at a jarring pace for what seemed like hours, and Akira desperately wanted to speak to her brother. She had to know if Isobel was safe and being cared for.

She jabbed him again, harder this time. "I have need to stop."

None too soon, the man reined in his steed at a nearby brook. Her brother slowed to a canter beside them, but with a commanding gesture from her captor, Kendrick and the other warriors continued on.

Akira jumped off. "Kendrick, wait!" she yelled at her brother's fleeing back. He glanced over his shoulder, but kept riding until he disappeared over the knoll. What was wrong with him? Why in all o' Scots did he not stop?

She turned to scrutinize the man astride his warhorse. His plaid was a woven gray-blue and olive crossbar pattern. The woolen cloth hung loosely over an exposed bronze thigh. A double-edged claymore graced his hip, and the black hilt of a *sgian dubh* poked out of red deerskin boots lacing up his braw calf. Unruly dark auburn hair lay disheveled about his shoulders with a thin braid falling from each temple. His entire being emanated authority. What power did this man have that he could control Kendrick with a look?

"Who are ye? What clan are ye from?"

"I am MacLeod."

He was a MacLeod? Kin to those vile worms who'd taken her from her family? She didn't care how much coin he'd bartered for her, she was promised to another and the last thing she wanted to do was cross the isles with another MacLeod.

"Tend to your needs, lass. We must put more distance between us and *Tigh Diabhail*."

She stared at him and the barb she had prepared already danced on her tongue, but she admitted distancing themselves from that barbaric place suited her tastes just fine. She darted to the stream and splashed cool water on her face, then drank heavily from her cupped hands, wondering if her throat would ever feel wet again. A silvery film concealed the sun and the scent of summer rain permeated the air.

Tigh Diabhail smelled like a cesspit, a nauseating odor she never wanted to inhale again. But today's air had the distinct aroma of freedom. A freedom she intended to revel in as soon as she separated herself from her riding companion.

She tightened the laces of worn leather brogues and properly pleated the sturdy plaid at her waist. She secured it over her shoulders with his silver clan brooch—the head of a bull, the MacLeod crest. Every clan in the isles knew the crests of their neighbor's flags. The bastards had been trying to claim Kinnon ground for years in an ongoing battle against the Lowlanders to regain the Lordship of the Isles from the crown. She overheard one of the Kinnon warriors discussing the battle at Ross with Kendrick just a few months back. Mayhap the MacLeod knew her benefactor and thought to trade her in exchange for a piece of Kinnon soil. This would explain why he hadn't taken her virginity. A moment of gratification crossed over her as she contemplated the disappointment he was sure to endure when he discovered she was landless.

As she climbed the hillside closing the space between them, her every step grew seven stones heavier. He looked down at her, his face a solemn mask of control. Her pulse tripped. She was fearful of the warrior, but Kendrick wouldn't leave her with anyone who meant to harm her. As soon as possible, she intended to find out exactly who the ox was and why Kendrick abandoned her into his company.

He kicked his boot from the stirrup and extended his hand to her. Akira ignored his offering and slammed her fists onto her hips—an action Mam always did when perturbed. "I wish to ride with my brother."

"Ye ride with me." His tone left no room for compromise.

"After what ye did to me?"

"What *I* did to ye? Ye ungrateful wench."

"Ungrateful?" If he thought his performance at *Tigh Diabhail* chivalrous, he was sorely deceiving himself. "Ye practically raped me in front of your brethren."

"I saved ye back there. And those men are not my brethren. Had ye simply told a wee white lie about your virtue, I wouldnae have had to slice my thigh open to prove the deed done."

"Mayhap I did lie. What say ye to that?"

He responded with a brooding frown. A few moments of silence heightened the tension between them. "Ye ride with me," he repeated his demand.

Akira tapped her foot and scanned the landscape. Past the blue haze swirling around the ancient stones, she knew the mountainous terrain was treacherous. With the morning so young, she could only assume he intended to ride the majority of the day, and the gray hue of a summer's eve would make traveling a probability long past eventide. Already chilled to the core, not to mention hungry and tired, she conceded. If she were being honest with herself, she would admit that this MacLeod had, in fact, saved her and for that she owed him her gratitude, but she couldn't quite ignore the possessiveness in his tone.

She tucked her toe into the stirrup and extended her hand. He lifted her into the saddle in front of him. She sat with her spine stiff, expressing how little she liked the arrangement. When he didn't urge the mount forward, she twisted to scowl at him.

One thick brow lifted higher than the other, giving him a constant inquisitive look. The chestnut hue of his eyes was surprisingly gentle, and his strong nose didn't appear to have ever been broken. Poorly groomed whiskers beaded with morning mist hid the majority of his face, but outlined the finest set of full lips she'd ever seen on a man.

"Are ye able to go on?" he asked, drawing her attention back to his eyes.

"In a moment. First, I would know if the MacLeod who so *gallantly saved* me has a Christian name?"

"Calin," he answered in an even tone as if unaffected by her sarcasm.

"Calin," she echoed. "'Tis a decent name."

The MacLeod's one eyebrow rose yet higher at her strange compliment. "I'm glad ye approve."

The warmth of his breath whispered over her cool cheeks, and his crooked grin suddenly made her realize their close proximity would not please her benefactor. The MacLeod was certainly braw. She couldn't imagine being wed to a man so well-favored. The women, no doubt, flocked to his bed like bitches in heat.

For some insane reason, she felt the prick of jealousy. Where in all o' Scots did that come from? She'd been promised to another for as long as she remembered and never had her loyalty to her benefactor wavered. Not even when Hugh

Og tried to kiss her when she was but ten and two. Of course, the boy looked like a toad, which made restraint effortless.

Wanting to distance herself from his eyes, Akira turned her attention to the stallion. "Has your mount a name?" She brushed one hand down the beast's sleek black neck. Its nose bobbed up and down in answer. "Or do ye just call it Horse?"

"His name is Sirius." The horse pranced forward, stomping its white front hooves in a swaggering strut. The beast was as haughty as its owner.

Instead of voicing her opinion of their shared character, she opted to change the subject. "How much longer afore we stop?"

"I'd like to reach the waters of the Minch, but if ye need to stop for the night we will do so now."

Insulted, Akira stiffened and made a conscious effort not to touch him. A difficult task, given the size of the saddle. "I dinnae need to stop."

"Are ye weary, lass?"

"Nay, I am beyond weary. I feel as though my bones have turned to ash inside my body. Not to mention, I am freezing and have never been hungrier in my life."

The MacLeod opened his mouth to respond, but she wasn't finished.

"I've spent more than a sennight in a pitch-black cavern with nary more on than a web for a gown and a cold slab of limestone for a pallet. And had my stomach not been empty, I probably would have retched on ye in the last few minutes I spent in that devil's keep. But what I find the most tiresome of all is the fact ye have not given me leave to speak with my brother. I've a sister who depends on me, and I only wished to inquire about—"

The MacLeod put one finger over her lips. "Isobel is being taken care of as weel as your mother. Your sister . . ." he paused in thought, and Akira waited with great anticipation for him to finish, ". . . the one married to a Donald. Maggie is it?"

Akira nodded vigorously, because his finger still denied her speech.

"Maggie is at the cot-house with her husband. Ye dinnae need to worry yourself over them."

She pushed his hand away. "Is someone working Isobel's legs? Morning and night?"

His brows stitched together with this question. No one in her family ever understood why she insisted on moving Isobel's legs and toes twice a day. Akira still clung to the hope that her sister might one day have need of them, and she wanted them to be strong when that day came.

"I cannae answer your question, lass, but I can promise to fill your belly when we reach the Minch." He lifted her so both her legs draped over his right thigh, paying little attention to her protests. Then he loosened his plaid from behind him and wrapped them together in a tight cocoon. Pushing her head beneath his chin, he pulled her to his chest, and kicked Sirius into motion.

Exhaustion denied her the ability to argue her position. His body was as warm as a toasted brick beneath the wool, and she had tired of being cold long ago. She nuzzled into him, yawned, and relaxed with the knowledge he'd provided her in regards to her family. She would be home soon. That thought alone was enough for her to let down her guard.

"Thank ye," she mumbled against his chest, not certain if he'd even heard her.

"Och, lass. Ye are a feisty one."

Calin pulled on the reins, slowing Sirius to a walk behind the others when they reached the glen just outside the Minch. He inhaled the salty air and studied the landscape. Dew already moistened the short grasses and gray mist settled low on the foothills. His thighs ached from many grueling hours in the saddle, and his arm was numb from holding Akira while she slept. Her cheek rested against his chest, tilted slightly upright, and her arm curled around his waist. Her fingers worked unconsciously to draw tiny circles on his lower back. A woman never felt more perfect in his arms.

A contented smile curled the corners of her mouth making his physical suffering more bearable. She really was a bonnie lass. Black lashes, thick as a raven's feather, fanned over smooth creamy skin. His fingers poised above her heart-shaped lips itching to touch them. The warmth of her breath teased his fingers and was nearly more than his warrior's will could resist.

Her full bottom lip hinted at a constant pout, reminding him of the night he placed a squalling babe in his friend's arms. He'd wanted to take her to his aunt Wanda on MacLeod soil, but knew the babe would not survive the journey. His steed had been seized along with the rest of the horses and the trek back to the MacLeod keep would have taken him a day or two on foot. She'd been so tiny then. Her lip quivered with her cries, and Calin had feared being caught with her.

The pad of one finger brushed her bottom lip.

Her eyes flew open and brought him out of his musing. She jerked upright out of her peaceful position. For the next several minutes, she sat with her spine stiff while both her hands gripped the pommel. The moment Sirius came to a halt, she sprang to the ground only to wince and then falter. Both hands rubbed her nicely rounded arse until her totter turned into a race to Kendrick.

Five hundred groats Calin had parted with to rescue her, and Kendrick was her savior.

She greeted her brother with an ardent hug, wrapping her arms around him. The joyful reunion, however, was short lived. She boxed Kendrick's ears with the palms of both hands then poked his chest repeatedly with her finger. "Have ye any comprehension what could've happened to me in that wretched place? What took ye so long?"

"Forgive me. I thought—"

"Kendrick. Not now," Calin interrupted. "This is not the time or the place. We must hunt while the light holds and much work needs to be done to make camp."

Before Akira could protest further, Calin delegated duties to everyone except her then grabbed his crossbow and headed for the moorland. Two of his men and Kendrick followed, leaving his most trusted warrior with Akira. He wanted her safe, yet far enough away from Kendrick to keep the two of them from conversing.

Now hidden in the underbrush beside Kendrick, Calin stalked a covey of grouse. His gut tightened and his mouth watered at the sight. The oatcakes they'd eaten for the past sennight had done little to satisfy his hunger. God knows what kind of fare had filled Akira's belly while held prisoner at *Tigh Diabhail*. He hoped to see her smile when he presented her with one of the fat little birds.

"What are ye grinnin' about?" Kendrick whispered.

"Your sister."

"So ye talked?"

Calin shrugged. "She asked my name. I told her. She asked my horse's name. I told her that, too. Then she said a few things that werenae so pleasant, after which she inquired about her sister's weel-being and went to sleep. I promised her I would kill something for her to eat, and this is what I'm trying to do. So if ye would still your tongue and take aim, I would like to uphold my vow."

With this said, Calin drew the arrow back and took aim. Kendrick did the same. They released in unison. The hissing noise of the arrow whistled through the air just before piercing two plump grouse through the neck. The flock scattered, but soon another warbling covey began nipping the damp ground. They repeated their actions, landing them two more birds for the spit. After walking in silence to a small pool of water, they plucked the first two birds clean of feathers. Calin felt Kendrick's question rising before it ever slipped off his tongue.

"Ye dinnae tell Akira ye were her benefactor. Did ye?"

"Nay. Not yet."

"And when do ye think ye might be doin' that?"

Calin narrowed his eyes. "Think ye I am going to feed her, then say, 'Your father is the evilest mon I have ever known. He killed my father and I seek my revenge on your father through a union with ye. Do ye accept?'"

Kendrick shook his head and threw his hands in the air, causing a flurry of feathers to tickle Calin's nose. "Weel, I can assure ye that wouldnae go weel at all, but ye have to trust the lass. She is smart and cares a great deal about her kin. She knows how important it is to have strong allies for protection. We've kin in the Lowlands that were slaughtered just last year by those English dogs. She hates the English as much as any other hot-blooded Scot and wouldnae want that fate for anyone in our clan. Ye'll at least tell her your intention to marry her."

"Give me time." Calin shoved another bird into Kendrick's empty hands and gestured for him to pluck.

"Ye've had eighteen years. She has known and respected ye as her benefactor the whole o' her life. Ye are like a king in her eyes. She has been loyal and protected ye when her sisters mocked ye. For the love o' Scots, the lass saved every missive ye ever sent."

Calin grinned knowing he'd done the same. Every rock, feather, stick, and drawing was locked safely away in an antechamber at Cànwyck Castle.

"Ye cannae keep her from speakin' to me, and I'll not lie to her if she asks why ye came to her aid."

Calin stopped gutting a plucked bird long enough to offer him a threatening glare. "Ye will say naught. I'll tell her when she has food in her belly and calms down a wee bit from her ordeal."

Kendrick snorted. "Think ye this will happen with Akira? The lass does not know what calm is." Kendrick stopped pulling feathers long enough to study Calin as if he were deciphering some riddle. "Do ye fear she will deny ye?"

Deny me? He hesitated just a bit before dismissing the thought straightaway. He pointed the sharp tip of his bloody *sgian dubh* at Kendrick's nose to emphasize his statement. "I fear naught. I am laird and a warrior. No mere woman can strike fear in me, especially one who has belonged to me since birth."

Kendrick snorted yet again and Calin sorely wanted to stuff grouse innards up his snickering nose.

"Dinnae be arrogant, MacLeod. Ye know as weel as I, she can oppose the alliance because of her blood ties to Laird Kinnon. She holds as much power as ye, my friend. She is the heir to Clan Kinnon and the only one who can sanction the power o' chieftainship."

"She is too smart. 'Tis why ye must give me time. If I tell her Laird Kinnon is her father, it will not take her long to figure out she can choose her own husband. Then she will know she does not have to marry me. 'Twould be foolish of ye to tell her the truth now that we have waited so long."

"Tell her the truth and let her choose ye as husband."

Calin shook his head. He would not give Akira a chance to deny him, nor would he be made a fool of by another woman. "Once I make her my wife, I will hold power over her. I will tell her the truth after we consummate the marriage. When she carries my heir, she will understand the necessity of protecting our clans."

"That's your plan?" Kendrick looked at him as if he had two

heads. "Woo her, bed her, then tell her she is the daughter o' the most vile mon she has e'er known? Ye are addlebrained. Your union will be based on lies. She'll never trust ye after that."

"Aye, but she trusts ye. Ye are her brother, and she'll listen to reason from ye." Calin lifted his brows and wiped a feather from his nose with his forearm. He handed Kendrick the gutted bird for washing then flung the blood and muck from his hands.

"She trusts me now, but I fear the lass's faith in me will slip when she learns I've lied to her the whole of her life, even if it was to protect her."

"I know ye despise your laird for what he did to Vanora and Neala. The man's crime has festered on ye like a rotting wound for a decade. I have nursed my hatred for him twice that long. If I am forced to tell Akira anything about the alliance prior to our vows, I will tell her what the bastard did to your kin. Then she'll seek the same vengeance as ye and I. My only fear is that she'll act on it as we have not."

Kendrick nodded his agreement, but remained silent. Calin struggled with the same regrets. Cowardice weighed on a warrior's pride.

Too much was at stake to trust her with the truth of her lineage just yet. He would not afford her the opportunity to endanger those living in his clan or stand in the way of fulfilling the vow he made to his father. "I ask for your silence until I feel the time is right to tell her. My father promised Lena he would protect her daughter. I mean to uphold that promise. I'll not allow Akira to endanger herself by confronting that monster. He has nay soul and would kill her just as he intended eighteen years ago. Then there would be nay one to transfer the title of laird unto ye, Kendrick. She must be protected."

Kendrick picked up the dressed birds. "I'll give ye the eve to tell her of your union before I tell her myself. With or without your permission, as I dinnae need it."

Chapter Four

Akira kneaded the aches out of her bum and lower back while helping her new companion gather kindling for the fire. She was grateful to be free of the man who'd taken possession of her. She knew nothing about this Calin MacLeod, other than he needed a bath. Of course, she couldn't hold that against him. She was in dire need of a good scouring as well.

The evening hadn't improved with the MacLeod's scowling guard. After he'd tended to the horses and the fire was ablaze, she made an effort to be congenial. "Have ye a name, sir?" When he didn't reply, she tried again. "'Tis good the rain has stopped."

Not even a grunt.

"How long afore we reach our borders?"

Nothing. Not a shrug of his shoulders, a curious glance, a snort. He knelt and cupped his hands out to the flames. Akira tried again in the Gaelic tongue. Then French. Try as she did, he refused polite conversation. Was he mute? Deaf? Dumb?

Crouched at the fire's side with his elbows resting on his knees, the man completely ignored her questions. Frustration picking at her patience, she leaned in close. "Have ye nay tongue?"

His stoic expression faltered and he tossed her a look—
a menacing look. *So he isn't deaf, just rude.* She refused to
waste time on him and left him to his duties. She found olive
oil soap and a shell comb in Kendrick's saddlebag. When she
turned around, the man stood directly in front of her with his
arms crossed over his chest, looking down his hawk-like nose
at her.

"I am going to the brook," she offered and walked around
him, but his footsteps crunched behind her. She spun on her
boot heel and poked her index finger into his breastbone. "I
dinnae know what your orders were, but I can assure ye, I need
nay guard to watch over me while I tend to my ablutions."

She waited for him to back down, which took longer than
she expected, then walked unattended to the brook.

Akira bathed in the brisk water, washing the squalid memories of *Tigh Diabhail* from every inch of her body. After
giving her hair equal attention, she was content with her
cleanliness, but now wished for a proper sark. She worked at
the laces, tightening them as modestly as one could with such
a flimsy shift. The material would better serve as a fishing net
than an undergarment. She'd never worn anything so indecent
in her life. A dozen ribbons fastened the shift from midbreast
to just below her navel, and only three ribbons secured each
side together. She fashioned the MacLeod's plaid around her
waist then held the wool over her shoulder with his clan
brooch. Noting the intricacy of the etched bull's head, she
stroked the gold.

Her family had never known such finery. The wool of his
plaid was as soft as doeskin and undoubtedly heavier than both
her threadbare kirtles. Clan MacLeod was a wealthy clan.
Why would Kendrick solicit them to come to her aid? Why not
bring the Kinnon warriors? Of course, mayhap he tried and
failed. *Tigh Diabhail* was on MacLeod soil. Kendrick must
have had no choice, but why would a MacLeod care a morsel

about the well-being of a Kinnon? She'd heard Clan MacLeod had recently come under the reign of a new chieftain. Word traveled on the wind in the Highlands. Mayhap the new chieftain was trying to mend the strife between their clans.

Determined to question Kendrick upon her return to camp, Akira combed through an abundance of black wavy tangles until the masses dried. Feeling rejuvenated, she picked a few sprigs of *siùcair* blossoms and a skirt full of red currant berries along the way. The men wouldn't be the only ones to provide food. Ignoring the knifelike pain in her stomach, she vowed not to eat even one berry until she returned to camp.

Her stomach growled—a mean vibrating noise she felt clear to her toes.

Who was she trying to fool? A handful of tart currants slid down her throat as she scurried up the foothill.

When she neared camp, the smoky aroma of fresh-cooked meat reached her nose. Her knees quivered when she saw the five men feasting on roasted grouse. She licked her lips and stared at the wild fowl sizzling over the fire. At least a month's time had passed since she'd tasted meat of any sort. She spilled the berries and *siùcair* blossoms into the lap of the man who ignored her pleasantries earlier and gawked at the cooked bird like a mangy wolf eyeing a lone sheep.

Calin lifted the skewer from the fire. Grease dripped into the flames and hissed on the coals. "Ye hungry, lass?"

"Ye know I am." Akira fisted her empty palms, but could do nothing more than stand in front of him like a starving dog awaiting his scraps. If he took one bite from *her* bird, she feared she would eat his hand. "Ye said ye would feed me. Is that my fare you're holding?"

"Aye. Come, sit, and fill your empty belly."

He didn't have to tell her twice. She sat beside him with the intent to devour every juicy morsel clean off the bone. The questions for Kendrick could wait until later. The first bite melted on her tongue, and she closed her eyes and moaned. Mayhap the MacLeod wasn't so awful after all.

Calin watched how ravenously she enjoyed her food. She played havoc on his senses. His eyes fixed on the sheen of grease the meat left on her lips. Her sweet and heady fragrance tempted his nose, and the moans vibrating from her throat with every savory bite had him wishing she dined on him.

His muscles clenched and his blood rushed to his loins.

This arousing attraction caught him unguarded. He'd spent the majority of his life knowing he would marry to protect his clan. The fact he found his bride extremely desirable came as a pleasant surprise. Part of him always questioned whether he'd be able to conceive an heir with the woman whose sire murdered his father, but Akira was not Laird Kinnon. She hadn't been raised by him, nor influenced by him. She was innocent of her father's sins. He couldn't count how many times he'd repeated this statement in his head over the years trying to convince himself it was true.

He intended to press the alliance with the Kinnons quickly, but he needed a bit more time to woo his bride. Her blue eyes studied him between bites, and he recognized a hint of stubbornness. Undoubtedly, one eve was not going to be enough time for her to warm to the idea of being his wife, but it was all Kendrick seemed willing to give him.

After the bones of her fare had been picked clean, Akira's eyes followed the juicy bird leg he was about to savor. He didn't have the heart to take the bite. She'd eaten like a woman who hadn't seen a crumb in days and would nary a doubt ache in the gut for it, but the lass obviously thought she was still hungry. When he offered her the meat, she shook her head and lowered her lashes.

"Eat it, lass." He put the leg in her empty hand.

"Thank ye. 'Tis verra good," was all she said before biting into the meat. He couldn't keep his gaze from lingering on her lips and was shocked when those lips curved into a bashful smile.

"I trust we'll go our separate ways at first light and bid ye much thanks for your help in my retrieval. I need to return quickly to my family."

"'Twill take two more days before we reach our homelands, and ye and Kendrick will be better protected traveling with MacLeod men."

Akira used the back of her hand to wipe her lips. "Ye've just disbursed a rather wealthy sum for my safety, for which I am verra grateful. But, I am not fool enough to believe ye expect naught in return. I'd like to end any claims ye might feel ye have to my person here and now. We will part ways on the morrow, and Kendrick will see that your siller is reimbursed."

Kendrick almost choked on a bone. Calin wasn't the only one shocked by this statement. Unwilling to give her brother any leeway in the conversation, Calin rushed to speak. "Are ye of such financial independence ye've five hundred groats at your disposal?"

Pride lifted her blue eyes, along with her chin. "The queries may take time, but I have a benefactor who'll be pleased to know I've been rescued. I'm confident he will graciously send funds by month's end."

Calin forced his teeth together to keep his laughter caged. Kendrick opened his mouth, but Calin cut him off before he could explain the error of her statement. "Then if we are to part ways on the morrow, might we enjoy the pleasure of each other's company tonight?"

Akira eyed him cautiously, then studied Kendrick with a curious look. "Though I suspect I may regret it, I see nay harm in obliging ye for the eve. Since ye've fed me and provided me with a warm plaid—even if 'tis your plaid. Howbeit, I am certain your men are not fit to be called pleasurable company. Truth be told, I fear their new laird may have cut out their tongues." Akira laughed aloud and paid no heed to the somber gazes of his men.

"And why would ye make such an absurd remark?"

"Weel, first and foremost, ye are MacLeods. If that is not reason enough, then I think the fact I've yet to hear them speak is a strong second argument."

Calin smiled with a broad-faced grin. "They can speak when spoken to."

"But I spoke to that one earlier . . ." Akira pointed at a tall, brooding redhead perched atop a decaying log, ". . . and he dinnae respond in any of the languages I spoke to him in. So he's either rude or has nay tongue. Or mayhap both." She gave the man a piercing look of disapproval.

Calin had asked for his men's silence in her presence until he informed her of his intent to marry her. They'd honored his request. Even Jaime's tongue remained unmoving, which was a most difficult task for his cousin. Overly proud of his men's conduct, Calin crossed his arms over his puffed chest. "I can assure ye, he has a tongue, but he'll not use it unless given permission to do so."

"Permission? Are ye insane? Permission from whom?"

"From his laird."

"What kind of barbarian would send his mon on a quest with nay permission to speak? Is your new laird so dim of wit he would deny the mon speech because of some foolish loyalty?" Akira shook her head, and muttered more insults under her breath. Insults directed at him since he was the new chieftain of Clan MacLeod. He found no reason to hide that fact from her. Mayhap she would show him a wee bit of respect if he revealed his status.

A trace of sarcasm laced his next query. "Gordon, is your laird a dimwitted barbarian?"

"Nay."

He laughed at the sweet and innocent shock that enveloped her features. That is, until one winged brow arched. "Are ye the new laird o' Clan MacLeod?" she asked, giving him a sidelong look.

"Aye," Calin said quietly.

Akira pressed her fingers to her temples. "Forgive me, m'laird. I dinnae know." She glared at her brother, who sipped whisky from a silver flask.

Calin caught Kendrick's sympathetic look and feared he might one day understand it. Akira Neish was going to be difficult to woo.

Calin scooped a handful of rosehip berries from where Gordon had dumped them then snapped off a sprig of *siùcair* blossoms. He sucked the nectar from the septum and tucked the yellow flower behind her ear. She flinched when his finger lingered over the outer edge of her ear, then the sweetest blush stained her cheeks. He reached for her small hand and dropped a few berries into her palm. "Enough about me. Tell me more about this benefactor of yours."

"Ye mean in reference to whether he can be trusted to return your siller?"

"Aye. Is he trustworthy?"

"I suspect he is."

"And does he treat ye weel?"

"Verra weel. He's generous with his monies, but in truth, I have yet to meet him. Kendrick says he will be good to me, and I trust my brother's opinion."

Calin dipped his head in approval toward Kendrick. "So your . . . benefactor, what do ye presume are his intentions for ye?"

"I suspect he wants a wife to maintain his holdings and see to personal matters of finance. 'Tis important to him that I am weel-educated. This leads me to believe he will be content with my intelligence, which is to my benefit, since I lack in qualities of face. Truth be known, I am not certain why he chose me over my sisters. He's sure to be disappointed when he realizes he's getting the raven when he could've had a dove." Akira's chin lowered to her chest and her gaze fell to the red berries in her hand.

The raven? Was the woman wowf? How could she possibly think herself less beautiful than any one of her sisters? "I am certain he'll not be disappointed."

Akira shrugged her shoulders.

Since Kendrick scrutinized his every move as though he were an English spy, Calin decided to save explanations of her beauty for a more private moment. For now, he focused on the subject of her education. "Ye consider yourself weel-educated?"

Her head popped up and she answered brightly. "Verra much so. I speak three languages and Mam tells me I'm a walking abacus."

"I counted four."

Akira laughed. The sound of her merriment, and the way her smile brightened the sapphires of her eyes, tickled Calin's senses. He inched closer, ignoring her brother's threatening gaze. Kendrick looked ready to end the farce when Akira began chattering again.

"The fourth language ye heard, my sisters and I made up when we were younger. Only my family understands it."

"How did ye come by your education?" Calin asked, though he already knew the answer.

"When I was eight, Kendrick sent me to Beauly Priory."

"Nay," Kendrick corrected. "'Twas your *benefactor* who sent ye there. Not I."

Only after giving Kendrick a sour look of disgust, did Akira return her attention to him. "As I was saying, my benefactor sent me to the priory in Inverness. Sister Esa taught me to read and write when I was just eight. When the Prioress gave me reprieve from kitchen duties, I studied in the library. After nigh two years, the Abbot nay longer felt I deserved the same education as those who had taken their vows and assigned me to the stables. I borrowed a few books and came home."

"A few?" Kendrick interrupted in an accusatory tone. "Ye pulled a cart behind that auld nag ye brought home."

"Mayhap more then," she confessed. "Ye shouldnae complain. I taught ye to read and write from those books. Besides, they werenae using them at the priory, and my benefactor sent ample funds for my education which the Abbot spent on frivolous luxuries for himself. Nay mon o' God needs gold rings to adorn every finger or whisky to fill his cupboards."

"Books werenae all ye stole."

"I dinnae *steal* anything." Akira sternly corrected Kendrick then threw a berry at him for emphasis. "My benefactor sent those monies for my education, not for the Abbot to purchase a gold crucifix encrusted with diamonds and rubies. In my way o' thinking, that crucifix belonged to my family, whom if ye will recall, was starving in ninety-four."

"Akira came tottering home with the Abbot's crucifix twinkling 'round her neck."

"Ye stole the Abbot's finery?" Calin asked, not sure if he was appalled or proud.

"I made her return it when I took her back to the priory," Kendrick interjected. "But—"

"I returned home two months later with a herd of sheep, a couple of fence dogs, and a *few* more books."

"When ye were a lass o' ten?" Calin questioned, not believing his ears. The Abbot never once mentioned this, and Calin had sent monies for five consecutive years to the Beauly Priory.

"I had help from two o' the lay brothers. It took us six sennights to guide that herd home."

The memory even received a chuckle from Kendrick. "A

sight to make your eyes laugh. Akira atop her palfrey leadin' a nayin', bell-ringin' herd of at least a hundred sheep down the dirt path o' Dalkirth. The village sounded like an English court full o' jesters."

"The Abbot wasted the monies, and I was teaching Sister Esa more than she was teaching me." Akira defended, then explained further to Calin. "Ye see, as punishment for taking the crucifix, the Abbot refused the sisters to educate me, all the while, my family was trying to get broth from a turnip. The Ionas' ribs were near to poking through their skin when Kendrick made me go back to the priory the second time. Our borders fell into the hands of reivers that year, since half our kinsmen were off on some foolish exploit to regain the Earldom of Ross from King James. Their absence left our borders unprotected. After four raids, the villagers of Dalkirth and my family were starving."

"So ye stole from the Abbot to feed your clan." He should've been angry with her, but the fact she held such compassion for her people not only pleased him, but filled him with pride. This quality would be well-received by the MacLeods.

"I would have if The Beast hadnae slaughtered the herd after a fortnight."

"The Beast?" Calin questioned, although he had a hunch who *The Beast* was.

"Our chieftain—The Beast of Brycen. He slaughtered the whole herd for his warriors, because nay one would reveal where they came from. The bastard even wasted their wool." Akira's eyes lit with contempt, revealing her obvious hatred for Laird Kinnon. This would probably not be a good time to inform her that the man she spoke so venomously of was her father.

"Akira!" Kendrick shouted. "Ye would do weel to hold your tongue."

All traces of courage drained from her face at the scolding.

"Why do ye protect the mon's status as our laird? He is not fit to hold the rank, and ye weel know it. He's a horrible mon who has raised the levies until the villagers have nothing. And the women are at his mercy when he wants them."

Akira rubbed her arms as if the mention of the man gave her chills. "He's sculpting his dreadful son into the verra essence of himself. Darach has not left the walls o' Brycen Castle in nigh eight years. The villagers have coined our laird's son 'the devil's spawn.' A name he has rightly earned from my perspective." Akira glared again at her brother, and Calin wondered what secrets were hidden there.

A dark mood surged to the surface when Kendrick chugged a large swill of whisky, then stood. "Ye are blatherin'. Nay one calls the laird's son that name, 'cept ye. The villagers dinnae even know if the boy still lives." He marched into the grove until his form became nothing more than a shadow.

"Crivons. I love the mon dearly, but he can be such an ogre."

Calin offered her a half-hearted smile and inhaled a breath of courage. Knowing his time ran short, he needed to take advantage of the situation. A brief look was all it took to send his men crawling inside their plaids for the eve. He retrieved a fur pelt from his steed and spread it out at the fire's edge. Jaime's snoring rumbled before Calin finished smoothing the pelt. His cousin had never had enough worries to keep him from sleep.

Calin reclined on his side, crossed his legs at the ankles, and extended his hand palm up for her to join him.

Akira's eyes widened. "Think ye I am going to bed down with ye?"

"Nay." He chuckled at her bold question. "I dinnae compromise ye at *Tigh Diabhail,* and I've nay intention of taking what belongs to your . . . benefactor. I just thought we might talk a wee bit closer to the fire."

She hesitated and looked to the grove where Kendrick had gone. When Calin made no attempt to force her, she accepted his offer, but sat so rigid he feared her back would snap. His presence obviously made her uncomfortable, hence making his task all the more difficult.

"So . . . what do ye know of this . . . mon ye are to wed?" He brushed his finger over her hand resting at her side.

She quickly brought her hand into her lap and glanced again into the grove. "Kendrick has told me little about him, but he has been good to my family. When Papa moved us from the bailey into the cot-house, my benefactor sent monies to ease the transition. Papa went to war shortly after and died fighting for the royalists, leaving Kendrick with the responsibility of rearing six girls."

Her tone revealed her political position. He had fought alongside Sir Alexander of Lochalsh to reclaim the Lordship of the Isles from the crown, but his motivations had been different. He supported the chief of Clan Donald to form alliances to protect their clans. Debating the issue with this headstrong woman would cost him valuable time, so he avoided the subject. "Kendrick has done a fine job rearing all o' ye."

"He has done his best, but I suspect his burdens will lighten ten-fold after he finds husbands for the Ionas." She laughed, which smoothed the nervous tension from her brow.

"And the husband he has found for ye. What do ye hope he is like?"

"I hope he is like Papa." Her answer came quick, and Calin wondered if he would ever live up to that standard. Murrdock Neish had been a good man.

"What else? Do ye hope he is a braw mon?"

Akira's head cocked on her shoulders as if to call him an idiot. "Truth is, I hope he's a wee bit older and not much to look at. Mayhap with a pack of weel-mannered bairns needing cared for."

Calin chuckled. "Why would ye want such a fate?"

"If he is older, then he will be finished with the rutting, and if he is homely then I'll not have need to chase the women from our marriage bed."

Mulling over her bold explanation, he sat up beside her. Her chin tilted upright as she awaited his reply. *Say the words*, he told himself. Soliciting such personal details from her this way was wrong. He tucked a stray black curl behind her ear, and this time she didn't shy away. He leaned closer, fully prepared to tell her he was her benefactor, but the words held tight to his tongue. Her lips separated as if to speak, but she only breathed, and he felt her air on his face. Their eyes locked and the silence seemed to go on forever. He raised his hand to touch her cheek, but his fingers only hovered beside. "I doubt ye should be worrying yourself over such matters. I would wager any mon would give his eyeteeth for your loyalty."

A loud crackle popped from the fire and gave Akira a swift kick in the gut. What was she doing? She felt herself staring into the laird's amber eyes while he spoke, and she had no business getting lost there. She glanced back at the grove. *Where in all o' Scots was Kendrick?* Her brother hadn't left her in the presence of another man since . . . well, her brother had never left her alone with a man.

When the laird twirled her ebony curl around his finger, she froze. He may as well have chained her for she lacked the ability to move away from him. A ferocious tingle flitted beneath her skin, and she rushed to continue the conversation. "In all actuality, I expected my benefactor sooner. I am already three years past marriageable age. I should have a bairn at the breast and one tugging at my kirtle by now."

"Ye are hardly past your years. I think the mon will be eager to see ye swollen with his child." He stroked her forearm with the back of one finger. In a flash, gooseflesh covered her skin beneath his simple caress. She giggled like a half-brained maiden and fought with a loose thread on her skirt. She was acting a fool. Kendrick would bruise his hand on her backside for talking to the laird in such a way.

She blew a relieved breath when her brother's stealthy footsteps crunched out of the grove.

Kendrick gruffly interrupted. "Did ye talk?"

"Akira was just telling me her expectations of her benefactor. She hopes he's auld and homely with a pack of weel-mannered bairns to rear." Laird MacLeod smiled at her brother, and she regretted sharing such details with him. The look of disgust on Kendrick's face made her feel as if she'd betrayed her benefactor. Her body, in fact, had. But the sour expression curling her brother's lip was directed at the laird, not her.

Kendrick stepped closer, shook his head, and glared at Laird MacLeod. "Ye've not told her, have ye?"

"Ye went to take a piss. 'Twas hardly enough time for me to broach the subject."

"Ye've had plenty o' time, MacLeod," Kendrick growled. "Ye will tell her or I will. She deserves the truth. Now!"

"Tell me what?" Akira sensed Kendrick's agitation. She'd seen that scowl before. He'd worn the same disappointed look a hundred times when scolding her for disobedience. "Tell me what, Kendrick?" she asked again when no one spoke.

Her brother stared at Laird MacLeod, giving him ample opportunity to answer. When he didn't, Kendrick proceeded. "The new chieftain o' Clan MacLeod is your benefactor and has come to claim ye as his wife."

"What?" Akira's hands flew to her face to cool the hot humiliation flooding her cheeks. *This* cunning, arrogant man, who just asked her a dozen questions about himself, was her benefactor? "Nay! 'Tis not true."

Recalling the details she'd provided him caused her further

embarrassment. He deceived her, which told her more than she wanted to know about his character. And the innocent smile he offered her bit into what little pride she felt she had left. The air thickened and grew too stifling to breathe. She stood and gave Kendrick a glare she hoped passed for righteous indignation. "How could ye? He is not what ye promised me."

"He is what he is," Kendrick offered without emotion.

She bolted into the timberland. A full moon reflected off the firth, which lit her way to the thickest tree in the grove. Digging her fingers into the bark, she started climbing.

Chapter Five

"By the saints! What did ye do that for?" Calin jumped to his feet, annoyed with Kendrick. He'd been learning so much about his new bride. He'd even come close to swindling a kiss from her sweet lips. The wooing had been going well.

"Cause ye were makin' a fool o' her." Kendrick retrieved a plaid from his saddlebag. "Ye should go after her. I assure ye, she'll not be comin' back on her own."

"Why should I go after her? Ye are the one who sent her fleeing." He squinted into the grove, searching for signs of movement.

"Ye are the one who humiliated her, and she'll be goin' home with ye in two days. I strongly suggest ye make amends. She is thick-brained. If ye keep the truth from her, she'll sense your deception and all the vengeance we have waited so long for will be lost." Kendrick kicked dirt and debris onto the fire, reducing the short flames to orange embers. "A word of advice before ye continue the wooing. Dinnae tell her she's bonnie. She'll think ye lie."

"Why?"

"She believes she's cursed. I have never been able to convince her otherwise."

"Cursed? Is she as blind as ye are loose in the head? What are ye blathering about?"

"She believes she was marked by the devil and condemned to live among those blessed by angels. When Akira was a wee lass, I caught her in a cavern burnin' goat's hair and dead frogs. She said she was castin' a spell to fix her face. She showed me a hand-scribed book she got from an old crone at Retterseils' fair. I never seen the likes o' such a book. Scrawled in a language I dinnae know. The lass bawled like an auld starvin' cat when I burned that book, but I suspect she had memorized every page anyway."

Calin winced. Branding her had been the act of a foolish boy, who thought she was no more than another possession. An act that had caused her to think ill of herself. He would right that wrong quickly. He spat on the dying embers just to hear the sizzle. "She is not marked by the devil."

"Think ye I dinnae know that? But even I wouldnae tell the lass ye branded her like livestock when she was born." Kendrick reclined beside a hollow log. "Ye should start with an apology, and look up."

"Why am I to look up?"

"Cause she's in a tree. Probably the tallest in the grove."

Calin found yellow petals scattered between the roots of a thick oak—ten decades old if it were a day. Looking up, he saw nothing but a twisted mass of black limbs outlined by colored moonbeams. However, the rustle of branches revealed Akira's refuge.

He definitely had to do something about her disposition before he presented her to his clan as the new Lady of Cànwyck Castle. The laird's wife couldn't throw tantrums every time she didn't get her way. Never would he allow another woman to disgrace him.

Knowing Akira felt deceived, he would indulge her this one time and try to solicit her willing acceptance of their union. Calin filled his lungs with fresh air. "Akira Neish, ye will come down at once."

Silence sliced the crisp air.

"If ye intend to sleep in this tree, ye will freeze to death by morn."

He didn't expect a reply, but he didn't expect to be pelted with acorns either. Muttering a slew of curses, he climbed the oak until he saw her boot dangling from a limb. Before he could reach her, she ascended. The higher she climbed, the more exasperated he became.

"This is ridiculous," he grumbled. "The chieftain does not chase women up trees."

"Then go back and send Kendrick."

"Why would I send anyone? Just come down."

"I cannae."

"Why not?"

"I can climb with the grace of a cat, but going back down is a whole other matter," she confessed, yet continued to twist around the branches away from him.

"Then why would ye be foolish enough to climb higher?"

"Because up is the only place I can go to rid myself of ye."

Calin reached up and grabbed her ankle, ending her escape. He secured his balance and perched himself over the breadth of a thick limb projecting nearly straight out from the trunk. Muttering his opinion about her unruly behavior, Calin propped both feet against two lower branches and pulled on her calf. She didn't budge. This was foolishness. He sat in a tree pulling at his bride's skirts like a wee laddie tugging on his mam.

Aggravated by her defiance, he jerked her down, catching her around the waist when she landed on her backside in front of him.

"Ow!" she complained while the limb bobbed up and down, protesting their combined weight. Leaves rustled and the angered caws of birds filled the air around them. She struggled to put space between them.

"Be still! Else we'll both be on our arses." Calin sat back against main trunk and coerced her to straddle the same limb as he. Their knees knocked and the slight angle of the limb forced her to lean into him.

"Think ye I care if ye fall to your death?" She splayed her hands around the limb between her legs and snapped herself upright.

"Cool your tongue, lass. I just want to talk."

"I think I've talked aplenty for one nigh'. Ye've had your fun, m'laird," she retorted through clenched teeth.

She jerked back in an obvious effort to escape him and nearly toppled out of the tree. Snagging her around the waist, he raised her clear off the limb and brought her closer to him. "I'll talk, and ye will be still and listen," he said in a husky voice.

He paused, searching for the appropriate words. Her animosity had taken him by surprise. He'd been good to her, provided for her, seen her reared with few hardships by a loving family. Did she really find him so repulsive? Why did the notion of marrying him make her so hostile?

Kendrick had suggested apologizing, but that wasn't something he was accustomed to doing. But he'd made a fool of her and mayhap he owed her that much. "Forgive me for deceiving ye. I was simply curious to know my wife's opinion of me."

"I am not your wife." Akira enunciated every syllable with irrefutable clarity.

"Ye will be in a matter of two days."

"Two days!" Akira shrieked in shock, then searched her mind to finagle a means to prolong it. "But the banns. The banns have to be announced every Sabbath at the kirk for three sennights."

"Aye. The chaplain has made this announcement for over a month. And not one member of the congregation has objected."

She wasn't impressed with his wit or his crooked smile.

"I've provided for ye and treated ye weel. 'Tis time ye marry."

Akira couldn't argue this. She'd known most of her life her benefactor would one day come for her. A man she felt a sense of loyalty to. But Laird MacLeod wasn't the person she'd imagined a thousand times over the years. Her benefactor was supposed to be older, more fatherly, much less well-favored. She didn't possess the beauty to keep a man like Calin MacLeod faithful to their marriage bed. She had nary a doubt he would be philandering moments after they wed.

Calin raised her hand to his lips, then pressed a tender kiss over the bruises on her wrist. "Would it be so bad? Being wife to the laird?"

"Aye. 'Twould be bad. 'Twould be horrible. I am not competent to be a laird's wife. My tongue acts of its own accord, causing me to behave in a way some may deem inappropriate for a woman, much less a lady. Ye should reconsider. I'll not make ye a good wife." Her excuses were futile, but they were all she had. Akira wrenched her hand out of his grasp, but couldn't escape his stare. Those eyes. So gentle and loving, reminding her of autumn leaves. How could anyone with such warmth in his eyes be so deceptive?

"Ye are disappointed I am not auld and homely with a passel of bairns for ye to rear?"

She'd let him stew over her opinion of his handsome qualities and, instead, directed her attentions on the more tangible portion of his question. "So ye have nay bairns?"

"Not yet. I had hoped ye might help me with that," he said

with a devilish edge that lit her face afire. Again, he reached for her hand and blew a sigh of relief when she allowed him to have it.

His obvious advances made her uneasy. No one had ever shown an interest in her, since the beauty of her sisters overshadowed her. Even if someone had, they needed to get through Kendrick first. Only two men had proven courageous enough to brawl with Kendrick, and those two were now husbands to Neala and Maggie. But Calin was a man of status. He put Kendrick in his place with a bold look. His constant arrogance implied he never had difficulty gaining a woman's attention. Undoubtedly, a more advantageous marriage would benefit his clan. She had no tocher or title or ground for that matter. She only had two kirtles to her namesake.

What could he possibly gain from their union?

A breeze swirled through the branches and brushed a chill over her skin. Hugging herself, she gazed off into the amber mist swirling around a full moon and searched for her next response.

His warm hand glided up the underside of her cheek. So strong, yet gentle.

When she returned her attention to him, his lips were a breath from hers. Did he intend to kiss her? Should she let him? Before she could answer either of these questions, he leaned closer. The moon reflected in his golden eyes just before he closed them and gently drew her bottom lip between his. He repeated the action with her top lip before he pulled away.

Crivons! "What did ye do that for?" she asked while her heart pounded with a fervency she'd never known.

"Ye dinnae enjoy it?"

"Is it necessary for me to enjoy it?"

"If ye are to be my lady wife, I'd like ye to enjoy it."

"If?" she questioned, with a bit too much enthusiasm. "Then I've a choice in the matter?"

Calin reached for her again, and whatever she intended to say got lost between his lips. Her arms flailed out to her sides searching for stability. The quest came up short as the only anchor her hands found was against his chest. His very brawny chest, flexing with muscles beneath a woolen *léine* shirt.

Pressing one hand against the small of her back, he drew her closer to him. His finger stroked the curve of her lips, as if he wanted her to open to him. The voice in her head begged her to allow him in, to experience all the things she'd denied herself while waiting for this man to come for her.

She didn't. She pushed him away. "M'laird, please. How are we supposed to discuss aught if ye continue to silence me?"

"And what would ye like to discuss?" His lips found their way up her neck. "Mayhap the way your creamy skin glows beneath the colored lights of summer or the smell of the *siùcair* blossom lingering behind this ear?"

Calin's full beard tickled the side of her neck as he nibbled her earlobe. Her skin prickled over her scalp. "M'laird, we should discuss our marriage contract." The man was a heathen—with a particular fondness for kissing. She couldn't deny his touch excited her. The newness of kissing exhilarated her, but she was smart enough to know she entered into a contract she had no gain in. Since she lacked charm, she'd use her wit to get his agreement to certain stipulations. "I'd like a boon or two of ye before I agree to this union." Holding him at bay with a palm against his chest, she thought she may have gained his attention.

"I'll consider your requests, if they're reasonable." No sooner had he spoken, did he turn her palm upright and graze over the skin of her forearm with his lips.

"I would like my kin allowed onto your land for the wedding."

He didn't respond.

"M'laird, do ye agree?" A heavy frown pulled her face downward.

"Do I agree to what?" he carefully asked.

"That my sisters and Mam will be allowed to attend the wedding?"

"Done. Mayhap ye'll not be as demanding as I thought."

And mayhap I will. Akira decided to push the laird. He'd been generous over the years with his monies, and she intended to see how far that generosity would extend. "Ye will allow me to return to the cot-house when Maggie delivers."

"Who's Maggie, and what is she delivering?"

Akira frowned. Surely he jested. She must have mentioned Maggie a dozen times in her missives as a child. "Maggie is my sister. And she is to deliver her first bairn soon."

Calin shook his head as if to free himself of the addle in his brain. "Aye. Forgive me, my mind is elsewhere." He repositioned her onto his lap, her thighs draped over his. Their position, though stable, was most improper. His closeness made her insides quiver and her pulse flutter.

Then he grew beneath her.

The only time she'd ever seen a man's parts was when she caught Kendrick in the barn with a village maid. Of course, after she caught him he shrank. This felt nothing like shrinking. She was flattered that she'd caused a state of arousal in him.

Calin brushed her hair over her shoulder and trailed delicious kisses up and down the column of her neck. Her body tightened when a breeze cooled her moist skin, contradicting the heat of his mouth. He drew back briefly. "For how long do ye wish to return?"

"Return where?" Akira breathed, and fought to regain her senses. What was he talking about?

He donned a sly smile as he reminded her of her question.

"Ye were requesting to go home when your sister delivers. I inquired how long ye wish to be gone."

"Aye. Of course. I'd like to return for . . . a month or two. Until Maggie is capable of getting along on her own."

The man made her wanton. The warmth of his lips heated every nerve ending in her body, and the trail his bushy beard left in the wake of his kisses raised gooseflesh across her chest. She never expected kissing to be so . . . so painfully arousing. A spiraling sensation tickled her lower belly, causing her to squirm.

She needed to remain focused—a task she found extremely difficult in his embrace.

"A sennight. Ye may return for a sennight," he rebutted.

"A fortnight," she countered.

"Done. Aught else?" he queried as he wrapped her hands around his thick neck where she held on as though she might be in danger of falling out of the tree. His roving hand released the three laces of her shift to find its way beneath her plaid. The shock of his swiftness startled her as much as the feel of his fingers against her bare skin, now caressing the ridges of her backbone. She wondered if he might actually be attracted to her or if he made such bold advances on all women with such ease. After all, Calin was the laird and a wealthy laird at that. She decided to allow him enough freedom to keep him agreeing to her requests.

She tested his leniency. "I want my sister, Isobel, welcome in our home and allowed to stay for as long as she desires." When the hair dusting his knuckles tickled the curve of her waist, she drew a sharp intake of air. "And I want ye to pay for the advancement of her education."

Calin's warm hand stilled over her hip. "Ye want me to send her to the priory like I did ye?"

"Nay. I wouldnae wish that place on my worst enemy." Had she known Calin was her benefactor, she wouldn't have revealed so much information. Nonetheless, he deceived her and she had never once felt remorse for stealing his monies from the Abbot. Still, she wanted this promise from him. "Isobel is good with herbs and salves. I want ye to provide the funds necessary for her to be tutored by someone knowledge-able in medicine."

She played coy and looked at him from beneath her lashes. She entwined her fingers at the nape of his neck, hoping he would agree.

While he contemplated, he circled the ridges of her spine. The tightness behind her breast increased with each motion. Lower . . . lower still. A shudder ripped through her, and her nipples hardened.

He was dangerously close to taking liberties that did not yet belong to him.

"Verra weel. I'll speak with my seneschal about the monies." Calin pushed her plaid around her shoulders to trace his fingertips across her collarbone. He followed the feathery path with his lips. "Is this all?"

"Nay," Akira quickly answered. There was more. Lots more. Her mind became a void. Dammit, what else had she intended to ask? And . . . och, what was he doing to her? The man was a thief and a heathen, robbing her of principles and wit. And what was worse, she only wanted him closer. Pressing herself against him, she ached and didn't know why, but this intimacy made her pulse beat between her legs. A squeak came with the air she exhaled. Had she not heard it with her own ears, she wouldn't have believed the noise came from her throat.

Her resolve was slipping. Calin knew it. Her curvaceous bottom wiggled in all the right places. Her breathing came in gulps. This pleased him. A few more kisses would quell her tenacity. After all, that had been what he wanted. A submissive bride. One untouched by another. One who entered their union without qualms and warmed his bed. One who would give him sons and be faithful to him.

As he caressed the smooth skin of her back and hips, he was glad he hadn't brought her a sark to wear. Unfortunately, knowing she sat practically naked beneath his plaid only furthered his discomfort. The lust coursing through his blood would taint his responses. He needed to be careful or he might relinquish every blade of grass on MacLeod soil before she finished her boons.

He should have eased his needs with one of the village maids before he retrieved Akira, but that had never been his way. He was partial to sharing his bed with only one woman at a time. A fleeting moment of disgust niggled through his body when he recalled the woman who last held that position.

He pushed the image from his head and pressed Akira's shapely hips into his pelvis.

"Cease, Calin! Crivons, I can barely breathe, much less think."

"I dinnae want ye to think." He leaned her back then suckled her tender lips again. The hand that had nearly descended all the way down her back, now fondled the base of her full breast.

And a bonnie fine tit it was indeed. Heavy in his hand with the nipple aroused to a tight peak. She was so clean, and fresh, and soft, and making him completely wowf with her incessant chatter.

"Dammit, Calin. Stop!" Akira shoved him back, pulling his wild hands out of her plaid. Both her slender, dark eyebrows wrinkled in frustration. "Is this how ye would have me? In a tree like some rutting animal afore we are wed? If this be your intention, ye may as weel have taken my virginity at *Tigh Diabhail*."

"Ah, then ye are a virgin."

"Of course I am. Dinnae insult me. I have been promised to my benefa—to ye for as long as I can remember. I have never even kissed a mon before this moment. Since I have guarded my favors while the other maids lifted their skirts, I dinnae think it is much to ask for ye to grant me a boon or two. 'Tis the least ye can do."

Relief flushed through him. He had hoped she came to him untouched. A virgin had never found her way into his bed. Finding a woman of such ilk within miles of Cànwyck Castle was like discovering a diamond in a pile of horse dung. The fact he would take a virginal wife to his bed increased his desire for the woman sitting astride his hips. He blew an audible exhale while trying to reposition himself beneath a rigid erection he knew she could feel, as she sat directly atop him. *'Twould be so easy to . . . Nay. Stop it! She's not a whore. She's your betrothed. Treat her with a wee bit of chivalry.*

Calin struggled, but did regain control over his thoughts. "What else would ye ask of me?"

"I'd like permission to educate the kin of your clan alongside your chaplain, given the council and your elders agree. Both girls and boys."

"Boys, too?"

"Aye. Until they're old enough to train under your command."

"If the council agrees, I'll see what I can do. Aught else?"

Akira smiled bashfully. "I want bairns. Lots of them. Dozens. And ye will let me have as many as I like. Maggie says I will be a verra good breeder."

Calin's heart leaped. He couldn't keep the corners of his mouth from curving upward. He'd always dreamed of filling Cànwyck Castle with a brood of heirs. He wanted to start fulfilling this request as soon as possible. "We can have as many as ye like. And this is all?"

Akira reached for his hand and folded his fingers into a

tight fist. Though confused by the gesture, he allowed her reign over his hand.

"My brother promised me a gentle husband, but my sisters always claimed 'twould take a brutal mon to break me. I disagree with them, as I dinnae wish to be broke. I would have your word that ye will never lay your fist to me in anger. Nay matter how provoked ye may be by my tongue."

Calin jerked his hand from hers and shook out his fist. "Ye are bold, and ye shame me by suggesting I would mistreat ye. I have never struck a woman, and I have nay intention of starting with my lady wife." Disturbed by her last request, he couldn't quell the question. "Have ye been beaten, lass?"

"The Prioress struck me once; the eve I departed Beauly Priory. Howbeit, I've seen such women. Seen their faces after their husbands bruised their flesh. I've been blessed to not yet know such pain. Albeit, I received a fair amount of whippings from Papa and Kendrick. Most of which were weel-deserved. Their hands were flat on my bottom and the humiliation alone sent me into nightmares."

Akira's puckered lips gave him a glimpse of that rebellious child. She had already proven to be stubborn. He could only assume she had been a difficult lass for Murrdock and Vanora Neish to rear. Still and all, she wouldn't live in fear of his hand. "Ye will never know such pain as my wife."

"Nay matter how provoked?"

"I vow it. I'll never strike ye."

Akira gripped his face between her palms, gaining his full attention. Based on the seriousness of her expression, he worried about her next request. Up to this point, she hadn't asked for anything he couldn't willingly give her.

"I am not finished," she said. "This one is particularly important to me, m'laird. Ye may think me foolish, but I—"

"What is it?"

She drew a breath. "Ye'll not take a mistress until I have

borne your first child . . . nay your second . . . your third. Ye'll not take a mistress until after I've given ye four bairns. And even then, ye will do your duty as my husband if I choose to have more." Akira lowered her eyes after this request. Her sooty lashes rested against her flushed cheeks hiding any emotion he may have searched for. Her hands fell to her lap and twisted a loose thread. "I know most men of your status keep a leman, but my papa never did."

Was she jesting? She actually expected him to take a mistress? She had a lot to learn about him. He was no monk, but he'd ended all his relationships and intended to take his responsibility as laird seriously. She obviously wanted bairns. Why would she make such a request?

Then a thought struck him. Did she intend to spurn him after she carried? He definitely didn't like the thought of his own wife refusing him in the marriage bed. He bargained. "I'll have nay need for a leman in my bed, if . . . ye dinnae deny me my conjugal rights."

Even in the pale moonlight, he could see the crimson crawling up her cheeks and around her wide shocked eyes. Her mouth opened, then closed. She chewed her bottom lip and contemplated heavily. Och, the lass searched for words. Hot barbed ones, he was certain.

"I wouldnae deny my lord husband."

My lord husband. Those words were forced from her tongue. Calin kissed the corner of her tight lips. "Then ye've my word. I'll not take a mistress." He raised her chin. "Is this all?" He smiled at her patiently, awaiting her next request—knowing she would have one. Mayhap she would ask for gowns and gold or expensive jewels and scented water.

"For the nonce. But considering ye are distracting me from thinking clearly, I would reserve the right to add a boon or two as the notion strikes me."

Her smile melted his heart, and her requests pleased him.

The fact he distracted her from thinking clearly pleased him even more.

"I am ready to go down now. If ye would be so kind as to take me back to the fire."

He drew her close by her chin. Briefly, he considered the circumstances of their betrothal. If she knew who sired her, she probably would refuse to wed him. He had two days to woo the lass and ease her rebellious nature. Kendrick hadn't told her the truth in all these years, and his men could be trusted to hold their tongues about the alliance. He needed her to believe she had no choice in the matter. The guilt he felt for deceiving her was quelled by his sense of duty to protect his clan. He also admitted he enjoyed the wooing.

He stroked her lips open with his thumb. "I have a boon or two of my own I'd like ye to agree upon before I take ye as my lady wife."

Akira remained compliant.

"Ye will allow me to kiss ye every morn . . ." He kissed her bottom lip. "And every eve . . ." He kissed her top lip. "And anytime I feel the need to press your sweet lips to mine." With this request, he tilted his head and flicked his tongue in her mouth. She jerked, but he held her firmly until she returned his kiss with equal abandon. Their tongues circled, vigorously pursuing one another until he released a hoarse groan. The nectar of her mouth tasted sweet and delicious like the honey from the *siùcair* blossom.

He forced himself away, but lingered on the pulse in her neck still beating wildly against his lips. "Will ye agree to my conditions as I have agreed to yours?" he whispered in her ear, waiting for her to catch her breath.

"'Tis all ye ask of me?"

"For the nonce."

"Do I have to return your kisses?"

"Aye." Calin nearly laughed.

"I'll do my best to honor your boon, m'laird . . ."

This time he did chuckle at her attempt to be less than enthusiastic, but he saw a glimpse of flirtation behind her batting lashes. Holding her tightly, he slipped into her mouth for another foray of savory kisses until his body threatened his head with impure thoughts once again. He pulled away. "I'll carry ye down now and warm ye for the rest of the night."

"I'm certain the fire will warm me weel enough."

Knowing full well the fire had been doused to hide them from brigands, Calin ignored her comment and focused on the task of descending. When he supported his weight on the lower branches, she held tightly to his torso. "Is there a particular way I should go about this, lass?"

"Nay. Kendrick always just made me hold tight and cursed me the whole way down. I would prefer ye not curse at me, but if it helps your descent I would forgive ye."

Calin laughed, but when he repositioned himself on the lower branch, she tightened her hold. Her arms wrapped around his neck nearly choking him, and her legs curled around his waist. Any other time he would have welcomed such an embrace, but the woman had the sheer strength of a warrior. "I'll not let ye fall."

"Please just go."

He shimmied down the trunk only knocking her head against one branch. When he jumped to the ground from the last limb, a grunt escaped him. She slid to her feet, smoothed her skirt, and rubbed the side of her skull.

"Sorry, lass. That branch snuck up on me."

"'Tis no harm. I appreciate ye not cursing at me." She turned and started back to camp.

Pulling a congenial "thank you" from her could prove more difficult than pulling teeth. Instead of fighting that battle, he followed her dainty footsteps through the woodland. When they reached camp, they found the others buried in their wools and snoring soundly. Calin quietly laid out a second fur pelt for her beside the one he'd spread earlier and willed his aching body to find rest.

An hour later, his internal request remained unfulfilled. His ears wouldn't allow him sleep. The men snored like pipers, and the north wind had developed a howl. Obviously uncomfortable with the close proximity of their sleeping arrangements, Akira had curled into a ball at the edge of the palette. Her teeth chattered a tune that made his bones ache.

His patience taxed, Calin reached a bold arm around her waist and closed the foot separating them. He added the weight of his fur to her shivering body and whispered into her hair. "Your teeth are stealing my sleeping hours."

"F–f–forgive me, m'laird. I am used t–t–to sleeping with my sisters. Could ye not build up the fire?"

"Nay. We'll not be on my land until we cross the Minch. A fire could reveal our position to brigands. I dinnae want ye in danger." He probably should have assigned one of his men to stand guard, but like him, none of them had slept in days.

"Would ye think me brazen if I used your body for warmth this night?" she asked.

"Nay. Ye may use my body however ye like," Calin said with a lewd grin. But the rakish comment and his smile were wasted on her innocence and the dark.

Akira turned into him, folded his beefy arm around her, then wiggled her way into the niche of his chest. The woman was freezing. Like the glass atop the loch on May Day.

"Ye are warmer than my sisters," she whispered against his chest as her body relaxed and then drifted to sleep. Though the flutter of her peaceful breathing soothed his ears, her soft curves now had him in turmoil. A wool-covered thigh had wormed its way between his, while the swell of her breasts pressed gently against his chest. Her feminine scent could drive a man to murder, and just when he thought his cock couldn't possibly get harder, she slid a hand between them and unconsciously massaged his earlobe.

She'd make a good wife—once he tamed her temper.

He wished his father could see the man he'd become. He was confident Da would be proud of his dedication to the alliance. Calin dwelled on little else over the years. Having apprenticed under Uncle Kerk, he'd been trained by most of the men now in his charge—men who were loyal and dedicated to the clan. He would do anything for kin, and his union with Akira would protect them and their lands.

He closed his eyes, wishing he never had to tell her the truth.

Chapter Six

Laird Baen Kinnon sat at his trestle table and clutched his throbbing skull. Morning always brought the same damned ache. The same frigid cold. Dawn's light had already cut through the mist and crawled up the tower wall. Gray light cast a shadow over the young girl cowering in the corner of his solar. He pointed to a satchel atop a three-legged cuttie stool. "Fetch me that poke o' herbs and come fill my cup with ale, wench."

The girl shuffled across the moldy floor rushes to do his bidding. She'd spent the night curled up with a few orange cats in front of an empty hearth. Had he not been blind drunk, her pathetic bawling would have kept him up half the night. Luckily, the drink had swiftly overcome him.

Her tear-spiked lashes rose just enough for her to peek at him through dirty, pale hair as she handed him the satchel.

She shivered.

He grinned. Just being in his presence terrified her, and he had yet to touch her. He retrieved the satchel from her shaking hand and proceeded to crush the dried herbs with the mortar and pestle, letting the biting smell penetrate the fog in his head. The mixture had been one of the sparse bits of knowl-

edge his father left him. The concoction had softened his old
man's fists in the early hours of day and, by twilight, his father
had always been too drunk again to stand, much less beat him.

He sprinkled the dust into his cup, stirred the ale with his
finger, and then consumed the drink in a single swallow. He
held out his cup for the girl to refill. Her hands shook with
the task, but once completed, she attempted to scramble away.
He snagged her wrist and pulled her onto his lap. Her soft
young skin contrasted with the leathery hide of his hand. He
stroked her cold neck and felt her shake beneath his fingertips. Leaning into her, he watched her pulse beat in her throat.
"How auld ye be?"

"Ten an' three, m'laird," she mumbled, her lips near blue,
her jaw quivering.

He could feel her panic. Could smell her fear. He needed
to intensify her terror before her father came. His hand
slipped into her loose bodice to cup her small breast. She
jerked against him, her ice-cold fingers clutched his forearm.

"Ye are auld enough to marry. Have ye a laddie in mind?"

"Nay, m'laird."

"Mayhap I should take ye to my bed. Teach ye how to pleasure a mon."

The girl's response came in the form of a shuddering sob.

Her future held no import to him. He sought her revulsion.
He intended to use the little innocent to coax information
from her father. Something had been amiss for months. He'd
sensed his warriors' betrayal on the training field. There was
a snake among them, and he needed to find the vermin before
he bit. Once he discovered who he was, he would force
Darach to carry out the traitor's punishment. The wretch had
yet to kill a man, much less torture a prisoner. Darach needed
to spill some blood to gain the respect of the Kinnon warriors
before he claimed chieftainship.

Kinnon scoffed, lost in his thoughts. Darach couldn't lead

a frog to water. The whore he'd bought the boy from long ago claimed he had the blood of a Spanish aristocrat. But Darach had turned out to be a sniveling twit without a trace of backbone. How many years had the boy been skulking about in the north tower—hiding away from dusk to dawn?

His named heir possessed no character for leadership. No skill for manipulating others. The only pawns he managed to maneuver were the armies of cats scuttling throughout the interior walls of the tower. The closest Darach got to the training field was a crow's flight from the parapet atop the north tower. The knave was of no more value to him than his four dead daughters. At least they might have filled his coffers through marriage.

If only Lena had borne him a son—a male bairn possessing his own noble blood, things would have been different. Thoughts of her still infuriated him eighteen years later. He awoke often at night to the hollow sound of sorrow and the cries of babes in the nursery. She haunted the walls of Brycen Castle, of this he was certain. Nigh every chamber remained irritably cold like her betraying heart. Her lavender scent was the only smell that didn't reek in this Godforsaken keep. How could the bitch still live inside his head?

He ceased the mild assault on the skittish doe in his lap and flung her to the floor. "Get off me."

The girl tripped over a pile of old chicken bones as she scrambled to reach the farthest corner of his solar. Laird Kinnon stood abruptly, knocking back his chair. A sharp pain coursed behind his eye. He refilled his tankard and in one swallow, he emptied the cup. With his exhale came the hot plumes of anger.

Lena had turned him into the monster he was today. He'd been respected by his clan before he married that whore, and she betrayed him with the MacLeod. Dalkirth had belonged to the Kinnon ancestors for decades and he would see his soil in English hands before a MacLeod dare own a blade of his grass.

He finished the flagon of ale then wiped the back of his hand across his mouth. The ruckus outside his solar door reminded him of his present task. The girl's father had arrived. He crossed the chamber and pulled her up by her hair. She yelped then he forced her hand beneath his plaid and pressed her icy palm against his semi-hard erection. She blanched, and he thought she might swoon. Not giving her the opportunity, he gripped her around the waist and threw her atop a feather tick buried beneath shrouds of drapes.

A high-pitched scream rang out of her mouth at the same time the chamber door burst open and slammed against the stone wall.

"Let her alone, m'laird!" Niall Kinnon yelled as Kinnon's warriors threw him into the room. He scurried to his feet and rushed across the floor to get to his daughter. "She's all I have left in the world."

Laird Kinnon motioned for his guest to sit.

"I mean ye no dishonor, m'laird, but I'd rather stand," Niall said, while pushing his daughter behind him.

With a single nod, Kinnon dismissed his men standing beneath the doorframe, then returned his attentions to Niall. "Do ye decline your laird's hospitality? Like ye refused my order for an audience? Your daughter would be safe in her bed had ye come when I summoned ye."

He marched over the planks of his solar and rammed his fist into Niall's gut, sending him to his hands and knees. "A Kinnon warrior does not fall after one blow. Get up! Ye are a disgrace to my clan. I should strip ye o' my name and your bitch daughter, too."

He kicked him in the ribs. "Get up, ye worthless cur."

Gasping for air, Niall stood clutching his side. He stared remorsefully at his daughter and took a place at the trestle table. He didn't turn away the silver flask of whisky Kinnon offered him. Instead, he took a hearty sip followed by another.

Laird Kinnon joined him in the drink, giving him ample time to comprehend the seriousness of his situation. "Ye pledged fealty to me a decade ago. I took your family in when ye had nowhere to go. I've been verra good to ye and trained ye beneath my own sword. After all I've done, why have ye betrayed me?"

Niall's eyes widened. His skin turned ashen. Knuckles whitened around the flask. He took another gulp. Kinnon recognized fear easily.

"Answer me!"

"I have not betrayed ye, m'laird."

Kinnon was sick to death of the lies. He crushed Niall's head to the table. Blood spilled from his nose and mouth. "Ye lie! I have protected these lands for my kin, and my warriors repay me with lies." He pulled his *sgian dubh* from his stocking and held the blade firm behind Niall's ear.

His daughter cried out.

"If ye e'er wish to hear her screams again, ye will tell me who leads the rebellion against me," Kinnon threatened.

Niall's head shook and sweat gathered at his temple. "I dinnae know. I swear it. I dinnae know."

More damned lies. Kinnon launched off him and grabbed the girl by the back of the neck. Holding her tight in front of him, he pressed the blade against her breast. A dab of crimson bled into her sark. "I'll cut out her heart and feed it to ye raw if ye dinnae answer me."

"Please, have mercy, m'laird."

"Give me the traitor's name, and I'll release her."

Niall pinched his eyes tight. His loyalty to the enemy sparked a fury in Laird Kinnon that summoned the beast inside him. "I'll give ye the time it takes me to rape your daughter to reveal the traitor's name then I'll kill her in front of ye." With a rip, the girl's bodice hung from her waist.

Niall's eyes flooded with unshed tears. His head fell and his lips moved in prayer. "Kendrick. Kendrick Neish," he confessed. "Now please, free my child and do with me what ye will."

Laird Kinnon smiled. Kendrick was a traitor just like his father, Murrdock Neish, and could be dealt with the same way. He could enjoy using each one of Kendrick's sisters until he flushed out the bastard. The same way he had Murrdock. The same way he handled all those who rebelled against him, including Niall.

Tossing the girl aside with the flick of his wrist, he turned his blade on her father. Strong fingers laced over Niall's forehead as Kinnon pulled his head back then sliced his throat open. He couldn't have the informant infecting his new plan, nor would he tolerate disloyalty.

"Da!" Niall's daughter screamed and fisted her hands over her mouth.

Satisfaction filled Kinnon's chest as he met the girl's horrified eyes. "It seems your father has met with an untimely death. As your laird, 'tis my duty to see that ye are fostered accordingly."

He licked his lips and followed the screaming girl to the floor.

Chapter Seven

Akira awoke to Calin's moist lips seducing hers. He tasted sinfully delicious. His warm inviting mouth aroused her senses. Until those senses fully awoke, and she realized what she was doing. She shouldn't return his kisses so willingly, so wantonly. They were not yet wed and she wanted his respect—and the strength of his arousal pressing against her thigh had nothing to do with respect. Mam had not taught her propriety for her to lay beside this man and allow him to have his way with her.

She tried backing away, but the ground prevented her goal. "Have ye plans to rut with me now, m'laird?" she asked, displaying a congenial smile.

"By the saints, lass. There is nay reason to be so wicked so early. Try again. This time mayhap ye could say something a wee bit more pleasant."

Akira looked past him into a gray sky and searched her mind for pleasant words. *It would be pleasant if I could go home. It would be pleasant if I wasnae cursed. It would be pleasant if I dinnae enjoy the fact that your hand just slipped beneath my wool.*

The man had her wanton again, "If ye dinnae remove your

person from me, I'll introduce my knee to your bollocks. I might add, this may not be *pleasant* for ye."

He laughed at her threat. "Those werenae pleasant words. Try again."

Spiteful words came easily to her. She'd known harsh words as a child and learned long ago how to deflect the jeering. No matter how many barbs she threw at Calin, he dodged them and pressed forward. Mayhap he was a good match for her. The tightness of her face smoothed into a genuine smile. She conceded to his game. "Good morrow, m'laird."

"There. That wasnae so difficult. And my response would be: 'Tis as beautiful a morn as the vision I awoke to." Calin smiled at her as if he'd known her a hundred years and could wake to her face a hundred more.

The man was born with a silver tongue and a reckless ability to lie with it. Not for one second did she believe he thought she was beautiful. What was his game? She'd agreed to be his wife. Why was he making such great efforts to flatter her now?

Calin continued. "And your sleepy eyes and supple lips are all a mon needs to arise in good spirits. Of course, the fact I've managed to untie these three pesky ribbons brightens my morn all the more."

Now he was the one being wicked. The palm of his hand lay over her stomach while playful fingers danced circles around her navel. She wished her body would quit betraying her. The man's closeness had her near scorched with foreign desires. She squirmed just enough that her knee brushed the base of his heavy sac causing him to flinch. She wondered if he awoke every morn in such a state of arousal. The fleeting question sent a jolt of expectancy through her mons.

Calin leaned in to kiss her, again, but she placed a finger over his lips, removed his hand from beneath her plaid and stopped him. "Why are ye kissing me, m'laird?"

"Ye agreed to this condition. That ye would kiss me every morn, and every night, and anytime I felt the need to kiss ye."

The grin splitting his face reminded her of how improper she'd been the night before. "This condition was made based on our union, and we are not yet married. So your kisses will have to wait along with the rest of ye that has arisen." He looked crestfallen, staring down at her like a child who lost his pet.

"And if I dinnae want to wait?" Calin questioned.

"Then I'll have to make more demands of ye." Akira held back the smile threatening her face while contemplating her options. Her curiosity about their betrothal had been piqued the night before when he readily agreed to her requests. She wondered why he chose her so many years ago. Why not Maggie or Neala? Did Papa or Kendrick owe him a debt? Kendrick had known him longer than she'd been alive and her brother would be the only one who could answer her questions. Not that Kendrick had ever been loose with his answers in the past. She gave up trying to pry information out of her brother long ago.

She needed to know what Calin would gain from their union, but the man guarded her like a knight protecting his king. She had to ride with Kendrick today. But how?

As she stroked Calin's dense auburn beard and inhaled his masculine scent, a mischievous idea developed in her head. She traced a fingertip over the brow that always seemed to be raised. "If ye intend to take liberties on my lips prior to our union, I would request that ye bathe with soap a minimum of once a sennight. Starting this day."

He snorted loudly at her blatant insult. "M'lady, are ye implying that I smell?"

"I am *implying* naught. I am telling ye that ye stink." Akira batted her thick lashes at him. "And this"—she tugged roughly at his beard—"I fear may be infested. If ye've any inclination of kissing me prior to our vows, then your beard will need to go as weel."

Calin's eyes widened. "M'lady, a Highlander without a beard is as rare as a sheep with nay wool. I have nary a doubt, ye are testing me."

Akira crossed her arms over her chest and raised both brows to challenge him.

"Ye cannae be serious. Ye want me to . . . shave. The bath is acceptable, even desirable at this point, I admit. But the beard? 'Tis a most unreasonable request. Ye cannae ask this of me."

"Then ye refuse?" She shot him a contrived glare to reflect her stubbornness.

Calin stroked his beard, contemplating briefly. "I'll not do it. I refuse."

Akira pushed him away then stepped out of the blankets of their pallet. "Then I refuse to ride with ye, too. I'll not subject myself to another day suffocating on your repugnant odor. Nor will I have my skin crawling with your lice. Nor will I allow ye to chaff my face." Stomping away in mock rebellion, Akira went to the brook for her morning ablutions.

Pleased as a sheared sheep in the summer months, she brought her hand to her mouth to cover her giggle then quickly asked God for forgiveness for the ruse. Granted, it was a wicked thing to do, but today she would seek answers from Kendrick.

Calin sat up and scowled. The little vixen was playing him like a fife. He agreed to every one of her requests the night before and, still, she wasn't satisfied. This had to stop. He couldn't have her thinking he would dance every time she opened her mouth or flashed those big blue eyes his way.

He tossed a murderous glance at Kendrick, who obviously overheard the entire quarrel as he grinned like a day-old groom.

At least he was safe from the badgering of his men. His dear cousin, Jaime, would thoroughly enjoy this if he wasn't still snug inside his plaid.

"Och, the lass is a shrew. Did ye raise her with extra spit and fire just to spite me or did she come that way?"

Two bushy eyebrows rose and curved Kendrick's eyes into half moons. "Akira's been spittin' flames since ye laid the squallin' dragon in me arms. Ye've verra much to learn about her. Other women—as I'm sure—may have fallen over themselves tryin' to gain your attentions. Akira will not. I fear ye may labor hours on end to have her melt in your hand." Kendrick burst with laughter. "I've a straightedge in me saddlebag, if ye've need of it."

Calin gaped at the witless man as if horns suddenly sprouted from his head. "Are ye wowf? Think ye I am actually going to concede to this? I will be the laughingstock of my clan. Why would she make such a request o' me?"

"I suspect the lass is testing your loyalty."

"I *am* loyal," Calin responded sharply.

"Ye are loyal to Clan MacLeod and the alliance. Mayhap Akira wishes to test your loyalty to her."

Admittedly, this decision might be less taxing if Kendrick wasn't so obviously enjoying Calin's quandary. His auld friend was starting to grate on his nerves.

"If ye dinnae wish to shave for Akira then do it for your clan. Do it for the alliance. By making such a bold sacrifice, you are ensuring her acceptance of your union. And ye will flatter her in the process."

Calin guffawed at Kendrick's back-minded persuasion. "And how do I benefit?"

Kendrick's grin turned into a toothy smile. "Ye get to ride with the lass and protect your secrets."

A deep throaty growl vibrated out of Calin's throat.

"Damnation! I'm the chieftain of Clan MacLeod. Why in the name of Saint Margaret am I contemplating this?"

Pushing himself to his feet, Kendrick left Calin with a final thought. "Think o' it as a means to subside some o' the guilt ye must feel for branding her."

Calin pushed air through his nose like an old bull.

A brilliant sun broke over the ridge, cutting through a hazy mist as the men waited atop their steeds. Sirius pranced impatiently among a patch of wildflowers while Akira sat pillion behind Kendrick, her nerves as fragile as an autumn leaf. Because Calin's men hovered over them, she restrained herself from asking her brother any direct questions involving her union to Calin. She didn't know how much these men knew or even if they could be trusted.

Feeling comfortable and safe again, she leaned into Kendrick and took a deep breath in an effort to ease her tension. She quickly recoiled. Not even the wildflowers beneath their horse's hooves could lessen what this journey had done for Kendrick's pungent odor. "Ye might consider a bath yourself, dear brother. With soap."

"Think ye this is funny? I cannae begin to understand why ye made such a ridiculous demand o' him. The mon has been verra good to ye. To our entire family. Laird MacLeod is chieftain o' the clan ye are marryin' into on the morrow, and ye make a fool o' him in front of his warriors. A mon has his pride ye know."

"But I just—"

Kendrick jerked a flat palm into the air and shook his head. "Quiet lass."

Akira held her tongue, but wasn't the least bit concerned about making a fool of him. Of course, Calin wouldn't shave.

She glanced at the other MacLeods. Their expressions filled with accusations, but not a single man voiced his opinion.

As the seconds passed painfully slow, she regretted her actions. She had goaded Calin to speak with Kendrick alone. Made a request the chieftain would, nary a doubt, not fulfill. She didn't really expect him to shave, but he'd been at the brook far longer than any of the others. It was madness to believe he would fulfill her request just to kiss her. Did the man lack control of his lusts so much he couldn't wait another day until they wed? Was it possible he might actually be attracted to her?

Akira shook her head, dismissing her foolish thoughts.

Calin emerged over the knoll, bare-chested, clasping his *léine* shirt between rigid fingers. The tails of his plaid swayed from his waist while the sun glistened off damp bronze skin dusted with golden hairs. His arms were as thick as her thighs and proudly displayed the rings of battle many warriors inked into their skin. The top blue ring, being thicker and more prominent than the other three, bespoke of a warrior's loss in battle. Dark eyes met his men's curiosity. He cringed.

Akira followed his line of sight and found his men gawking at him open-mouthed.

Gordon was the first to find words. "Who are ye, and what've ye done with our laird?"

Calin stabbed him with another piercing look. "Did I give ye permission to speak?" He sidestepped to Kendrick's mount, grabbed Akira around the waist, and then jerked her to the ground. "Ye ride with me," he demanded, more than a little perturbed. Turning to his men, he ordered, "Ye will ride ahead. We'll meet ye at the Minch. The vessel should be waiting to ferry us across. Gordon, handle the funds with the captain."

There was no movement—not man, nor beast. They were still gaping with slack jaws at him as if he were a bogie that slithered up from the underworld. "Ye'll do as ordered. Now begone!"

Calin smacked the flanks of Gordon's horse sending it racing. The others followed suit. His harsh tone and abrupt actions startled her, but she knew he was holding onto what pride he hadn't just sheared off and left in the brook.

True, Calin wasn't the man she had envisioned for her husband, but he proved capable of changing that image. She tried to hide her joy, all the while, ogling the handsome creature standing in front of her. Strength lined his face from strong cheekbones to a distinguished nose. The golden color of his eyes, though lit with anger, sparkled beneath dark lashes, and his rousing woody aroma stimulated her senses. But most of all—what tickled her innards and curled her lips—was his smooth jaw. She wouldn't be riding with Kendrick, but she was nonetheless pleased.

He pulled her possessively to his chest and raised her hand to his cheek as if awaiting her inspection. She didn't deny him. He did this for her, and she intended to reward him with her approval. Her fingertips touched his freshly shaven cheek. "'Tis better," she murmured.

"I should hope this pleases ye," he responded gruffly.

"It pleases me verra much. Verra, verra much." She played over the slight cleft in his chin and along his strong jaw.

"Then I would have my kiss now," he demanded and made himself ready for her by bending down.

Akira considered pecking him on the cheek just to be obstinate, but she secretly wanted to taste what he offered. Standing on tiptoes, she threaded her fingers into his darkened hair, flowing loosely in wet clumps over his brawny shoulders. Drawing him close, she skimmed a feather-light kiss over the ridges of perfectly chiseled lips before nuzzling her cheek against his jawline.

Settling back on her heels, Akira wavered beneath his

smile. His grin creased his face with three dimples. Two set
in his cheeks and one that winked at her from the corner of
his eye. The longer she stared at him the deeper the crevices
became until he flashed white teeth. Akira clutched her chest
and inhaled deeply. He was certainly easy to look at.

Calin growled, ripped his *léine* shirt on, and rushed past
her. "Ye are becoming difficult to woo." He mounted and
hauled her up in front of him. He whisked her raven locks
aside and took a moment to dine on her neck. "I'll not always
do everything ye ask of me."

"I know." Akira warmed with amusement at the victory she
won. Having only known him a day, she was elated with his
willingness to please her. She resolved to be content with their
arrangement, regardless of why he chose her. For her own
safeguard, she would accept the fact he chose her because she
was smart enough to manage the keep: As long as she kept her
wits, she'd have a bounty of bairns to love her and a bonnie
fine man to wake to every morn. She *would* make him a good
wife.

"If ye dinnae wipe that smirk off your face, I may decide to
take liberties that dinnae belong to me, even if ye refuse me,"
he threatened while his hand inched up her thigh beneath
her skirt.

"Ye will not!" Her smirk faded and defiance took its place.

Calin removed his hand and conceded. "I know."

He dug his heels into the underside of his steed, and they
broke into a sprint over the green marsh of the moorland.

The passage across the aqua-blue waters of the Minch took
the better part of the morning. Otters, seals, and a variety of
sea life entertained Akira while Kendrick, Calin, and his men
quietly discussed a topic that caused them all to scowl. Akira's
attempts to eavesdrop were not successful, though she caught

a snippet about the lordship of the Isles before they blatantly changed the subject. She didn't know why they would be discussing the age-old battle. That title had been forfeited to the crown years ago and enough Scots had died fighting to regain possession of it, including Papa. She suspected their deliberations also involved her pending marriage to Calin, but couldn't surmise why that topic would make them frown so. Unless the MacLeod kinsmen disapproved of his choice. She felt certain at least one of them didn't like her. Gordon was scowling at her now.

She scowled back.

Mayhap he thought she was a witch like the two MacLeods who'd taken her to *Tigh Diabhail*? She rather hoped to enter her new clan without those accusations looming over her.

Regardless of Gordon's opinion, she was determined to earn the approval of Calin's kin with her quick wit—a task which could prove difficult since they refused to converse with her.

The MacLeod men harassed Calin mercilessly about his abrupt decision to separate himself from his facial hair. Calin only grinned, ignoring their banter, all the while casting her devilish winks to let her know he was man enough to withstand their ridicule.

Upon reaching the steep cliffs of the Isles, they traveled across valleys blanketed with purple heather. Only when crossing the shallow lochs did they slow their pace. He purposely fell behind during these leisure periods to take full advantage of the stipulations Akira agreed to—kissing her any time he felt the need. And over the course of several hours, he felt the need on more than one occasion. If he wasn't kissing her, he was grazing her neck with his new smooth face and sneaking tiny bites of her earlobes between his teeth.

Every time he pressed his lips to hers, a wave of excitement flowed through her. The man seemed genuinely attracted to her. The stiffness of his manhood pressing against her backside the whole of the day was enough to prove that point, and she had difficulty denying his magnetism. The same frustrating ache she'd known the night before tormented her all day, but she managed to hold firm. Though only a peasant, she was a woman of virtue, and she refused to let the man have free roam over her person before they spoke their vows. Unfortunately, what would be expected of her after they wed terrified her. She would be his wife and no longer able to refuse him. If she intended to gain his respect, she would have to prove her intelligence and worth to him.

She shared her ideas in regards to the children's education and asked him endless questions about Cànwyck Castle and Clan MacLeod. He seemed pleased with her ideas and inquiries. Akira decided he could be a reasonable man, that is, until she drifted to sleep only to awaken with his hand nestled neatly over her breast inside her plaid.

Once inside the sanctuary of their homelands, they made camp and settled around a low-burning fire. Akira's entire body hummed with an uncomfortable ache she didn't know how to soothe, but somehow knew Calin's seductions were responsible for her turmoil.

A bitter wind swept out of the darkness, chilling her back. Akira shivered and inched nearer the fire. Calin instantly moved to sit beside her, his arm curled possessively around her back. Strong fingers squeezed her hip. She glanced up at him, but his eyes roamed over the golden flames and locked with his men. Briefly, she exchanged a quick glance with each of his warriors. The moment became awkward and she suddenly felt very small.

Pulling from his embrace, she moved to stir the fire. "Kendrick, ye five deliberated over a matter of great importance today on the vessel. What had all of ye looking so somber?"

"We were discussin' how many drams o' whisky would be consumed at your weddin'."

Rolling her eyes at the blatant lie, she studied the five men with avid curiosity. In the ease of their safe surroundings, each man warmed his belly with a flask of malt whisky. Akira resolved if they didn't want to return pleasant conversation then she would prove her endurance and dabble in the strengths of their spirits. Papa never shied away from a healthy dose of whisky after a long day of shearing. Mayhap that was just the remedy she needed to ease her nerves after such a grueling day. Returning to stand in front of Calin, she held out her hand. "May I have a drink?"

"Of whisky?" He made a sour face she hadn't seen yet.

"Aye." She grabbed his flask out of his hand and took a hearty sip.

She nearly choked. The peppery flavor scorched her throat. The flames coated her insides clear to her toes. Her eyes widened as she inhaled large gulps of air, but still she maintained composure.

Crivons! No wonder Mam never let us touch the stuff. She loosened her white-knuckle grip on the flask. If she meant to socialize with these brutes, she'd have to match their stamina. After taking another plentiful drink, she broke into a fit of coughing.

Calin shot to her side, patting her back, and pushing a flagon of spring water beneath her nose. "Are ye wowf, woman? Ye dinnae drink whisky like wine."

When she regained her breath, she forcefully shoved his offering away. "If these barbarians will not converse with me then I'm forced to join in what appears to be the only form o' enter . . . entertain . . . fun. If I'm to be your wife, I'll need to be able to hold my whisky."

Calin broke into a wide grin. "But our women dinnae drink whisky."

She shot him a lethal glare and jerked away from him when he reached for the flask. "If your women dinnae participate in your social gatherin's, what do they do?"

Calin shrugged and eyed his men, who shrugged back. "I suspect they tend to their husbands, and birth their bairns."

Akira gave a quick hoot to his comment, squeezed her eyes tight, and downed another generous swig. She hiccuped once, twice, then swayed side to side. Calin steadied her with one hand. There must be something besides whisky in the flask to affect her so quickly. Mayhap a potion? Or poison? Someone spoke to her, but she couldn't place the voice. She blinked several times when the three men on the log transformed into trolls. She laughed, but not aloud. Her arms felt light like the wings of a dragonfly. She conceded to her own stupidity.

This had been a verra bad idea.

She shoved the flask back into Calin's grasp then staggered out of the fire's circle. She stumbled into the grove, dodging low-hanging branches, and supporting herself from one tree trunk to the next until she found one sturdy enough to hold. She closed her heavy eyelids and the world seemed to stop between her ears.

Oddly enough, the only thing she saw on the back of her eyelids was a gentle warrior whose smile made her weak in the knees and whose kisses made her forget reality.

She was soused.

Chapter Eight

Calin looked at Kendrick. "Did I set her teeth off again?"

Looking equally puzzled, Kendrick shrugged. "I've never seen Akira act so odd, nor can I recall e'er seein' her drink aught stronger than watered wine—much less Scots whisky. Howbeit, I'd worry 'bout her scalin' another tree if I was ye."

If the woman climbed a tree, she was liable to break her wee neck. Frustrated, Calin ripped through a batch of stinging nettles while the forest floor snapped beneath his footsteps. He found her hugging the trunk of a silver birch just inside the grove. Her cheek pressed against its peeling bark, and her eyes lay shut, but the curve on her lips didn't appear to be hostile. She looked . . . content.

"I think I'd like ye to wear that face when ye hug me," he said, his voice laced with a touch of foolery.

Akira didn't move. "Ye poisoned me."

He laughed and drew closer. "'Tis not poison. Just the finest Scots blend to pass between your lips. The brewer claims 'twill put hair on your chest."

"I dinnae want hair on my chest." Akira moaned. Actually, the sound came out more as a whimper. "How do ye drink that wretched stuff?"

"Och, ye dinnae *drink* whisky. Ye sip it. I've been nursing that flask for a month." He placed his hand on the small of her back. Her entire being quivered. He'd upset her. Damnation, but he hated to see a woman cry, especially this woman. "Forgive me if I said something to offend ye, but please dinnae cry, lass."

Akira continued to shake until she released her hold on the tree and doubled over holding her gut. Just as he was certain she would retch, she surprised him by bursting into laughter.

"Tend to their husbands?" she choked out between giggles. "Think ye this is what women do? Tend to their husbands like a herd of sheep? I can almost see the image in your head. Buxom women filling a trough with slop and shoving it beneath their husbands' noses just before shearing their beards off and plopping out a bairn or even two during the whole affair."

Akira swayed slightly in small circles then cocked her head as if in recollection. "Come to think of it, Auld Bessie birthed her last son while feedin' the butcher his noontide meal." Her laughter sailed through the air again.

Though the description struck her more humorous than it did him, Calin shared in her contagious laughter—not a sweet giggle muffled behind her hand, but a booming cackle trickled with snorts. She laughed aloud for a longer period than he thought necessary before wiping streaming tears from her eyes. "Forgive me, m'laird. 'Tis really not that funny."

A few hearty quaffs of Scots whisky and the woman was completely blootered. The morrow would be taxing for her, and he didn't want her afflicted with a pounding head on their wedding night. Much-needed rest would find her quickly, and he wanted her tucked into his side when sleep overcame her.

He couldn't quite shake this feeling of possessiveness she evoked in him. Putting one arm behind her knees and another behind her back, he lifted her up and cradled her against his chest.

The smile disappeared from her face. Her eyes slowly focused on him. Just him. Women rarely looked at him and saw a man. They only saw the chieftain. The man with power and wealth. He'd spent a lifetime learning how cold and lonely those possessions were. He wanted Akira to see him, not his status. He attempted to read the emotions in her eyes, but the sheen glossing her sapphire irises was void of sensibility. Her lips parted, and he sorely wanted to suckle the moonlight off her full bottom lip.

"Ye are a delicious-looking mon, Calin MacLeod." She traced his brows, his nose, his lips. The tickle sent a flash of heat through his veins and straight to his groin.

Her gaze followed the path of her finger. "Ye've a mouth that tempts me in ways I shouldnae admit." She wrapped both arms around his neck then inexpertly pressed her mouth to his. Tilting her head, she grazed over the inside of his lips, his teeth, his tongue.

Her assault caught him unguarded, but he eagerly returned her advances. An age-old hunger thrummed through him. He had to cage that beast, else it would devour him. Or mayhap her. When he pulled back, she continued to kiss his face, his chin, his sensitive earlobe, anything she could get her hot mouth on.

"What are ye doing?"

"I'm upholding my end of our contract," she whispered in a breathy seductive voice that made his cock stiffen.

"But ye wouldnae even let me sit next to ye by the fire."

"Ye were claiming me. Marking me as yours in front of your men. I dinnae want to be your prey or your property. I want . . . I want . . ."

Her words ended on the pulse in his neck, taking possession of the life beating there. "What do ye want, my Akira? Ask, and it is yours."

"I want ye to kiss me." She forced his chin lower and

delved into his mouth once again. Her small fingers tangled in the hair at the nape of his neck. Pulling, tugging, tightening with the aggression of her kiss. But he wanted more. Much more.

"I dinnae know why, but I cannae get close enough to ye," she confessed on a breath.

He knew the whisky made her audacious, but months had passed since he'd bedded a woman. He wanted her, and she wanted him. Neither could deny the passion igniting between them. She was innocent, yet spirited. He could feel her soul coming to life inside her.

He dropped her legs. His free hands were everywhere—caressing her breasts, kneading her thighs, then he cupped her backside and pushed her pelvis into his. He wanted to throw her to the ground and taste every ounce of her naked flesh until she begged him to take her.

By the saints! He had to get the lust out of his blood, else his mind would turn to mush. The whimpers escaping her throat were his undoing. He lifted her ankle-length skirt and squeezed the soft flesh of her shapely bottom in both hands. "Sweet, sweet Akira. What are ye doing to me?"

She gasped. Her body tensed. A feeble resistance pushed against his chest.

"Please stop." Her words came out as a sad whisper.

Their gazes locked. He saw regret pooling behind her eyes.

"Forgive me, m'laird. Ye must think me wanton." Akira pushed him away further and held her face between the palms of her hands. "Nay wonder ye dinnae let your women drink whisky."

"Had we known our women would react this way, we would serve whisky at every meal." He reached for her, but she tottered backward.

"This is not funny."

"Ye were laughing enough a moment ago."

"That was before I threw myself at ye. How are ye supposed to respect me if I act like this after two days in your presence? This is not me. I promise to be the decent, respectable, intelligent woman ye've chosen to be your lady wife. Forgive me, m'laird. I've acted a fool." Akira tightened the pleats at her waist then smoothed wild black tendrils back into place. Her fingers shook with the task, after which she proceeded to fan her face with both hands.

Calin didn't know what to make of her erratic mood. Was the woman speaking in tongues again? "Why do ye think I am marrying ye?" he asked, even though he worried slightly over her answer.

"I have asked myself that question repeatedly. Since I have nay tocher, nor land or title, I suspect ye are marrying me because I am smart. Ye are the one who paid for my education at the priory. I presume ye want me to manage the keep and bear your heirs—heirs who will be intelligent. If ye wanted more, ye would have chosen one of my sisters."

"Why?"

"Because they are beautiful."

The nonchalant manner in which she made this statement angered him. "And ye are not?" Calin posed this as a question. Not a statement. But the dejected look on her face told him this is how she took it—as a cold, blunt statement.

Somehow, her creamy skin looked paler beneath the gauzy light of the moon. She bowed her head, letting her raven hair hide her melancholy. "'Tis true. I am not."

"Damnation, woman! Have ye never seen yourself in a looking glass? How blind are ye that ye cannae see your own beauty?"

Akira's lids snapped open, her brow curled in denial. "Ye say this to please me. I know 'tis a lie. I look nothing like them. I barely look like a Scot. My own papa told me I was special. That my brain was so full of information it burnt the red out of my hair. My sisters say I have nay a freckle on my face because the angels dinnae sprinkle me with dust when I was born."

"Childish banter! Why would ye believe such foolishness, and from your own kin?" He reached for her, but she was nimble for a half-drunk woman with the wiles of a wildcat.

"'Tis not foolishness. The devil marked me with his image at birth. 'Tis why Papa moved my family from the bailey and into the cot-house when I was just a child. Laird Kinnon burned three women for acts of heresy that year. He made the kinfolk watch. The bastard lit the fire before the accused had strangled beneath the noose."

Those living in Scotland knew the punishment for heresy was execution by fire. Of course, death only occurred after a merciful strangulation. Villagers flocked from far and wide to witness the horror with eager eyes.

Calin frowned as the image of him branding her with his father's signet ring came to life in his mind's eye. The act of a stupid boy who placed the MacLeod crest on everything he owned. He couldn't very well explain that folly to her now, but he was to blame for her feelings of inadequacy. The woman lived her entire life thinking her soul cursed because of him.

Hell and damnation! How was he going to fix this? "Your father moved your family to protect ye from Laird Kinnon. Ye are not cursed."

Both hands swiped her eyes and a quavering sniffle followed that action. "Ye dinnae know what 'tis like to be different. 'Tis a verra lonely life for a child." Her voice cracked.

He knew exactly how it felt to be different and lonely. From the night he lost his father, he'd felt imprisoned at Cànwyck Castle. Uncle Kerk may as well have shackled him in the dungeons. And when Aunt Wanda hadn't been coddling his cousin, she'd managed the maids and maintained harmony among the kinswomen when the men were at battle.

"I dinnae want to talk about this anymore. I shouldnae have told ye." She whirled and scanned the brush-ridden forest, obviously desperate to be free of the conversation.

When she tried to flee, he grabbed her and hauled her up against him. "Ye'll not climb a tree. Ye will remain with me until ye are convinced ye are not cursed and not a witch."

He held her firmly and kissed the tip of her nose. "If ye were a witch, ye would have hairy moles and a crooked nose, and ye dinnae. Your skin is flawless."

He stroked her lips with his thumb and kissed her damp eyelids. "Your eyes would be colorless, and they are not. They are the color of Heaven." Leaning her back, he pressed a kiss against the wool covering her heart. "And your heart would be made of stone. And I know 'tis not."

She smacked him playfully and bowed her head to hide her smile. Complimenting her seemed to cool her tongue, for she'd turned bashful. "Ye are the bonniest lass I have ever laid eyes on, and I cannae keep my hands from ye."

"This is because ye are a mon, not because ye think I am beautiful."

"Ye will stop this at once. I dinnae lie."

"And I dinnae drink whisky, nor do I cry, nor do I throw myself at men. I think we are verra bad for each other. Mayhap ye should choose another wife." Even as she made this suggestion, her fingers held tight to the front of his *léine* shirt.

"I'll need Saints Peter and Paul to survive another night without ravishing ye. But tomorrow, Akira. Tomorrow I'll make ye my wife in every sense of the word. And tomorrow ye will know what 'tis like to feel beautiful. I vow it." Gripping both sides of her face between his palms, he kissed her with conviction. A kiss so laced with promise it scared him to death.

Akira wanted to believe his words. Her mind denied his

flattery, but her racing heart felt something different in his kiss. Or was she being foolish again? Calin could woo any maiden out of her kirtle. She wondered how many maidens there might have been, then scolded herself for adding jealousy to her emotions.

Calin picked her up and carried her back to the fire. When he set her on her feet, the men meekly closed their flasks then tucked them inside their plaids.

She stifled a shamed giggle behind her hand. "Dinnae worry, gentlemen. I've had my quota of your spirits this eve, but m'laird tells me ye might reconsider sharing your drink with your wives." She smirked at Calin's grin before returning her attentions back to the men sitting like stepping-stones on the log, all three covered with unruly tufts of golden-red hair.

Gordon, who was easily the oldest, wore a surly frown. The skin beneath his eyes weighed heavily downward, which told her laughter didn't find his face often. He would undoubtedly be the hardest to befriend. She stood before him, matching his scowl. "That is assuming ye have wives. One might think it a difficult task to find a wife when one does not speak."

Gordon didn't respond, as she expected, nor did he return her look. Crossing her arms defiantly over her chest, she spoke to Calin, but never once removed her stare from Gordon. "M'laird, when I am your lady wife, will I have the authority to give your men permission to speak?"

"Aye."

"For the nonce, I'd like ye to give them permission to speak to me." Akira thought she caught the hint of a smile threatening Gordon's face, but she doubted he would crack so easily.

"Just because I give them permission does not mean they will exchange pleasantries with ye."

She spun around to glare at Calin, her long tresses whipped over her shoulder with the sharp action. Pain stabbed her temples. This did nothing to improve her temper. "Then order them to converse with me."

Calin's eyebrow rose in that pleasingly wicked manner. "Men, Akira is to be my wife. Ye will address her as 'm'lady' and give her the same loyalty and respect ye've always given me. If she asks ye a question, ye will respond without raising your voice to her."

After smiling sweetly at Calin, she turned back to Gordon and raised both eyebrows triumphantly. "Have ye a wife?"

"Aye."

"Are ye good to her?"

Gordon frowned heavily, glanced around her, then answered under obvious duress. "Aye."

"I'd like to know her name, and the names and ages of all your bairns."

This line of questioning continued until she had Gordon talking in full sentences. He never offered more information than she demanded until he slipped into a memory of his grandson's first brawl.

Having squeezed between the first two brutes on the log, she redirected her attention to the warrior on her right. He licked his lips and swallowed repeatedly. The man appeared quite frightened of the forthcoming inquisition. "And what be your name, sir?"

"My name is Alec, m'lady. My wife is Aileen. We've five bairns, Alec Og, Albert, Andrew, Alexina, and Anice, and another wee one on the way. I'm good to my wife as I am to my bairns."

She held Alec's gaze as he answered each question with a tender smile. She liked Alec immediately. When she had no more inquiries, Alec reached for her hand to kiss her knuckles. "I'd like to be the first to welcome ye to our clan, and say that our laird is a verra lucky mon."

Gordon expelled a disgusted snort.

Akira ignored his obvious disapproval of Alec's congeniality then moved to sit next to the third man. "And ye. Have ye a name?"

"Aye, m'lady. The name's Jaime." He, too, pressed his lips to her knuckles, but didn't release her hand as Alec had. "I have nay wife, but if ye've any sisters as bonnie as ye, I'm sure to be lookin'."

A blush heated her cheeks beneath Jaime's flattery. Calin's kin certainly excelled in the art of wooing. She fell into a trance under the dreamy hue of aqua-blue eyes. Jaime had a hint more blond streaked through his beard, and she knew he would be strikingly handsome beneath his whiskers. Certainly, he would have no trouble finding a wife with his face.

"I'm cousin to m'laird. Our aunt Wanda raised us as brothers since both our mams died birthing us."

Akira glanced at Calin and felt a pang of sympathy for him, along with a twinge of guilt for having called his mother such horrible names at *Tigh Diabhail*. "I'm sorry," she said more to Calin than to Jaime.

"'Tis the past." Jaime brushed his thumb in circles over her hand. "Aunt Wanda has been a verra good mother to us."

Calin glared at Jaime. "Had Aunt Wanda been a wee bit harder on ye, ye may not be lacking so much discipline."

"I've discipline," Jaime argued.

"Ye call downing a buck in the middle o' mating season, discipline?"

"Are ye still sore my kill was bigger?"

Calin rolled his eyes, but Akira could tell Jaime heated his blood, and she knew all too well the emotions that simmered from being provoked by kin.

"We didn't even need the meat, else to feed that big head o' yours."

Jaime smiled at her and winked. Did he instigate Calin on purpose or did they always converse with such derision? She spoke similarly to her sisters, but Calin didn't seem to enjoy Jaime's banter. Just as she was about to divert the topic, Jaime perked up.

"Ye see the laird and I have always enjoyed a challenge. Truth is, Uncle Kerk started us sparring against each other with wooden swords when we were but laddies. We fought together in Ross where I slaughtered more Lowlanders than he." He raised his sleeve to proudly display two blue battle rings.

"Those men were your Scots countrymen," Calin said. "I wouldnae be a braggart about such a feat."

"Ye fought with the royalists?" Her question, directed at Calin, came with a frown she couldn't control.

Calin opened his mouth to answer, but Jaime cut him off. "Aye, we did at that. With the Donalds at our side, we were sure to regain the Earldom of Ross back from the crown. I believe one of the Donalds is still being harbored on MacLeod soil."

Jaime proceeded to boast of his battles, but Akira's mind lingered on the fact Calin had fought against his king in the same war that killed her papa.

With every word Jaime spoke, he inched closer until she thought he might kiss her. This MacLeod breed was undoubtedly an arrogant lusty bunch of men.

"Then there was the deer," Jaime continued. "And what was it, cousin, that got ye so riled last year?" Jaime stared at her, but his question slithered disrespect. "Och, I remember. I took cat—"

"Jaime, if ye move an inch closer to her or speak another word, I swear I'll gut ye like a swine where ye sit." Calin's tone held no humor when he delivered the threat.

Akira didn't know what the cat had to do with Calin's ferocious look, but it stopped Jaime cold.

Jaime jerked back with a devilish grin. "Have ye more questions for me, lass?"

"Nay, she does not," Calin snapped with the edge of jealousy hanging from his words.

She didn't like him speaking for her, but the angry wrinkles on his forehead warned her not to test him. She pulled free from Jaime's hand then walked to stand in front of Calin. "Dinnae frown so, m'laird. 'Tis not becoming." She smoothed the sulky expression from his face with her fingertips.

Calin glared at Jaime and forcefully yanked her down beside him. Akira's bum protested the impact. Moments later, the fire's dance hypnotized her mind. She hugged herself, yawned like a nursed kitten, and allowed herself to rest heavily against his strong arm. Would it be so bad being the laird's wife? Akira asked herself the same question he posed the eve before, only this time she wondered if the prospect would be so horrible. She was certainly smart enough to manage the keep, and she relished the thought of being surrounded by kin who wouldn't see her as different.

Unwillingly to move, she watched Kendrick, Jaime, and Alec settle beneath fur pelts for the night. Her eyes then locked with Gordon's from overtop the low-burning fire. He made no effort to hide his dislike of her.

"Why did ye make him do it?" Gordon asked. "Why did ye make our laird shave his beard?"

Akira stole a glance at Calin through sleepy eyes and stroked his face. "I should think 'tis obvious. Look at the mon. Would any of ye have guessed he would wear such bonnie dimples?"

She enjoyed the tint of embarrassment coloring his bronze cheeks, but Gordon's heavy grunts ruined the moment.

"So ye find our laird more . . . appealing? This is why ye asked him to deface himself?"

"Of course not, the dimples came as a pleasant surprise," she defended and decided against expanding her reasons unless the man pushed.

Gordon pushed. "I've answered all your questions. I'd like to know why ye made the mon remove the signature o' the Highlander."

She couldn't exactly blurt out that she wanted to speak with Kendrick alone. They would all frown upon her game. She would gain no allies with that admission. She contemplated a reason that would appease Gordon without making her sound ridiculous. She had told Calin she refused to kiss him unless he shaved. Somehow, she had to explain this reasoning to Gordon. She forced her weary body to its feet and slipped into the grove.

Behind her, she heard Calin threaten Gordon. "If she climbs a tree, ye'll be the one fetching her this time."

She didn't have to look hard to find what she was searching for. Calin had just stood to come after her, she assumed, when she returned minutes later with her hands hidden behind her back. She stood directly in front of Gordon. "Please, close your eyes, sir."

He didn't.

"M'laird, make Gordon close his eyes so I may answer his question."

Gordon closed his eyes without being ordered, after which she reached for his burly hand. "When ye kiss your wife, this is what ye feel." She cupped his wrinkled hand around the satiny smooth skin of a mushroom. Once he examined the texture, she reached for his other hand. "And when your wife kisses ye, this is what she feels." Akira closed Gordon's callused hand around the needle-sharp pricks of a thistle.

"Ow!" Gordon bellowed, then threw the thistle into the fire. Ignoring the snickers from the other men, he crawled under his plaid and turned his back on all of them.

Feeling pleased with herself, Akira turned to find Calin laying out the two fur pelts they shared the previous night. Her amusement diminished when she realized he intended for her to join him. Nervously, she glanced at Kendrick who offered her a nod of approval before turning his back on her. She was sorely tempted to march over there and kick him, but her interest became diverted.

Calin slid between the wool and propped his cheek upon his hand. "Come and seek your sleep, lass. We've a big day on the morrow."

She gripped her fingers to keep them from wringing while she searched for some reason to deny his request. Or did she even need to deny his request? She certainly didn't want to. She'd lain with him the night before out of necessity for warmth. The fire provided heat aplenty this night, giving her no reason to accept his offer. It would be improper for her to bed down with him even to just sleep before they wed. Wouldn't it?

Kendrick obviously gave her his opinion when he cast her that all-knowing smile and rolled over. Her brother had been shielding her virtue his entire life and now seemed grateful to be free of the duty.

Torn between protecting her morals and wanting to curl up inside Calin's arms, she remained unmoving like a lost child.

"Come, lass. I'll warm ye." He raised the fur.

"We've a fire this night. I dinnae need your warmth. Toss me a pelt and I will seek my sleep over here."

A victorious smile crossed his lips. "I'll have my kiss first."

"Rogue," Akira grumbled through her teeth.

"I shaved my beard for that kiss, and I mean to have it. Ye have nay reason to worry over your virtue. First and foremost, ye have guarded your favors better than some nuns and second, ye have saved yourself for me, remember? Come now. Retract your claws and uphold your promise."

As much as she hated to admit it, his argument seemed acceptable. It was just a kiss. A harmless good-eve kiss that meant nothing. She only hoped she could get through it without attacking him again.

She knelt beside him, preparing to fulfill his boon, when his arm curled around her and pulled her flat against his chest. He kissed the top of her head and wrapped the cover over her shoulders. Shocked by his swiftness, she stiffened.

"Relax, lass. Even dragons require sleep."

The chortles of his men mocked her, but she resolved to let the matter rest. Her weariness won this battle. She awkwardly twisted and wiggled until her back rested against his chest and she closed her eyes. The light caresses he drew up and down her forearm eased her anxiety. She allowed herself to hope for a life far greater than she ever expected. A life filled with passion and devotion—one like Mam and Papa had shared.

Papa used to hold Mam this same way at night with her and her sisters tucked in every nook. They must have looked like lambs curled around each other in the small bed of their home, nuzzling each other's warmth during the endless winter nights. There was nary a doubt that Papa had loved Mam. Part of her now greedily pined for a similar affection from Calin.

"Put your mind to rest, my sweet Akira." His fingers laced with hers and the gate guarding her heart unlocked.

Chapter Nine

Akira awoke early and studied the man she would marry today. Today. The startling realization had her stomach fluttering with a peculiar thrill. Certainly, waking to such a handsome face every morn wouldn't be horrible. Or allowing him to adorn her lips with his tantalizing kisses—per his request.

She recalled the many queries and worthless trinkets she'd sent Calin when she was a mere child. He must have thought her so foolish, much the same as her sisters. Regardless of the barbs her family had thrown at her, never once did her loyalty falter for her benefactor. Propped up on her elbow, she studied his lips—full, smooth, perfect for kissing. A flash of heat sizzled beneath her skin. The image she had conjured in her head of him over the years was far different from the man who could make her skin heat just at the sight of him. Never had she expected to have such strong feelings for him, but after two days with Calin, she couldn't deny the attraction between them. He was respected by his men, protective, witty, and gentle to a fault.

She couldn't help but think of how their marriage might benefit her family. Isobel had always wanted to learn more about medicine. Now her sister could have that dream. This made

Akira smile all the more about their arrangement. Mayhap she could convince him to provide a tutor for the twins as well. The many prayers she offered as a child were finally being answered. Or mayhap the spells she and Isobel had cast in childhood play from that damnable book were taking root. She giggled silently at the memory.

But why was she—a peasant cursed with misfortune—suddenly so blessed? The question niggled at her relentlessly. The chieftains of Scotland married to improve the quality of life for their people. They gained allies and lands through marriage to protect their kin. What did she possess that would benefit his clan? It certainly wasn't wealth or land. Everything she owned belonged to the chieftain of Clan Kinnon. No noble titles graced her name, making her worthy of such a substantial marriage. She wasn't even first born. So why had he chosen her?

She soaked up the heat radiating from his body. He was a giant of a man, yet so gentle with her. She traced the pad of her finger over his soft lips and purred, "M'laird?"

Calin's lips lifted slightly from the tickle, but his eyelids remained closed. "Mmm," he murmured inside his drowsy state.

"Why are ye marrying me today?"

"To form the alliance," he mumbled.

An alliance? Her chest tightened. Her pulse raced.

Akira moved away, not wanting to touch him. She'd been naïve to think he wanted her for more. At least, believing her intelligence attracted him was far greater comfort than knowing he wanted her because she belonged to Clan Kinnon. She'd been blinded by his kisses and sweet words.

Stupid, stupid fool. She cursed her ignorance. *No one would marry ye for your intellect.*

As the full expanse of his comment set in, her mouth went bone-dry. The pieces of this puzzle seemed so clear now.

Kendrick had gathered an army to rebel against King James. With her sister Maggie married to a Donald, and she to a MacLeod, the Isles would unite to regain possession of the Lordship of the Isles from the Scottish crown. Akira wanted no part of a political uprising. Those who tried to rebel against the king in ninety-three had been executed for treason. She didn't know the extent of this plan nor did she care. She'd known clans destroyed by greed and a lust for power. She couldn't live with herself knowing her union to Calin might bring such calamity to the livelihood of Clan Kinnon and to her family. How could Kendrick be in favor of this marriage?

Her brother had betrayed her. He'd sold her like an animal to breed with the enemy all in an effort to go against his sworn allegiance to his king.

Tears blurred her vision. She rose to her feet, raised her head, and then realized she had an audience. Four men staring at her with pity in their expressions told her the hurt was evident on her face. She tried to read Kendrick, to understand why he'd done this, but he looked away as if to hide his shame.

"I'm going to the brook." She turned on her heel and walked away.

Calin's heart gave a quick jerk. His eyes flew open. He bolted upright and pressed his hand against the fur pelt still warm from her body. He then saw the four pairs of shocked eyes. "Tell me I dinnae say that aloud," he pleaded in a state of confusion.

"Ye dinnae say that aloud." Jaime fulfilled his request with a sardonic lift in his voice.

Gordon, Alec, and Kendrick snorted in unison at the blatant lie.

"Hell and damnation!" Calin jumped to his feet then raked

his fingers through his already aching scalp. "Damn! Damn, damn, damn," he muttered while kicking a smoldering chunk of wood. "*To form the alliance.* This is what I say to my bride on her wedding day? I am such a dunderheid."

"Ye'll not be gettin' an argument from me," Jaime clucked with a grin then crawled out of his blankets to stretch.

Calin's temper peaked. The last thing he wanted was to watch Jaime gloat over his folly. He wanted to brawl, but he only had himself to blame for the mishap. He hit Jaime anyway—one steel-fisted punch in the gut. The moment of gratification didn't curb his mood.

While Jaime was doubled over, clutching his stomach and groaning, Calin started giving orders. "Gordon, take Alec and ride to Cànwyck Castle. Prepare the clan. I want twice as many flowers adorning the kirk as before. I want twice as much food prepared, and I want every villager to bathe, and display full Highland dress; men, women, and children. Alec, ye will retrieve Elsbeth. Tell her to add two ells of French silk to Akira's gown. Have the maids prepare my solar again. More flowers. Lots of flowers. I want flowers everywhere. And berries. Akira likes berries. Right?"

He glanced at Kendrick for confirmation.

Kendrick nodded.

Calin paced with his hands locked behind his back. He had been molded for leadership his entire life, been taught loyalty and commitment by his father and uncle. Now, the fate of the Isles rested on his ability to subdue this hot-tempered woman. How in the name of all the saints, both living and dead, was he supposed to accomplish that feat exactly? Akira was bold, reckless, stubborn . . . beautiful, witty . . .

His heartless words probably ruined the most important day of his bride's life. But what seemed more ludicrous, what he couldn't begin to comprehend, was why he cared.

She had belonged to him since the day of her birth. She

lived and breathed because of him. He paid five hundred groats for her to be his lady wife and share his bed. Though these reasons sounded logical in his head, Calin couldn't deny he wanted to please her. He wanted her to enter their union willingly, wanted to see passion in her eyes when he took her for the first time. He wanted their union to be more than just a sense of obligation of duty.

Determined to do everything in his power to make sure nothing else went amiss, he stopped pacing and looked at Gordon. "See to it Catriona does not attend the ceremony or the festivities and be sure Father Harrald is of sound mind before we return. Nay one drinks a drop until after the ceremony. And nay one utters a word of *Tigh Diabhail*."

Calin raked his fingers through his hair. "Kendrick, ye will return home to fetch your family. Jaime will wait for ye at the waterfall to escort ye back to the keep."

"And what important task have ye for me while I wait?" Jaime asked, his damned haunting eyes sparkling with the desire to prove himself.

Jaime had always mimicked Calin's every move, trying to best him at hunting, fighting, wooing. A devil's grin crossed Calin's lips when an idea struck him. He wouldn't be the only one returning to Cànwyck Castle with a smooth jaw. "Kendrick, loan Jaime your straightedge. He's going to shave."

"What?" Jaime bellowed.

Calin would have laughed had he not been in such turmoil. "Ye heard me. This will please Akira. Ye have your orders. Now go!"

"What are ye going to do about Akira? Woo her?" Kendrick asked as the men untethered their mounts. His red-gold eyebrows raised and his head tilted, telling Calin he should prepare for war.

"Nay. Your sister is beyond wooing. I'm going to instruct m'lady on the necessity of accepting this union. If she does not comply, I suspect I'll have to bind her to Sirius for the remainder of this trek." He pivoted on his heel and reluctantly walked over the dew-covered knoll to the brook.

Calin tried to relate the upcoming confrontation to a strategically planned battle. He'd spent sennights at a time on battlefields. Led infantries into hand-to-hand combat. No amount of training could've prepared him for this war. Bloodied fists, swords, men of brute strength. These battles were no competition to the fire-breathing dragon he would make his wife. Akira was undoubtedly the most obstinate opponent he had ever encountered.

Though it was a blow to his ego, he knew he wouldn't be able to force her into submission. Never had he met a woman as smart, or as proud. She would do anything to protect her family. The only way to gain her agreement now would be to convince her the alliance benefited her as well as Clan Kinnon. If he told her Laird Kinnon was her blood sire, she would hold the power to deny him. He would not afford her that option.

· The time had come for her to know what The Beast did to her family.

Chapter Ten

Clear, cool water spilled over her feet along with a school of minnows. Akira hugged her knees and buried her bare toes into the pebbled rock. The sun's early rays peeked over the top of the ridge while she slipped into a bout of self-pity. She would never let Calin know how badly his words hurt her. She refused to let him see the foolish girl inside her. The innocent who dreamed of love and commitment.

Calin's interest resided in his desire to acquire an heir—one of both MacLeod and Kinnon blood. He'd provided for her all these years simply to breed with her and align with Clan Kinnon. Although she hadn't quite wrapped her mind around how that was possible. She was a peasant living on Laird Kinnon's land. She held no ties to any of the Kinnon ground. Neither Calin, nor Kendrick, appeared bothered by that detail. Truths were being hidden from her, and her brother's involvement in that deception made her heart ache further. With Kendrick as her guardian, she couldn't refute the life he'd chosen for her. If she didn't comply with this arrangement, Calin could force her, as was his right.

Mayhap then she could hate him. A tear left a cool trail down her cheek and plopped into the trickling stream.

Immersed in her thoughts, she flinched when Calin's fingers webbed through her hair. She jerked away, bolted upright, and splashed through the brook in her haste. A flock of black birds took flight overhead, startled by her abrupt action. Humiliation kept her eyes downcast as she moved past him. "I am ready. I'm sure ye are anxious to get moving, m'laird."

"There is nay rush. I've sent the others ahead." Calin reached for her.

"Why?" She sidestepped just out of his grasp.

"Because I wanted to speak to ye alone . . . to apologize."

She laughed to keep from sobbing. "Why would ye apologize? We will be married today. Our clans will unite, and the MacLeods will hold the utmost devotion for their new laird— a laird who selflessly took a homely bride to improve the livelihood of his people. I see nay need for explanations nor apologies for becoming their hero. Ye've made your reasons for wanting this union abundantly clear, m'laird." Even as she said the words, she couldn't believe she'd fallen victim to his seductions.

Calin lunged for her. She spun away, but not swiftly enough. He caught her skirt causing her to slip on the slick grasses, then held her tight around the waist. He pressed her to his chest and looked down at her. "There are many reasons I wish to marry ye."

"Then having me in your bed will be a reward. Or will that be your duty to the clan as weel?" Clenched fists pumped against his chest, sending the blood in her veins racing.

He released her. "Akira, please."

She glared at him through narrowed eyes. Her fate might be to bear him an heir, but she would never submit to him willingly. Their union would be nothing more than a contract between them. Never would he take her pride or her heart.

"I'll not marry ye," she declared and guarded her expression, knowing it was futile to refuse him.

His nostrils flared, and she saw a glimpse of the temper he'd been hiding. "Ye *will* marry me, and ye will wear a smile when ye speak your vows. Ye belong to me. I paid five hundred groats for ye, and ye will submit and become my wife." Calin advanced toward her.

With both hands planted firmly against his chest, she pushed him away. He faltered back, and she gained some satisfaction knowing she possessed the strength to fight him physically. Carrying Isobel all these years had made her as strong as an ox.

He closed the small gap between them, and again she pushed him back. His brow curled in confusion, and she cast him an all-knowing smile.

"I'll not argue with ye, nor will I fight ye like a damned brigand." He moved to circle her like prey. Arms bent slightly in front of him and poised to attack. She grabbed his wrist with both hands and twisted it until he twirled away from her. He nearly fell to one knee.

She'd fought with Kendrick on several occasions. She only bested him once, granted he was soused, but that one time gave her hope she could fend for herself.

"Damn the saints, woman! Ye are a hoyden. And how did ye get so strong?"

She didn't answer his question, but prepared herself for further battle.

Her attempts were in vain.

He caught both her hands, knocked her feet out from under her, and then lowered her to the ground. The fresh dew slicked the backs of her calves as he captured her wrists above her head. "I'll not brawl with my betrothed on the day we are to wed. Ye will cease this behavior and cool your wicked temper. A bride should be happy on her wedding day."

"Happy?" Akira reared back to slam her head into his like she had at *Tigh Diabhail*, but he was wise to her tactics. The way he restrained her, prevented her from hurting herself. Damn the man. He even imprisoned her gently.

"Can ye not see that I can provide ye with a better life? From the moment ye enter the gates o' Cànwyck Castle, ye will be treated with reverence."

"Ye want me to ride up on your beast and greet my new clan with a smile? Weel I will not. Nor will I leave my family behind to starve to death while ye seize their lands. Ye are a fool if ye think I'll happily speak my vows knowing ye intend to coerce another member of my family to die battling against your sovereign king."

"What? Is this what ye think?" His brows stitched together. "Allow me leave to explain."

Akira squirmed beneath him. The skin around her wrists wrinkled when she tried to pull free of his grasp. "Ye may own me, m'laird, but ye cannae control my emotions," she hissed, her tongue her only weapon.

"Nay, but I can prove ye have emotions—emotions ye are denying even now." He released his grip, clutched the back of her head, and then ravaged her mouth with a soul-searching kiss. Their tongues entwined, and their teeth clicked by the sheer power of it.

Her mind screamed at her to refuse him, but her mouth acted on its own behalf. She wanted to despise him even as the pulse in her neck paced itself to the rhythm of his kiss. Fast and fervent at first then slower, until he pulled away, leaving her gasping for air.

Calin could ravish her here and now and no one would think less of him, but his hands never dropped below her chin.

He pressed his roughened cheek into the crook of her neck. "This is not about the Lordship of the Isles. I have wanted this alliance my entire life, as my father did before me. I can give ye anything ye ask. Anything your heart desires. I can protect ye for the rest of your life, and someday, mayhap ye will respect me."

She eased him off her and pulled herself into a sitting position. She hugged her knees and stared at her bare toes. "I dinnae want your wealth or your protection. I want my family safe. I want the truth."

Settling in beside her, he took her small hand in his. He held it in silence for a long time, stroking the heel of her palm with his thumb. Finally, his thoughts formed into words. "When ye brought the flock of sheep into your village, why did your kinsmen protect ye from their laird?"

She thought his question odd, but she answered him without pause. "Because of loyalty. Ye may not believe it, but we are a loyal clan."

"Ye are loyal to each other, not to your chieftain. Laird Kinnon is supposed to offer protection to his people. Instead, he is what they need protection from."

"This is about our chieftain?" she asked, trying to understand his words.

"Laird Kinnon must be denounced for his crimes, and his son must be banished before he holds the power of chieftain. Havenae your people suffered enough?"

Akira knew he spoke the truth about Laird Kinnon, but Kendrick had protected her family from The Beast's treachery. She'd never heard her brother speak about an alliançe. However, he'd been collaborating with scores of Kinnon warriors. Maggie's husband, Logan, had been at the cot-house more frequently, as well, with the Donalds' warriors in tow. Had Kendrick been preparing for this alliance all along? Is that why he married Maggie to a Donald? Did he want to unite the clans of the Isles? She wished he had confided in her and expressed his desires for their clan's well-being. Then she would know whether or not to trust Calin.

"Laird Kinnon is a lying, thieving murderer, and God

knows what kind of influence he has had on Darach. How will ye protect your clan from his spawn? How will ye protect the twins or Isobel if Kendrick is away at battle? Or worse, dies at battle, fighting to protect the borders Laird Kinnon dinnae defend."

"And this is why ye, a MacLeod, want the alliance? To protect the Kinnons from their evil laird?" She was far from stupid. She didn't believe for a moment that Calin MacLeod wanted to protect the people of her clan, but she intended to hear him out.

"There are many reasons, but this is one. The alliance will protect both our clans along with the Isles. The English are pressing their way up the Lowlands. We would be fools to believe they'll not send soldiers up the coast and into the Isles. It is imperative that we unite to protect our borders from an invasion. I can promise ye, I'll not evict your kinfolk, but nothing will stop the bluidy English from seizing property for their king. Laird Kinnon cannae be trusted. I believe the man would sell his kin for a silver coin before agreeing to fight alongside the MacLeod warriors.

"We have agreed to unite with the Donalds and fight for Scotland's freedom. Our King James already grows verra weary of the battles betwixt our clans. He has a greater purpose for our country, and we may all suffer if he is not placated."

"Then ye have the king's approval?"

"I'll seek my liege lord's approval after we're wed."

"King James will see this alliance as an uprising against the crown. He will see our union as an attempt to regain possession of the Earldom of Ross and reclaim the title of Lord of the Isles. Is that what ye seek?"

"Nay!" He shouted the word with such vehemence she almost believed him. "I have nay desire to abolish Clan Kinnon for such a cause, nor do the Donalds. I have pledged allegiance to my king and to Scotland. I would fight to the death to protect this country and my kin, as would Kendrick. Clan Kinnon will not suffer from our union, but thrive beneath the leadership of a new laird. One who will protect his borders as Laird Kinnon has not."

Akira pondered his words, struggling to suppress her personal emotions with what was truly best for her kin. The English were the vilest of God's creatures. She'd oftentimes wondered if the scores of English soldiers weren't part of Satan's army. Their men of war raped and pillaged the Scottish villages without remorse. If he spoke the truth, an alliance could protect them. "And who will be the chieftain, if not Laird Kinnon's son?" When Calin didn't answer, she tilted his chin, forcing him to look at her. His rich brown eyes hid so much anger. She'd been so consumed protecting her pride, she hadn't considered how much responsibility weighed on his shoulders. She stroked his bristled cheek. "Who, Calin? Who will protect my clan?"

"Kendrick."

Her eyes widened with this announcement. "Though I agree Kendrick would make an honorable laird, he is the son of a peasant. 'Tis blessed blood of the chieftain that holds the line of the Kinnon laird, not honor. Some clans are not like this, but our elders wouldnae ordain a mon as chieftain unless he is blood of a blessed marriage."

"There is much ye dinnae know, but believe me when I tell ye Kendrick will be the Kinnon's chieftain. And because ye are his sister, our marriage will bind our clans together."

"'Tis not possible. Ye cannae just break centuries of law because he's honorable. He must be of blessed blood. If ye want me to trust ye, then ye must trust me as weel. Tell me how ye intend to bestow the power chieftainship unto the son of a peasant."

Calin released her hand and stared vacantly at the traveling waters of the brook. "Laird Kinnon abuses his power as chieftain. He buys his warriors' loyalty with the villages' taxes and treats his kinswomen like dogs. How many bastards do ye think the man has running amuck in Dalkirth?"

"I dinnae know. He has never laid claim to any of them." She concentrated on his question. A long pause filled the air with silence. While awaiting further explanation, realization set in. Her jaw dropped. "Are ye implying Kendrick is one of Laird Kinnon's bastards? 'Tis nay true. Mam was never unfaithful to Papa!"

Slowly, he turned to her, his expression guarded. "Vanora was never unfaithful. Laird Kinnon raped her two months before she wed Murrdock Neish."

Akira felt sick. Her hand covered her mouth. The muscles in her throat contracted. "The Beast raped Mam?"

Calin nodded. "Kendrick is Laird Kinnon's son. Murrdock never knew, and Vanora never intended to tell Kendrick either. Ten years ago, Laird Kinnon suspected Murrdock of treason and sent for Neala to draw him out. Your sister was fourteen— the same age as Vanora when The Beast planted his seed inside her."

Akira struggled to comprehend his words while choking on hatred. "Had Papa returned from fighting with the royalists, he would have killed him."

"Murrdock dinnae die in Ross as ye were told. He died in Brycen Castle trying to protect Neala from Laird Kinnon."

How could she have not known this? Hands shaking, pulse pounding, she forced the question from her throat. "Did Papa get to Neala in time?"

Calin closed his eyes and shook his head.

Her heart clenched. Her abdomen convulsed. A painful sorrow escaped from her in a flood of tears over her cheeks. She didn't want to believe Neala had been raped by The Beast or that Papa didn't die in honor. Anger replaced her sorrow. "Ye lie. Kendrick would have killed him."

Calin's strong hand circled around her clenched fist. Gently, he swiped the tears from her cheeks and bore his amber stare into her eyes. "He tried. When Kendrick gathered warriors to kill The Beast, Vanora told him he was Laird Kinnon's son and could one day hold the power of chieftainship. She charged him with a greater purpose—to free Clan Kinnon from The Beast. She dinnae want Kendrick to suffer the same fate as Murrdock. She begged him to be patient and wait for aid from my clan and the Donalds."

Damn him and his evil blood! Rage and an undeniable taste for revenge consumed her. She wanted The Beast's head for his crimes against her kin. She always knew he was evil. "Why in all o' Scots has he not been denounced before now? Clan Kinnon's warriors cannae be more than three hundred. The MacLeods alone triple that number. Why have ye not revolted before now?"

"Your laird holds favor with the king of Scotland. Laird Kinnon dinnae join forces with the royalists, which not only gained him the king's protection, but the Lowlanders, as weel."

"I'd have killed The Beast myself had I known what he'd done to my kin," she stated with conviction.

Calin brought her hand to his chest, pulling her closer. "Kendrick couldnae deny your mother, nor his duty to protect ye and your sisters. When your brother is chieftain, Laird Kinnon will get his punishment. Kendrick has promised this to your kinsmen for more than a decade. 'Tis why he married Maggie to Logan Donald. He is the third-born son of the chieftain o' Clan Donald. The Donalds are already Kendrick's allies and await our union to unite the Isles."

Akira steadied her breathing and unclenched her fist, but held tight to his hand, thankful for his strength. She studied the puzzle Calin presented. Kendrick had been building a rebellion within the Kinnon clan to revolt against Laird Kinnon's garrison. Her brother married Maggie to Logan to align the Kinnons with the Donalds. But Neala was first born and married to a Kinnon crofter. Had Neala been betrothed to Logan before The Beast ruined her?

Akira hated the laws of the land. Hated the way men of status formed allies through pure marriages. She tried to hate Kendrick for selling her sisters to form such alliances, but she understood that he had been part of a greater plan to protect, not only her sisters and Mam, but the Isles. If Kendrick and Calin intended to make her part of their machinations to unite the Isles, then Calin had to know how Kendrick intended to assume power of chieftainship.

"Ye will tell me how Kendrick is to become laird," she demanded in a tone more forceful than she intended. "I am not ignorant to the law. The council will not honor my brother as laird over the Kinnon's named heir. Kendrick is illegitimate. He wasnae born to a blessed marriage as Darach is."

Calin studied the landscape. The black birds had resumed their feast in the lush green grasses, and the sun had already begun to burn through the mist. Akira knew he searched for words. She also sensed there was so much he wanted to tell her, but couldn't or was afraid to. She held his hand, pleading with him silently to trust her.

Calin's chin fell to his chest, and a muscle pulsed in his jaw. "If Laird Kinnon's heir decrees Kendrick as chieftain, then your council will agree."

Akira gave a quick hoot. That was their brilliant plan to oust The Beast? They were muddleheaded fools—both her brother and Calin. "If ye think Darach will agree to this, ye are mad, Calin MacLeod."

The lines of his face broke into mischief. "I am mad. Mad about ye." He crawled overtop her, lying her back against the velvet grasses, and then laced his fingers in hers beside her head.

He leaned into her face. The heat of his mouth warmed her

lips and quickened her pulse. "I've already told ye more than I should have, but I need ye to trust me. Marry me today to protect your clan. To protect Scotland, and soon I'll tell ye everything. I vow it."

Kendrick must have known their union would protect so many people. Not only would Calin be a hero, so would her brother. The people of Dalkirth could be free of The Beast and could live respectable, happy lives under Kendrick's reign. This vision filled her with peace. Her acceptance of this union would prevent The Beast from ever hurting anyone again.

She felt empowered. "I'll marry ye."

His smile came quickly and the arrogant bluster returned to his eyes. He was gloating, so she teased him. "To protect my family and my clan, but I'll not submit to ye."

Calin's eyes brightened with mischief at this challenge. A broad, luscious grin sprang over his face as he started in with his antics. The bodice of her shift dipped low from her earlier struggles, revealing far more flesh than she knew was proper. He bent over her and nuzzled his nose over her chest. His eyelashes swept over her skin, tickling, tingling. He placed whisper-soft kisses across her upper breasts making it difficult for her to be quarrelsome.

She closed her eyes and tightened her clasp on his fingers. She didn't know why, but his kiss and his touch made her ache. He would be her husband by day's end, and she didn't have to deny the way he made her feel, even if she didn't ignite the same desire in him.

Her betraying body arched, craving his attention.

"Ye keep squirming like that and your rosy nipples will be exposed."

Excitement pebbled the nipples he spoke of so freely. "And what would ye do if that happened?"

He nipped her bottom lip, but withdrew before engaging the kiss. "I would be forced to taste each one verra slowly."

Akira inhaled a deep breath of cool mist, wanting to know what that would feel like. Raising both brows, she wiggled beneath him.

Calin groaned. "I am a weak mon. Ye must not tease me. Now please quit trying to seduce me, and allow me to take ye properly as my wife after we're wed."

She fought the undeniable hunger pooling low in her stomach. Refusing to give in to her stubbornness, she challenged him. "I'll not smile when we are wed, nor will I give myself to ye willingly."

"Och, my wee fire-breathing dragon, ye will do both." Calin's arrogant grin broadened just before he released her.

Chapter Eleven

The morning sun warmed the top of Akira's head on their journey across MacLeod soil. They stopped at three tenant farms along the way, where Calin accepted wedding gifts from his kinfolk as if they offered the king's gold. He appeared humbled by these peasants, and his earnest thanks touched her heart. One of the matrons presented him with a lace kerchief to catch his bride's tears. Another gave a spotted feather from the tail of a capercaillie for luck, and the third gifted Akira with a hollow egg. The elderly rawboned woman supplied instructions to crush the egg after the wedding night. Akira giggled nervously when the woman told her the egg represented the status of her womb.

Calin guided Sirius at a canter around Loch Ceardach, all the while answering her questions about his clan, his council, and the alliance. She was elated when he asked for her opinion on educating the young boys of the clan. No one had ever treated her with such regard.

Soon, a strong scent of sea mingled with the wind. A falcon screeched overhead, a leather strap hanging from its leg—circling, inviting them home. *Home*. The thought alone terrified her. The haunting melody of pipers echoed in the distance.

At the peak of the knoll, Cànwyck Castle came into view. Her eyes widened at the sight before her. A fortress of stone basalt blocks loomed atop a steep coastal cliff and overlooked the open sea. Double towers, erected on both the east and west corners of the keep, tied a great curtain wall of stone around the bailey of cottages within the stronghold.

Clan MacLeod tripled the size of Clan Kinnon, mayhap more. And they would, no doubt, be expecting a woman of dignified grace. One who possessed qualities much nobler than those of a peasant. Akira had lived her entire life in a two-room cot-house with an earthen floor, tending to a herd of sheep and the needs of her sisters. This was madness. How could she possibly play the role of Lady of Clan MacLeod?

Her thoughts plagued her until they reached a deep moat separating them from Cànwyck Castle. A massive drawbridge began to lower. The rattle of metal pulsed in her ear as the porters raised an iron lattice gate to allow their entrance. With every clang, Akira fretted over another reason why she couldn't possibly become Lady MacLeod. The portcullis rose higher until she thought she might retch. She clutched Calin's forearm and beads of sweat pooled between her breasts. If she held the reins, she would have coaxed Sirius into a pounding gallop in the opposite direction.

"Halt! Please, m'laird. I cannae go in there." Her voice shook with panic. "'Tis too much. Too grand. Please, just another night. I'll be ready on the morrow to become your lady wife. I vow it."

"Nay. This request I am denying ye. My kin have waited for ye too long, lass, and I assure ye, they will adore ye."

Akira pulled on the reins and twisted in the saddle. "How can ye say that? Gordon does not adore me."

"Gordon doesnae like anyone."

"Those men who dragged me behind their horses to *Tigh Diabhail* showed me nay adoration."

"Those men will be hunted and exiled."

"Then name one of your kin who will *adore* me."

"Aunt Wanda. She has a pure heart, and she will see that ye do, too, even though ye hide it behind your barbs. Now, release the reins, lass, and smile." Calin clicked his tongue and nudged Sirius over the drawbridge and through the barbican.

Akira huffed then smoothed her hair and fidgeted with the pleats of her skirt. She did not smile. "I look like a hedgehog. I need a bath. I must have more time."

Calin leaned into her and kissed her temple. "Ye are the most beautiful hedgehog I have ever seen."

Her breathing increased while her hands continued to tremble, and the reassuring squeeze Calin offered her did little to ease her anxiety. "Ye must not show fear. They look to ye for strength," he whispered into her hair.

Standing before each whitewashed cottage were men, women, and children garbed in multicolored plaids pinned with the MacLeod brooch. She thought the weaver must work dawn to dusk dying all the wool for such beautiful garments.

Calin halted at the base of a sloped embankment covered in the thick foliage of summer grasses. Two rows of pink-frosted primroses dabbled with bluebells bordered the worn path leading to the keep. The floral bouquet scented the air with an overwhelming sweet aroma, which explained the hum of busy bumblebees.

Calin dismounted then lowered her to stand beside him. Two spit boys scrambled to tend to Sirius and offer greetings to his new bride. The incessant skirling of bagpipes was soon drowned out by the high-pitched screams of a brood of children racing for Akira's skirt. Five in all, each one taller than the next, skirmished around her kirtle staring at her with anxious interest. Beneath the fighting elbows came a crop of pale blond hair that framed the sweet cherub face of a little boy with giant blue eyes.

He raised his arms to Akira. "Choose me, m'lady."

Not caring about the propriety of her new status, she bent to lift the young boy. Before she could stop him, he stretched his chubby arms around her neck, latched his fingers together, and embraced her with an affectionate hug.

"Welcome home, m'lady." His sweet voice rang in her ear.

Her heart nearly exploded from the little innocent's greeting. Her vision blurred with tears and a lump formed in her throat. This little boy could never know how powerful his words were. She refused to cry. Instead, she unveiled the smile she was determined not to share with Calin. She turned, knowing he studied her face. He seemed to want her approval. Had he granted her another day, she may have willingly given him that approval. As it stood, she decided to be stubborn and a wee bit selfish with her merriment. But the sweetling clutching her neck made being dismal difficult.

Alec, and a woman Akira guessed was Alec's wife, Aileen, scurried after their children. Red-gold locks fell over her face when Aileen bowed. "A thousand pardons, m'lady. They dinnae know their manners." Aileen attempted to peel the boy from Akira's neck.

He wouldn't let go. Wrinkling his nose, he gave his mother a sour expression and tightened his grasp.

Aileen apologized repeatedly. "Andrew, release m'lady this instant."

"I cannae, Mammie. I love her."

That did it.

Akira laughed outright while a blush burned her face to the tips of her ears. Aileen forcefully pulled Andrew off and dropped him to his feet beside her. "Ye can love her from a distance."

The boy snuggled into his mother's skirts then gave Akira a tiny wave before sticking his thumb in his mouth. The boy had far too many teeth for such a habit and Akira knew, with nary a doubt, lil' Andrew had been coddled.

"Forgive them, m'lady." Aileen pleaded then lowered her eyes. "I fear our children lack discipline. Alec and I have, by far, the most ill-mannered litter within the walls o' Cànwyck."

"I think they are wonderful. All of them." She gave Aileen a gentle hug then bent to pop a kiss atop Andrew's pug nose. She wanted very much to have a friend in this foreign place, and Aileen seemed a decent prospect.

"Have ye anyone to help prepare ye for the ceremony, m'lady?" Aileen asked.

"Elsbeth awaits her," Calin informed coolly from behind her.

Akira ground her teeth while continuing to smile at Aileen. "I am sure to need more than one maid to help prepare me."

Aileen eagerly hustled Andrew around her swollen abdomen to Alec's side then accepted Akira's extended hand. Andrew popped his thumb out and gave his father a shamed look. "Da, she is not feisty. She's bonnie."

In a flush of mortification, Alec herded his bairns back into the bailey, leaving his blushing wife in Akira's hands.

If she received such warm greetings from all the kinfolk, she would settle very nicely here. She interlocked elbows with Aileen, and the women started to ascend the path to the keep.

Calin called them to a halt. "Akira, might I have a word afore we part ways?"

She studied him. His manner had transformed the moment they passed through the barbican. He emanated a regal bearing—dignified, authoritative and proud. Part of her sought to be the reason for that pride.

She walked back to him, no longer intimidated by his size, and looked into his strong eyes. "Aye, m'laird?"

Calin curled a loose tendril of hair behind her ear and pressed his lips to her cheek. She felt his breath in her ear. "Ye are smiling."

* * *

Akira stood in her wedding gown before the looking glass and didn't recognize the person staring back at her. Three rays of golden light fluttered in through the arrow-slit windows and illuminated the yellow bodice hanging modestly off her shoulders. A chiffon cape flowed in wisps behind her back making her feel ethereal. The remainder of the gown hugged her ample curves with a French silk train trailing the floor like melted butter. Ebony braids and curls gathered into a six-pointed headdress encrusted with rubies.

The damp scent of wildflowers permeated the chamber from her bath. Aileen and Elsbeth had catered to her every need. Not an ounce of her lacked for attention—from the floral creams used to moisturize her skin to the mint leaf placed on her tongue.

Akira traced the contours of the gown over her breasts and thought the seamstress must be gifted with magic. For the first time in her entire life, she felt beautiful.

Wishing she didn't care, she hoped Calin would be pleased. She now wanted the alliance as much as he did and knew this wedding served a greater purpose, but a part of her wanted this day to be special. She'd saved herself for her wedding night, and she would afford herself a few dreams even if the reality of their union destroyed those dreams on the morrow. Soon enough she would be no more than a woman to bear his heirs.

"Our laird will surely lose his heart when ye grace his vision," Aileen said in a breathy voice.

Elsbeth added the final article to Akira's ensemble—a sash of blue and green plaid draped diagonally over her right shoulder then pinned loosely at her hip. The weaver designed the sash to match the one Calin would wear during the ceremony, a symbol of their union. Elsbeth smoothed the creases. "I fear our laird has already lost his heart."

Akira wondered if she would ever possess a part of Calin's heart.

She graciously held Elsbeth's soft hands. "Thank ye for your labors on the gown. 'Tis beautiful."

"What you wear, m'lady, is mere threads. It is you who makes the gown beautiful," Elsbeth mumbled in a weak voice and lowered sheepish hazel eyes.

Akira smiled while examining the young woman's fragile demeanor. Unlike Aileen, who endlessly chattered, Elsbeth portrayed a more docile manner. What few words she did speak lacked any hint of the Highland burr. A tight red-gold braid fell to the middle of her back and her pristine clean garments were modest. Holding her hand, Akira noticed the bloodstains speckling her fingertips from multiple pinpricks. But what intrigued her more were the faint remnants of bruises on her wrists and forearms, and the yellow tint of an aged bruise alongside her high cheekbones. Why would such a timid woman carry such marks? And especially one with child?

"Elsbeth, do ye stay in the keep or have ye a family?" Akira queried nonchalantly, wanting to know more about her.

"I live outside the bailey with my husband, Ian, and my son."

"So ye already have one child. Ye and your husband must be excited about the arrival of your second." A wave of excitement fluttered through her with the question as always did when discussing children. It seemed more than half the women in the clan were with child. Which didn't surprise her. If the other men were aught like their laird, they were certain to be a randy breed.

When Elsbeth didn't return her smile, Akira knew she'd overstepped her bounds. Elsbeth really wasn't showing to the degree anyone might notice, but Akira had seen her hand flatten over her stomach at least twice while the woman had dressed her.

Elsbeth caressed her stomach. "I am not very far along. Ian does not yet know."

"I'm certain he will be overjoyed," Akira assured her.

"I am sure he will be . . . I must go. Ian waits for me."

While Elsbeth gathered her sewing supplies, Akira noticed her trembling. "Ye are not attending the wedding?" Her tone reflected her genuine disappointment.

"I was called to finish the gown and prepare you, m'lady. Now I must return to my family."

"But I insist ye stay for the wedding."

"Much thanks, m'lady, but I really must decline." Elsbeth didn't return eye contact when she walked to the door. She paused to address Aileen, her words barely audible. "Ian needs to be the first to know that I carry his child. I would ask for your silence until then."

"Aye, Elsbeth. I wouldnae say aught," Aileen offered quickly.

Elsbeth left the chamber, closing the door behind her. Akira would seek her out and find out where those bruises came from. As Lady of Cànwyck Castle, she intended to make one of her duties to oversee the protection of the womenfolk. The power to help the women of Clan Kinnon had never been within her reach.

That was not the case here.

A rustling came from the corridor followed by a swift kick to the bottom of the door. Already nervous, Akira jumped. Aileen frowned, but quickly waddled to open the door. Aileen's balled fist landed on her hips, and Akira wondered if all women struck that pose naturally. Aileen was quietly scolding whoever stood on the other side of the entranceway.

Akira smiled when Andrew pushed around his mother's skirts completely oblivious to Aileen's tongue-lashing. He carried two satchels—one blue, one green.

"But, Mammie, I bring gifts for—"

"Dinnae 'but Mammie' me, 'tis—"

"Aileen, let the boy speak."

Turning toward her, Andrew's blue eyes slowly widened in awe and his arms fell loose to his sides. A flush of warmth washed over her cheeks from the innocent flattery. If only Calin would look at her like that, she might be less apprehensive about their marriage bed. "Have ye something for me, Andrew?"

Andrew nodded and held out the satchels. "A bridegift. M'laird said bring ye these and dinnae leave till ye smile." Akira took the satchels from him, after which he spread his legs, crossed his pudgy arms over his chest, and adamantly waited. The once peaceful expression on his face hardened with the duty Calin had bestowed upon him.

Akira would have laughed at the boy's pose if he didn't appear to be taking his duty so seriously. Calin was toying with her. Of course she would smile for this little boy. Calin could be as iron-headed as she when it came to a challenge. Why was he so determined to see her happy? The man was a riddle.

Curiosity overcame her, and she opened the first satchel.

Her heart jumped when she withdrew a necklace. A trio of red heart-shaped rubies fixed along a gold chain. Never had she seen anything so extravagant. She considered its value and how much food could be purchased with it before realizing she would never have to worry about such things again. With the tip of her finger, she stroked the two smaller rubies suspended alongside the larger red stone.

"Hearts united," Aileen whispered.

"Hearts united?" Akira echoed and raised her brows.

"'Tis symbolic of ye and m'laird's union," Aileen explained. "The smaller stones represent the bride and groom."

Akira stared at the woman smiling like a teat-fed cat as she took the necklace and clasped it around Akira's neck. It was heavy and cold against her skin. "And the larger stone?"

"Represents the love ye will share after ye are wed."

Love. A tickle danced in her stomach at the mention of the word. She wanted that. Unfortunately, love was not forcing Calin to the altar. Duty was. She wouldn't lose her heart on this day, regardless of Calin's efforts.

"Mammie, she is not happy," Andrew interrupted from below, his frown reflecting Akira's.

"Then mayhap she should open the other bridegift," Aileen suggested.

What Akira found inside the second satchel sent her into nervous giggles. A silver flask of whisky. She was tempted to take several hearty quaffs in the hopes she would survive this wedding. Instead, she handed it back to Andrew. "Ye tell m'laird, he will have need of this gift more than I."

"I'll not fail ye, m'lady." Andrew gripped the hilt of his wooden sword hanging from his side and stomped out of the chamber.

Aileen and Akira continued prattling for another hour until the chamber door burst open with a bang. Akira gawked in astonishment at the odd couple filling the archway. Jaime held her sister, Isobel, in his arms, and she looked as irritated as he looked happy.

"Put me down, ye heathen." Isobel slapped Jaime's chest while he twirled her into the chamber. "I swear ye are a swine, Jaime MacLeod. The mon tried to kiss me the whole way here."

Although Isobel spoke to Akira, her stormy eyes never left Jaime's face. He set her in a high-backed chair.

"Why did ye not ride with Kendrick?" Akira couldn't contain her smile. Jaime was a devil, and she didn't have to guess why he was clean-shaven.

"The brute insisted I ride with him." Isobel's flame-kissed locks fell in disarray over angry green eyes when she scowled at Jaime standing possessively overtop her.

"But Isobel, I only wanted one wee kiss from your bonnie-fine mouth," Jaime retorted.

"I gave ye one wee kiss to keep ye from wagging your tongue, and ye still dinnae act a gentleman."

"Cause your sweet lips left me wantin' more."

Isobel growled at Jaime. "The only thing ye want is a woman who cannae run from ye. As I am certain all the rest do."

"This is not true." Jaime flashed his handsome smile at Isobel then planted a kiss on her lips.

Isobel pushed him away. "Brute!" She then looked at Akira for the first time since entering the chamber. Her face smoothed and her lips parted, but Isobel spoke no words. Akira hadn't seen her sister in over a month. Filled with relief to see her so healthy and full of life, Akira wanted to run and embrace her, but she froze, awaiting Isobel's approval.

"Ye look beautiful," Isobel said, her voice breathy and full of adoration.

Akira looked away embarrassed by the compliment. No one in her family had ever called her beautiful.

Jaime followed her line of sight and crossed himself. "Dear God 'n Heaven. I have died and stand before an angel."

Aileen pushed Jaime toward the door. "Dearest Jaime, ye have nay hope o' gettin' to Heaven."

The women fell into a heap of giggles and then continued to converse overtop each other while they waited for the soft sounds of the fife to float into the windows. Akira was comforted by the camaraderie, but her insides were rebelling. She smiled at both Isobel and Aileen, though she had no idea what they were talking about and offered a prayer to God to bless her on this day. She prayed for her soul and stroked the large ruby hanging in the hollow of her neck. Before she could stop herself, she asked God for a tiny piece of Calin's heart.

* * *

"Ye look good enough to eat," Aunt Wanda told Calin after Uncle Kerk left the candlelit chamber. She smoothed the creases of his saffron *léine* shirt before pinning his plaid at his right shoulder with the MacLeod brooch. He warmed with her approval, but at the same time felt like a lad of ten again preparing for Sabbath. Still, it was good to be home. His aunt's familiar scent of cinnamon eased his nerves just as it always did.

"Aunt Wanda, quit fawning over me. 'Tis embarrassing." Calin stilled her hands after she brushed lint from the front of an indigo jacket Elsbeth had tailored for him months before.

"Forgive me for wanting ye to look braw for your bride." Tucking a dark red lock of hair back into the knot behind her head, she forced him to stand with his arms outright so she could fasten the decorated sporran to his leather belt and read-just the broadsword at his hip. "Your uncle Kerk has taken his leave, and I would like to hear more about your betrothed."

"Ye will like her," he said without hesitation. "She is smart and will be good for the clan."

She pulled his arms back to his sides then stepped back to inspect him. "Stop talking horseshite. Of course I will like her. And I dinnae give a wit how good she'll be for the clan. I want to know if she'll be good for ye?"

Her arms crossed and a silk-covered toe tapped beneath dark blue skirts. Always forthright, she was a rock, and he knew she wouldn't cease her badgering until he gave her something solid. "Akira is as stubborn as an auld mule and gives me trouble every time her tongue starts moving, which is often."

"And?"

"She is strong."

"Ye mean she is strong-willed. Determined."

"Nay." Calin laughed, thinking of the brawl they'd had just that morning. "I mean she is strong. Like an ox. I dinnae know why, but she nigh brought me to my knees. I think she could take Jaime."

"Dinnae speak ill o' your cousin when he is not here to protect himself."

Calin rolled his eyes. Jaime was three and twenty. The woman really needed to quit coddling him.

"What else?"

"Naught else," he lied.

"Dinnae play games with me." She poked him in the chest with a long bony finger. "I know ye better than that. A mon does not show up on his weddin' day clean-shaven in the Highlands with nay story to tell."

"There is not much to tell. She wouldnae kiss me lest I bathed and shaved, so I did."

Aunt Wanda curled a tale-telling smile. "So ye like the lass's kisses?"

Och! Aye. Her kisses are warm and sweet and make me forget who I am. A trickle of sweat slid down his back as the faint scent of the *siùcair* blossom floated beneath his nose. He inhaled deeply wanting to savor the memory, but Aunt Wanda waited impatiently for an answer.

He didn't intend to reveal the intimacies between him and Akira with his aunt, but he had to offer her something, else she would continue to tap her damnable foot. "She has soft lips."

"Soft lips, aye." Narrowing one green eye on him, she circled him like a vulture. Calin felt very small, even though he towered over the woman by two heads.

"Is she fair of looks?"

He sighed. Fair didn't even begin to describe his Akira. He couldn't put into words how one look at her sent his heart to jumping. "Aye. She is easy on the eyes."

"Easy on the eyes, stubborn, strong, and good for the clan. These are the words ye take to your marriage bed. I hope the woman ties ye to the bed and lashes ye."

Calin gave a quick hoot. "How can ye wish such ill on me?"

"Do ye like the lass?"

"I like the fact that our union will seal the alliance with our neighbors and protect Clan MacLeod from those English dogs."

She scowled her disapproval, and he knew he'd yet to appease the woman.

"Take those words to your marriage bed and I can assure ye, there will be nay hope for bairns."

Calin looked at his feet and focused on the granite tiles sparkling beneath the dying rays of the sun. He didn't want to talk about his marriage bed with his aunt. He didn't want to talk about his marriage bed with anyone for that matter. He'd been trying to rid his mind of the fact he would take his virginal wife's maidenhead, and now his aunt had brought the matter back to the forefront of his mind. He moved to wash again at the basin and noted the tremble of his hands along with the agitated cadence of his heart. He would have ridiculed himself, if he weren't trying desperately to maintain an ineffectual composure in front of his aunt.

Internally, he behaved like the young boy who'd taken a woman ten years his senior for the first time. Remembering the interlude, reminded him how aggressive he'd been, and how briefly the encounter lasted. But this night would be different.

"Sit," Aunt Wanda ordered. "I am not finished with ye."

Calin fell into a wooden settee while she slipped into the antechamber and returned with his father's signet ring. When she attempted to place the ring on his finger, he withdrew. "Nay. I dinnae wish to wear it." The ring reminded him of what he'd done to Akira. He wouldn't be haunted by such memories while he spoke vows of devotion and trust.

"But the ring symbolizes your status as laird."

"Mayhap 'tis wrong of me, but I dinnae want to be laird

today. I just want to be a mon who's marrying a woman before God and his clan."

He felt Aunt Wanda's smile as she bent and kissed his temple. After placing the ring on the mantel, she tied his brushed hair in a queue at the nape of his neck. "Tell me, Calin. Can this woman be trusted with your heart? I dinnae want to see ye hurt again. Catriona nigh ruined ye. She was a whore, and ye must not let what happened prevent ye from sharing your heart with your wife."

Calin's frown was fierce. Even he could feel it wrinkling his face. "Akira is naught like Catriona or Laird Kinnon for that matter. She is smart and giving and passionate about the people she loves. She looks like an angel and smells like a valley of spring flowers. If anyone dares to say otherwise or speak ill of her, I will slit their throat and ask questions after I bury them in unholy ground."

Instead of balking at his rebuttal, Aunt Wanda grinned. "Those are the words ye should take to your marriage bed. Forget about the clan for one day. Enjoy your bride and dinnae be stingy with your heart."

He stood abruptly and crossed the chamber to stare out the narrow window. Kinfolk filled the lawn and awaited the sounds of the fife. He thought of how easy it would be to let Akira into his heart. He wanted that, but he also had a duty to his clan and a vow to fulfill to his father. Had Da pursued the alliance solely to protect Lena? Had that goal been more important to Da than the fate of the MacLeod clan? Calin could not allow himself to be weakened by such sentiments. "My father died because he fell in love with a woman. I'll not suffer the same fate. I am a warrior and a leader. Men who take love into battlefields, die."

Her comforting hand pressed against his back. "Ye are misguided, Calin, for love is what drives men to battle. Love for freedom and for Scotland. Your father dinnae die because he loved Lena. He was murdered by a mon who dinnae know love. Hate and evil killed your father, nay love. Promise me, ye will at least give the lass a chance to love ye."

"I fear she guards her heart more than I." He wondered over his own words. He suspected it would take a great deal of time for Akira to open up to him. That time was certain to turn into an eternity when she discovered the secret he'd hidden from her.

Turning him to her, Aunt Wanda put a mint leaf on his tongue and drew a ragged breath. "'Tis still hope both o' ye will be defenseless in the marriage bed. Mayhap then ye will learn to trust each other. But be gentle with the lass. Ye are a big mon and liable to split her in two."

"Aunt Wanda!" Calin was aghast. Uncle Kerk sorely needed to instruct his wife on sharing her opinion.

"What? 'Tis my duty to offer ye guidance on your wedding day."

Refusing to let the conversation go any further, he took her hand and escorted her from the chamber. "Welcome Akira to the clan and dinnae speak to her about love or the marriage bed. Ye will send her up a tree."

Chapter Twelve

Calin stood at the entrance to the kirk beside Father Harrald when Akira floated through the procession of people and into his view. His knees locked, and what felt like a small animal jumped inside his gut. When a constricting force clutched at his heart, he gave his head a quick shake. What was wrong with him? He was a leader. A warrior. He refused to believe the woman he was about to marry for the sake of protecting his clan shared part of his heart, but the undeniable weight pushing against his lungs challenged his theory. As the timeless moment whirled around him like Highland mist, he realized Akira would be more than just his lady wife. She would be his companion. His friend. His lover.

As she stood before him, her silk gown brushed his bare knee and sent a rush of tingles up his thigh. Her sweet scent consumed his senses, and the stars in her blue eyes glittered with excitement. Summer's breeze pushed the coiled black tendrils against her slender neck. With every breath she took, the rise and fall of her chest hypnotized him beyond sensibility. And her lips. Her generous rosebud lips held the slightest curve—until they parted.

Calin was lost.

The crowd, Father Harrald's garbled words, the squawking bairns, all dissipated. There was only her. Only Akira.

He whispered her name then closed his eyes and leaned in to kiss her.

"Calin," Father Harrald whispered. "M'laird, ye must declare first."

Calin looked down and found Father Harrald's age-spotted hand braced against his chest. Narrowed eyes scanned his surroundings with an acute warrior's regard. He experienced a sense of intoxication, like he just woke from a dream, but the fantasy was real. He stood before God and his clan, and from their expressions, he was making a complete imbecile of himself. He cleared his throat, shook his muddled head, and then looked at Father Harrald. "Ye may begin."

"Begin?" Father Harrald chortled behind a thick white beard. "I am awaiting your vows so I might proceed to the second ceremony."

Once realizing he missed the dialogue to the entire first ceremony, Calin grinned sheepishly, reached for Akira's hand, and then recited his vows in Gaelic as was the custom.

A few moments later, she did the same then the congregation pushed them inside the kirk. She gave him a sideways glance. "Ye may want to give attention to the Latin version. It might behoove ye to know what ye agree to."

Calin ignored her parry, focusing on her smile. He didn't care why she smiled, only that she did. Just before the second ceremony began, Calin leaned close to her ear. "By the saints, Akira Neish, ye are a vision."

"Ye are looking quite braw yourself, m'laird." Akira batted her thick lashes shyly and held his hand.

Calin had been quite pleased with his appearance when he left his solar. Clean-shaven and resplendent in regal Highland dress. As he walked to the kirk, he mused that his little dragon wouldn't be able to resist him. But she duped him once again, for he was spellbound by her as she recited her vows, again in Latin.

Father Harrald nudged him, and he followed suit.

After completing the second ceremony, Father Harrald announced them, but before the priest gave permission to kiss the bride, Calin's lips gained possession of Akira's and refused to let go. He lost himself in her soft, warm mouth until one of his warriors pulled him off her and rushed them both into the Great Hall. He couldn't be certain which man ended his wedding kiss, but intended to kill the bastard as soon as he figured it out.

The assembly cheered, and the pipers exploded, marking the beginning of the festivities. Guttering torches cast the hall into an array of golden light, revealing tables strewn with pewter cups of heather ale, viands, meat pastries, and loaves of honeyed oatcakes. In little time, the trestle benches lined with kinfolk swapping flasks of malted whisky. After Father Harrald blessed the meal, a rush of gillies and maidservants tended the guests. Calin pulled his delicate bride into a ring for the first dance, and the merriment was underway in a whirlwind. Muffled voices hummed throughout the hall and, despite the melee, Calin's gaze never left his bride.

Uncle Kerk and Aunt Wanda formally welcomed her to Cànwyck Castle, and he found himself longing for his father's presence. For a fleeting moment, he glanced into the ceiling of the Great Hall. An eerie tickle curled around his spine as it once did when he was a boy. He felt his father's spirit and wondered if he had found peace with Lena. A sense of contentment washed over him. His father would have liked Akira. And Lena would be proud of her daughter's spirit.

Aileen played the role of hostess, hustling Akira through the kinfolk, and introducing her to nearly every member of the clan. A passel of children followed her like baby ducklings everywhere she went. Akira's foster mother, Vanora, blushed wildly over an abundance of praise offered by his kinswomen. The twins danced with every child in the clan, and Isobel was at the mercy of Jaime's attentions most of the evening. Maggie's husband, Logan, had all but confined her to a bed due to her advanced condition, and Neala stayed behind with her husband to tend the herd.

Calin held the utmost respect for his clan as they welcomed Akira's family without reluctance. Not one of the Kinnons had been shunned from any conversation, and Kendrick joined the MacLeod men with ease as they tormented their laird about the absence of his beard. But Calin paid little attention to their raillery, as he was mesmerized by his bride's composure.

Mayhap he saw her differently now because she was his wife, but he'd never known a more dignified woman. So proud and brave. A born leader.

His conscience niggled to the surface. He hated the secrets he would bring to their marriage bed. The deception. Would she trust him if he told her the truth? Or would she leave to lead Clan Kinnon as was her birthright? The weight within him expelled the breath from his lungs.

He would gain her trust. He had to.

Eventide passed in a haze of anticipation. Anxiously, Calin stood beside a hearth large enough for him to stand in when Kendrick pulled up beside him. "She looks happy."

"Aye, she does," Calin agreed and watched her toss her head back in laughter as she conversed with Gordon's wife.

"Will ye tell her tonight?"

"Nay. Tonight is for us. I'll not ruin it with nightmares. I'll tell her after the games. Ye will give me that before she hates me again. I will take my men and ride to meet with King James to gain his approval. This will give ye time to secure your family with the Donalds and then prepare the rebels. I dinnae want any of your womenfolk to suffer the wrath of Laird Kinnon when we declare war."

Kendrick nodded his acceptance. "Ye'll be good to her. I have promised the lass a gentle mon for a husband. Dinnae make a liar o' me, auld friend."

To Calin's surprise, Kendrick embraced him and clapped him on the back with a forceful slap. He lost sight of Akira as he finalized arrangements with Kendrick, and the Great Hall suddenly felt cold. For the first time all eve, he couldn't smell her floral scent. Instead, the bitter tinge of smoke and ale twisted through him. He pushed out of the circle of warriors to search for her when Father Harrald's booming voice caught his attention.

The opening of a toast rang out. The hall fell into a veil of silence. Too much whisky glazed Father Harrald's wrinkled eyes, and his words came out garbled. "Join me in salutation one an' all, as I toast the bride an' groom." He wavered. "I've awaited this day nigh twenty years myself. May your hearts be filled with happiness an' Cànwyck Castle be filled with your bairns."

The crowd rumbled in agreement. Father Harrald raised a quaff of whisky. "To the chieftain o' Clan MacLeod an' his bride." Brown droplets trickled to the floor when he raised an unsteady hand yet higher, gaining everyone's undivided attention. "To Calin and Lena."

Father Harrald dipped his head back and poured the whisky down his throat. Escalating sounds of question pitched throughout the hall. Confused looks crossed between the attendants, followed by a few passing shrugs. Ignoring Father Harrald's folly, a handful of men cheered, raised their goblets, and then quickly followed his actions.

Calin's eyes popped, as did Kendrick's. He scanned the assembly. Some still lingered in puzzlement. Most didn't care, but Vanora sat in the midst of five elderly women with her hands over her mouth in an obvious panic.

"Hell and damnation!" Calin cursed at no one in particular. This upset would send Akira into upheaval. She would insist on knowing who Lena was. He didn't want to lie to her anymore, but . . .

Calin moved swiftly through the maze of people dreading the inevitable discussion. He stood in the center of the Great Hall and slowly turned a full circle.

Akira was gone.

She must have heard Father Harrald's toast and ran. His eyes rolled beneath his lids when he pictured her climbing a tree in that gown. The attendants in the corridor hadn't seen her leave, but she'd vanished from the hall. Calin sent a dozen men onto the lawn to search the trees while he and his clansmen stalked the castle.

They returned empty-handed.

Anger replaced worry, and he wondered if this woman would make anything easy on him. Calin flinched when Aileen cupped his elbow from behind.

"Come with me, m'laird." She led him to a blue drape, shrouding a small mural alcove off the entrance to the keep. An audible exhale came from his throat when he found Akira buried beneath the puddle of her gown atop a multitude of pillows stuffed with dried heather. Curled into a ball, snuggled lil' Andrew, sleeping soundly atop her bosom. A burgundy smudge of rowan marmalade stained the corner of his lips.

She appeared at peace, content. She must have slipped out while he spoke with Kendrick. Relief flooded his insides as he realized she hadn't heard the toast. His saints had been with him this time.

Akira looked up at them with lethargic eyes. "I fear the festivities have exhausted us both. Forgive us for hiding."

Calin never took his eyes off her. "Aileen, could ye please take your son? I'd like to escort my wife to our chamber."

"Aye, m'laird."

As soon as Aileen removed Andrew, Calin lifted Akira into his arms. He was about to make this woman his wife in mind and body and every nerve sprung to life. He would know the taste of her milky skin, and the feel of her soft body beneath him. A passion had been forming between them, and he was eager to see if her spirit followed her into their bed. Before he ever took a step, he was raging hard beneath his plaid.

He glanced at Aileen. "Have Alec convince Father Harrald he already blessed our marriage bed. I dinnae wish to be disturbed."

Akira stiffened in his arms. A flush of terror washed over her face. "Nay!" she shouted.

Chapter Thirteen

"Have ye lost your wit? I'll not consummate this union on an unblessed bed." Akira couldn't allow this, but Calin seemed determined to escape the ritual. What was he thinking?

She suspected his wits were no longer in charge of his actions. All evening his eyes had followed her, and she fantasized about his heated gaze traveling the length of her naked body. Such impure thoughts had never entered her head before she met him.

The bed must be blessed!

She began to visibly shake as Calin carried her to the base of the stone-cut stairwell.

"Please, m'laird. Ye cannae do this."

He halted on the bottom step, and she knew he'd heard the slight quiver in her voice. "I am cursed. I dinnae want our bairns conceived in an unblessed bed. They are sure to be born deformed or scarred. Please, m'laird. Have Father Harrald bless the bed. I vow to never cause ye trouble ever again."

"Ha! Ye are incapable of fulfilling such a vow. Do ye know what ye ask? Father Harrald is blootered. I have nary a doubt he will never survive the climb to our solar."

"Then have Kendrick carry him."

He blew a long breath of air and shot her an incredulous look. "Ye are serious."

"Please. I have not saved myself for ye, confessed my sins, and married ye before God and the kirk to consummate this marriage on an unholy bed." Akira looked into his eyes and cupped his jaw, praying he would see her reasoning. Her pulse flitted like a frightened bird as she awaited his decision.

He turned back to Aileen. "Have Alec, Gordon, and Kendrick escort Father Harrald to my solar," he practically growled. "Stuff an oatcake down his throat first and dinnae let him wash it down with whisky."

"Aye, m'laird." Aileen bobbed off, leaving Andrew sleeping soundly in the alcove.

He popped a quick kiss onto Akira's nose, and the lines on his face smoothed after the action. "Just because ye have a forked tongue does not mean ye are cursed."

Calin carried her gracefully up the spiral stairs of the west tower to his solar, her heart knocking against her chest with every step.

The fresh rushes strewn about the floor scented with a hint of chamomile stimulated Akira's senses. A dancing fire warmed the air and ignited the golden hues of his eyes. Tallow candles flickered in a pair of six-tier silver candelabras on a dressing table, casting a haze of subtle light over the richly decorated chamber. Over the mantel hung his shield, claymore, and battle-axe. All of which were engraved with the MacLeod crest.

Sprigs of pink and yellow blossoms decorated the walls and furniture, transforming the solar into a miniature garden. In the midst of the solar stood the massive centerpiece—an ornately carved four-poster canopy bed, draped with red wine curtains trimmed in gold. The matching bedding was embellished with a mosaic of white rose petals.

As Akira examined the elegance of his solar, she observed their reflection in an oval mirror. Mayhap it was wishful thinking, but they looked like they belonged together. Her hands clutched behind his neck. Her silk-covered toes dangled over the cradle of his brawny arm. He stood in the middle of the chamber, not making any motion to let her go. He resembled a god from a Greek tragedy, and she was to be his virginal sacrifice. No curve touched his lips as typically did when he awaited her approval. He appeared serious, determined, and, oddly enough, slightly nervous. He inhaled and lowered his lids, hiding his amber eyes.

Turning into him, she stroked his brow. "The devil himself could seduce a maiden in this solar."

Calin lifted his one brow beneath her fingertips. "I have nay intention of seducing ye."

"If ye dinnae intend to seduce me, how are ye to take my . . . virginity?"

A rogue's grin curled one side of his mouth, as if he knew something she didn't. "I'll never force ye to do anything ye dinnae want to do. Nor will I touch ye anywhere ye dinnae want to be touched. Tonight, Akira MacLeod. Tonight, ye will take your own virginity. I'll just offer my . . . assistance."

Akira hooted. "Though I admit to being ignorant to . . . matters of . . . coupling, I am certain ye will need to participate in . . . this."

"I intend to participate fully," he assured then dropped her to her feet. He turned from her and proceeded to disrobe to his plaid. Pale white scars veining his back spoke of the time he'd spent in battle, and she knew he displayed them and the blue battle rings with pride. She wanted to know the depth of his losses, but now wasn't the time to speak of war.

He washed briefly at the basin then turned back to her,

exposing the golden ripples of a magnificent chest. He settled casually onto the high-backed bench cushioned with burgundy damask. Careful not to topple the two goblets of wine on the dressing table, he scooped up a handful of rowan berries from a wooden bowl and popped them, one by one, into his mouth. "Would ye like to start seducing me now or wait 'til the bed has been blessed?"

She knew nothing about seducing a man, but the thought of it made her insides thick and her breasts heavy. Her nerves spiked and she could do little more than banter with him. "I think ye are arrogant, Calin MacLeod. And if ye think I'll be the one ravishing ye, ye are deceiving yourself."

"Tsk, tsk, wife. Ye must conserve your energy. Ye are going to need it." Calin revealed his dimples with this threat while his eyes traveled leisurely over her body.

She remained standing in the middle of the room, hoping Father Harrald would arrive quickly. Calin's heated gaze made her feel naked and vulnerable. *How did he do that?* The heavy gown she wore suddenly felt as thin as a threadbare shift. Her skin tingled against the silk and she wondered if she'd just married the devil. Only a hex could make her feel this wanton. He chewed slowly on the berry he'd just popped in his mouth, and her body tightened, wanting to know the feel of those lips on her skin. She crossed her arms over her breasts in an effort to subdue the sensations flitting inside her. Closing her eyes, she asked God's forgiveness for her sinful thoughts.

Her prayers were answered when Father Harrald staggered through the open door, bringing with him the smell of burning frankincense. Kendrick, Gordon, and Alec guarded the entranceway behind her as if she might bolt from this duty. Admittedly, the thought had occurred to her.

Silent reverence filled the room as the priest spread a cloth over the tabletop and prepared the oils. Calin remained seated while Father Harrald made the sign of the cross against his forehead. The priest then wavered slightly when he turned to her and did the same. He proceeded to sprinkle the bed with holy water and recite the prayer that would bless their union. Her tension eased when the priest turned and stood before her again. His dark eyes glazed with approval when he opened his mouth to speak.

"Father Harrald," Gordon shouted from behind, "your duty is done. 'Tis time we return to the festivities."

Father Harrald offered her a faraway look and kissed her on the forehead saying nothing more.

Alec stepped forward, his eyes downcast. "Aileen is in the corridor if ye have need of a maid to prepare ye, m'lady."

"She has nay need of a maid. I will prepare her."

Even Father Harrald grinned at Calin's comment, and Akira was sorely tempted to kick all of them. Before she could offer her own barb, the men ushered Father Harrald from the room and left her in silence with her husband.

"The bed has been blessed, and I believe ye were about to seduce me." Patting the tiny space beside him, he encouraged her to join him.

Observing the wolfish grin lifting his face, she doubted she could contrive any barb clever enough to dissolve his good cheer. Instead, she sashayed toward him. When she stood within his grasp, he pulled her onto his lap then tickled her lips with the soft skin of a berry until she conceded to his game and opened her mouth. He lazily let his fingers linger over her moist lips after the third berry, tempting her to lick them. He was good at his game and she felt no reason to battle him.

She suckled the red juices from his fingers until he held no more berries in his hand. Flutters of angst filled her stomach. She felt his eyes searching her soul. She was afraid to think, knowing he could somehow read her thoughts. Thoughts that would have made her blush a sennight ago, but now only made her ache. At least she found comfort knowing he was equally affected and aroused. Fully aroused, in fact. The length of his erection had hardened beneath her bottom the moment he pulled her into his lap.

He handed her a goblet of gooseberry wine. She poured the contents down her throat in one gulp then realized he meant to offer a toast. She held out the empty cup. "Might ye have the flask of whisky ye gave me as a bridegift?"

"Ye returned my offering, and ye dinnae need it. Ye may have whisky another night, my sweet."

"But I fear I need it tonight."

His thumb caressed her parted lips while she tried to make light of their situation. He leaned in and brushed his lips across hers. Still, he withheld the kiss. He only breathed in her air. "Would ye like me to kiss ye?"

Even as she held on to a sliver of her rebellious thoughts, her body told her she wanted that kiss. She wanted anything this man was willing to give. Her eyes slid shut. "Aye," she whispered into his mouth.

He drew her bottom lip into his mouth, suckled it, teased it, then did the same with her top lip. The tangy mixture of wine and berries cooled her hot mouth. She slanted her head and darted her tongue between his lips, pursuing the depths of his mouth in an aggressive race. Her heart pounded so hard against her breastbone she could feel the vibrations in her throat. She needed to calm down. Instead, she intensified their kiss.

Calin pulled back. "Relax, my sweet. I want this night to last forever, and I want ye to want the same."

Akira wanted this night over. His desire to go painstakingly slow only intensified her anxiety. Her nerves were going to ruin her wedding night. She feared making a fool of herself.

What if she fell off the bed? What if her limbs wouldn't position themselves the way they were supposed to?

This was insane. Maggie had explained the physical mechanics of consummation after Calin's first query came a year prior. Akira reassured herself that she could manage the task. He was her husband, and he would expect her to perform certain . . . duties. Duties she had no knowledge of, or experience in, but was secretly excited about learning all he could teach her.

A wife's duty, her duty, was to please her husband. And this was exactly how she intended to approach the matter. "I am your wife, m'laird, and I'll perform as your wife. This is my duty unto ye."

"Nay! I dinnae want this to be a *duty*. I want ye to want me like a woman wants a mon. Not out of duty. Not for the damn alliance. For us. Submit to me and say that ye are mine and mine alone." His tone bordered on possessive. All traces of banter were gone, leaving his expression one of insistence.

What did he want from her? She'd agreed not to give him any more grief. There was no question as to whether or not she would be faithful to him. Why did he need to hear her say it?

The man was contrary and domineering. She did want him and would admit that she belonged to him, but she had to protect her heart. Calin was a warrior and couldn't possibly return this powerful affection churning inside her. "M'laird, I belong to ye. I'll do as ye ask."

"I dinnae want to be your laird. I want to be your husband. Your protector. I want ye to give me a chance to touch your heart. I want ye to trust me."

Her heart ached to do just that, but there hadn't been enough time between them for her mind to trust him. Was it possible he felt as vulnerable as she did? The question was hopeless and ridiculous. Calin MacLeod was the laird. Men of his status did not love women like her.

After a long period of silence, he lowered his eyes. His sad expression told her he accepted defeat on the matter. He stroked the exposed area of her collarbone with his fingertips and nuzzled her cheek with his jaw. He poised his lips a hairsbreadth from hers and waited for her to kiss him.

She explored the hollows of his mouth. Dancing with his tongue, she felt innocent, yet seductive. He kissed her as long as she wanted, and never once did his fingers stray from the curves of her neck. But now she ached to have his powerful hands caress her.

She pulled away with a soft moan. The tip of her tongue licked her tingling lips. She removed the sash and cape of her own accord. The silk material of her gown sculpted her aroused breasts, swelling overtop the hem of her bodice. Sparks ignited in her womb as she waited for him to touch her, but he remained gallant.

"M'laird, I could kiss ye all night, but my body tells me I want more. Howbeit, I feel a fool to ask."

"I am your husband. Ye've nothing to be ashamed of." He held her hand and kissed the blue vein in her wrist adding to the fever growing inside her. "What do ye ask of me, my sweet Akira?"

The way he looked at her made her inhibitions fall away. She wouldn't shy away from his question, nor did she want to. She cupped his hand over her breast and hid her eyes beneath her lashes. "I want ye to touch me . . . here."

Her chest tightened beneath his gentle caress, and the ache intensified when he kissed the exposed skin of her shoulder. Heat leapt beneath her flesh, and the short hairs prickled behind her neck. Leaning forward, she allowed him to release the laces at her back until the bodice of her gown fell to her waist.

He tilted her chin back up to him. "Dinnae look away. I want ye to see the passion in my eyes. The passion I hold for only ye. My bride. My wife. My Akira." Calin held her gaze, but trailed his fingers over the fullness of her breast until the tip of his thumb swirled over a peaked nipple.

On the table beside, he reached for a sprig of *siùcair* blossoms. After sucking the sweet honey from the septum, he offered another bloom to Akira. She mimicked his lead. Plucking a third from the sprig, he squeezed the nectar between her breasts. His tongue warmed her skin as he licked away the tiny droplets. He proceeded to lave her upper breasts with the ambrosia and ritually bathe it away.

But Akira wanted more. She needed more and feared exploding into flames if he didn't cease his torment.

"More," she whispered and guided his mouth over her aching nipple. A satisfied moan escaped her throat when his warm mouth suckled her. All thoughts of protecting her heart left her as she set her body free to enjoy his touch. The sensation that had been building behind her breast plummeted into her stomach then seeped lower until a fire ignited between her legs. She wiggled in his lap and hoped this ferocity was normal.

His hands stilled the movements of her hips. "Dinnae do that."

She studied his pained expression. "Do ye ache the same as I?"

He nodded slowly, almost cautiously. "But 'tis a good ache. One I know ye will soon remedy."

She smiled and accepted his words as a compliment just as her hands found their way over the contours of his chest. The fresh scent of sandalwood permeated her senses while she tasted the spice of his skin—down his neck then over the breadth of his strong shoulders. She showed him the same attention only more aggressive as she bit and tugged at his small nipple.

She twitched and yearned to move faster, still Calin didn't break his poise. He continued to titillate her breasts, until she pushed off him then stood. She wanted him—now, and he showed no signs of advancing.

After releasing her arms from the sleeves, she pushed the gown over her hips. A pool of yellow material fell in a silken whisper to her feet. She repressed the urge to cover herself when his eyes followed the contours of her body. The way he looked at her made her dizzy as if she were the most sensual creature in the world.

The sight before him made Calin's manhood jump. Every ounce of Akira's creamy flesh curved into the next. Her flaring hips were wide and every bit as full as her breasts. Arms and legs sculpted lightly with feminine muscle, and the small patch of dark curls only whispered at what treasures lay beneath.

A rush of excitement spiraled up his spine as he walked to her then traced the edges of those exquisite curves with one finger. Under both breasts, down the middle of her torso to her navel, then rounding out over one hip. "May God blind me now and leave your vision tattooed upon my eyes." With his knuckle, he raised her chin to him again. "I dinnae lie when I tell ye, ye are beautiful."

She blushed under the glow of the room, and he thought she might actually believe him this time. He hoped she did, for it was true.

He clutched her head between his hands then fiercely kissed her swollen lips before carrying her to the bed. Undeniable passion turned her sapphire eyes to near black. He proceeded to adorn her petal-soft skin with tender kisses, lingering over her hipbones until he swirled her navel with his tongue. She was exquisite. The taste of her. The smell of her. The feel of her. He'd never wanted to please anyone the way he did her. The desire he felt for her not only filled his erection to a painful size, but his chest ached with an emotion stronger than devotion. He'd never felt more alive.

He wanted her to want him. Calin MacLeod. The man. She could trust him with her heart. He would never hurt her.

He pressed a kiss over her heart and felt the vibration pounding against his lips. He splayed his palm over her breast to feel the pulse stronger. She wanted him. Her words may deny it, but her heart mocked her. The more her breathing increased, the faster he wanted to go.

She released the leather thong gathering his hair then weaved her fingers through it. She whimpered and urged his head back to her rigid nipples, all the while grinding her pelvis against the knee firmly planted between her legs.

Her heat scorched his bare thigh, and nearly stripped him of dignity. He wanted to suck harder, to bite, to taste the warm nectar between her legs with a savage ferocity that would send her screaming, yet pleading for more. As he drew her delectable skin between his lips, a fever coursed through his veins that begged him to take her. The muscles in his arms and legs tightened against his inner battle until he groaned in misery. A voice in his head reminded him, *Be gentle. She is a virgin. Ye will tear her in two.*

The chamber became unbearably hot. Perspiration beaded her temple, and above her lip, then over her throat, and between her breasts. The wisps of hair falling from her headdress clung to her neck in laced swirls. He didn't know the source of the heat. Did her body burn his hands? Or was it his hands that scorched her body?

"I dinnae know what to do. Your touch, your kiss . . . ye are inflicting great pain on my person. I dinnae know how, but I cannae bear it."

Calin saw the fright wash over her face, and sought to end her torment, along with his own. "Do ye want me to touch ye?"

"Aye, please."

Grinning with satisfaction, Calin slid his callused hand up her thigh. She sucked in air when he slowly eased her folds apart then grazed the damp frills. Akira drew a quick gasp of air at the contact. One deft finger entered her, stroking the slick walls, only penetrating the surface. She was swollen, and already quivering against the unfamiliar sensation. She panted into the sultry air. He sensed her confusion. She didn't know whether to push against him or pull away.

She did both.

When his thumb found her hidden gem, she screamed— quick, heated squeals that vaporized into whimpers. Her arms flew to the bedding, grasping fistfuls of rose petals and silk between her fingers. Her back arched off the down-filled mattress. "Oh, *mon Dieu!*"

Her eyes flew open. "Cease!"

He did.

But within seconds she had changed her mind. She bucked against the hand lying motionless between her legs. "Och, Calin, dinnae cease."

His arrogance swelled. Grinning, he continued his masterful touch. "Say my name, again."

She obeyed him. Again and again.

Calin was sure he would explode beneath his plaid just watching the mixture of pleasure and pain unfold over her confused face. When her inner walls convulsed, he stepped off the edge of the bed to remove his leather belt, sending his plaid to pile beside her gown.

She was crying his name when he returned. His muscles ached from restraint, but he intended to hold a piece of her heart before he finished with her. Even if that piece were only a morsel.

Gripping her firmly by the hips, he flipped her atop him to straddle his cock. He clutched the soft flesh of her backside, sliding her up and down the length of him. He wanted to bury himself inside her, and her heat was more than he could bear. Sweat broke out in a flood over his chest. He knew she was ready, but he wanted her to say the words. "Do ye want me?"

"I am afraid."

"I'll not hurt ye. I'll let ye control it."

"But I dinnae know how. This is not the way I know."

"Lean into me and kiss me, my sweet."

Akira was frightened, but did as he asked. His hand reached between them to circle the nub pulsing inside her. She quit kissing him and only moaned into his mouth.

"Do ye want me?" he asked again.

"Aye."

Calin increased the pressure and speed of his thumb then stopped all at once, removing his hand completely. "Say the words, Akira," he demanded.

"Nay. I'll not let ye break my heart." She fought the urge. She would not succumb. Would not give into her body's desires. A desire so primal it scorched her loins. "Damn ye, Calin MacLeod."

This time when he stroked her flesh, he teased harder, with more promise. Her mouth opened and undulated whimpers that sounded like sobs. *Crivons, Akira. Control yourself. Ye are acting brazen, and a fool,* she scolded herself then a jarring ache stabbed the back of her head just before her mind clouded into a surrealistic haze. She was falling.

But, once again, he ceased.

A powerful force had been escalating inside her. It terrified her, at the same time exhilarated her. But now, only the intense craving returned. He clutched her skull between his hands then crushed her mouth with his kiss.

He pushed her back with a jerk. "I vow I will never hurt ye.

Trust me with part of your heart. Submit to me. Say it. Say ye belong to me and me alone."

The temptation was unbearable. He was her husband. She was being foolish. *Oh, damn it all to Hell!* "I want ye. My husband. My Calin. I am yours and yours alone. I want nay other."

He raised her hips above him then guided her over the tip of his erection. With an open-mouthed groan, he released her. She placed her hands on his chest, bracing herself up above him. Her body told her what to do, still she panicked.

"Dinnae be afraid," he whispered through a breath ripe with agony. The fan of her lashes hid her fear. "Open your eyes, my sweet. I dinnae want ye to feel alone. Look at me."

She did and was comforted by his gentleness. She bore down onto the thin shield of her maidenhead and then pushed through it. Drawing her bottom lip between her teeth, she held his gaze. She did not scream.

Calin held her hips still while she adjusted to his size. She saw the torment in his face, saw the sweat dripping down his temples, felt him throbbing inside her. She didn't realize she wept until he wiped the tear from her cheek. A moment later, the pain passed, and he began to slide her up and down him again, showing her the rhythm. She mimicked the motion then pulled his hand to stroke the center of her.

A film clouded her mind as she was blinded by ecstasy. Digging her nails into his sweat-drenched muscles, she cried out his name and gave in to the sensation at last.

Her climax poured over him.

"Ah, sweet Akira . . . sweet, sweet Akira." Calin surrendered to his own zenith with a hoarse roar. His hands shook while he held her motionless and pumped into her.

Sated, Akira collapsed against his chest, inhaling gulps of air through her mouth. His heart beat rapidly against her own. Filled with emotions and trembling, she didn't care if she did it right. She only knew what they had just shared was beautiful and even though she felt foolish, she cried.

Calin raised her head and dabbed the tears from her lashes. She couldn't contain her smile. "That was divine."

A flood of relief washed over his features. "Aye. Ye are divine. Every ounce o' ye is sumptuous."

Laying the side of her cheek against his chest, she straddled him for a long while, frolicking in the sensuous feel of him still inside her. Reality soon drifted back to her senses. Hidden beneath the musky smell of their lovemaking, wafted the aroma of flowers. The faint whistle of pipes were muffled by the hum of people and shrieks of children. Children. Akira's head popped up. "Am I with child now?"

Calin laughed at her. "I hope so, but we will have to keep trying in the event my virility fails ye." He pulled her off him then tucked her into his side.

"Keep trying. Ha! I have nay intention of doing *that* again," she teased and circled his flat nipple with the tip of her finger.

"Ye will do *that* again, and ye will do it willingly, and ye will wear a smile." Though his words were pretentious, he lay listless with closed lids. Had she done that to him? The only movement he seemed able to muster was to stroke her forearm draped across his chest.

She, on the other hand, erupted with energy. She welcomed the return of his arrogance and curled her toes around his beefy calves. "The next time we dinnae do it, and I dinnae do it willingly, and I dinnae wear a smile, will ye please douse the fire first?" she jested, feeling particularly feisty.

He only grinned, and nodded.

Moments later, his eyes slid open. "What did ye mean when ye said ye dinnae know that way? Ye were a virgin. What way do ye know?"

Akira couldn't help but laugh. The way he made love to her wasn't like Maggie had described. "My sister, Maggie, explained to me the way 'twould happen so I wouldnae be afraid. She said I'd just lay there and ye would do all the work." Akira suckled his nipple and rubbed her leg between his. "But I fear I've married a lazy mon, for my husband was the one lying there with me doing all the work."

Calin only smiled. He appeared too exhausted to laugh. "I never had a virgin in my bed, and I dinnae want to hurt ye. I thought that way might be easier for ye."

She didn't even try to hide the shock that lifted her brows. Though surprised he'd never had a virgin, she was more surprised he shared that information with her. Deciding to allow him to keep his oversized ego, she swallowed the retort she had already conjured for him and focused on the fact that he'd been concerned about hurting her.

"Thank ye for being gentle. Ye are a good husband, and I am glad ye chose me to be your lady wife." She coiled into his side, wondering if every man took his wife so tenderly her first time. She considered herself fortunate, but she was also afraid. Knowing the reality of their arrangement, if she didn't protect herself, she could easily lose her heart to her husband. She suspected part of her had already let him slip in. If he insisted she trust him with part of her heart, then she would insist he do the same.

On the morrow.

Chapter Fourteen

The pale light of dawn sliced through the crevices of the tapestry covering the narrow window. Akira stared blindly at a peat fire she'd saved from smoldering. Tucked inside a plaid blanket atop a cushioned bench, she was dressed in a simple sark. With eyes wide and in a trance, she stroked the etched crest of Calin's broadsword and recollected the night she'd spent with the man who was now her husband.

"Why are ye so far away from me, wife?" She heard him ask in a deep sleepy voice.

Her lips bowed as she looked at him buried beneath the disarray of their covers. "I was too excited to sleep."

"Aye, I am excited as weel." Rolling to his side, he raised the fur coverlet for her to join him. "Lay with me, kitten. I want to hear ye purr for me, again."

Crossing the chamber, she stood beside the bed and gawked at the glow of his sculpted body against the pale of sheets stained with her innocence. Her curious eyes followed the path of sparse hair which tapered into a most impressive erection. The remembrance of their union set her cheeks on fire, and she wondered how he'd actually fit inside her. The dull uncomfortable ache at her woman's core reminded her of why she'd crawled out of his arms and dressed earlier. Peeling her stare away from him, she found his face. "M'laird, I am your wife, not your pet. Ye cannae keep me caged in your solar. I want to meet with the chaplain and the council to discuss educating the children."

Calin's forehead wrinkled. He dropped the covers and exhaled. "Now?"

"Aye. Ye promised me this." Akira jutted her full bottom lip in a pout just to tempt him.

"The cock has yet to crow. The elders will be in their beds or snoring in the hall with the rest of the kin. We will not be expected to appear until well into noontide."

"Noontide? What am I to do until then?"

Calin arched both brows and exposed broad dimples in response to her question.

Akira curled around the bedpost, snubbing his obvious attempt to bed her. "I told ye I wasnae doing *that* again."

"Ye lied, and ye know it," Calin accused, and watched her glide to the opposite bedpost.

She twisted a loose tendril around her finger and peeked at him from beneath her lashes. "Ye vowed ye wouldnae force me. And I dinnae want to right now."

"Why not?"

"Because I am sore," she admitted without shame, yet rubbed her knees together beneath her skirts when her body reacted to his invitation.

He winced. "I'll give ye time to heal. For the nonce, just lay with me. I swear to Saint Jerome, I'll be a monk."

Akira didn't trust him. Never had she known a monk to have such lust in his eyes. "Forgive me if I dinnae believe ye, m'laird. Furthermore, I want a bath first."

"By the saints, woman, ye certainly like to be clean. Ye just bathed yestereve, and the day before that. And the day before that."

"I dinnae like to smell like a goat."

"I'll have the maids prepare ye a bath." Calin paused for a moment, his eyes flashed a naughty look. "Howbeit, I may have to search the bailey to find out whose bed they ended up in. I saw them sipping whisky."

Akira hid a shamed laugh at his comment. Having maids would be an adjustment. In all actuality, her new life was going to take a great deal of adjusting. Having servants cater to her. Having people ogle over her because she was the laird's wife. Just being the laird's wife. But what would take the most adjustment, was sharing a bed with this man. A man who'd given her everything she'd asked—including gentleness.

Still and all, the hour was dreadfully early. Having the brook behind her cottage had always simplified tending to her ablutions. Her penchant for cleanliness would, no doubt, cause a ruckus within the keep. She didn't want the servants to think her a nuisance already. "There's nay need to disturb the maids."

"Ye are not disturbing them. 'Tis their duty to tend to your needs. I suspect they will become verra strong hauling pails of water for ye every day, but the cistern is just at the end of the corridor. Ye are the Lady o' Cànwyck Castle. If ye want a bath, they will oblige."

"I am certain I'll not need a maid's services to bathe. Is there a spring within the bailey?" Akira turned to pack a satchel of toiletries, determined to rid herself of the chamber, her husband, and dutiful maids. If he simply inhaled, he would probably smell the arousal escalating between her thighs.

"Aye, but there is a better place. 'Tis outside the walls. I'll take ye there." Calin threw off the thick fur coverlet, and crossed the chamber to retrieve his attire. Akira grinned. The man hadn't a modest bone in his body. And what a wonderful body he had. Chiseled muscles corded every ounce of him, and all were covered beneath bronze-colored flesh. All except his pale-white little backside and midsection, both of which held their own qualities. Qualities making her taut with desire. She hoped she healed quickly.

The thought occurred to her that he probably intended to bathe with her. "I am more certain, I'll not need your services to bathe."

His head snapped back, and he caught her watching him dress. He flashed a grin while tying his hair back in a thong. "And I am certain ye will."

"And ye will be a gentleman?" She asked coyly as she flushed her back against the solidity of the bedpost when he approached her.

"Aye."

"Ye will expect nothing from me until I have . . . healed?"

"Only my kiss." Calin cupped her neck and kissed her— a simple, gentle, good-morrow kiss, without intensity. "I do have a boon of ye. I wish for ye to call me Calin. At least in the privacy of our solar."

"As ye wish, Calin." She liked saying his name outside the heat of anger or passion. He kissed her again and when he drew back, she asked, "Will ye always be so gentle with me?"

"I will try." He led her to the door.

"When we return, may I meet with the council?"

He laughed at her persistence. "The games begin late today. I'll introduce ye then, and ye may have a cordial conversation with the elders. Ye must state your reasons for wanting to school the children. But ye cannae just demand from them. They'll not find your audacity as appealing as I do."

Her jaw dropped at this insult. "I am not audacious."

Calin grinned, and quietly opened the door. So as to not wake anyone, he leaned into her ear. "Ye are audacious, and bold, and reckless, and stubborn. And these, wife, are your good qualities."

She punched him playfully in the gut, but hard enough to

solicit a grunt from him. They escaped the castle walls, only disturbing two porters in the barbican to lower the iron-spiked grating of the portcullis behind them.

A powerful cascade of water roared over a cliff into an aqua-blue pool. Lush green grasses and bright pink rhododendron blanketed the embankment surrounding the lagoon. Akira gazed in awe, overwhelmed by its natural beauty. The waterfall was twice as grand as her own. Twice as beautiful. Twice as tall. Everything in Calin's world seemed more impressive than what she was accustomed to. After dismounting, she looked up at him. "I'll not be long. Ye may return for me shortly."

Calin ignored her dismissal, and dismounted behind her, leaving Sirius to graze alongside the water's edge. "I have need of a bath myself." Without a morsel of shame, he stripped to his birthright, stepped atop a jutting rock, and then dove head-long into the depths of turquoise water. He emerged with a quick yelp and shook his hair like a hound.

Akira's throat suddenly felt like ash. Her fingers itched to touch him. The man could tempt her to follow him into the fires of Hell. Was it wrong for her to want him so?

Leisurely, he swam to the middle of the lagoon. "Ye must not come in," he yelled. "The water is cold enough to freeze the blood of the burliest Highlander. I fear what it might do to a woman."

She narrowed her eyes. His statement was nothing more than a challenge. After removing the headdress, her fingers worked to detangle the braids and curls from the confinement of pins. A quick scan of the area assured her of their privacy, still, she hid behind Sirius' massive form and nervously removed her garments. The air tickled her bare skin or mayhap it was the prospect of exposing herself to her husband in the full light of dawn that excited her. She leapt from the rock in a perfect dive just before disappearing beneath the water's surface. Her blood crystallized to ice instantly.

She emerged with a gasp. "Crivons! 'Tis freezing."

Swiveling, she saw him paddling in her direction. Plunging below, she escaped him, swimming to where she thought she could touch bottom.

She couldn't. With only an arm's length separating them, she tried to splash away from him, but the cold water made her movements sluggish. She was easily caught, for in truth, she wanted to be. "I hadnae intended to swim. The water is like ice."

Standing chest deep, Calin lifted her up by her backside. "I'll warm ye."

She wiped a trickle of water from his cheek and traced his classic features. Calin MacLeod was a beautiful man. Hair dripped all around a face boned with strength and dignity. Yet his sincere eyes were what spoke to her. The promise a life she'd only dreamed of filled her with a mixture of both terror and hope.

Could their marriage ever be more than just a contract? This question arose a hundred times since she'd awoken that morning. And she continued to count herself fortunate. He vowed to give her bairns and never strike her. She would be content with what he offered, which was far more than most women ever received. His earlobe found its way between her fingers as she drifted into her thoughts.

"What do ye think of now?" he asked.

Akira gave a shiver and found his warm gaze again. "Us."

Calin's brow lifted as he drew her tighter. His voice was soft, yet seductive. "I think of us as weel. Would ye like to know what we are doing behind my eyes?"

Akira nodded, and hooked her legs around his waist, no longer embarrassed by her nudity.

"There is grass on the bank." He pointed. "Its texture, soft as silk. My lady wife is lying naked in those grasses, warming her skin beneath the sun."

Akira laughed aloud at his vision. "And where are ye in this fantasy, husband?"

"I am trying to heal her." Not only was his answer wicked, so were his hands. They rounded her backside to find their way into her most intimate of crevices.

She sucked in an audible breath at his swiftness and slapped him on the shoulder. "Ye promised to be a gentleman."

"But the vision of ye brings out the devil in me."

Crawling up his shoulders, she pushed him under with both hands. He resurfaced a few feet away. "Swim with me. I'll resist ye for the moment," he hollered over his shoulder, and then broke into a vigorous glide toward the pounding fall. She followed, matching him stroke for stroke. They emerged behind a curtain of white water. The waterfall created a booming echo inside the cavelike hollow. Calin stabilized his footing on a projecting rock then reached for her. When he raised her up, she stood waist deep out of the water, her erect nipples a testament to the frigid temperature. The narrow space of the rock left little distance between them.

"Ye swim like a selkie, and ye are as enchanting as a mermaid, my Akira," he said in a husky voice then bent to suckle the fresh water from her lips. He raised her up by her bottom, forcing her legs to wrap around his waist.

The intensity of his fevered kiss contradicted the icy gooseflesh sprouting from her skin. He wove his fingers into her heavy mane and drew her back, exposing the flitting pulse in her throat. His lips grazed her flesh just before his hot mouth found her breast.

Twisting her rigid nipple between his teeth, he moaned.

"Och, Calin." His name came out as a squeak. Though tender, the craving to have him inside her returned with a vengeance. "'Tis too soon. Ye are too much for me to take so quickly," she whined, yet rubbed herself against him.

Calin laughed. "The water is far too brisk for me to ravish ye. I only want to bathe ye with kisses." As he spoke, he did just that.

She dipped her head back, surrendering beneath his lips. Her body responded to him in ways that made her question her morals. "Ye make me wanton, husband. Nay mon wants this quality in a wife. I fear your clan will accuse me of behaving like a whore."

Calin stopped abruptly and dropped her to her feet with a splash. Brown eyes darkened to burnt anger. His strong nose flared. His lips thinned. Akira confessed to not knowing all his moods, but the face he wore now was one she never cared to see again.

For the first time, she feared him.

Looking down his nose at her, he delivered his words in a harsh clipped tone. "Ye will never refer to yourself as a whore again. I dinnae lay with whores. I am faithful as my father was to my mother. Ye are my wife, and ye may act as wanton in my presence as ye desire. If anyone in my clan dares to name ye a whore, they will be exiled. Is this understood?"

Akira nodded and bowed her head like a reprimanded child. Embarrassment doused the flame inside her, causing her teeth to chatter. "Forgive me, m'laird," she murmured and hugged herself to cover her breasts.

"Ye need not apologize. There are some matters in which I'll not yield. This being one of them. Whores are not faithful. Ye've vowed faithfulness to me. Ye'll not break the vows ye spoke before God and the kirk. Ye've said ye are mine and mine alone. 'Tis all I need."

Dumbfounded by this outburst, she found herself lost for words. She'd asked him not to take a mistress until after she had borne their fifth child, but she never thought for a moment he'd think she would lay with another man. He obviously had a streak of possessiveness running through his veins. She tried to move away from him.

"Dinnae cower before me." He raised her trembling chin and kissed her cold lips. "Ye are forgiven. Now . . . I believe ye were acting wanton." The last of his words were delivered in a tone that flirted with her.

Peeking up at him, Akira watched his eyebrow arch above a wink he snapped her. Inspired by his wicked grin, she pushed him off the ledge then plunged out in front, racing him back to the water's edge. Calin retrieved soap from his saddle-bag and sprawled out beneath the rising sun on a bed of lush green grasses. "Come, lie with me. I'll behave. I vow it."

Crawling up beside him, she tucked herself partially beneath him on the slope.

She followed a trickle of water over his broad shoulder and studied the battle marks circling his thick arm. The wide top ring was near gray with age compared to the other three, which were sharp thin blue lines. "Did ye go to war young?"

"Not 'til I was one and twenty. Uncle Kerk wouldnae allow it."

She traced the top ring with the tip of her finger. "This mark is older than that."

"The rings dinnae signify the number of battles a warrior has fought. They represent a mon's losses."

"Ye lost many men when ye were young?"

"Nay. I lost my father when I was ten. I had the blacksmith mark me to remind me of my father's aspirations."

She met his tormented eyes and saw an age-old longing there she hadn't intended to uncover. "I'm sorry. I know what 'tis like to lose someone ye love," she whispered, overcome with the desire to comfort him.

"'Twas a long time ago." He lowered his eyes, but not

before she saw how much pain her last statement caused him. She desperately wanted to fill that void.

She reached up and caressed his bristled chin. "Calin?"

"Aye?"

Could ye ever love me like that? The words dangled so loosely on her tongue, she felt all she had to do was open her mouth and they would come out. But the fear that his answer would crush her made her swallow the question and instead ask, "Will ye shave while we are here?"

His eyes flashed back open with the abrupt change in subject, and the air of humor returned to his grin. "Aye, but not until I bathe ye." He ran the soap over her wet skin. Lathering her neck, her breasts, her stomach, her thighs. He set the soap atop its leather satchel and finished the job with his hand.

Though she enjoyed his touch, she couldn't help but throw barbs at him. "I told ye I dinnae need your services to bathe. I can clean myself ye know."

"As I am certain ye can, I thought ye might return the service." He picked up the small cake of soap and placed it in her hand. Rolling onto his back, he cradled his head in his laced fingers and grinned. "I fear I need a stringent scrubbing. Would ye oblige me?"

Lusty barbarian. Her husband proved to be very wolfish with his seductions. A playful trait she intended to learn, practice, and then master. She explored his body with the intrigue of a curious innocent. Her teasing fingers slicked over his shoulders, down his stomach, and around his corded thighs.

Then she stroked his cock—twice.

A robust moan rumbled from his throat. Hooded lids flickered over his rolling eyes. Intrigued by his response, she studied the pained expression on his face. She chewed her bottom lip wanting to touch him again.

She did.

She swirled her index finger around the tip of his cock,

learning its smooth texture. She became bold in her perusal and gripped him firmly, unable to touch her fingertips to her thumb.

"Ye are being wicked, wife. Verra, verra wicked."

Feeling her insides crackle with desire, Akira crawled overtop him, sliding her slick body over his. She brushed her breasts up and down his arousal then kissed him wildly. She pulled back. "Do ye want me, husband?"

Calin growled into her mouth, roughly pinched both her nipples, then spanked her bare arse with a whack. Throwing her off him, he jumped to his feet. "Hell and damnation! Of course I do, but I'll not hurt ye. I swear ye are the devil in angel's skin. Ye will pay for your wickedness, wife." He dove headlong into the frigid water.

Laughing aloud, she sat up, curled her arms around her bent legs and watched her husband's graceful dance in the rippling water. A sense of pride swirled behind her breast, warming her. She would make Calin proud to call her wife, and somehow she intended to find a way into her husband's heart.

"Enjoy your merriment, you Scottish whore. 'Twill not last long," Catriona murmured to herself behind the thick cover of gorse. Her nails sliced into her palms while a jealous fury erupted within her. "Calin belongs to me."

Chapter Fifteen

Brycen Castle had never been so quiet. No squawking bairns running amok. No young maids scurrying with duties. The simple tapping of his guest's fingertips on the stone council table sounded like a drum in his ear. The silence pecked at Laird Kinnon's brain like a vulture on a rotting corpse.

It was cold enough to chill wine in the hearth. A hearth that hadn't held a fire in nigh twenty years. Thick moisture slicked the stone table and dripped in black rivulets down the once smoke-tinted walls of the council chamber. He felt the end of summer in his bones. Or was the ice passing through his soul the spirit of his late wife taunting him again?

He hated this chamber. The chill was worse here than any other room in Brycen Castle.

Laird Kinnon itched for upheaval. Something to heat his blood and set his mind free of this haunted place. And Kendrick Neish would soon provide what he hungered for.

A war.

As of late, his training field reeked of male sweat and fresh blood. Every lad in Dalkirth who could wield a sword trained alongside their fathers, uncles, and brothers. Just yestereve he sent missives to his brethren in the Lowlands. The survival of

Clan Kinnon resided in the loyalty of its kin. That loyalty didn't extend to Kendrick. Laird Kinnon knew why Kendrick failed to train with his kinsmen. The traitor sold one of his bitches to the MacLeod. It took the blood of a prized warrior to gain that information.

The Kinnon garrison was strong, but not strong enough. His warriors would lose a battle against the MacLeods even with the aid of his Lowlander cousins. Which is why he now stood in his council chamber staring into the pitch-black orbs of Logan Donald's eyes.

Laird Kinnon needed an ally.

He pulled at the loose-fitting woolen trews beneath his plaid as he paced around the stone table where Logan sat in apparent boredom. Long, dense fingers propped up his black-bearded chin and clouds of mist swirled evenly out his nose. A pile of cats by the empty hearth held his interest. Four in all. And every one as scrawny as the next. Laird Kinnon hated the mangy creatures, but had never been able to rid the castle of their presence. He'd tried to poison them, but the damned things wouldn't die.

Lena had coddled them like bairns.

Logan brushed a piece of lint from the pleated wool draped over his shoulder. His nonchalant demeanor infuriated Laird Kinnon, but he tempered that anger and feigned interest in Logan's personal affairs. "Your wife is about to deliver your first bairn, is she not?"

"Aye. Our midwife has confined my Maggie to a bed as her time draws near. Methinks she may be carrying bairns o' two."

"I have not seen Maggie's brother among my warriors. Kendrick bears my name and lives on my lands, yet finds nay time to train with the Kinnon brethren to protect the verra ground he reaps."

"Our country is at peace with England for the nonce," Logan offered congenially. "Ye train your warriors as if war awaits ye on the morrow. There is really nay need to deplete your men's endurance during such times as these. Kendrick devotes his time to tending to his herd and his womenfolk. Now I know ye have not dragged me away from my wife on the Sabbath to speak to me about the absence o' my brother-in-law. What do ye want from me?" Logan's brows drew tight as he rose from the table, towering two heads over Laird Kinnon. The trestle bench scraped across the floor and echoed off the empty walls. The cats scattered.

Laird Kinnon looked up at him and swallowed his pride. "I have asked ye here to propose an alliance."

A treacherous smile played at Logan's lips. "The chieftain o' Clan Donald would sooner dig his own grave afore aligning with ye."

Angered by Logan's sardonic tone, Laird Kinnon's pulse tripped a beat. "But your father would unite his clan with a shepherd's son. A peasant who holds nay status and is disloyal to his chieftain."

Logan bent over the stone table and looked Kinnon straight in the eyes—not a trace of fear could be found in his expression. "Kendrick dinnae sell his borders to the English for a bride and enough siller to fill the caverns beneath Brycen Castle. Ye would do weel to remember that ye did."

Laird Kinnon spat in the empty hearth and paced the chamber in frustration. That English bitch hadn't been worth the gold attached to her name. The same gold which had prevented him from aligning with either of his neighbors. The same gold that was now gone.

He gripped the dried ox hide from the chamber's sole window and tore it from its fastenings. He searched the bailey. Smoke swirled in wisps from the cot-houses. Matrons herded their bairns down a path to the kirk.

A woman's weeping echoed in the corridor behind him. His head snapped in the direction. Logan's head cocked with intrigue, but Laird Kinnon knew that cry all too well. The strong fragrance of lavender suddenly filled the chamber. Despite himself, he shivered. "I fear ye leave me nay choice then. I have need for an audience with Kendrick. Ye are wed to his sister and can bring him to me. I have a proposition for the mon."

"And what might that be?"

"As laird of Clan Kinnon, I wish for naught more than the same peace King James provides. Peace among my clan and the Isles. Kendrick has conveniently bound the Isles together for me by marrying his sisters off to my neighboring clans. 'Tis my intention for my son to marry Kendrick's twin sisters and strengthen the loyalty within our clans."

"'Tis bigamy and punishable by death according to the kirk. Kendrick will not allow it, nor will King James. Now, if ye have nay further need o' me, I've a wife to tend to." Without waiting for a dismissal, Logan scuffled through the molded rushes stirring up the stench of cat piss.

It infuriated Laird Kinnon that he held no status with this man. The Donalds had never been his enemy, but neither were they allies. For him to remain in power, he would have to get to Kendrick. "Darach will choose. One for his wife, the other for his leman. Ye will send Kendrick and his sisters to me, or I'll send for your Maggie."

Logan swiveled on his heel. The broadsword hanging from his hip swung wide with the action. A surge of trepidation flushed through Laird Kinnon, warming his skin. He poised his palm over the hilt of his *sgian dubh* in preparation.

Logan's black eyes bore into him. "Ye cannae threaten me, auld mon. Ye may seek loyalty among your warriors by threatening their women, but ye have nay reign over my person or my Maggie. Touch my wife, and I can promise ye a slow and painful death. Kill me and suffer the fury o' Clan Donald."

Laird Kinnon would not be swayed by the obstinacy

exuding from Logan's eyes. These bastards had been after him for years to unite. Now that he makes one of them an offer, he is threatened for his generosity.

After Logan turned beneath the doorframe, Kinnon unsheathed the *sgian dubh* from beneath his right arm. Darach would have Kendrick's sisters and Kendrick would regret he'd ever crossed Laird Baen Kinnon. Pinching the blade between thumb and forefinger, he flung the *sgian dubh* into Logan's upper arm.

The man didn't flinch, nor did he cry out. He simply pulled the blade from his arm as if removing a splinter. Laird Kinnon's pulse skidded when Logan donned a broad smile from over his bleeding shoulder.

"Ye waste my time, auld mon, but I'll give Kendrick your message. He has awaited your summons too long and will relish an audience with ye." Logan wiped the dark blood from the blade then sheathed it next to his own in his wool stocking just before he left.

Alone in the chamber, Laird Kinnon tried to ignore the woman's laughter.

Heat flushed through him. Perspiration slicked his skin beneath his fur vest. The walls instantly bled streams of black.

He drew a breath of lavender.

A feather-light weight brushed over his shoulder.

Hair prickled at his neck.

Laird Kinnon rushed from the chamber and headed for the training field.

Chapter Sixteen

"I swear when my sister returns, she will have ye drawn and quartered, Jaime MacLeod."

Calin heard the futile threat just as he passed beneath the archway with his wife at his side. Jaime spun Isobel in circles, clearing a path through the chaos of the Great Hall. Two matrons sweeping out the old rushes reared back to avoid a foot in the face. Isobel shrieked and wrapped both hands tightly around Jaime's neck. His cousin's eyes were alight with mischief, while Isobel's cheeks stained a rosy red.

Isobel thwarted Jaime's advances in much the same way Akira had. Most women went willy-nilly beneath Jaime's charms, but Calin concluded Isobel, like Akira, wasn't most women. Untamed and obstinate, Isobel was just what his cousin deserved. The sight of their feuding struck him as comical. Feeling no need to keep his merriment contained, Calin's boisterous laugh echoed into the tall ceiling above him, bouncing off the carvings of cherubs.

When he stole a glance at Akira's stunned expression, he knew she didn't share his opinion. Wide blue eyes and a gaping mouth verbalized her opinion more than words. He couldn't determine if she was appalled or angry. He decided both.

Akira rushed around a man rolling a wooden barrel of heather ale, then tore Isobel out of Jaime's arms with possessive force. Even though they were the same height and proportion, she carried Isobel at an alarming pace up the stone stairwell. Calin followed and tried to pry Isobel from Akira's arms, assuming she would have difficulty with her sister's weight.

Akira glared at his interference. "I'd like a moment alone with my sister."

"Of course, but let me assist ye. 'Tis not fitting for—"

"I've been carrying Isobel for a decade. Ye insult me by implying she's a burden to me." Her firm countenance didn't invite argument.

Calin backed away, nearly toppling over Jaime, who stood on the step below him. He swiveled to shoot Jaime a warning look.

"I dinnae treat her unkind in any way, m'laird," Jaime defended, even though no verbal threat had been given. He crawled around Calin in the narrow space of the tower stairwell. Standing in front of Akira, he halted her steps.

Calin glimpsed the troubled glint in Jaime's eyes when he touched Isobel's cheek. Furthermore, he recognized the victorious expression on Isobel's face when she drew her finger across her throat.

Jaime turned to Akira. "M'lady, dinnae believe what Isobel tells ye. I've been a perfect gentleman in her presence."

"Ha!" This reaction was unanimously delivered by all three of Jaime's accusers.

"Ye are nay gentleman, Jaime MacLeod," Isobel said. "Ye are a rakish swine."

A lock of blond hair fell over his brow when Jaime's chin fell to his chest. The crushed look on Jaime's face reminded Calin of the young lad who'd been pushed back to Aunt Wanda's skirts when Calin had been old enough to train with the MacLeod warriors. He brushed aside the familiar pang of sympathy and watched Jaime descend one step. Calin had never seen such a look of defeat on the man's face as he did right now.

Akira took advantage, and pushed forward. But Isobel halted her. "Wait."

Jaime turned, his eyes wide and hopeful.

"I'll need an escort today," Isobel said. "If ye promise to behave, I'll allow ye to accompany me to the games."

Jaime dipped into a regal bow. "With m'lady's permission, I'd be honored."

Akira just stood there staring at Jaime, the look of shock still clinging to her face. "I need to speak with my sister in private." Her voice faltered.

Calin followed the sisters up the stairs and into the solar adjoining his. He held Jaime at bay beneath the archway, giving Akira the privacy she'd requested. Akira sat Isobel atop a three-legged cuttie stool in the corner of the chamber then smoothed her red plaid kirtle around her. Try as he did, Calin couldn't hear the women's conversation, but he watched intently.

Akira had difficulty swallowing. She thought her eyes must be playing tricks on her. Did she really see Isobel's leg move? Kneeling in front of Isobel, Akira held her hand then noticed the blush in her cheeks and the dimple at the corner of her eye. Never had she seen her sister look so happy.

Isobel's face exploded into a flurry of exhilaration. "Is Jaime not the most delicious rogue ye've e'er laid eyes on?"

"Nay. My husband is. Never mind that. Isobel, your leg. I saw your leg . . ." She couldn't find words to finish her sentence. Akira had catered to Isobel for more than half her life. Bearing Isobel's weight somehow lessened Akira's guilt about the accident. Isobel never asked for anything. Simply existed from day to day in silent frustration.

But now, Akira was filled with such hope she could barely breathe.

Isobel leaned close to Akira and kissed her forehead. "Do ye remember the tingling I got just after the accident?"

"Aye." Akira's stomach jumped, but too often she'd prayed for her sister's recovery and too many times she'd been disappointed. She waited patiently for Isobel's continuance.

"Jaime took me to—"

"Enough about Jaime. I want to know if I imagined the movement in your leg."

Isobel soothed her with a smile. "My toes started burning about a month ago. It wasnae like the tingle. 'Twas different."

"Why did ye not tell me?"

"I dinnae want to get your hopes up, again." Isobel massaged Akira's earlobe as she continued. "Ye will think me brazen. And I swear if ye tell Mam, I'll pull out your eyelashes."

"Crivons, Isobel. Tell me." Akira couldn't stand the unknowing on a subject so close to her heart.

"Yestereve when Jaime took me to my quarters he wouldnae leave. I wouldnae admit it to him, but I dinnae want him to leave."

Akira followed Isobel's line of sight over her shoulder and saw the two men standing in the entranceway—a frightful expression now engraved on both their faces. She turned back to Isobel. "Please, do go on."

"He touched me," Isobel said softly. "Weel, he . . . I dinnae give myself to the mon, but no one had e'er paid me any heed and . . ."

"Tell me, Isobel. I swear on Papa's grave, I'll not judge ye." Akira's hands visibly shook in anticipation.

"When he touched me, my entire body came alive. I felt my legs burning. Not a tingle in my toes, but an ache. 'Twas so powerful. And after . . ." Isobel blushed. "This morn when I awoke to his teasing—"

"He stayed in your chamber?" Akira interrupted.

"Ye promised ye wouldnae judge. I told ye I dinnae give myself to him."

"Forgive me. Do continue." Akira pressed her lips to Isobel's palm, and held her tongue. Isobel's words were so hushed Akira could barely make them out.

"He kissed my legs, and I felt his lips. I looked down and saw my toes moving. Look." Isobel raised her kirtle and wiggled her big toe.

Akira burst into joyful tears, and collapsed onto Isobel's lap. Her whole body shook as she hugged her sister around the waist. Never had she known a greater happiness than she felt at this moment.

At this sight, Calin turned to Jaime. "If ye've hurt her, I'll kill ye."

Calin crossed the chamber and raised Akira to her feet. Brushing her hair from her face, he wiped the tears from her eyes. "What has he done? Tell me, and I'll punish him to the fullest extent of his crime."

Her face smoothed into what appeared to be happiness, but her big blue eyes overflowed with tears. He wanted to console her, to listen to her, but instead of explaining, she ran into Jaime's arms. She embraced him so ferociously he gasped for air. Grabbing both sides of Jaime's face, she kissed his cheeks, his chin. Then, damn the saints, if she didn't kiss him on his mouth.

"I fear I love ye, Jaime MacLeod."

Jaime turned a bright shade of pink, which infuriated Calin to a state of insanity. "Ye what?"

"Jaime, mayhap we should give my sister and her new husband some privacy." Isobel waved him in her direction.

"Nay. I want ye to stay," Akira insisted.

"Nay! I want them to leave," Calin insisted stronger and actually felt his nostrils flare as he pointed at the door. Anger heated his skin, and his patience ceased to exist.

Blowing a relieved breath, Jaime crossed the chamber and lifted Isobel into his arms. "There is an herb garden just outside the walls. Would ye like to see it?"

"Nay. Isobel ye—" Akira started to protest, but Calin interrupted.

"Wife, let them leave."

Isobel wrapped her arms around Jaime's neck as he carried her with ease toward the open door. She gave Calin a "be-nice" look over Jaime's shoulder that only irritated him further and waved to Akira with one finger as they left.

Akira's cheeks streaked with tears, but she donned a huge smile. Calin was furious when he crossed the chamber and slammed the door. "Damn the saints! Ye will tell me what that was about? Ye kiss another mon and tell him ye love him, and I am the one who has promised not to take a mistress?"

"Ye are overreacting." Akira's smirk enraged him all the more.

"Overreacting? We have been married a day, and already ye are throwing yourself at another mon and right in front of me!"

"Calin MacLeod, I think I found your temper," Akira teased then closed the space between them. When she reached up to caress his cheek, he roughly seized her wrist.

"Ye tell me what Isobel said. I'd like to know what makes my wife fall instantly in love with another mon and cover him with kisses. Kisses that belong to me." Calin's tone bordered on cruel, and the hold he retained on her wrist was unbreakable.

Ignoring his obvious rage, Akira's smile became even

broader. "He found her legs. Jaime found her legs. Isobel has been crippled for a decade, and that lusty bastard found her legs."

Calin's frown lessened, but he wasn't satisfied. He waited for her to elaborate.

"I love Isobel, and I am the reason she's crippled. There is nay greater gift I could've ever been given."

He released her wrist, but the image of his wife kissing Jaime blinded him from fully comprehending her words. "How did he *find* her legs?"

A glint sparkled in her eyes. "He touched her the way ye did me."

"I'll kill him." Calin pivoted to leave.

"Nay! Ye must not say anything. Isobel threatened to pull out my eyelashes if I told anyone." Akira locked her arms around his neck. "I dinnae love Jaime. I spoke out of haste. I promise not to attack him again." She stood on her toes and gave Calin a quick kiss on the cheek. "Dinnae be jealous."

But he was jealous. Damned jealous.

Love. She used the word so freely. He selfishly wished he'd been the one to give Isobel back her legs. He wanted to be the one she said those words to. They'd come so easily for her. But she was passionate about Isobel. He wanted her to be that passionate about him.

Damn the saints! She was rubbing his ear again. But, that too, she shared with Isobel. He'd seen them do it. That, too, he wanted to be his and his alone. "I am jealous," he admitted in a gruff tone. "I'm jealous of Jaime, of Isobel. I'm even jealous of Andrew. Sit down, I want to talk." Calin hauled her beneath the ivory-lace dome of the canopy bed then forcefully sat beside her.

She twisted into him and slid an aggressive hand beneath his plaid. Skimming over the bristly hair of his bare thigh, she lewdly cupped his heavy sac, which caused his manhood to leap. The insatiable woman then had the audacity to actually purr. "But we have talked all morning. I am feeling rather . . . healed."

"I am not." Calin pushed her away from him then crossed his arms over his chest like a spurned boy. "Tell me why ye feel responsible for Isobel's injury."

She scowled at his rebuttal. "There was a boy, Gowan, son of one o' The Beast's favored warriors. He tormented me. Called me a witch and played tricks on me. He told the other children I'd been sent to Beauly Priory because I was evil. The day before the accident, he cut my hair. He said he needed the lock to cast a spell on me. Isobel and I snuck into his cottage that night and took his younger brother from his crib."

"Ye stole the boy's brother?"

"I am not proud of this. Now do ye want to know or not?"

His silence encouraged her to continue. "We *borrowed* the brother and put another piece of my hair along with a muddy toad in his place. That morning Gowan came running into Dalkirth screaming like a girl and accusing me of turning his brother into a toad. He was crying when Isobel and I skipped in with his brother, returning him with angelic smiles. We lied, and told his mother the lad came out that morning to play. The children laughed at Gowan's insinuations and ridiculed him."

"Like they always did ye?"

Akira nodded, her fingers working at a loose thread on her kirtle. "Of course, he dinnae have to put up with such mockery. Gowan and Darach Kinnon were as thick as cherry sap. That afternoon, Isobel and I were walking down the path at the base of the keep. When we looked up the slope, Darach and Gowan released a cart full of boulders down the hillside at us. Isobel pushed me out of the way, and the cart rolled over her back. She just laid there flat on her belly with her face pressed into the ground. The wheels never even touched her legs. But she never walked again."

Akira's voice was laced with sorrow, and Calin regretted making her dredge up the past. But at least now he understood her hatred for Laird's Kinnon's named son. "'Tis when ye quit sending the missives."

Akira nodded. "I dinnae feel I was of worth to anyone." Caught up in the memory, she squeezed in closer and reached for his ear.

Still irritated, Calin grabbed her hand. "Why do ye rub my ear?"

Akira's thin dark brows wrinkled as if appalled by this accusation. "I dinnae rub your ear."

Calin actually felt his eyes bulge. Was she jesting? How could the woman not know she did this? "Ye have been teasing my right lobe since I met ye. Every morn, every night, and every time your mind is preoccupied by something else. As it was just now. I want to know why, and I want to know why Isobel does the same to ye."

Akira looked genuinely perplexed. He didn't know why this would be such a revelation to her, but it was just the same, and he intended to know why.

"I dinnae remember ever doing this to ye. 'Tis not possible that I believe we are . . . Nay. 'Tis foolish thoughts of children. 'Twas just a habit I acquired in infancy—naught more. Isobel and I have always done this. 'Tis our . . . connection. Since we are twins, Mam said—"

"Twins?" Calin interrupted. Isobel had been two months old when he took Akira to Kendrick.

"Aye." Akira defended sternly. "Just because we are not identical like the Ionas makes us nay less connected. We were born on the same day. Mam says we rub each other's ears because we share a soul. The twins tickle each other's palms. Isobel and I rub each other's ears. I couldnae possibly do this to ye. How could ye possess something given to my sister upon our birth?"

"Ye mean to tell me ye rub Isobel's ear, because ye believe she shares your soul." Calin snorted at her.

"Dinnae laugh at me, or I'll turn ye into a toad," Akira taunted playfully.

"Dinnae tease, Akira. Do ye believe this? And if ye do, why would ye do this to me?"

"I know not. Mam filled our heads with such stories when we were but wee ones." She crawled onto his lap then smoothed the lines of tension from the corners of his eyes. "I think I rub your ear, because I want ye to make love to me," Akira cooed and slipped her hand into his *léine* shirt to toy with his chest.

Lusty wench. Calin squeezed her bottom, forcing her legs wider around his hips. When she rubbed herself against him, his brain nearly shut down. Still, he was unable to rid himself of the mystery. "Tell me what your mother told ye. She has a theory behind this ear rubbing."

"'Tis foolish," Akira said while she kissed his neck.

"I'll determine if 'tis foolish. Tell me."

Akira blew a breath. "Mam says when a child is born, their soul awaits them outside their mother's womb. In the case where there is only one child, the soul easily finds its way into that child's body. But in the instance of twins, the soul must split to allow both babes to have life." Akira giggled. "Mam says sometimes a soul gets confused and will split even when there is only one child. Giving half to the babe and half to the person who would love them throughout eternity. Of course, they have to be present at the time of birth to receive the soul. Mam used a term she claimed to have coined." Akira tapped her chin, trying to recollect. "I remember. Mam said that person was the child's soul mate."

Calin jerked back, his mind a blur of confusion. He was there when Akira was born. The story her mother wove was preposterous. He didn't believe in soul mates. His heart started to pound. His head exploded with old memories. The lifeless body of his father still branded on his brain. A tiny babe nestled at her mother's breast. He'd thought about her every day his entire life. He was possessive of her. And protective of her. And jealous of anyone who received her affection.

By the saints, I am in love with her! Warriors didn't fall in love. He had a duty unto his people to protect the clan. This duty didn't require him to fall in love with his wife. In fact, his responsibilities demanded that he not become distracted by her. This emotion would only weaken him. He'd watched his father die because of his love for a woman. He'd be damned if he'd allow Akira to coerce him into such a folly.

"Hell and damnation!" He pushed her off him and instantly condemned himself for believing such a fairy tale.

"Dinnae be angry with me," she hollered at his fleeing back. He stormed out of the solar in a fury, leaving her to dwell on his mood.

"Crivons."

She started to follow, then decided if he wanted to be addle-brained about the whole ordeal with Jaime, she would let him stew. The afternoon games would soon begin, and she needed to make herself more presentable. Especially if she intended to meet with the elders. Stepping into the corridor, she found two young maids. In white smocks, they were dressed alike with copper hair tucked beneath linen coifs. They matched Akira in height, but were both slender in frame. Both bowed their heads and splayed their skirts in perfect curtsies.

"Forgive me for speaking without permission, m'lady. We are your maids. I am Evie, and this is me older sister, Tara."

"I am Akira," she offered mechanically, as she'd introduced herself at least a hundred times the previous day. She hoped she was near to meeting everyone. Remembering the names of every clan member was going to be near impossible.

"Aye, m'lady, we know."

Akira laughed at herself this time: Everyone knew her. She was the one who had to acquaint herself with the servants, the *mesnie*, the stewards. "Please forgive me. Have ye any idea what I am to wear to the games?"

The maids circled around her into the chamber. Evie stepped into an anteroom and presented Akira with an array of finery. Granted, half the garments were plaid *arisaids*, but the others were gowns of silk embellished with lace—garments more fashionable of England than those of the Highlands. Evie swung her hand wide over the assortment. "Ye may choose, m'lady."

Akira's interest strayed as she studied the chamber for the first time in a different light. The luxurious décor reflected a feminine style. Whitewashed stones brightened the chamber filled with ornately engraved furniture. In addition to the stool next to the hearth sat a settee upholstered in mauve damask. Pink floral paintings decorated a washbasin next to a privately placed chamber pot. The solar was as big as her family's cot-house. Walking to the dressing table, she picked up a gilded brush then noted a dozen different perfume bottles lining the top. Unable to resist, she pulled the stopper from a cool lavender crystal and held the fragrance beneath her nose. Akira's eyes fell shut as she inhaled the exotic aroma. A smile lifted the corners of her lips. "Who does this solar belong to?"

"'Tis your solar now, m'lady. And everything in it belongs to ye." The maid named Evie displayed an eager grin. "If the scented water pleases ye, ye might want to tickle your eyes on the contents o' the top drawer."

Akira pulled two ivory knobs to open a thin drawer just below the tabletop. This was the closest she'd ever come to an actual swoon. Secured on rose silk lining were three jeweled necklaces—the first, diamond, the second, ruby, and the third, sapphire. In addition, there were a multitude of bracelets, earbobs, and pendants, all encrusted in gemstones, and all suitable for a queen. She was in awe and felt unworthy of the display.

Akira looked at the maids, hoping her eyes weren't as wide as they felt. "These are . . . mine?"

"'Tis all yours, m'lady. The perfume, the gowns, the jewels." Evie stepped away from the wardrobe to open two adjoining doors connecting to Calin's chamber. "This solar belongs to the Lady o' Cànwyck Castle."

Akira stood in the archway between the two chambers and noted Calin's solar had been flawlessly cleaned. The wooden bowl of berries was gone, along with the crystal goblets, and the bed was neatly made. She then scanned the white laced bed in the other chamber—her solar. "Am I expected to sleep in here?"

Both maids snickered and covered their naughty smiles behind their hands. "'Tis your business where ye sleep, m'lady."

· Akira cocked one eyebrow, scrutinizing them carefully. If anyone knew the happenings of the keep, it would be the servants. "But I presume 'twill quickly become your business, as weel, when ye check to see if my bed has need of making." As she spoke, Akira sauntered to the bed to select one of the multicolored pillows decorating the bolster.

"I doubt your bed will have need o' makin' for quite some time, m'lady." Evie flashed pearly white teeth.

"Evie!" The scolding came from the passive maid named Tara.

Akira didn't try to hide her bashful grin. Already, she liked this Evie. She was bold, and outspoken, and a lot like her. "We are certain to spend a great deal of time together. We must not be so formal. Now, how long have ye resided in the keep?"

"The laird took us in five years ago when our father died at battle. We helped in the kitchens then, as we were only twelve."

Akira crossed the chamber to trail a finger over the well-polished dressing table. "Who did this solar belong to before I came?"

"The laird's wife."

Akira almost fell over. Calin was previously married? She had to start asking him more questions. "How did she die?"

"She is not dead." Evie grinned.

Akira's demeanor faltered then, but before she could ask another question, Tara took a step forward. "Our former laird, your husband's uncle, is still married, and moved to the east tower last year when your husband took over chieftainship. This solar belonged to your husband's mother prior to that who died a sennight after his birth. My younger sister is being a trickster, and if we dinnae serve ye with respect, ye may choose to have us replaced." With this final statement, Tara glared at her sister.

Akira blew a relieved breath then walked to stand in front of Evie. "Mayhap I'll have *her* replaced, since she cannae be trusted to be loyal."

Evie's face fell, and her light gray eyes filled with remorse. "Please, m'lady, a thousand apologies. I had heard ye were spirited and only meant to tease for a moment. Forgive me, I've been foolish and offer my undying loyalty if ye choose to keep me on."

Akira smiled and hugged Evie. "I was just toying with ye. I should, nay doubt, keep ye on my good side. Ye could prove to be a verra valuable friend."

Evie beamed at the inept compliment and hugged her back. "I'd like verra much to be your friend, m'lady."

"Now. Tara, ye will choose a gown. And, Evie, ye will tell me everything ye know about the new laird."

Within an hour, the maids had Akira attired in queenly garb. Tara had chosen a ripe-plum gown with ivory sleeves adorned with silver trim. Amethysts ornamented a boned bodice, sloped provocatively into a square neckline. The skirt hugged her hips and gathered at the base of her back where a train dragged the floor.

Akira stood before a full-length looking glass, smiling her approval. Tara returned to the dressing table and reopened the jewelry drawer. "Would ye like to choose, m'lady?"

"That one." Akira pointed to a simple chain with a silver cross holding a single amethyst in its center.

Tara agreed then clasped the circlet behind her neck. While the maids remained at attention, Akira pulled the stopper from the exotic scented perfume then trailed a line down her neck. When she returned the bottle, she eyed the gilded brush with avid curiosity. Her black hair now webbed overtop pale blond hair neglectfully left in the bristles. She had met Calin's aunt and recalled her hair to be a very dark red.

"Have ye need of aught else, m'lady?"

Evie's words broke her speculation. "Ye've done more than enough. I trust I'll see ye at the games?"

"Aye, m'lady," Tara and Evie answered in unison. They popped curtsies then scurried to leave.

"Evie, did someone occupy this solar after Calin's aunt?"

"M'laird's mistress," Evie answered quickly and then closed the door behind her.

Chapter Seventeen

Calin hadn't uttered nary a word to her since his ridiculous outburst, nor had he retired to his solar the previous night. Akira had waited for him, fighting much-needed rest. But sleep-deprived, and exhausted from the ongoing celebration, she lost the battle in the small hours of the night. She awoke alone in his bed and determined he still sulked over the incident with Jaime. That conclusion had been easier to accept than the possibility of him retiring to another chamber with his *mistress*.

After worrying herself into blotches, Akira had forced herself to attend the second day of games. Though she'd been nervous about attending the festivities without Calin at her side, she'd found an ally in his aunt Wanda. The woman was forthright in her instructions, but Akira quickly grew to appreciate the older woman's wisdom. Her role as Lady of Cànwyck Castle felt less daunting after an afternoon spent under Wanda's tutelage. She intended to make Calin proud to call her wife on this day, and if that failed, she would at least begin the task of gaining the respect and loyalty of his kinfolk. A daunting effort, considering jealousy caused her to mentally question which of the many women had been Calin's mistress.

Evie and Tara dressed her for the final day's activities in a scarlet overdress. A gold bodice cinched tightly in the waist hugged her curves more than the gown she'd worn the day before. Akira decided to take Wanda's advice and send for Elsbeth to tailor the gowns more suitably to her shape. For today, she added a matching twill ruanna, fastening the folds above her breast with a Celtic brooch. Evie pinched color into Akira's cheeks while Tara secured the last pearl-tipped pin to create an elegant braid all around her head.

Akira didn't question the maids further about Calin's mistress, as she was sure she didn't want details from them. But she intended to discuss the topic in detail with her husband, just as soon as he broke his silence. If that moment didn't present itself soon, however, she would confide in his aunt Wanda.

The festivities continued as they had the day before, and Akira was pleased with her dignified performance as she presented the winners with a ribbon and a chaste kiss. This not only included the young lad who shot the straightest arrow, but Alec and Aileen's youngest lass, Lexi, whose bullfrog outmaneuvered her competitors over a battleground of leaves and muck. Though Akira felt no remorse for her impropriety with Jaime, she sensed Calin's undeserved anger each time she awarded his warriors for their victories.

However, today she wasn't the only one glaring at his behavior. A battalion of MacLeod kinswomen came to her defense with crossed arms and puckered brows. Obviously his distant behavior hadn't gone unnoticed. Wanda's scowl could scare the hair off the burliest Highlander and Akira couldn't help but smile when Calin tucked his chin to his chest like a scorned boy.

A man, stout in size and odor, reigned undefeated in the swine chase. This man, who answered to Angus, pinned the peach-colored pig into the crook of his arm. Both the pig and Angus were mud encrusted from head to hoof. Wearing a snaggletooth grin, he proudly approached the dais where Akira stood, ribbon in hand. After tucking his award into his belt, Angus pulled her flatly against him then planted a muddy kiss on her mouth. With a smirk, he released the swine into her arms. "Fer yer next meal, m'lady."

Fortunately for Akira, the pig was already vexed. The animal dove from her arms to scamper off the dais, escaping between the ankles of spectators. One of whom was her husband, whose speculative glare and matching frown told her more than she cared to know about his disapproval.

Calin watched the scene dutifully. Knowing how Akira disliked being sullied, he wasn't surprised when she removed her soiled ruanna and accepted a towel from a maid. What did surprise him, in fact infuriated him, was her attire beneath or lack thereof. Her gown had been tailored for a smaller-framed woman, this much he knew. A ruby hung from a teardrop pendant, falling neatly between the shadowy crevice of her breasts which overflowed her bodice. When she bent to hand her ruanna to a young gillie, Calin followed the obvious direction of his warrior's interests. Irrepressible jealousy surged through him.

The sun descended behind Cànwyck Castle, bringing a slight chill with its shadow. A horn announced the start of the final event. Like a flock of sheep, the kinfolk followed Akira across the landscape to gather around the ring of stones, circumscribing an area twenty feet in diameter. The same he used for training. Two warriors, equal in height, fought within its boundaries. No weapons were allowed, only their strength. When any part of the man's body fell outside the stones, another stepped in to challenge. Ten, twenty, thirty men found their way in and out of the circle.

At present, the contender was Lyel Og, an overgrown man

with arms the size of tree trunks, but with the face of a child. "Who will challenge?" Lyel Og repeated when no one entered.

Just as he clasped his hands above his head in a victorious gesture, Calin stepped into the ring. "I challenge."

"Take no insult, m'laird, but ye cannae challenge. 'Twould be disrespectful to strike ye," a man protested from across the circle.

"'Tis my game, and I give ye all permission to try and best me."

The faces of his warriors lit with mischief. Calin pushed them to extreme limits in training for battle. At this moment, he sensed he would receive some well-deserved revenge. Still and all, he intended to win. The last ribbon would be his, along with the last kiss.

In truth, he sought more. He wanted her affection, her praise, her admiration. Akira gave her smile to everyone. However, she'd only frowned at him for two days. Granted, he left her in a huff. The foolish story about soul mates had his mind reeling. Now, he regretted losing a night against her body to a temper that landed him in a cold bed by the brewery.

Calin took a stance and outwitted the reigning giant. Ten more challengers followed. Most of them younger lads eager to prove their strength in front of the maidens. Another dozen men passed through the circle, and he began to waver. One eye had swollen shut, and given the opportunity, he would spit a mouthful of blood in any given direction. As he hugged what he was certain was a cracked rib, he debated the sanity behind each battle.

Between each challenge, he glanced at Akira. Her face was closed to emotion, but he sensed her disapproval of his arrogant show of physical prowess. Still, he fought on.

"Is there no one left to challenge?" he asked with arms splayed and a wide grin, tasting victory amid the tinge of his own blood.

"Can we agree our laird is conqueror and deem him worthy o' the last kiss from our lady? Shall we hail him triumphant?" Gordon's baritone voice hollered.

"Nay!" Before the assembly could roar their agreement, a young voice denied Calin of victory. Weaving through the crowd, Andrew stepped onto the trampled grasses of the ring— wooden sword in hand and a scowl to make King James proud. "I challenge ye, m'laird."

Calin peered down with one good eye at the boy and bit the inside of his cheek to stifle his amusement. "This is a warrior's game, young Andrew."

Engulfed in Calin's shadow, Andrew held up his wooden sword. "I am a MacLeod warrior and protector o' Scotland. And I fight fer m'lady's honor."

Calin was further impressed with the boy's courage. Not to mention, his speech was impeccable for a lad standing slightly higher than his kneecaps. When Aileen ran to retrieve her son, Calin halted her with one hand. He studied Andrew and wished he'd possessed half this much courage at his young age. The boy held a perfect warrior's stance and appeared ready to run him through. Calin considered his options and decided Andrew set a brave example for any young page wanting to join Calin's garrison. "This battle is typically fought without weapons, only skill and strength. But considering I am a wee bit bigger than ye, I'll allow ye use of your sword."

"Thank ye, m'laird." This was all the encouragement Andrew needed. With legs braced wide, Andrew swung his mighty sword and caught Calin in the shins. He winced at the contact then lunged for the boy, who escaped between his legs. Before Calin could swivel, Andrew had sheathed his sword and scaled up Calin's back with the agility of a squirrel. Andrew's chubby arms clasped around Calin's neck, and his legs dangled as Calin whirled him around in circles.

Calin slowed enough to see Akira rushing past the bystanders to console Aileen, who looked near to tears at the edge of the ring. Observing them, Calin quickly decided he'd win more affection if he let Andrew best him. Opening his mouth, Calin made a theatrical gurgling noise from his throat. He feigned defeat and collapsed like a fallen stone with Andrew still attached.

Andrew crawled off his back and pushed Calin until he rolled over, his efforts delivered with grunts. The boy then straddled his chest—not one of his toes touched the ground. Calin grabbed him by the head to whisper into his ear, after which Andrew rose, unsheathed his sword, and held the dull tip beneath Calin's chin. "Do ye give up, m'laird?"

Calin conceded with a nod, thankful the battle ended. He hoped to find Akira smiling at him when he found the strength to stand.

Andrew vaulted off him. "I won! I won!" he chanted and skipped around the circle.

Akira stepped into the ring and tucked the last ribbon into Andrew's belt. "Congratulations, Andrew. Ye have proven your loyalty to me and to Scotland. Ye are a brave and noble warrior to have slain such a mighty dragon."

"'Tis not a dragon. 'Tis m'laird." Andrew looked confused, but gripped both sides of Akira's face as all the others had done and kissed her firmly on the mouth. "Thank ye for the ribbon, m'lady, but in truth, I only wanted the kiss." Andrew dashed off with a group of children holding his ribbon out for all to touch.

Calin stood behind her. He gripped her shoulders and bent into her ear. "That was the last kiss ye will place on another mon's lips, my lady wife. I expect to be rewarded for my efforts accordingly in our solar after ye bid the women a good eve." He nipped at the rim of her ear and spanked her playfully on the rump before making a hasty retreat to the keep.

* * *

Akira whirled around, fully prepared to question his conduct, but he was already halfway up the foothill. *Coward,* she accused with a narrowed eye on his fleeing back. At least he was speaking to her again. Mayhap the hint of mischief in his voice and that love pat to her rump were his way of telling her he wanted to make amends. They would talk about his jealousy before she let him take her to bed. Then, if she had the courage, she would find out where he'd slept the previous night.

Vowing to deal with him sternly, she fanned her hot face and sought out Wanda, Aileen, and the other kinswomen who were clearing tables behind the stables. Little remained of the bounty, save for rinds and crumbs. The sun disappeared behind the grove in the west, leaving only the pink dust of day overhead. The fife ceased, and the laughter of children followed every family back to their cottages. Once the last trestle table had been cleaned and sent back to the Great Hall, she turned to take the path back to the keep, eager to end this foolish quarrel with her husband.

A woman emerging from the woodland caught her eye.

The courtyard was vacant, so Akira donned a cordial smile and awaited her acquaintance. Akira thought she'd been introduced to everyone, but evidently not. This woman was not one who would be easily forgotten. Floating over the lush foliage of the knoll, the woman glowed beneath the fading sun. Beauty and grace surrounded her every step. Flowing pale blond hair bounced at her waist. A slim figure curved neatly into slender hips under a plain ivory gown. No jewels graced her bodice or her neck, nor did she wear a plaid, but the woman carried herself with the dignity of a noble. As she stepped even closer, Akira was mesmerized by the perfection of her face. High cheekbones pointed to a mouth most men would betray their country for. Then Akira looked into a pair of silver eyes. Not a blemish of color hid in the flecks. Foreboding crawled up her spine. Immediately, Akira felt uncomfortable in her presence.

The woman embraced her in a cold hug. When she spoke, her teeth sparkled. "You must be Calin's new wife. 'Tis such an honor to finally meet you."

"I am Akira. And ye are?"

The woman's smile broadened when she brushed her long blond locks over her shoulder. "I am the laird's mistress, Catriona."

Chapter Eighteen

Stunned, Akira gave her head a little shake, certain she'd either misunderstood the woman or fallen into another trap as she had with Evie. Then, she remembered Evie's words and the pale yellow hairs in the brush in the lady's chamber.

The woman sauntered a full circle around her, and Akira felt eyes scrutinize her body. With a long slender finger, the woman traced Akira's gold chain then followed the ribbing of her bodice over her shoulder. Akira's jaw lowered to speak, but shock kept her from moving or forming a sentence.

"Do take care not to stretch the seams of my gowns. Elsbeth slaved for days to get each stitch perfect."

Catriona stepped closer. Her eyes closed, and she inhaled deeply. "Ah. You are wearing my scent. Jasmine. Those decanters came all the way from the Indies. Do be careful with the lavender atomizer. My aunt was quite fond of that particular piece." Catriona's accent twirled like that of English nobility.

The rhythm of Akira's heart became erratic. The words caught her so unguarded, she froze in a dumbfounded stupor, wishing the earth would open up and swallow her.

Catriona continued to scrutinize her with her soulless eyes. "I trust you are treating my Calin well?"

My Calin! Akira repeated the words in her head. "He is not *your* Calin."

"Aye. I suspect not completely anymore. But I am not a greedy shrew. I have already generously given you three days with him. But he'll soon come back to me, unable to resist what's become so habitual for us."

With her gut churning in denial, Akira scanned the landscape. She didn't know what she searched for, but she could no longer bear the woman's presence. She swiveled around Catriona, only to be trapped between her words and the wide trunk of an ash tree. A tree she considered climbing.

Akira swallowed hard. "If ye are so certain of Calin's loyalty, why did he not marry ye?"

"He chose Scotland over England. But I can assure you, your King James will not support your marriage." She twisted a loose tendril of Akira's hair around her finger, pulling roughly at the temple before releasing it, only to reach for Akira's hand to circle the Celtic wedding band. "Calin did not marry you. He married Scotland. And once Scotland provides him with an heir, he will await me with open arms. He promised me a place at Cànwyck Castle and in his bed."

The woman's wicked assertions couldn't be true. Calin promised her he wouldn't take a mistress until after she had borne him six bairns. The woman must be deluded, or Calin lied. The cold steel of betrayal knifed through her heart. Akira clasped her trembling hands together then moved away from her. "Whatever role ye may have once played in m'laird's life is over. He has vowed fidelity to me before God and the kirk," she declared with words as stern as she could muster.

"Do not be naïve." The woman slithered around Akira, brushing her breasts against Akira's back. "I am certain you have discovered my Calin is a virile man. 'Twill take more than one woman to please him. And once you carry his heir, he will need an experienced leman to tend to his needs."

"He'll not take a mistress. He has promised me this."

The humorless laugh vibrating out of Catriona's mouth mocked Akira's innocence. "You have known the man a sennight and already you trust his word?"

"Aye." Akira's sounded confident, but at the moment she wasn't sure.

"We shall become dear friends. The role you undertake requires a significant amount of responsibility. You will reign over the servants, and I shall tend to Calin. Of course, when your time comes, I will share him long enough for you to provide him an heir."

Akira's mouth parched from her rage. "Catriona, ye may return to whatever pile of English refuse ye crawled out of. There is only one word for a woman like ye. 'Tis not mistress. 'Tis whore. I dinnae associate with whores, nor do I befriend them. Ye are deranged if ye think I'll give leave to sharing aught with ye. Least of all my husband." Akira drew a breath and turned to separate herself from Calin's mistress. "Heed me, or ye will be exiled."

Akira's threat didn't seem to affect Catriona in the least. "I agree. We mustn't share everything. We shall have separate solars, as well as pet names. He probably calls you . . ." She ran a finger over Akira's collarbone while contemplating, ". . . his sweetheart. Wait . . . that wouldn't be fitting for a wife. Too . . . sweet. Yes, that's what he calls you. 'My sweet.' 'My sweet, sweet Akira.' Am I right?"

Akira didn't answer. How could she have knowledge of this? Had Calin called her this as well?

"Or perhaps you have already progressed to 'kitten.' My Calin called me his kitten for a while. But after a year of purring in his bed, I became his cat. So you may be his sweet kitten, as long as you remember I'll always be his cat."

Akira ripped Catriona's hand away from her chest and held her at arm's length. "Ye'll not be his anything. Not his mistress, his whore, or his cat. Ye will be banished for disrespecting my status as his wife."

"Tsk, tsk, kitten. You must tame your claws." Catriona pressed closer, trapping Akira against the tree. "You cannot threaten me. I'll have my Calin back in my bed. This I promise you. The MacLeod men are loyal to me. I have only to bat my eyes, and you will find yourself on the auction block again."

"Get away from me." Akira pushed her away with one hand then smashed a clenched fist into the side of her face. Catriona withered gracefully to the ground. Akira clutched the sides of her skirt, sprinted up the rampart, and into the front of the keep. Whirling past the laundress carrying linens, Akira climbed the steps two at a time. She entered the dimly lit corridor screaming, "Evie! Tara!"

Following the maids into her solar, she barred the door then dashed across the solar to do the same to the adjoining doors of Calin's solar. The scarlet gown felt like a swarm of bees crawling over her skin. Reaching awkwardly behind her back, Akira groped with the fastenings, but escaping the gown would be impossible alone.

"Get this gown off me!" Her hands shook violently when she outstretched her arms. "Loosen the laces. Now!"

Tara flinched. "M'laird's been patiently waiting in his solar. I am certain there is nay need for such haste, m'lady."

Akira tried desperately to control her tongue. The maids did not deserve her rage, but her teeth couldn't hold back her anger. "If either of ye speak another word, I'll have ye relocated to the scullery. I want Elsbeth in my solar at first light."

Evie fumbled with the task of gloving Akira in a pale blue nightshift. Trembling fingers pulled the silk material snuggly over her hips. "Would ye like me to tend to your hair, m'lady?" she asked cautiously.

"Nay!" The word came out as a bellow, and Akira regretted

showing her temper. Her mind whirled around blond ringlets and smooth creamy skin. Catriona's face smirked at her behind her eyes. She felt faint. Her knees knocked. Her throat constricted. "Forgive me. I'll not send either of ye to the scullery. Please, go. I wish to be alone."

"But m'laird said to send ye—"

"I care not what he said. And I can assure ye my solar will need tending to on the morrow." Akira's words were short, clipped, and full of anger.

Evie stepped through the archway behind Tara, but held the door slightly ajar. "M'lady, I saw ye with her after the games. I can assure ye, whatever Catriona said was a lie."

Akira slammed and barred the door. Bitter tears stung her eyes. Her body became too heavy to hold. She slid to the floor in a heap of muffled sobs. A fool. That is what she was. To believe she might be privy to the same love that Mam and Papa shared was a little girl's dream. Calin had agreed not to take a mistress, but he hadn't mentioned that he already had one. Hiding the truth was as deceptive as lying. He admitted he married to form the alliance. Another truth he tried to hide. Once she carried the MacLeod heir, he would hold true to the vow he made to his mistress.

She was so beautiful. Her every movement spoke of nobility. How was Akira supposed to vie for Calin's attentions against such grace and dignity? Deep down, she knew she was a peasant trying to be something she wasn't and never could be. She didn't want this life. The hurt felt unbearable, and the painful pinch on her heart made breathing a chore.

The latch rattled. A slight movement shook the adjoining doors. Then she heard him.

"Remove the bolt." Calin's tone was calm, yet held merit.

Akira searched the walls of the chamber. She was trapped. Trapped in another woman's solar. Dressed in another woman's gowns. With another woman's man. Her perfumes. Her bed.

She couldn't breathe.

She clapped her hands over her ears to stifle the incessant rapping on the adjoining doors. The fevered knock escalated. Then stopped all at once.

Heartbeats later, she lurched forward when he came to the door at her back. Forcefully, he rattled the handle. The beating rumble of his fist against the wooden door pulsed in time with her heart.

"Unbar the door, or I swear I'll break it down. By the saints, wife, dinnae push me this night. I've had enough of your temper to last me ten lifetimes."

"*Thalla gu Taigh na Galla!*" Akira screamed. Her feelings of rejection quickly turned to anger—an uncontrollable fury she intended to unleash. She crossed the chamber to the dressing table, grabbed the lavender atomizer that reeked of Catriona's exotic scent, and then hurled the crystal at the door. Three more bottles of expensive scented water followed in its wake. "I hope ye choke on your lies! *Déverminage enfer*, husband!"

The aroma wafted from beneath the door as a puddle of heady scents seeped through the glowing crack. Calin expected her to be perturbed, but to cast him to the flames of the netherworld in multiple languages seemed a bit much. His neglect of her seemed childish now, still and all, he should be the one throwing a tantrum. Following the fourth crash against the door, his patience reached its peak. Weary from the day, he wanted to end this bickering and seek his reward, but he would talk himself to death before his wee fire-breathing dragon opened the door.

Hard muscles corded in irritation. Biting back a curse, he stormed into his solar and retrieved the battle-axe from its mount above the hearth. Raising the weapon high above his head, Calin pummeled the steel edge into the adjoining doors.

Fragments of wood shot like arrows across the chamber. The force of one fierce blow sent the heavy doors crashing against the interior walls. He caught Akira around the waist as she made an escape into the hallway.

Wrenching her back into the chamber, he chucked the axe to the floor, and then barred the exterior door. Confusion engulfed him. Only a fire lit the chamber, but even with one eye sealed shut, he saw her anger. Fisted hands, heaving chest, flaring nostrils. If she held a weapon, he would be inhaling his last breath. Behind swollen eyes lay a rage he meant to subdue. "Ye are wild and untamed, Akira MacLeod, and 'tis time ye learned your place."

The gilded brush she threw at him nicked his shoulder. She sidestepped barefooted to the hearth. "There is nay place for me here. Not this solar. Not yours. This all belongs to someone else, as do your affections. I am only here because my presence will unite the Isles."

Calin's brow furrowed in the middle as he walked toward her. The material of his plaid swayed loosely from his waist. He had her cornered. When he reached for her, she held him back with both palms against his chest. Prepared for her strength, he pressed closer. "Your place is here, with me."

Hatred crawled from her eyes to her hand. Rearing back, she slapped him. "Your words mean naught to me. I've been blinded by them. Words ye used to coax me into your bed. I made a grave mistake believing your lies. Ye are nothing more than a mon owned by a country. Controlled by a king."

Blood trickled into his mouth from an earlier wound. He'd never struck a woman, but never had one provoked him to such a breaking point that raw fury seeped into his fingertips. Calin spit blood into the hearth then reached for her again.

And again, she held him at bay. "Ye will never touch me again."

The shock of her words sent his teeth to grinding. The

chieftain of Clan MacLeod didn't cower to a woman, nor did he take orders from one. He'd given her everything, hoping for a morsel of praise, of attention, but all she gave him were spiteful words he didn't think he deserved. She treated him like the enemy. "Ye are my wife. Ye belong to me, and I'll touch ye whenever and wherever I please."

His edict seemed to infuriate her further. For a brief moment, he thought she might suffer an apoplexy. The soft flesh beneath her darkened blue eyes quivered uncontrollably. "Why are ye so angry with me? Ye are the one who spent the last two days kissing my kinsmen."

Akira exhaled a sarcastic chuckle. "This is why ye've avoided me for two days? Because I awarded a few filthy warriors with a peck on the cheek or at most a puckered kiss as is customary?"

Calin backed her up to the settee, giving her little choice other than to stand atop the cushion. Matching his full height, she edged close. "How dare ye accuse me of betrayal for paying heed to your kinsmen when ye are the one who spent the last year rutting with an English woman. The same woman who believes she belongs in your bed. And probably, the same woman whose bed ye were in last night."

The cause of her sudden spike in temperament became evident. His wife had met Catriona. Guilt overwhelmed him.

Still, he had broken no vows. "I spent the night in a vacant chamber in the east tower. I wasnae in her bed, nor will I be in her bed in the future. I've promised ye this."

"Ye promised me ye wouldnae take a mistress until after I delivered ye seven bairns. Ye failed to mention ye already had a mistress."

Had that number nearly doubled since her boon in the tree? The woman was wowf.

"Your promises mean naught to me. Ye speak half-truths. I'll not be married to a mon who deceives me." She crossed her arms over her breast and raised a victorious eyebrow. "I want an annulment."

Shock bulged his eyes. Rage so raw he could taste it on his tongue flared within him. He was a man of honor, a man of pride, a man sick to death of trying to win his wife's affections. Without so much as a grunt, he grabbed her around the waist then hauled her kicking and screaming into his solar. He threw her atop the bed. "Our marriage cannae be annulled, *wife*. We have already consummated our union. And I intend to consummate it some more."

Akira tried to escape him, crawling across the bed on her hands and knees, but he snagged her ankle and slid her back to its middle. He climbed overtop her. She struggled beneath him, but he held her down. He gripped her wrists above her head with one hand while the other curved around her waist. His thighs straddled one of hers, forcing the thin silk of her nightdress to tighten over her breasts.

"If ye pursue this, I assure ye, ye will have to rape me to get me with child."

He matched her temper and vowed to no longer yield to her tantrums. "I should've taken ye at *Tigh Diabhail*. I made promises to ye nay mon of my rank would ever be expected to keep. Ye've nay reverence for my oaths. Ye disrespect me as your husband and your laird. Ye are my wife. Ye are under my power, and I have owned ye since the day ye were born. I'll feel nay guilt if I have to force myself upon ye." He leaned in to kiss her.

She turned away.

He diverted and kissed her upper breasts. Short fingernails dug into the hand that bound her wrists. He only tightened his hold. Damn her! He hated that she'd weakened him. That she'd made him no better than her sire. Is this what Laird Kinnon had done to Lena?

The firelight glittered off the single tear escaping over the bridge of her nose. He had never seen her so afraid. If he made good on his threat, she would never look at him the way he desired. He didn't want her body. He wanted her heart. A heart he knew he was breaking.

"Hell and damnation!" He shouted then released her. He rolled to his back and buried his face between his palms. "Catriona was a mistake. King Henry sent her to me as a peace offering. Half the chieftains in the Highlands were gifted with her English cousins. King James has been negotiating a peace treaty and has encouraged Scotland's nobles to marry English to further peace between our countries. Hell, King James himself is entering an English union with Henry's own daughter.

"Catriona was bound and gagged when she arrived. Tied to the back of an auld roan. Her escorts murdered en route. I gave her duties in the kitchens, but she proved to be verra . . . persuasive. I intended to find her a husband, but she found her way into my bed instead."

"For a year?" Akira turned her back on him. "And is it common practice for the laird to attire the kitchen maids in silks? The woman owns more gowns than all my sisters combined."

"Her father is the Crown Prince of Malaga. He sent ells of silk a couple of months after her arrival. Another bribe, I suppose."

"And the jewels?"

"Those belonged to my mother. They are yours now."

Silence fell between them. Calin wanted to reach out to her, to say he was sorry for being high-handed with her. But mostly he wished he could go back to the day Catriona had arrived. He would have sent her fleeing before she dismounted.

"Her presence here could have been prevented had ye come for me sooner."

"I know." This was all he could say. In his first year as chieftain, he'd taken advantage of his power. He'd behaved like a man without purpose, accepting largesse from nobles without care for consequence. He would pay dearly for accepting King Henry's gift. "She means naught to me. She's a daughter of England and acts on behalf of their king."

"What hold does she have on ye?"

"Four months ago, after I denied her a place as my wife, she informed me that she carried the MacLeod heir. I had nay reason to doubt her until I found her abed with the cofferer. The child could've belonged to anyone as I discovered three more of my warriors had fallen victim to her seductions. But she lied. She never even carried. Her lies had been a ploy to keep me from attaining ye. She knew about ye the moment she stepped foot on MacLeod soil."

"Ye told her about me then bedded her anyway? For the love o' Scots, she is English. Ye are the chieftain, why did ye not banish her from the clan?"

"I appealed the council for her exile, but she flattered the elders as weel. She claimed she'd been defiled by the MacLeod kin. She threatened to have her father, along with his English gentry, seek retribution. The elders feared King Henry's wrath, so they agreed to put her up in a cot-house outside the bailey. This is the only reason she still resides on MacLeod soil."

Akira fell into a trance listening to him. She didn't know what to believe. Her heart searched for answers while her mind recalled Catriona's words. Certainly, Akira wasn't so gullible that she expected Calin to have been inexperienced in the way of women. He was chieftain, and ten years her senior. However, she didn't expect to come face to face with any of those women, much less vie for her husband's bed. Catriona already proved to be resourceful. "She knew about *Tigh Diabhail.*"

"She said this to ye?" Calin sounded confused.

"She said your men were loyal to her, and if I dinnae share ye with her, she would have me returned to the auction block. If ye dinnae tell her, then there is a traitor among your men. Or she played a role in the whole scheme herself." Akira wiped the tears from her eyes. Calin slid an arm beneath the down-stuffed bolster supporting her head. His hand cautiously pulled on her shoulder. She rolled into her husband, not fully trusting him, but having little choice in her position. She would accept his words until she learned otherwise. "I can see why a mon would do her bidding. She is so . . . beautiful."

"She is an English whore, and she's evil."

Akira had thought the same thing when she looked into her cold eyes. She realized now why Calin had become so enraged at the waterfall. "If she hadnae betrayed ye, would ye have taken her as your wife?"

"Nay. I have no desire to form allies with England." Calin stated without emotion which made his statement all the more difficult to bear. Catriona had been right when she said Calin chose Scotland over England.

"I want her gone."

"If she partook in your abduction in any way, 'tis all I'll need to banish her to King James' court."

Brushing back a lock of auburn hair, she trailed a finger over his discolored eye. The pang of betrayal subsided with his explanations. "Ye will tell me what ye discover. Until then, I dinnae want her name spoken in my presence again."

Calin caught her hand to kiss the pads of her fingers. "I am sorry ye ever had to meet her."

Her fingers rested over his lips. "I want to believe ye. I want naught more than to believe I am not just a body to carry your heir. I cannae take another shock like this. If there are others I should know about, I want to hear it from ye, not from them."

"Ye want me to tell ye every encounter I've ever had?"

"Nay. I am certain I have not the time, nor the patience for such a lengthy discussion," she stated sarcastically, but her morbid curiosity sought answers. "Have ye lain with the maids?"

"Nay." Calin answered in an appalling tone. "I am not a monk. Howbeit, I am not a rutting swine either. Their father died in my arms at Drumchatt."

"Fighting against your king." She hoped he caught the disappointment in her tone.

"Aye. 'Twas his dying wish that his daughters be cared for. I couldnae deny the mon. But if they displease ye I'll—"

"Nay. They dinnae displease me."

"There is nay other woman I want as my wife or in my bed."

"Who is Lena?"

Calin felt nauseous.

"Over the past two days, I've overheard at least a dozen kinswomen refer to me as Lena. Why would they make this mistake?"

In her current emotional state, if Calin told her everything now, she would probably hurl herself over the tower parapet into the moat. Though his courage shriveled, he knew she deserved some explanation. "My father cared for a woman named Lena. Father Harrald was verra close to both of them. He confused us for them and mistook her name for yours while giving a toast at the festivities. Those who spoke of her, just repeated his error. She has been dead a verra long time." Calin's eye fell shut as the horrid memories surged into his head. Akira mirrored her mother's appearance. Her black hair, her blue eyes, the color of her skin. He held her hand tightly. "I dinnae want to fight with ye any more. I leave on the morrow for Scone to meet with King James. I dinnae wish to take your anger with me, my love."

He leaned in to kiss her.

She halted him once again. "Did ye ever call *her* 'my love'?"

Though her question odd, he knew it held relevance. "Nay. Ye are my wife, my Akira, my love. Please, forgive me for not coming for ye sooner." Calin pulled her up against him then buried his face into the crook of her neck. His hand slid over the smooth silk of her nightdress and encouraged her thigh to wrap around him.

"I am not ready to forgive ye just yet. My heart feels as though it has been trampled by a dozen auld nags. Ye may have to grovel a wee bit more, husband." Her fingertip brushed over his flat nipple.

Calin raised his head to see a tinge of fire rekindle in her eyes. He hoped his dragon had returned. "I fear I may have years of groveling afore me to earn your forgiveness, but I have just this one night."

"How long will ye be gone?" Akira's lips skimmed his shoulder where an old scar whelped.

"A fortnight, mayhap longer," he informed, then chanced a gentle kiss on her neck. She allowed it.

"I'll miss ye," she said, twining her leg around his.

Calin inched her nightshift up over her hips. One hot hand squeezed her backside. "Show me how much."

Akira lifted her arms and allowed the removal of her shift. "I am going to enjoy this."

Calin couldn't agree more, but he worried slightly that they may not be talking about the same thing. "Enjoy what?"

"Retaliation. I'm feeling a wee bit victorious, and I've yet to begin my game." Akira removed his belt and stripped him of his plaid, then pushed him back to the bed.

Calin ogled her swaying buttocks as she crossed back into her solar. So full and round, each cheek tempted him with every step. And one bearing the faded pink blemish of his mark. The MacLeod crest. He itched to study it closer. She returned with the blue and green sash she'd worn at the games. "And what do ye intend to do with that?"

"'Tis your ribbon. Andrew clearly cheated, and I think ye deserve your reward now."

Calin probably should have protested when she tied his wrists rather snugly above his head. If Akira brought her temper into their bed, Calin was sure to endure the most exquisite torture of his life. He couldn't remember the last time a tremor of fear slid over him. He liked it.

Akira crawled atop him, straddling the side of his erection. She tweaked his nipples between her thumbs and fingers—hard. "I am going to make ye forget ye ever shared your bed with another woman."

Chapter Nineteen

The scream sounded distant. The stench of death unchanged. His father's murdered body lay in a pool of blood at a woman's feet. A slender blonde with wicked gray eyes seeking vengeance.

Laird Kinnon stood behind her. Lena cried out, and clutched her child in a desperate embrace.

Calin floated around the hall at Brycen Castle. He no longer hid. His form that of a man, not a boy. Through the haze of the Kinnon keep, his eyes focused on the black blade. But not in the hand of a masked warrior. The hand clutching the sgian dubh *belonged to Catriona.*

A light flashed, blinding him.

Calin stood close. He could touch Lena's terrified face, her blue eyes filled with sorrow. Then her face took shape. The pale blue of her eyes darkened and the lips of his lady wife smiled sweetly at him.

Another burst of white stole his vision.

A sound from Heaven struck, and Catriona's mouth curled in evil satisfaction as she sliced the blade across Lena's throat. But no longer were his eyes branded with Lena's face. She was Akira.

His wife. His love. His soul mate.

And crimson seeped from her throat, stealing her life from him.

"Nay!" He lunged for her.

Another boom deafened his ears.

He held her lifeless body. Slick warm blood slid between their skin.

"Nay, Akira! Nay!" *A crash shook his insides. Then a howl, sounding like a tortured soul, tore through his body.*

"Calin! Calin, wake up!" Akira yelled at him. "Calin, please, ye are hurting me."

His eyes flew open. Hysteria touched his mind. He scanned the chamber, searching the shadows for the murderers. He crushed her with his weight. Sweat-drenched and trembling, his arms engulfed her. His throat dry, and his lungs burned, searching for air.

The storm outside unleashed a gnarled streak of white light revealing the terror painting Akira's face. Calin tensed and tightened his fists behind her back.

Another impaling clash of thunder jarred him physically.

His body slowly found reality, but his warrior spirit still combated the dream. The same nightmare that haunted his childhood arose in his mind anew. Calin released her then shook his hands, relaxing his white-knuckled fists. Rolling to his back, he inhaled gulps of air. At least a year had passed since the nightmare had disturbed his slumber. The players had never been different. Could his dream be an omen?

Nay. He refused to allow such thoughts of loss into his mind. God would not punish him again.

Akira crawled from the bed to set a tallow aflame in the hearth. Within seconds, the candelabras flickered, casting golden lights over her pale skin. She pulled a threadbare shift over her head and knelt beside him. Her small hand flattened over his heart. Calin placed his hand overtop hers and felt his pulse pounding through her palm. He'd acted like a fool. She would see him as a lesser man for showing such fear.

"Are ye weel?"

"By the saints, put out the flame and come back to bed." Draping one arm over his eyes, Calin tried to act nonchalant, but the vision clung to his mind's eye so vividly. So much so, he still smelled the tinge of torn flesh.

He heard her at the washbasin then felt the cool cloth on his chest, up his neck, over his jaw. Gentle fingers pushed his arm back. Akira mopped his brow and skimmed the damp linen over his face just as Aunt Wanda had done so many times before.

"Do ye fear the storm?" she asked, her voice a caress.

Opening one eye, he snorted at her then latched her around the waist and pulled her into bed beside him. "Do I strike ye as the kind of mon who would be afraid of storms?"

"Ye cannae fool me, husband. Fear still clings to your brow." She stroked his coarse cheek and persisted. "Something terrified ye. What was it?"

"Ye. Ye terrify me." Though galled to admit it, Calin spoke the truth, as much to her, as to himself. He couldn't fight these feelings anymore.

He was in love with his wife.

He feared the success of the alliance and the vengeance he sought against Laird Kinnon for eighteen years would soon come to pass. The blood in her veins gave her dominion over Clan Kinnon. Only she could unite the Isles. But the truth would turn her against him, and the deceptive role he played would destroy them. He couldn't bear her hatred.

He trembled.

She gathered him against her tiny body. Her cool fingers wiped his damp cheek. "Did ye dream of a monster?" she asked as if trying to salvage his manly pride.

"Aye. 'Twas a verra scary dragon with shiny black scales covering her body." Calin pulled the shift over her head and slid her naked body beneath him before he continued his tale. "With blue eyes sparkling like midnight." Calin suckled the soft flesh at the base of one breast then the other until she arched into him.

"And what did the dragon do to ye?"

"She bound my hands and tortured me with the fire in her mouth until I begged for mercy. But she devoured my heart in one bite."

Only a few hours, at best, befell since he'd made love to her, but she stirred a passion in him he couldn't fight. She weaved her fingers into his hair as he kissed her. Her knees straddled his hips, and the thickness of his manhood grew against her belly. He chided himself for believing his lust would lessen once he took her virginity. Instead, his compulsion for her increased and the desire to know every ounce of her flesh consumed him.

He became more assertive. Nibbling each rib with his teeth, his feast trailed lower over the soft valley of her stomach. His tongue filled her navel, but he didn't possess the strength to deny his hunger for more.

"Did the dragon kill ye?" Akira's fingertips followed Calin's trail, but one hand remained behind to pleasure her own breast. Calin watched intently as she pulled and twisted her nipple between her thumb and fingers. Her mouth opened, and he felt a shiver course through her.

"Nay. I hunted her down and tamed her," Calin answered, licking his lips.

She squeaked when he parted her legs wider and kissed the creamy skin of her inner thigh. He could smell her arousal. He was shameless. He didn't care. He'd wanted to taste her nectar since he'd met her. Separating her satiny flesh, he delved two fingers into velvety honey.

She moaned. "And then . . . what did ye . . . do to her?"

"I ate her." His mouth replaced his fingers and molded to the most private area of her body.

Akira tensed. "What are ye doing?"

He paused and cocked a grin while peering at her from between her legs. "I am tasting my wee dragon."

"Is this done?"

"I am doing it, am I naught?" Calin proceeded to his loving task. He kissed her and savored her sweetness. His thumb worked its magic soliciting whimpers of ecstasy while his tongue tormented the secret hollows within. Her moans encouraged his plight. Wanting to give her fulfillment, he drew her polished nub between his teeth. A hoarse vibration traveled up his throat when she pulsed against his tongue. The same aching pulse beat painfully within his arousal.

Akira cried out his name, unable to find any level of reality. The culmination of her soul surged into her core. Humiliation added to the heat burning her skin. Such a carnal act must be sinful. Could a woman kiss her husband in the same manner? A quiver pulsed through her body at the devilish thought, but her morals refused to subside. "Och, Calin . . . does this help to get me with child?"

"Nay, Akira. This is all for ye. Not for our child. For ye."

Rolling her hips, she clutched the back of his head and panted. "Ye are a . . . good husband . . . Calin." Unleashing her desires, she screamed until the warm trickle of a shattering climax flowed over her thighs.

"Crivons!" She added exclamations in French, Gaelic, and the language only she understood, but the tone sounded all the same. Bliss. Satisfaction. Her mind wandered in bewilderment when he arose to kiss her. His tongue filled her mouth, and she tasted what he'd tasted. A foreign, erotic, wildly sensual flavor. She buried her modesty and returned his kiss.

Immediately, she ached for him. "I want ye, husband."

Calin scooped one hand behind her back and carried her lithe body with him as he sat upright at the edge of the bed. She felt like a rag in his arms as his positioned her over his lap. With his feet flat on the floor, he gripped her waist. "Wrap your legs around me and open your eyes."

She wondered why he always took her in this position, why he always forced her to look at him when he made love to her. She tried to protect her heart against his searing gaze, but her husband's eyes chipped away at her resistance. She held tight to his shoulders as he raised her overtop him and entered her slowly. Perspiration rolled from his temple as he pumped short draws in and out of her.

"Och, love. Ye are still so tight."

Akira felt his desire. Felt his undeniable passion for her. Yet he held back what she so desperately sought. "I am yours, Calin. Ye'll not hurt me. I want all of ye."

His mouth opened, enabling him to inhale more air. He lowered her onto his stiff rod until he buried himself inside her—all of him. His pace quickened, and she could do little more than hold on. The muscles in his arms flexed while his fingers clutched her hips, moving her up and down in a rhythm that filled her with pure pleasure.

Just as she reached the pinnacle his eyes slid shut. He pressed his cheek to hers and whispered her name.

She collapsed against his shoulder. Her breaths bordered on cries.

Once regaining his energy, he fell onto the bed's softness dragging her with him. Tucking her into his side, he threw a leg over hers and pulled her fingers to his earlobe. Did he want more than just her body, more than an heir? Would she be a fool to allow herself to love him? Could a man of his position ever return such love? Such fanciful dreams only belonged to the faint of heart. She closed her eyes and nuzzled in tighter to him. The peaceful patter of raindrops, and the silk of his earlobe between her fingers lulled her into relaxation.

He stroked her arm. "Did I hurt ye?"

"Hurt" isn't the word she would use to describe their love-making. The way he treated her when alone made her feel desirable. But guilt clutched at her. She didn't know if making a child should feel so wonderful. "Ye dinnae hurt me. Ye make me feel . . . beautiful. I like the way ye touch me. But I know not if I should receive such enjoyment from making our child."

"We are husband and wife. If we choose to seek pleasure with one another, we may do so without guilt."

Akira worried she wouldn't be able to please him. His insatiable appetite seemed a hunger she could never feed. "When I carry the MacLeod heir will ye still want to touch me, even if it is not necessary?"

"All o' Scotland couldnae keep me from ye."

Calin leaned over her to douse the candles and then cradled her body tightly against his. One hand nestled over her breast, the other cupped her backside.

The darkness brought insecurity. Stroking the muscles of his back, she questioned whether or not she'd be able to satisfy him the way Catriona must have. She tried to block the woman's face from her vision, but the gray eyes lingered. Jealousy overwhelmed her.

Calin belonged to her now, and no one would take him from her.

Chapter Twenty

"M'lady."

Akira opened her eyes sluggishly. The soft tap escalated to a vigorous knock.

"M'lady, pray forgive me for waking ye, but I am worried ye might be ill."

She heard the knock again. "Please, m'lady, are ye in there?" the muffled panicked voice pleaded.

She jumped from the bed and swayed a little from a sudden burst of dizziness. Her husband stole all her sleeping hours and now the inside of her head weighed heavy. Concealing her nakedness with a silk robe, she opened the door. Evie and Tara's ears were flattened against the lady's chamber door. Elsbeth stood beside with a basket of sewing supplies.

"Evie, what is it?" Akira asked. "Do quiet your voice. Ye will wake the entire west wing."

Relieved faces lit up when the maids scurried down the corridor and entered their laird's solar. Evie's footing came to an abrupt halt between the two chambers. Her gaze fixed on the adjoining doors—splintered and partially hanging from the hinges. Cautiously, Evie stepped into the lady's solar and retrieved the battle-axe from the floor, which probably weighed as much as she. Tara assisted her in returning the weapon to its mount above the hearth at which point both the young maids pinched their noses in an effort to extinguish the potent smell of mixed perfumes. Evie made a dramatic production out of fluffing the decorative pillows atop the untouched bed.

The wicked smirk touching the dimple in Evie's cheek spoke louder than the words Akira felt certain were near to jumping off her tongue.

"I apologize for the muss. M'laird and I had a wee bit of a disagreement. I think I won, but I cannae be sure until I've the chance to fully awaken. What are ye doing here at such an early hour?"

"Early." Evie giggled and lifted the tapestry covering the arched window. "'Tis past noonday. Ye've missed mornin' mass, and the council has been awaiting ye since they broke their fast."

"The council! Noonday!" Akira darted to the arrow-slit window and cringed. It would do naught for the kinfolk to think their new mistress such a sloth. Thankfully, she'd bid her family farewell the eve before. Though hesitant, Kendrick left Isobel in her care. Akira insisted she stay at least until Maggie delivered her baby. She heard water sloshing and turned to find Tara carrying two pails of water.

"M'laird has arranged for ye to meet with the elders and the chaplain. He said ye would want another bath, though I argued ye just bathed yestereve, he insisted ye would be wanting another. I fear the water is not verra warm anymore."

Her cheeks heated. Calin already knew her so well. Akira's fixation for cleanliness stemmed from a young age. She scoured for hours at a time to remove the demon-shaped mark on her backside, which caused her such turmoil as a child. Once old enough to realize the blemish was simply a birthmark, she'd already become obsessed. She accepted her flaw and the habit didn't seem to bother Calin. She assumed he enjoyed the taste of her skin, as he'd dined on almost all of it. The remembrance of all the places he'd kissed her brought the heat in her cheeks to a fevered flame.

Akira ran her fingers over the coverlet of the disheveled bed she and her husband shared. Her mind became lost in the memory of the passion they'd shared just hours before. She straightened the linens and smoothed the coverlet over the bolster.

"M'lady, please. If ye clean the solar, I'll be out of a job." Evie scuffled in behind her gathering loose garments from a cuttie stool for the laundress.

Akira snatched back Calin's *léine* shirt out of the pile overflowing Evie's arms. She shoved the soiled tunic beneath the bolster on his side of the bed. "I dinnae want that laundered until m'laird returns."

"Aye, m'lady." Evie dipped her head dutifully, but still, she giggled.

Akira would miss him. She'd grown to like having him near. His smell seemed so familiar, and if she closed her eyes, she could feel his kiss. A tickle fluttered through her stomach.

Shaking off the giddiness making her head light, Akira focused on her duties. His absence would allow her time to prove her value to Clan MacLeod—starting with the council. She already discussed schooling the children with four of the five elders at the games and each of them seemed favorable to her ideas. The fifth elder, however, would prove difficult to sway. She'd been informed Gordon resided on the council. The man made no effort to hide his dislike of her. Fortunately, his wife took to her like a cow to a salt lick. Nonetheless, a formal meeting awaited her and she would respect the council's decision.

Elsbeth's timid voice mumbled over the ruckus of the maids. "M'lady, I can see you're very busy. I might be of service to you another day."

"Wait, Elsbeth. I have a verra important task for ye." Akira caught her arm as she attempted to back out of the solar. "If ye've the time, would ye listen while Evie and Tara transform me into something more appealing."

Elsbeth waited on a stool until Akira bathed privately and Evie and Tara completed her informal attire. A long blue-black braid fell to her waist, and her plaid kirtle pleated to perfection around her waist. Her toes clenched a bit inside new leather brogues while Tara fastened the MacLeod brooch to her shoulder.

"Do the gowns displease you, m'lady?" Elsbeth asked, somewhat contrite.

Akira sensed her disappointment, but had no intention of wearing any of them. Elsbeth probably labored for hours on each and every one of them, which made Akira's request all the more difficult. "The gowns are exquisite, Elsbeth. Never have I seen such artistry in clothing. Howbeit, I wondered if mayhap ye've ever quilted?"

For the first time since meeting the woman, Elsbeth smiled. A generous toothy grin. "Me and my grandmum used to stitch the most wonderful floral designs when I was just a child."

"Then ye wouldnae mind making a quilt for me? I would solicit some of the kinswomen to assist ye and have the children sift through the hen feathers to find the softest eider for stuffing."

"'Twould be an honor, indeed, but 'twould take ells of material for such a task. I would need to—"

"I have material aplenty for an entire quilted garden." Akira closed her arms around a handful of gowns from the wardrobe and dropped them at Elsbeth's worn leather toes. "As I am certain Catriona worked your fingers to the bone over these gowns, they dinnae belong to her anymore. They belong to me, and I dinnae want them. 'Tis not my intention to offend ye, but I'll not wear them. Return the precious stones to Calin's Aunt Wanda and as for the beads, mayhap, the children can make jewelry for their mothers. Use them all, but leave the plaids. I'll need something to wear. I want a quilt big enough to hold all the children for lessons."

Elsbeth raised a purple gown from the pile and brushed her thumb over the silk. "I am not offended, m'lady, but my si—I mean, Catriona will be—"

"What?" Akira caught Elsbeth's slip. Elsbeth looked more like a Scot than Akira did with her red-gold hair and freckled skin. How could she possibly be that vile woman's sister? Catriona was easy to hate. She was a whore and she was English. Two qualities Akira despised equally.

Elsbeth gave a sidelong glance at the maids, who made no bones about their interest in the conversation.

"Evie, Tara. Ye are dismissed. Apologize to the council for my delay and let them know I'll be there posthaste. Send for my sister, Isobel. I want her settled into the lady's solar by nightfall. Also, have Jaime and Alec repair the adjoining doors. Send word to Aileen. I'll require her assistance, as weel, after I meet with the council. There is much to prepare." The maids curtsied their way out the door after which Akira settled in beside Elsbeth.

"Forgive me, but I find it difficult to believe Catriona is your sister."

"Aye, m'lady. Though I do not like to admit either, Catriona is my half-sister. Our mother—God rest her soul—was King Henry's niece. Catriona is of blessed and noble blood. Her father is the Crown Prince of Malaga and our mother's legal husband. I, howbeit, am daughter to my mother's paramour." Elsbeth appeared to have found her emotions. As if she held Catriona's limbs in her hands, she ripped the garment at the seam then tore each sleeve from the bodice. "Mother spent her days fawning over her prized daughter. She attended the finest schools. Wore the most luxurious gowns. Mother worshipped her and flaunted her beneath the noses of every prince and duke betwixt London and Venice. Before Mother could secure Catriona a title, she died of an ague. Being the eldest, I cared for Catriona and she repays me with her . . . well, suffice it to say, she . . ."

"She beats ye?" Akira guessed then reached for Elsbeth's cold quivering hand. The pads of her fingers were completely callused. "Does your husband not protect ye?"

She shook her head and pinched her eyes tight when a sob overtook her body. The purple material in her hand now served as a kerchief to catch her tears.

Akira desperately wanted to help this woman, but worried about trusting a woman of English blood. "First, I would know how ye came to live among the kin of Clan MacLeod, then ye will tell me how your husband and sister mistreat ye or I'll send for them and hear the words from their mouths."

"No, m'lady. That will not be necessary. Catriona was sent as a gift to your laird by our most gracious King Henry to further his ongoing machinations to maintain peace with Scotland. Arrangements were made for Catriona to travel under the king's guard alone, but she insisted on having a maid in tow and King Henry obliged her request to take me. Your Scotsmen brothers murdered our escorts then tied us to a couple of ailing garrons and pointed us in the direction of MacLeod soil. We traveled for two days unattended until your kinsmen found us. Brady suffered the most."

"Your son?" Akira interrupted.

"Aye. He is just a child. Only years of five now."

"Then your son does not belong to Ian?"

"No." Elsbeth answered forcefully. "Brady belongs to Robert, my English husband."

Akira's brows pinched. "Your late husband?"

"No." Elsbeth lowered her lids.

"Ye were married when ye came here? Why did ye not tell m'laird?"

"Catriona forced me to hold my tongue about my marriage and accept Laird MacLeod's gracious offering to find me a husband. My Robert had been at battle for three months prior to our leaving England. Catriona told m'laird my husband died."

"Do ye believe him dead?"

"I did when I left England. 'Tis why I accepted my place with Ian. Brady needed a home and a father. Ian was kind at first. But Catriona used her wily ways on him after the laird dismissed her, as she has half the MacLeod warriors." Elsbeth paused to blow her nose and Akira patted her on the back. "It would be most improper for me to discuss my sister's relationship with your husband. I do not wish to insult you, m'lady."

"Calin has told me about her, and I dinnae wish to hear about their relationship either. I am more interested in the way she mistreats ye." Akira's gut clenched at the subject. The knot in the pit of her stomach grew with every heartfelt word coming from Elsbeth's mouth.

"Catriona is easily angered. She tosses me around a bit from time to time when she is refused."

The casual tone of her voice infuriated Akira. "Tosses ye around? Elsbeth, I saw the bruises. Why would ye protect her after what she has done to ye?" Akira laid her palm against Elsbeth's stomach. "Ye are with child and Ian does not protect ye from her abuse. If I am to help ye, I must know what I am dealing with. I cannae understand why ye wouldnae tell m'laird ye were married." Akira spoke in a relentless tone, but by accepting Ian as her husband, Elsbeth broke kirk law. The act of bigamy was punishable by death.

Elsbeth burst into a torrent of cries. She fell against Akira's shoulder and clutched her around the waist. "I thought my husband dead, but when Catriona's father sent gifts I learned my Robert had returned home. I did not want to betray him, but

Catriona insisted I forget England and accept my duties as Ian's wife. She's evil and I am ashamed to call her sister." Elsbeth inhaled several shaky breaths. "Ian likes for Catriona to watch us. At first, they were discreet. Catriona would hide in the larder while Ian had his way with me then he would ask me to leave whilst he lay with my sister in our marriage bed. I feel so unclean, m'lady. And I desperately want to return to my Robert. 'Tis why I am telling you this. I beg you to help me."

Her confession sickened Akira and made her hate Catriona all the more. She smoothed Elsbeth's hair and allowed her time to weep. "I dinnae like your husband, and I've never even met him," Akira calmly stated, unable to contain her opinion.

Elsbeth popped her head up, nearly catching Akira's chin, and wiped her swollen eyes. "If I provided you with information that could banish Catriona from Clan MacLeod and send her back home to her father, would you protect me and my son?"

"Of course." Though afraid of what Elsbeth might reveal, Akira wouldn't deny this woman refuge, nor could she stand by idle while a boy's safety was at risk.

"Vow it," Elsbeth insisted.

"I vow it." Akira wiped a tear from Elsbeth's cheek and brushed the loose hair from her scared eyes. "I will do everything within my power to help ye. Please, trust me."

Elsbeth held tight to Akira's hand as if what she was about to say would send her racing. "My husband, Ian, and his brother abducted you. They are the ones who took you to *Tigh Diabhail*. They acted on Catriona's behalf. When I tried to go to the laird, Catriona threatened my son. She gave me no choice but to remain silent."

Akira would have smiled if Elsbeth hadn't been so distressed. Elsbeth trusted her with a great deal of information, and Akira intended to use what Elspeth told her with discretion. "I'll petition King James to have your marriage to Ian annulled.

The marriage is not legally binding as ye were physically threatened into accepting the contract. I'll send m'laird's seneschal to retrieve your son before I meet with the council. Ye and Brady will move into the keep until the arrangements are made to send ye home." Akira's gaze fell to Elsbeth's belly. "Will Robert still have ye, if ye carry another mon's child?"

"Yes, m'lady, but I cannot return to England. The child I carry will be born with Scot's blood—enemy blood. I cannot put my child's life at risk or my husband's. My return will be perceived as a treacherous insult by the English nobles. My Robert is a soldier to England and would be accused of seditious acts, punishable by imprisonment or even death."

"Would your Robert betray his country for ye?" Akira asked while she considered their limited options.

"Yes. I believe he would." Elsbeth held her hand tight. Hope shined in the tear falling from pale green eyes.

"I realize the danger ye've put yourself and your son in by trusting me, but I can assure ye, ye will suffer the cruelties of your sister nay more, nor Ian. I am going to help ye, but I need time."

"Thank you, m'lady." Elsbeth kissed her knuckles as Akira stood to leave. "And I will never reveal your secret either."

Akira halted beneath the archway genuinely perplexed by her comment. "What secret?"

"That you are a witch."

Chapter Twenty-One

Calin said a fortnight. He'd been gone three times longer. Akira vowed if her husband didn't return by this Sabbath she would go in search of him herself. Neither the elders, nor a single member of the *mesnie* seemed the least bit concerned by his delay.

Granted, not a moment of her days were spent in boredom. She worked with Isobel's recovery every morn, and she'd acquainted herself with the servants, the baker, the brewer, the butcher, and devoted a great deal of her time to the elder kinswomen who worked diligently on the quilt. The children consumed the remaining hours. The first few days only a dozen matrons brought their children to the keep following morning mass. But within a sennight, Akira relocated her entourage to the front lawn when more than sixty children arrived, eager for tutoring.

Elsbeth and Brady had settled into a vacant chamber near the scullery and the kinswomen arrived in droves to help her with the quilt. They stitched the last patch the day prior and presented it to Akira beneath the shade of an old oak as she schooled the children in French. Unable to control her sentiments, Akira had cried outright at the kindhearted display.

Never had she seen a more beautiful quilt. Multicolored flowers surrounded the focal point, which oddly enough was a deep plum dragon with eyes of tiny sapphires. Elsbeth wouldn't divulge how she conceptualized the creative motif, but Akira was nonetheless pleased.

Catriona had not shown her despicable face, and for that Akira expressed eternal gratitude to her Maker. Her responsibilities elevated without facing another confrontation with the woman she felt inferior to. Elsbeth assured her Ian wouldn't seek her out. He had admitted to Elsbeth that he was a wee bit frightened of Akira's pagan powers. Akira had assured her new friend she possessed no unearthly powers, but Elsbeth only winked and grinned.

The women befriended her, accepting her as part of their kin, and Akira warmed with their attentions. Mam would be proud of her and she felt Papa's presence as she walked among her new family with honor. She hoped Calin would be pleased with her accomplishments when he returned. His absence made her heart ache, and the fear that something horrible happened to him grew in her gut daily until the worrisome knot became too much to bear. She had learned it was useless to fight the deep-seated emotions she felt for her husband. Instead, she tried to focus her energy on the children.

Andrew was perched in her lap sucking his thumb, while Akira occupied the children. She entwined their minds around the tale of a mighty dragon. Her voice altered in high and low pitches for each character, making the story more dramatic. ". . . And after the brave knight buried the steel of his sword into the heart of the fire-breathing dragon, he fell to his knees. A bright pink light beamed from the dragon's wound. Suddenly"—Akira paused, every child's eyes rounded like silver shillings—"the dragon transformed into a—" her words caught in her throat, for over top the knoll she sighted her husband.

Calin walked alone.

Her heart pounded against her ribs when his strides lengthened. Akira tossed Andrew into a quartet of young lasses, raised her kirtle, and rounded a corner of the quilt.

"M'lady, ye cannae leave. What did the dragon turn into?" A tiny voice asked from within the throng of children and then a multitude of begging voices protested.

Akira blew a breath then quickly concluded her tale. "The dragon turned into a beautiful maiden with hair the color of a raven's wing and eyes of sapphire blue."

"And did she fall in love with the brave knight?"

"Aye, she did," she hollered over her shoulder. "And they lived happily ever after."

With the children content with the conclusion of her story, Akira's pace quickened. What had delayed his return? Had he been hurt? Attacked en route by brigands? Where were his kinsmen? Her feet couldn't keep up with her worries, and her walk turned into a fevered run. A cool wind pushed tears across her temples while the burning in her chest dried her throat.

She only wanted to touch his skin and be reassured he was unharmed.

Calin seemed to be in an equal hurry to reach her. They met at the base of the knoll, both inhaling air in starving gulps.

Sweat trickled down her spine.

An arm's length separated them.

Relief swelled in her throat. She feared she might burst into tears right here before him.

Dark auburn hair settled atop his shoulders in wet waves. His freshly shaven jaw gleamed and the clean scent of a recent bath clung to the air like a fresh mist of rain. Fatigue rested beneath his eyes in dark half-moons, but his one brow remained raised and ever perky. She touched his forearm. His skin felt cool and damp beneath her burning fingertips.

The muscles of his chest heaved. "Are ye angry with me?"

"Should I be?"

"Nay."

His answer cooled the tear-streaked path along one cheek. His eyes twitched as he studied her. He licked his lips.

She could no longer hide her feelings for her husband. No longer wanted to. She wanted to leap onto his chest and crush his mouth with her kiss.

The fire in his eyes told her he wanted the same.

The whoops and cheers of the many kinfolk gathering on the lawn jarred her. His strong arm shook beneath her fingertips. Her breathing sounded raspy in her ears. She could bear it no more.

"We have much to discuss," they said in unison.

Akira smiled and lowered her lashes bashfully, but Calin jerked her in the direction of the keep, nearly pulling her arm loose from her shoulder. By the time they reached the worn path, they were sprinting for the front entrance.

Once inside the keep, Gordon tried to stay them. "Welcome home, m'laird."

"Gather the elders," Calin tossed over his shoulder. "We need to meet after I speak with my wife."

Gordon spoke, but his words were incomprehensible behind her. They reached the base of the tower stairwell and Calin took three steps to her one. She clutched at her skirts trying to follow him up the stairs of the west wing. Evie and Tara ducked beneath a pitch-pine torch as they whirled past.

"M'lady, have ye need of anything?"

Akira didn't know which maid asked the question, nor did she care. "Nay." The single word echoed throughout the tower stairwell. Her body flashed with expectancy. Her nipples hardened against the coarse wool of her sark. She should inquire of his journey. A good wife would pay heed to his needs. Was it possible he felt the same sense of urgency as she? The same longing?

The stairwell seemed endless. She couldn't keep up with Calin's strides and stumbled. He jogged back down and carried her the remaining twenty steps to his solar. Kicking the door open, Calin dropped her to her feet and barred the adjoining doors while she did the same with his solar door.

"We need to talk," Calin said, but no words followed when he tossed his belt and claymore to the floor with a clank. He looked angry or mayhap impatient.

After removing the long pin holding his plaid at his waist, he jerked his *léine* shirt over his head. His hot hands closed over her wrists and pressed her open palms against his bare chest. The depth of desire in his eyes burned her face. The intensity scared her. "Have I displeased ye, m'laird?"

"Nay." His hands clutched her skull and tilted her head, then his lips covered hers. Their tongues spiraled each other in a frenzied chase. Calin pulled away, but not before nibbling at each lip. Teasing, taunting, promising so much more.

She inhaled deeply through her nose, trying to steady her turbulent emotions. Her mind, her body, her entire being felt trapped inside a storm. Moisture flooded between her legs. A proper wife would never conduct herself in such a manner. She should break free of him.

The task proved impossible. "I've verra much to tell ye. I started schooling the children." She panted between eager breaths. Gooseflesh sprouted over her collarbone when his mouth moved to the pulse in her neck.

"I've much to tell ye, too, but I need ye—now." Calin raised her kirtle and impaled his thumb into the damp curls between her legs while his fingers stroked the cleft of her backside. His eyes widened wickedly. "And ye need me as well." He looked starved, crazed—the same as she felt.

Embarrassed he found her in such a state of arousal, Akira lowered her lids and moaned. The intimate touch made her knees weak and her sensitive breasts tighten.

When she started for the bed, Calin pressed her against the door. "Nay. Here. Now!"

He gave her no time to rebuke his demand. He shed his plaid and raised her atop him. She latched her boots around his waist while strong fingers circled her bottom and opened her hot flesh to him. She bit her bottom lip when he slid inside her. Pressing her back against the solidity of the wooden door, he plunged into her.

She gasped at the intensity, but couldn't control her racing mind. So much needed to be said, and she couldn't hold back the information. "Jaime . . . has asked Isobel . . . to be his wife," she mentioned, while suckling his neck and searching for an anchor.

"I met with King James . . . and have his permission . . . to pursue an alliance." Calin ripped the brooch from her *arisaid* to free her of the heavy wool while she worked at the laces of her bodice. The thin linen of her sark didn't stand a chance. The seams ripped against his desperate need to get to her breasts. His teeth found her rigid nipple—bathing, sucking, biting, while he buried himself deep inside her. The door knocked within its frame with each thrust.

She whimpered, but continued their conversation. "I've petitioned the king . . . for an annulment."

Calin ceased abruptly. His amber eyes filled with upset.

She pulled his bottom lip between her teeth and smiled. "Not for us, for Elsbeth."

"Och, lass. Ye gave me a fright." Calin growled and lunged back inside her.

She squealed, then inhaled sharply. "I know who abducted me."

He silenced her with a kiss. His tongue swirled through the recesses of her mouth while he pumped hard and fast. He pressed the backs of her hands against the door and filled her with his seed. "King James wishes me to marry English," he said between sporadic breaths.

She fell against his shoulder when the deluge of ecstasy overcame her. "I missed ye."

"I missed ye more." Calin put his arms around her back and carried her across the chamber. After shedding the garment hanging from her waist, she fell onto the bed. Her body ached for him and her mind turned to mush. What did he say about marrying English?

"I met with Logan Donald and Kendrick," he informed her while he freed himself of his deerskin boots.

"Is Kendrick with ye?" She tried to sit up, but he pushed her back against the bolster and pinned her arms above her head with one hand. The other wicked hand rekindled the fire between her legs until she thought her bones would combust.

"Aye, he just returned from securing your sisters and mam with the Donalds," Calin answered, his voice raspy and out of breath.

She wanted to ask more questions. There was so much to discuss. So much to do. But she only wanted to make love to her husband and not worry about the problems they would face.

Crivons! What was he doing with his hand?

The thickness of his middle fingers spiraled in the most private area of her body, while his thumb flicked deep inside her. She rolled her hips in response and clenched her muscles around his teasing touch.

Calin pulled her fingers to titillate one breast while he filled his palm with the other, then proceeded to kiss his way down her belly—never once easing the exquisite torment between her legs.

"I need to meet with the elders." He breathed against her nether curls.

She squealed when he drew her swollen pebble between his teeth. Quivers of delight rippled beneath her skin. Icy air sucked through her teeth, then she exhaled her words. "I'll not be long now. I vow it . . . Ye must be . . . hungry."

"I am ravenous." Calin flipped her onto her stomach and gnawed on her backside. He was grateful he didn't make camp with the others, even though the inside of his thighs were raw from the saddle. The glow of a full moon lit his way back to Cànwyck Castle as he rode throughout the night. He missed his wife. The irrefutable ache in his chest drove him to push Sirius to near exhaustion. His hands had burned with the desire to press his wife's body against his own and feel her hands caress his heart.

An empty stomach begged him for two days to stop, but he'd ignored the cramps. None of it mattered now. She was here, with him and not even the king's demands would take her from him.

He closed his mouth over the pink MacLeod crest branded on her creamy cheek. The brand marking her as his. He wanted to fill her with life. A new life. A child. He raised her to her knees and filled his palms with the milky swells of her behind. By the saints, the woman presented a tantalizing sight. She was pink and swollen and glistening with need.

His manhood filled with blood instantly and jumped. He positioned his fully erect member between her silky mons. Running a hand up her spine, he pressed her shoulders to the coverlet and spread her legs wide with his knees. Sliding himself into her, he gripped her hipbones and rocked her against him, again and again. When she mimicked the cadence, he reached around to circle her tiny nub until she screamed in exhilarated rapture.

The muscles in his thighs clenched. The heat of her orgasm, along with the friction caused by the awkward position he twisted her into, snapped any restraint he may have still possessed. A peculiar, yet wonderful, sensation rippled through him as he poured life inside her womb. A life that would bond them together forever.

Loosening his hold on her, he gently caressed her hips and watched the red ovals fade where he'd gripped her pale flesh. Sprawling out beside her, he rolled to her side and wedged her against him. The silky softness of her damp body molded against his rugged skin. He kissed the back of her eyelids and wiped the sheen of sweat from her top lip. He caressed the base of her breast with his callused knuckles and speculated how any part of this woman could belong to Laird Kinnon.

The answer to a question, which had plagued him half his life, suddenly became poignantly clear. For eighteen years he wondered why his father hadn't put forth a battle the night he died. Why he sacrificed the last moment of his existence for a woman who wasn't even his wife. Now, he finally understood. His father loved Lena, just as he loved Akira.

He would die to keep her, regardless of what King James wanted.

Akira's warm fingers touched his cheek. He pushed her hand the rest of the way to his earlobe. He wanted her to admit they were soul mates. He knew it. He felt it in his heart. He just didn't know how to tell her. Or worse, feared she didn't return those feelings.

Beautiful blue eyes peeked at him from beneath fluttering lashes and her voice caressed his ears. "*That* wasnae the way I know."

His chest bounced with laughter. He'd never known *that way* either, but he'd been crazed to have her, and she had yet to protest any position his creative mind could devise. "We will do it your way soon." He kissed the curved corner of her reddened lips. "I missed ye, my love," he whispered into the whorl of her ear.

She giggled and toyed with his ear. "We already said that, but I fear we may want to start over."

"Gladly." Though exhausted, he slid his hand between her thighs. "Mayhap we will try your way now."

"Nay, ye lusty barbarian!" She halted his wicked fingers, but instead of throwing his hand aside, she cupped his palm over her breast and gave him an encouraging squeeze. "We are supposed to be having a discussion."

"Ye are too naked for me to discuss anything. I cannae concentrate with your bonnie fine tit in my palm," he protested and bent to nip the pink crest.

"Then I'll clothe myself, as will ye." Akira crawled out of his embrace and slipped into an ivory silk robe. She sat atop the bench and waited for him to do the same.

He groaned, but forced himself to retrieve a rust-colored robe from the anteroom and tied the matching belt about his waist. When he started to sit beside her, she held up her hand, palm flat. "Nay. Ye will sit over there. I dinnae trust your hands." She pointed at the three-legged cuttie stool across the solar.

Disgruntled, he followed her orders, and propped his elbows on his knees, all the while hoping the small stool wouldn't topple beneath his weight.

"I started schooling the children." Akira told him about Jaime and Isobel, the kinswomen, and then summarized her conversations with Elsbeth and how she petitioned the king four sennights ago for their annulment. Calin buried his face in his hands when she described Catriona's conduct. How could he have been blindsided by such a treacherous woman? Catriona's involvement in Akira's abduction would complicate matters even more with King James. Nonetheless, he assured Akira that Ian and his brother's punishment for their betrayal would be severe.

"Now. Tell me why Kendrick has need of securing my family." Akira steepled her fingers beneath her chin.

"Laird Kinnon knows Kendrick leads the rebellion. Your chieftain intends to give the Ionas to Darach in an effort to join the alliance."

"What?" Akira's hand flew to her chest. "He is mad! And King James has agreed to support such a union?"

"Nay. King James has other plans for the Isles."

Akira waited for further explanation, and Calin knew what her next question would be just as she asked it.

"Plans that involve an English union? How are ye to marry English when ye are already my husband, bound by God and the kirk?"

Calin had asked King James the same question. The king expressed his desire to maintain peace with King Henry for the good of Scotland. At which point, the archbishop unraveled a scroll. King James dissolved his marriage to Akira with the tip of a quill, but Calin ripped the parchment to shreds and threw the royal decree at His Majesty's feet. This act of stupidity gained him three sennights of imprisonment.

The kings of Scotland had been trying to dissolve the Lords of the Isles for decades. King James refused to support any alliance unless the chieftains of the Isles declared fealty to the crown and married daughters of English nobility as a selfless act to prove their allegiance to Scotland.

"I would know how the king wishes ye to marry English," Akira inquired again, when he gave no response.

Now parched, he cleared his throat. "I'll answer that question in the Great Hall with the elders. Mayhap ye'll not throw a tantrum in their presence."

Two black brows rose. "Mayhap, I'll bind your limbs and torture ye until ye answer accordingly." Crossing her legs, knee over knee, Akira let the robe "V" over her sumptuous thigh. The tip of her middle finger circled the shadow of her peaked nipple pressing against the silk of her robe.

His delicate dragon was indeed a dangerous creature. He

sensed her impatience, but her seductive tactics for obtaining the truth shocked him nonetheless.

"Or mayhap I'll offer my body to ye in exchange for what I want to know."

Minx! Calin tore his eyes away, unable to watch her toy with herself. He enjoyed her games. The play thickened his blood and made him want her all the more. He stared at the adjoining doors. "Are ye done blathering, wife?"

"Have ye an answer for me, husband?"

Calin turned back, disappointed to find her arms crossed in defiance over the sweet swells of her breasts. His eyes narrowed on her. "Touch yourself again, and I'll tell ye."

Her head tilted as if she might be considering his request. Excitement twirled up his spine when the corner of her lips rose, then she touched one finger to her exposed knee. "There. Now tell me."

"Nay. Ye know what I want."

Akira suckled the tip of her middle finger between her full lips then reached inside her robe to caress her nipple. Her mouth lay open and her pink tongue darted out to lick her heart-shaped lips.

"King James wishes for peace between England and Scotland. He has issued an edict for the annulment of our marriage and has ordered me to marry English, but I refused him." The words poured out of his mouth with astonishing ease, but the look of dejection on her face froze the fire in his loins.

Her eyes pinched together and the hand that had teased him in playful banter now clutched the edges of her robe together at her neck. She stood and then unbarred the door to her solar. He followed her into the darkest corner of the anteroom where she wept open-mouthed into her hands. He hated her tears and hated himself more for causing them.

He placed his hand on her shoulder and thanked the saint

she didn't pull away. "I'll not give ye up, my love. I promise this to ye on my father's grave and afore the saints I pray to daily."

"What if ye've nay choice?" Her chin fell to her chest, but her tear-soaked hand rested over his, quivering.

"A mon always has a choice. Sometimes those choices require immense sacrifice, but 'tis a choice just the same." Calin turned her into him and brushed his lips over her forehead then kissed her temple. He wished she believed in him, but that trust had not yet been built, and he hadn't the time to erect such a fortress.

"Ye have pledged fealty to your king. To refuse him would be treasonous. What choice did he give ye?"

"If I choose to accept the annulment and marry English, Clan MacLeod will receive His Majesty's full support in aligning the Isles."

"And if ye refuse your king?"

"King James has threatened to confiscate the MacLeod title and land. My kin will be evicted from their homes, and I will hang for treason."

Akira's hand covered her mouth, but not in time to hide her gasp. "I am not willing to make such a sacrifice." She slipped past him and dressed quickly. Her eyes avoided him and the words to console her never found their way off his tongue.

"I'll meet ye in the hall, m'laird." She quietly left her solar.

Chapter Twenty-Two

"God's teeth, son! King James makes ye an offer ye cannae refuse. I fear the peasant has bewitched ye to the point ye cannae think rationally." The insult freely tossed came from Calin's uncle Kerk. Deft fingers combed through graying temples in an obvious attempt to ease the tension writhing his brain.

"Your tongue is disrespectful, *Uncle*. Dinnae forget I am laird now. I am nay longer requesting your approval, so much as soliciting your aid," Calin responded, his tone obstinate.

Akira's patience had swelled, peaked, and snapped hours prior. She'd pushed back every cuticle of every fingernail and now worried if she didn't relieve herself soon, that part of her would burst as well. Fidgeting, she sat alone at the low table and continued to listen to the men quibble. Not a single subject had been rectified in over three hours of debate, and they sounded like a gaggle of cackling hens. Kendrick had ceased trying to make Calin's council see reason and was now drowning himself in spirits.

Three of the five prune-faced elders sitting behind the high table on the raised dais had held council status within the clan for decades. Gordon, the youngest of these five, voiced his convictions often and without qualms. His opinion didn't favor

Akira's marriage to Calin. The eldest dozed in and out of sleep. Drool seeped from the corner of his mouth into an unkempt white beard and from time to time, he sat upright and hollered, "Aye."

Calin and his uncle Kerk squabbled mindlessly and the verbal battle had reached a blockade.

"Ye've a greater purpose now," Kerk continued. "A union with Catriona would be advantageous to the greater good o' Scotland. Your decision to defy King James will not go unpunished for any of us living on MacLeod soil. Have ye nay reverence for your kin? All will suffer from your selfish tirade."

Calin slammed his fist onto the alabaster council table. The jarring noise reverberated off the stone walls and flipped Akira's innards upside down. She peeked up at her husband and saw the anger in his stance—narrowed eyes, fisted hands, legs wide and locked. She'd never seen him so full of rage.

"Selfish tirade? I've lived my entire life with a single goal driving me through my mundane existence. To protect the livelihood of this clan."

"Ye dinnae crave the alliance for the protection of your people," Kerk retorted. One bushy brow rose over his accusing dark eyes. "Ye seek the alliance to avenge your father's death. Our feud with our neighbor is not over land, and ye weel know it. 'Tis blood. The blood o' my brother. Have ye so quickly forgotten Laird Kinnon murdered your father?"

Akira's breath caught in her throat. The Beast killed Calin's father? She shot Kendrick a questioning scowl.

He looked away.

"I've not forgotten and dinnae accuse me of doing so." Calin peered at her from the corner of his eye. She sensed he hadn't wanted the secrets of his father's death divulged in such a manner, but her gut told her to trust her husband.

"Then appease your king and marry Catriona. Keep Akira as your leman, if ye so desire."

Akira choked on the acidic repulsion filling her throat. Kerk's suggestion was utter madness. Just as she thought the words, Calin acted on them. He lunged across the table, knocking pewter goblets to the floor. Both hands clutched Kerk's throat while he asked his saints for stoicism.

Unable to watch the men behave like their barbarian ancestors, Akira bolted upright from her chair. "Cease!"

The five elders sitting at the high table studied her as if she'd fallen from the sky. Even Dougall snapped awake and wiped the slobber from his chin. Had they even known she was still there? Calin's cheeks were red with fury and his uncle Kerk's face had gone pallid beneath the clutches of her husband's rigid fingers.

"I've a proposition for ye. Unhand your uncle, m'laird, and hear me." Trying to control the uneven cadence of her pounding heart, Akira smoothed her kirtle and clasped her hands to keep them from trembling. Calin was wrong. His refusal to annul their marriage put too many lives in jeopardy, including his own. She couldn't bear the penalty. Akira swallowed hard. "Your arrogance has hindered your memories, m'lords. Might I remind ye King James brought down the Lord o' the Isles less than a decade ago. Ye would be acting self-righteous to believe ye can ignore his requisition. I dinnae wish to defy him, causing the ruination of life as we know it. King James seeks peace, as do I. If ye will agree to send your warriors to my brother's aid and rid Clan Kinnon of their laird, I'll agree to the annulment and return to Kinnon soil."

"Aye." Six voices voted.

"Nay," Calin declined in unison.

Akira bowed her head and accepted the vote while her heart cleaved in two. "Your council has spoken, m'laird. Ye must respect their decision."

Akira held herself tall and departed the hall, but the moment she passed beneath the archway, she ran for the solitude of her solar as quickly as her brogues would carry her. Tears soaked the blue and green sash she wore so proudly.

"Ye should be ashamed o' yourselves." Calin's aunt Wanda rounded the entranceway and seated every man with a piercing gaze. Dark-red fiery tresses framed the ire burning in her cheeks. Calin sensed the wrath she was about to unleash would topple the devil's battalion. Though unaware of how long she'd listened to their deliberations, he could only hope she sided with him. He needed an ally.

"That woman"—she pointed at the empty archway—"is the Lady o' Cànwyck Castle and ye treat her with no more reverence than a pocked beggar. She has displayed more courage and nobility in two months' time than any one o' ye has delivered in a decade." Wanda filled her lungs with air, glared at Uncle Kerk, and redirected her long finger at him. "And ye. It galls me to call ye husband. Ye may as weel have branded her a whore. I've the mind to take a blade to your bollocks and have Mattie cook them slowly over the spit. Ye've nay use for them. Ye have displayed nay courage in the titles ye bear. Nay loyalty to your kinswomen."

Wanda crossed her arms over her breast and paced in front of the high table of gawping men. "Did any of ye know our Elsbeth had a husband when she came here?" Wanda didn't give them time to answer. "Nay. Ye cared not a wit to inquire. Ye married her off to a mon who lays with her sister. The same whore ye've all probably bedded down with. Including ye."

Uncle Kerk's adam's apple slid up and down while his eyes rounded. "Darling, ye—"

"Dinnae darling me, ye addleheaded arse. Think ye King James is a force to be reckoned with. Wait till your women hear o' your decision. Ye will all wish ye had unsheathed your swords for m'lady's place here with us. The children adore her, and she has bonded our kinswomen over the making of a quilt. A quilt I wager none of ye has laid eyes on. Weel, I for one think it is beautiful, and it represents the one thing ye auld fools have neglected—devotion." Her eyes narrowed yet further. "Ye are worthless men. Ye think with your cocks and not with your minds. Weel, I hope your cocks keep ye warm at night, for your kinswomen will not." Aunt Wanda ended her tirade with one final comment. "I trust by morn the brilliant leaders of Clan MacLeod will see the error in choosing the path your King James has conveniently laid for ye. Otherwise, I'll gather the women. Fare ye weel . . . *darling*." The word oozed off her tongue, just before she twirled out of the hall with dignified grace.

Calin was aghast. Women held more power in the tips of their wee fingers than any warlord he'd ever known. A tinge of hope rekindled behind his breastbone.

Kerk appeared ill, his face ashen, his hands cupped over his groin.

Kendrick grinned, and Calin was thankful for his presence.

"Weel. What say ye to that, Uncle?" Calin crossed his arms and gloated as if he'd just defeated England single-handedly. He always did like Aunt Wanda.

"'Tis horseshite," Uncle Kerk grumbled. "Women. They'll be the death o' Scotland."

"Aye. Horseshite indeed," Calin agreed. "But your lady wife has ye by the—"

"Dinnae say it," Uncle Kerk bit off his words. "I suspect we must find a way to keep your lassie part of our kin. Else, we find our bollocks skewered over the spit, as my *darling* wife so delicately explained. What do ye propose, son?" Kerk passed a flagon of whisky to one of the elders.

"We issue a plea for military aid to every MacLeod warrior in Scotland—from the Outer Hebrides to the few scattered over the Lowlands. Laird Kinnon's militia is not a force to be taken lightly, but some of the men who walk among him are rebellious. We can have five warriors to his every one within a fortnight, and Logan Donald's kinsmen are eager to lend aid now. We've only to light the torch and The Beast will have his war."

"And the king? How do ye intend to appease him?"

"I am nay concerned with King James' threat. The Highland Lords will rally against the crown on a dare, and this time I will take up my sword without guilt to fight with the royalists."

Uncle Kerk nodded once, the look of determination in his eyes reflected the warrior Calin knew still lived inside him.

Their deliberations continued until the pink light of dawn peeked through the stained-glass window of Saint Aidan. Too many warriors sacrificed their lives over the years to the ongoing feud between their clans. The council didn't intend to lunge into a war with The Beast's army haphazardly. Though Kendrick spent years building the rebellion, the majority of Laird Kinnon's warriors still pledged fealty to The Beast and an even bigger disadvantage would be Laird Kinnon's Lowland kin. Because Laird Kinnon had not fought alongside the royalist against the crown, he would have the king's support if he sought it.

Uncle Kerk rubbed both eyes with one hand. "We will summon military tacticians on the morrow and begin warfare strategies upon their arrival. Grant the blacksmith a staff for artillery preparation. The hunters will need to prepare for a militia of nigh five hundred men. A warrior cannae fight on an empty stomach."

"Unless ye've the mind to fill their bellies with raw meat, our wives will need to employ the aid of our kinswomen to offer suitable hospitality," Calin offered, anxious to conclude their session.

His uncle blew a snort of air, half chuckle, half dread. "Our women will need to be placated. This battle I fear may be the most difficult of all." Kerk stood and stretched his back. "We rest now. Go to your wife, son. We will reconvene midday."

Calin didn't argue. His lids were heavy and his body frail with exhaustion. He hadn't slept in three days. Crawling the stairwell of the west wing, he heard the cock crow.

The door to his solar squeaked open.

The curtains had not been drawn around the bed. Akira lay in the middle of the mattress, her raven hair spread atop the bolster, and the fan of her black lashes splayed over her cheek. He took a step closer and looked past her bare shoulder peeking out from beneath the coverlet. Clutched tightly in both hands beneath her chin was the blue and green sash Akira had worn since the day of their wedding.

He freed himself of his garments and slipped beneath the covers. Her smooth, milky skin felt like silk against his worn hands.

She turned into him, her eyes awake, alert, and filled with worry.

He kissed her and tasted her tears. He wanted to tell her she had nothing to fear, but mostly he wanted her to understand how much she meant to him.

"I'm not giving ye up, my love. We are going to war."

Chapter Twenty-Three

"'Tis a wealth o' tellin' ye blather about, wench." Laird Kinnon exhaled between rotting teeth.

The smell of his repugnant breath cut through the icy air and made Catriona's gut quiver. One filthy hand scratched his grimy beard, while the other did the same beneath his plaid. The Scot displayed the manners of a goat and his acrid stench ate through her nostrils like poison.

Catriona wouldn't have sought aid from Laird Kinnon if Wanda MacLeod hadn't ruined a decision weighing heavily in her favor. Calin's new wife possessed the ability to rapt people at will. The witch held Calin and his kin under the influence of black magic and Catriona needed a stronger ally to eliminate the peasant. Then she would never have to return to England or her father again. Catriona envisioned herself at Calin's side after the bitch burned for heresy. Then all would be as before.

The butcher's son proved ever loyal to her and most inform-ative. Not only did she know when and how Calin intended to attack, but also his intent to have her apprehended and sent to King James for crimes against kin and country. With little choice, she had fled to the foothills with Ian and his brother. But the abandoned cot-house filled with animal feces and infestation were not accommodations suitable to her tastes. A sennight later, Catriona convinced her lovers to escort her onto Kinnon soil.

The accommodations had not improved.

Now, Ian and his brother occupied a small chamber beneath the Kinnon keep where they had been stripped and chained to the stone floor. Catriona found herself at the mercy of Laird Kinnon and his mercenaries. Pitch torches flickered along the dank walls of the grotto and the rhythmic patter of rodents played a horrid tune in her ears. The leather straps binding her wrists behind her back made her fingers numb, and Catriona feared she'd made a grave mistake.

A chair, like none she'd ever seen, sat in the center of the antechamber. Sharp iron spikes protruded from every surface and the brown discoloration of aged blood painted the metal. Blades, axes, saws, metal hooks—all hung from brackets in the stone walls. When Laird Kinnon retrieved an iron claw from the selection of torture mechanisms, terror spiraled up her spine. She backed away from him and into the solid chest of a guard.

"I vow what I speak is the truth. The MacLeod plans to attack your fortress come the next full moon." Looking into Laird Kinnon's black eyes, Catriona repeated the information in an effort to divert his attentions from the device in his gloved hand.

"The MacLeod has tried to plunder my holdings afore and has always failed. I dinnae fear his militia. With the information ye've so eagerly provided, my warriors will crush him before he crosses Loch Ceardach." Laird Kinnon stroked her cheek with the cold steel of the iron claw.

"The MacLeod is powered by a force stronger than your warriors can conquer. He uses the sorcery of a heretic. A witch. One of your clan. She has the mark of Satan upon her flesh and her powers are fierce. You'll not reign the victor in your battle against him. Without the witch, you will fail." For the first time since entering the antechamber, Catriona saw a spark of interest in Laird Kinnon's eyes.

"A witch, ye say?"

"Yes. A master in her craft. She leaves the MacLeod stronghold every morn to practice her trade. Only I know her daily regimen." With this lie, Catriona felt a warm bead of sweat trickle over her frigid skin.

"Weel, out with it, lass. Dinnae let those bonnie fine lips quit blatherin' just when ye've somethin' interesting to finally say."

Catriona's opportunity to escape had arrived. "I will divulge that information as soon as my escorts are released, and we are safe from your stronghold."

Laird Kinnon's nostrils flared. Plumes of gray swirled beneath his nose like brewing storm clouds. "Your escorts will be executed by nightfall. Ye are in nay position to barter with me, bitch. Ye will tell me what I wish to know. Now!"

Laird Kinnon used the cat-like claw to slice through the laces of her bodice. The sentry dug his fingers into her shoulders, pinning her in place. Laird Kinnon's foul hand curved over her stomach and slid beneath the drawstring of her skirt. His palm pressed against her mound while his fingers screwed their way inside her.

She inhaled a quick scream at the abrupt contact.

The tilt of his wrist brought Catriona to her toes. "Speak or I'll feed ye to my warriors."

She knew the ways of men. Her father offered her favors freely to hordes of English nobility, but Laird Kinnon instilled a fear in her she'd never known. A fear so revolting she tasted the bile on the back of her tongue. "I will not be threatened by your primitive tactics. I am the daughter of the Crown Prince of Malaga. You will suffer the wrath of King Henry if you brutalize me."

"Your king strikes nay fear in me." Laird Kinnon ripped his

hand from her skirt only to grope at her breasts. He then forced her to her knees by her throat. "Tell me what ye know of the witch."

"Free me, and I will take you to her."

Catriona blew a sigh of relief when Laird Kinnon side-stepped away from her and tossed the iron claw to the floor. She would lead him to Akira, then return to Calin. A moment of calm flushed beneath her cold skin.

"'Tis to your good fortune I have nay taste for English whores," he said mildly then ordered his sentries. "Use whatever tactics ye need to find me the witch, then execute her escorts and chain lady English till her information holds true."

"Nay! I'll take you to her!" Catriona screamed, while the two warriors lifted her beneath the arms and then strapped her to a wooden table.

Chapter Twenty-Four

"Just five more, Isobel." Akira applied pressure against her sister's foot while bending her left leg back and forth. Isobel's heavy breathing told Akira her sister's physical endurance was near spent this morning.

"Please cease, Akira," Isobel whispered behind closed lids.

Easing Isobel's leg atop the feather tick, Akira stepped to Isobel's side and wiped the sheen of sweat from her temple. "Your legs are getting stronger every day." Akira smiled down at her lying atop the healer's bed and wished she could take away her sister's pain.

"Andrew, come and work Isobel's toes until the healer returns for your lesson." Akira directed her young guard to his daily regimen.

"I dinnae wish to be a healer like Isobel. I'm a warrior and protector." Andrew's face fell in a defiant frown, but he crossed the earthen floor of the healer's cot-house to do as instructed.

"Your laird wants ye to learn a trade and will only allow ye on the training field after your lesson. Now count to one hundred aloud in French today while ye wiggle each of Isobel's toes twenty times."

"Aye, m'lady."

Once Andrew focused on his duty, Akira moved to add a brick of peat to the fire and set water to warm in the iron pot for the herbs Jaime was collecting. The faintest blush of morn crept around the thin ox hide covering the window, and the drone of Andrew's numbers sent her mind astray. A wisp of black smoke held her gaze, and the bitter smell of herbs set Akira's stomach in motion.

She'd been ill every morn for ten consecutive days. A child grew in her belly, the MacLeod heir. More than anything, Akira wanted a brood of bairns to run circles around their father's legs. She played the scene out in her head often, and more than once she'd made plans to tell Calin. But the preparations for the pending war seemed to preoccupy the majority of his thoughts.

Tonight, she vowed. Tonight she would tell him about the babe. And before he went to battle, she would tell him exactly how she felt about him. She could no longer deny it. She was in love with him.

"Akira, ye look pale."

Akira heard her sister's words, but could do little to respond with her heart in her throat and her stomach churning. "Andrew, keep counting. I'll be back-a-ten."

Akira burst through the small door of the cot-house and emptied her stomach onto the leaf-covered ground. Clutching her gut and holding tight to the birch tree, she heard Jaime step up behind her.

"Ye need anything, lass?" Jaime asked as he rubbed her back with the hand not holding two bundles of wilted herbs.

Shaking her head in response, she sucked in cool autumn air until her breathing regulated.

"Have ye told Calin ye are with child yet?"

Akira shook her head again, vowing to never trust Isobel with a secret again.

"Think ye the mon should know before he goes off to war?"

Akira wiped her mouth with the back of her hand then offered Jaime a pitiful smile. "I dinnae wish to add to his worries, but I intend to tell him."

"When?"

"Tonight." Akira's smile matched Jaime's.

"He will be verra pleased. As will Aunt Wanda."

The nausea typically eased immediately, but another rumble rolled through her belly. What seemed odder, she heard pounding in her ears. Standing upright, she looked at Jaime. His pinched brows told her he heard the noise too, which was impossible. How could he hear the queasiness in her gut?

But the sound pulsing her innards was not her bodily protests. The thunder of hoofbeats vibrated the ground beneath her bare feet. Akira followed Jaime's wide eyes over the valley and saw the riders. A cloud of dust billowed behind at least a dozen Kinnon warriors.

Within seconds, they were close enough for her to recognize one of The Beast's sentries.

Jaime tossed the herbs into a heap on the ground then unsheathed his claymore. "Go inside. Dinnae be afraid, lass."

"Are ye insane? Ye intend to fight them? There are too many. Ye are but one mon."

"Go!" Jaime yelled and gave her an encouraging push.

Akira rushed to the useless cover of the cot-house.

"What is it?" Isobel asked as Akira helped her to a sitting position at the edge of the bed.

"Kinnon warriors."

"Rebels?"

Akira shook her head and willed herself to be calm. The water she had set to warm now boiled and filled the room with damp steam. Andrew raced to the window, wooden sword drawn. Akira heard the nickers of horses prancing just outside the door.

"Move aside. We've come for the witch," a man announced.

Witch.

The word that haunted her childhood echoed in her ears.

She moved closer to the door. Age-old panic surfaced behind her breast.

"There is nay witch here, and ye are trespassing on MacLeod soil," Jaime defended.

"We come by order of Laird Kinnon and will not leave without the witch. Now move aside or die."

The scrape of a sword being pulled from its scabbard lifted the hair on Akira's neck.

Isobel sucked in an audible breath as her hands flew to her mouth. "Jaime."

A thump on the thatch roof prefaced the crackle that soon followed.

Jaime burst through the door just as the tinge of smoke filtered through the rafters. He pulled Isobel to his chest with one arm and scanned the small room. When Akira saw the look of failure in his aqua-blue eyes, her heart hammered against her ribs. The situation at hand left no time for words. Smoke already filled the ceiling and orange flecks of burnt thatch and ash floated weightlessly around them.

"Andrew, swing your sword at anything that moves."

Isobel held tight to Jaime's neck as they ran toward the doorway.

"Stay at my back. I will fight them off while ye make a break for Calin's stallion," Jaime instructed Akira.

"With Isobel in your arms?" Akira asked and felt the helplessness of the situation wash over her.

"Hold tight to my belt. I'll protect ye with God at my side." Jaime jerked her up tight behind him and rushed over the threshold of the burning cot-house.

The warriors awaited them, building an impregnable wall of horseflesh. Their steeds blew clouds of fog from their nostrils, which only added to the chaos. Jaime set Isobel on the ground and then swung his sword wide as he attempted to back Akira in the direction of Calin's stallion. Amid the confusion, the drone of the flame-engulfed cot-house, and the biting pitch of Isobel's screams, Akira lost her grip on Jaime's belt. Andrew's small hands disappeared from her kirtle.

A hand wrenched her back by her hair. A stealthy forearm gripped her beneath the arms and then hoisted her up in the saddle in front of him. She swiveled to watch a warrior slap the flat side of his sword against Jaime's temple.

A stream of blood spewed from his mouth just before he sank to the ground at Isobel's feet.

In a panic, Akira screamed, "Send for Calin!"

The horse reared then all four hooves left the ground.

Calin sharpened his *sgian dubh* on a flat rock outside the chapel where Father Harrald administered the Sacrament of Reconciliation. Soul-cleansed warriors, preparing their bodies for war, had cycled through the kirk for two days. His garrison was prepared, and MacLeod warriors arrived in droves over the past sennight. The Donalds awaited the signal in the northwest, and Kendrick had sent instructions to the members of the rebellion. The vengeance that had consumed his life would soon come to pass, but, more so, he ached to be free of his secrets. Akira needed to know that Laird Kinnon sired her. If something went awry during the battle, he didn't want her secret still tucked inside his soul.

The horn sounded from the tower, breaking his thoughts. A falcon circled overhead. Both signaled an approaching rider.

Sirius appeared through the entrance of the gatehouse, barreling at a full-blown gallop. Calin jumped to his feet and studied the scene. A crop of blond hair bobbed behind the stallion's head. Andrew was bent over the mane of the warhorse clutching the reins and bellowing in high pitches. A sense of dread shot through his core, and the unknowing wreaked havoc on his mind.

"M'laird, they ran Jaime down with a sword and took m'lady!" Andrew cried out, tears filling the bottoms of his eyes.

Calin didn't pause to ask questions. He yanked Andrew out of the saddle and mounted the prancing warhorse. Setting Sirius back into motion, Calin kicked its flanks and raced through the barbican. Whoever had taken her would weep for death when he finished with them. He didn't care who they were or how big their number, he would kill them all. He drove Sirius hard over the valley, the reins digging grooves into his palms.

Terror thickened in his gullet to the degree he nearly choked with every pummel of hooves. Gray smoke mixed with the clouds above the healer's cot-house and tinged the air with an acidic smell. When he crested the hill, all four hooves left the ground. Then through the haze emerged Jaime with Isobel draped over his arms. A stain of crimson touched his temple, but, thank the saints, he was alive.

Before Sirius came to a halt on the slope of the knoll, Jaime had faltered twice beneath Isobel's weight. Calin dismounted and rushed to his cousin's aid. "Let me help ye."

Calin gently lifted Isobel from Jaime's arms. "Are ye hurt, lass?"

Isobel shook her head, fear puckering her face. "Ye must go after her, m'laird. They called her a witch."

"Who called her a witch? Where is Akira?" Calin could barely swallow.

Jaime nodded in the opposite direction. "Kinnon warriors took her. The Beast's blackguards. I tried—"

"How many?" Calin interrupted, now terrified.

"A dozen. Mayhap more."

Before Calin could form another question, a multitude of

warriors were upon them. Both MacLeod kinsmen and Kinnon rebels were armed and ready for orders, Gordon led the assembly with Kendrick at his side.

Calin sat a trembling Isobel in the empty saddle of a steed beside Alec. "Take her and Jaime back to the keep. Send for Aunt Wanda. Jaime needs tending."

"Nay. I'm going with ye," Jaime protested and wrapped his hands around Isobel's waist to bring her back out of the saddle. He pulled her tight, kissed her, and whispered in her ear.

"I love ye, too. Please be careful and return to me," Isobel responded quietly, tears flowing over her cheeks.

Jaime placed her in the saddle in front of Alec then moved to clasp Calin's forearm. His voice dropped low. "There is something else ye should know. I know it is a woman's place to tell her husband, but if Akira were my wife I'd want to know."

Calin turned to him, their eyes on the same level. "What is it?"

"Akira is with child."

Calin clutched his chest. "Oh God." The weight of Jaime's hand on his arm felt like a stone wall. His knees wobbled. He was going to be a father. A vivid picture of Akira holding his child flashed behind his eyes.

Jaime gave him a brotherly pat that almost sent him to his knees and mounted. "Now, I'm going with ye."

Calin nodded his agreement and turned to his brethren. "I'm going after her. Who is with me?"

The roaring agreement set him into motion. He mounted Sirius and focused on Gordon. "Prepare the clan. If we cannae reach her before they enter onto Kinnon soil, I will need the MacLeod warriors positioned outside Brycen Castle. The war has begun."

Chapter Twenty-Five

The smell had to be coming from the decaying carcass bound to the rock wall by all four limbs.

Akira held the wool of her skirt over her nose and mouth to deaden her senses. The odd heat thickening the air ripened the stench that had been gagging her for nearly an hour now. She questioned how the dungeon of Brycen Castle could be so hot with no sign of a fire.

The eeriness of this evil place filled her with dread, but she remained hopeful her husband would arrive soon. If only he could have caught them before Laird Kinnon's warriors burned the bridge. She prayed Laird Kinnon would stay occupied while Calin traveled around the mouth of Loch Ceardach. Ten lifetimes wouldn't be long enough for her to be free of the man's appalling presence.

Remembering the way he'd lifted her skirts to inspect her birthmark made her shiver. Though grateful the moment of humiliation passed quickly, what disturbed her more was Laird Kinnon's reaction to her. She expected him to order her burned straightaway, but he looked at her with the light of recognition in his demon's eyes. The Beast's expression of delight made her recoil in fear.

Could his curious smile have stemmed from some perverse excitement he received from torturing his captives? Or did he know she was sister and wife to the men who sought his destruction? The chilling questions were too horrifying to pay heed.

She had to escape.

The iron clasp around her ankle chaining her to the stone floor would prove to make that goal unachievable. A single torch lit the bottom two stone steps leading to freedom. The slightest illumination reflected off the damp floor where a woman lay curled into a ball. Soiled bare feet peeked out from what remained of her bloodstained chemise. Her hair had been hacked off close to her scalp with the exception of a few straggled locks hiding her face and neck.

Akira had touched the woman's back only moments earlier, but the simple show of affection caused her to jump so intensely Akira regretted startling her.

Was it possible the woman weeping beside her had been accused of witchcraft, as well?

Akira shook her head, answering her own question. This woman was no witch. Though her woeful mumbling could've just as easily been a plea to the Pagan gods, Akira knew those words. They were not of black magic. They were of prayer. The woman begged forgiveness for her adulterated sins and pleaded with her Maker to take her away from such an evil world. With her hands folded piously beneath her face, her body convulsed and rocked back and forth.

Akira called out to her again. The woman's only response, a woeful repentance.

The baritone voice of another prisoner hollered from the darkness. "Your God cannae protect ye in here. Now, cease your weepin', else they'll cut out your tongue."

Placing a protective hand over her stomach, Akira feared what might happen to the child Calin didn't know about and quite possibly never would. Her situation seemed hopeless. There was no way out of this dungeon. With hot tears rolling freely over her face, Akira flattened her palm on the warm floor beside the woman. "Lend me your hand, and we can try to help each other."

The woman's hand crept out from underneath her. The tip of her pinkie finger had been cut off at the second knuckle and then burned to seal the wound. Akira's heart jolted at the sight. Bruises and cuts circled her wrists where she'd been bound and grime filled the tips of chewed-off nails. Akira swallowed hard and accepted the mangled hand drenched with tears.

"Are ye a witch?" Akira asked, part of her hoping the woman possessed the power to free them from this swelter-ing prison.

The woman's head shook against the stone floor. "I am my father's whore."

"Please, come to me."

She crawled across the floor, her heavy chain scraping with the action. Her cheek fell against Akira's plaid, and her fin-gers twisted around the folds of Akira's kirtle. "Pray forgive me, m'lady, for the sins I have committed against you."

Though confused by her words, Akira brushed her thick chunks of hair then raised her chin to comfort her.

Akira recognized Catriona's gray eyes in the pale glow of torchlight. The single breath Akira inhaled tightened like a shard of glass in her throat. She released Catriona's chin. Her breathing intensified tenfold. Her sympathetic heart had ached for the woman who cried to her father and cursed him at the same time. A woman who asked God to reunite her with her dead mother. The same woman who set out to ruin her life now clutched at her waist, sobbing and begging for forgiveness. She'd been tortured and probably raped, and part of Akira wanted to believe she deserved it.

With her mind a deluge of whirling emotions, Akira questioned why God would couple them in such a horrific place. Then the answer struck her like a revelation. God. He was testing her, and she would not fail Him.

Akira wouldn't deny Catriona. Enemy or not, no one deserved such animalistic cruelty. She pushed past her hate and gripped Catriona's shoulders to embrace her. "If my forgiveness is what ye seek, then 'tis yours, but we must work together to leave this place alive."

Catriona raised Akira's hand to the side of her face. "I have nothing to live for. I can only pray for a merciful death."

"How can ye say such a thing?" Akira forced Catriona to sit beside her and dried her cheeks.

"The elders have agreed to banish me from Clan MacLeod. My fate lies at the hands of your King James. If he chooses to spare my life for crimes against kin and country, he will return me to England, to my father and my king. I am barren and am no worth to any man. 'Tis why King Henry gifted me to Calin. My father knew I would never produce an heir. When Calin didn't accept me as his wife, I feared my return back to England."

"Why would ye not want to return to your home?"

Catriona's face fell into her hands. "My father is greedy and cruel. He will not part with his monies or lands for my dowry because I cannot provide my husband an heir. He saves his wealth for his sons and prostitutes me to his gentry. I'd rather die than return to him. I have never known love or compassion from him or any man."

Akira couldn't stop herself from empathizing. Catriona had been sold by her own father and abused in ways more brutal than a man's fist. "Then mayhap 'tis time ye knew compassion from a woman."

"But I am the reason you are here. I told Laird Kinnon where to find you."

"There are many things I struggle to understand about ye,

Catriona. But hear me when I tell ye, I would have given up my enemy if someone took a blade to my finger."

Catriona gave an unladylike snort, revealing the side of her that probably kept her alive. "I am not worthy of your flattery, m'lady. Do not think me so strong. I forfeited your location after they cut off my hair and placed a blade to my breast . . . then they raped and tortured me anyway."

"They'll not hurt ye again. I promise ye," Akira assured her, not yet knowing how she would keep that vow.

Catriona's brow stitched together. A hopeful glint almost brought color to her eyes. "Then you *are* a witch. Might you conjure white magic?"

"Nay." Akira wiped the sweat from her brow and wondered briefly how the air could have possibly gotten hotter, then a shadow moved in the darkness. Glowing feline eyes winked at her from black folds of emptiness. Her heart flittered.

"But ye have the power to convince the laird ye *are* a witch." A hushed voice spoke to her from the pitch.

Catriona jumped and sidled up beside Akira, trembling.

"Who are ye? Show yourself," Akira demanded.

A figure garbed in a dark wool rounded the rock wall. Cats circled around deerskin boots. Most of the figure's face hid behind a hood, but when the person squatted in front of them, Akira realized he was a boy. Mayhap even a man, but no taller than she, and gangly. He absently scratched the gray ears of a purring cat with a hand puckered from fire. When he pushed back his hood, she gaped at his appearance. A long scar drew a pink line from his temple to his chin. Dark, thin hair laid flat against his scalp, yet didn't hide the fact that he was missing an ear.

He stared at Akira with glowing green eyes and then smiled. A childhood memory burst into her mind. *Darach.* This man had worn the same wicked smile just before he'd pushed the cart of boulders that had crippled Isobel down the hillside.

Catriona whimpered at Akira's side and gripped her upper arm with unyielding fingers. He reached out and stroked Catriona's head slowly, the same as he had the cat's.

"Shh," he cooed, seemingly seeking her trust. "I am not here to hurt ye."

One of the tabbies reared up on its back legs to rub its nose against his chin. His face smoothed, and he returned his attention to petting the three cats now mewling between them. Akira tried to summon the hate she felt for him. He'd ruined Isobel's life, and she truly wanted to despise him, but one only had to look at him to know he'd paid his penance. She couldn't begin to envy the life he must have lived in this loveless castle. But Darach was the last person she would have expected to help her.

"Why have ye come here?" Akira asked, unafraid of the man he'd become.

"I have come to help ye."

"To escape?" Catriona perked up.

"Nay. There are warriors at every entrance. The laird has positioned the Lowlanders on the Donald's borders and the Kinnon warriors guard the western crag."

"Lowlanders?" Akira questioned, certain she'd misunderstood.

"Aye. Hundreds arrived by vessel a sennight ago. The laird sent out a plea for aid when he learned of your brother's rebellion."

"Crivons!" She swallowed hard. "Does Laird Kinnon know I am Kendrick's sister?"

"Aye. And the MacLeod's wife."

Akira turned to Catriona.

"I swear to you, I did not tell the laird you are Calin's wife. I did not," she protested, shaking her head. "You have to believe me."

Akira suddenly felt as if a thousand insects crawled beneath her skin. Scrubbing the sensation from her arms, she feared a fate worse than death. Laird Kinnon would use her to get to both Kendrick and Calin. The same as he had Papa. The same horrific fate The Beast had forced on Mam and Neala. Akira's mind became paralyzed by the thought of that monster's hands on her. She cupped her hand over her mouth and closed her eyes.

Several heavy breaths later, she felt Darach's warm hand on hers. Opening her wet eyes to him, Akira wanted to weep. Wanted to cry out for help.

"I will help ye," Darach said, as if reading her thoughts.

"Why?"

"Mayhap to right a wrong."

To right a wrong? Did he mean Isobel? Could she trust him? Did she really have a choice?

"I wish for freedom from these haunted walls," Darach supplied. "I wish to ride a stallion beneath the sun and know the pride of my brethren."

Catriona sat up tall and clasped Akira's hand, giving her strength. If she intended to survive and give birth to her child, she needed fortitude. And her damnable pride wouldn't dissuade her from accepting their gift. "Tell me what I must do."

Darach smiled and nodded. "Ye must prevent Laird Kinnon from realizing ye are of nay value to him. Ye must convince the laird ye are a witch."

"I cannae! 'Tis blasphemy. I am nay witch. Ye place much trust in abilities I dinnae have nor wish to portray falsely." Akira had spent her entire life denying the accusations. God would punish her for such a sin.

"'Tis not blasphemy if the pagan words arenae spoken. God would see the right of it. Ye are saving his people. 'Tis a matter of war, of survival. I will be your eyes, and ye will be Laird Kinnon's."

"And I can be your voice," Catriona said in a deep rich

timber that sounded much like a man. "I have been able to change my voice since I was a child. I used my skill a time or two to trick my father. I'm verra good at it, lass. Think ye I sound a wee bit like your kinsmen?" The last of her words came out with a thick Scottish burr, and Akira believed they might actually be able to trick the old laird. But they needed time to devise such a plan.

"I can tell ye what to say, and the laird will believe it all because ye will use his fear against him," Darach said.

"Fear?" Akira asked trying to fathom what she could possibly do to scare a man of his demented mind. "What does he fear?"

"*Her* . . . ye. I saw it in his eyes when he entered the dungeon."

"I dinnae understand."

"Can ye not feel it? The heat?" He reached out and wiped a rivulet from her temple. A tabby's pink tongue licked the pearl of sweat in one swipe.

"Aye." She wiped sweaty palms down her kirtle. "I fear God has abandoned me and placed me in the fires of Hell."

"Nay. 'Tis not Hell in the Highlands." He chuckled and blinked his green eyes slowly in time with the cat's. "If God wanted to punish a mon in the Highlands, he would set him down in the middle of a frozen loch. The warmth ye feel is the presence of good, nay evil. Dinnae fear it, for 'tis her. I have seen her, and ye are her likeness. I followed her into the shadows when I was just a boy. She weeps in the nursery for the deaths of her daughters. She, and she alone, reaps a fear in Laird Kinnon he would never admit to. And ye must use that fear to gain an advantage."

Darach had obviously lost his wit over the years, which was understandable, but he spoke in riddles and Akira's mind struggled to make sense of his words. "Who is she?"

"Laird Kinnon's wife."

How could that be? The laird's wife died years ago in child-bearing. The clan never spoke of her, and Akira knew nothing more about her other than the cause of her death. Akira felt her entire face contort in confusion, then her senses came alive. Her cheeks burned, her pulse beat like a thousand drums in her ears, and a hum traveled through her body in a flash.

Suddenly, one of the cats arched, its fur ruffled. Another hissed a chilling sound of warning. Feline growls escalated until the cats scattered.

Darach stood and stared into the darkness, searching. "He is coming. Be brave, lass. Make demands of him. If he strikes ye, raise your chin to him. He feeds on fear. Dinnae let him see yours. I will find ye."

Terrified by his words, Akira summoned every morsel of strength within her. She caressed her stomach and asked God to protect her and her child.

"Please, ye cannae leave us here," Catriona pleaded and reached out to him, but Darach vanished into the pitch just as the wooden door crashed against the rock wall.

Laird Kinnon reared his ugly head beneath the archway, half his face cast in shadows. With his presence came an icy blast of cold that filled the hollows of the cavern, and chilled Akira straight to her core.

Chapter Twenty-Six

The blood in Calin's veins had flowed hot and fervent during the time it took him to reach Kinnon soil. He'd lost at least three hours because those bastards burned the bridge. But he was here now, standing knee-deep in seawater at the threshold of the cavern entrance, and he feared his limbs might combust from anticipation. The path ahead of him was as dark and heinous as Laird Kinnon's own soul, and the cold hilt of his broadsword offered him little comfort. His wife and unborn child were somewhere within The Beast's lair, and not even the deep-seated foreboding slithering in his gut could prevent him from finding her.

Calin prayed Laird Kinnon kept Akira alive. He could only hope the bastard wanted her for some belief in her powers, and not because she was married to the man about to wage war against him. The thought that Laird Kinnon might unknowingly rape his own daughter was a possibility he couldn't ignore. He pressed both palms against his eyes, fighting off the image that burrowed into his mind like a thousand rodents.

His entire future rested in the hands of the man who murdered his father.

Peering over his shoulder, Calin cooled with pride. Twelve

of his warriors merged with twelve more of the Kinnon rebels. Kendrick stood at his side, awaiting his command. Calin no longer fought for an alliance. Kendrick provided him with that. This battle was for the woman he loved.

Inhaling deeply, Calin gave a quick nod to Kendrick and led his warriors into the dungeon of Brycen Castle. A chain of linked men followed him as he groped his way over the jagged slick walls into pitch-blackness. The air was wet, and the vapors of death grew stronger the further they slinked into the grotto.

Soon, a low-burning pitch torch came into vision. Only two sentries guarded the prisoners. Calin held up his fingers and pointed to two stealthy warriors. The sentries hit the floor only seconds later, after which, twenty more members of the rebellion were freed from their chains.

"Find her." Calin gave the order and the search for Akira ensued.

In hushed tones, Calin conversed with Kendrick. "I dinnae like this."

"Too easy. Too quiet," Kendrick agreed.

"We've met little resistance. I cannae help but feel like I'm walking into a trap."

Kendrick shrugged his shoulders. "Mayhap God is on our side."

"God does not follow men into war. 'Tis the devil's occupation."

A prisoner, hollow-eyed and haggard with his hands still bound by shackles, hobbled to Calin. "Your men search for just one lass, but there were two. Kinnon's mercenaries escorted both lassies out o' the dungeon a couple hours ago. Just a short time later, Kinnon's men left their post on the western crag and swarmed through here like a band o' demons, leaving only the two sentries behind."

The slick blood drippings beneath the wooden table in the

torture chamber hypnotized Calin while the man conveyed the information. Calin closed his eyes. "Were they weel? The women?"

"I dinnae see them, but I heard one lass offering comfort to the other. The one that puckered my arse when the guards tortured her. A real screamer that one."

Calin's arm went into spasm. A guttural scream rose in his throat, but held tight between his lips. He would tear the bastards' limbs from their bodies for touching his wife.

"I cannae be certain, but I believe another came. Mayhap a gillie," the man continued while Jaime freed him of his shackles. "The voice was low and soft-spoken. Whoever he was, he came and went freely just before the laird took the women away."

Kendrick clasped Calin's forearm. "Akira's alive. 'Tis all that matters right now."

May Saint Margaret protect ye, my sweet Akira, and keep ye and our child safe. Calin checked his emotions, and then ordered two men to lead the weaker prisoners out of the cavern. The others awaited his order.

He had to find her, but walking into the belly of this fortress would be certain death to him and his men.

"I will take ye to them." The words spoken behind him were followed by the hissing sound of unsheathed swords.

Calin whirled around to find a small man standing at attention behind the threat of three swords. His hands were poised in front of him, and his chin rose, giving the warriors further access to his throat.

"Put down your weapons. He is unarmed," Calin ordered.

Kendrick circled the man, his narrowed eyes studied him. Pushing back the hood hiding his face, Kendrick didn't so much as wince at the man's scarred appearance. "Who are ye?"

"Who I am is of nay import." He returned the hood over his

head and nodded at Calin. "Follow me if ye wish to see the women." He turned and blended into the darkness.

Every warrior instinct inside Calin warned him not to follow this mysterious man alone. He would die acting reckless, making fool-hearted decisions.

So be it.

Calin quickly located the man's heels and followed him through a maze of hidden walls leading to the council chamber. The memory of the night he traveled the same path invaded his mind. The night The Beast stole his father from him. The night his soul found its mate. A cowardice child then, hiding in fear. But that boy no longer existed. A man had taken his place. A shadow who skulked through musky walls armed with a broadsword in one hand, a *sgian dubh* in the other, and a garrison of over five hundred warriors awaiting his signal.

His footsteps were muted when they rounded the bend. Then he heard her voice. Muffled by the wall, but her words sounded like a sweet lullaby in his ears. Akira spoke a mixture of languages garbled into words he didn't comprehend. Then came silence. Just as he pressed forward, another voice came to his ears. A voice he recognized as well—Catriona.

A manifold of questions overwhelmed him, but he gave them no heed and squeezed through the hollow wall. His guide stopped in front of him and pointed to a small slit in the wall which gave Calin a bird's-eye picture of the chamber. His gaze fell upon his wife and his heart pounded wanting to go to her, to touch her and take her away from this evil place.

She stood with her arms splayed out beside her, palm ups as if in prayer. Though pale, not a mar touched her beautiful skin. He followed her line of sight to Catriona, on her knees wearing a tattered blood-stained chemise. There was no mistaking who'd been tortured. Accompanied by ten warriors Laird Kinnon stood nearby wearing the same contemptuous scowl he'd worn the night he'd murdered Da. Sweat spilled over Calin's forehead.

His feet itched to run into the chamber and battle all of them, but the warrior and leader inside him kept his body in check. He would not survive such a foolish attempt and then Akira's fate would be sealed. He had to be patient.

Akira mumbled—a strange humming noise came from deep within her throat. What was she doing with her arms? Her head rolled atop her shoulders and her lids fell shut. Then with a jerk, her body stiffened, and her eyes flew open. The hair lifted on Calin's arms, and his body gave a quick shudder.

"Hear me, Guardian of the Night. I offer ye an unholy host as a sacrifice, if ye grant me your visions," Akira chanted in Gaelic, pausing to inhale deeply, as if her words stole her life source. "Hear me, Guardian of the Night, so I might free m'laird from the plight of the savages who hunt him. Show me the way of the warriors. Speak now through the unholy host." The last of her words came out as a bellow. With her arms raised high above her head and shaking violently, Akira chanted out the open window in the direction of the black sea. The incantation changed to the language only Akira understood, but at that precise moment her arms jolted and Catriona's chest and head snapped up as if a serpent just crawled through her body.

Calin was riveted.

Catriona's eyes were glazed over and wide when she responded. "They come by vessel . . . up the mouth of the firth . . . hundreds. The MacLeod leads the first boat . . . there is an order."

Hell and damnation! Calin's pulse became erratic. He crossed himself. *Akira is a witch?* Paralyzed, he could only watch, unable to tear his eyes away from the exhibition before him.

Akira's body convulsed. Her lips moved as if in conversation, but no words emerged.

Laird Kinnon appeared transfixed on the scene as well. The warriors aligning the wall stood at loyal attention, but even they were wide eyed.

"Kendrick, ye take the members o' the rebellion and scale the cliff." Catriona's voice changed tones. A perfect mimic of Calin's deep Highland burr. "The MacLeods will travel on foot. With the saints to guide us, we will meet inside the stable at the blackest hour afore dawn."

Akira pressed a hand to her breast and breathed heavily through her mouth, then turned to Laird Kinnon. "I'll need the blood of six swine, a garland of woodbine, the urine of a barren woman, and the bones of a rotting corpse. All this must be boiled in a cauldron for the remainder of eventide and given to the host just afore the moon crosses the sea at dawn. My host's body will need fed and rested before she is able to accept the vision from my Guardian. At dawn ye will see the slaughter of your enemy. The MacLeod is a fool to attack on Hallow E'en. The barriers are thin and the souls of the dead can only strengthen the Guardian from dawn to dusk on the morrow."

"Ye've done weel, my pet." Laird Kinnon grinned and brushed Akira's hair with the palm of his hand. He moved past her shoulder to give orders to his warriors.

Calin studied the scene, his heart still pounding in his ears. Just as he was about to turn away, he saw Akira's lips lift ever so slightly then she winked at Catriona. Though Catriona still appeared to be under some sort of trance, she returned the gesture just before she wailed out and collapsed onto the stone floor.

Unable to speak for fear he'd give away his presence, Calin silently ordered his guide to return to the dungeon. Once inside the safety of the grotto, Calin turned to Kendrick, a

smile as broad as the day of his wedding crossed his face.
"My lady wife is a witch."

"'Tis blasphemy!" Kendrick scolded in a harsh whisper
and drew his *sgian dubh*. "Akira is not a witch, and ye weel
know it."

"I know it. Ye know it, but The Beast is in the palm of her
wicked lil' hand."

Kendrick's scowl deepened in confusion. A dozen warriors
drew a circle around them while the small mysterious man
weaved his way to stand between Calin and Kendrick. "She
is safe for now, but ye must prepare your warriors."

"I demand to know who are ye?" Kendrick asked with the
tip on his *sgian dubh* pointed at the man's nose.

"The laird's son."

"Darach?" Kendrick lowered his blade at the same time the
collected warriors unsheathed theirs. Calin held up his hand,
ordering both his men and Kendrick's to withdraw their
weapons. This man-boy posed no threat to them. A summer
breeze would knock him down, and he'd already proven his
desire to aid them. He certainly didn't look to be the demon
Akira had painted him to be.

"Why would ye help us?" Kendrick asked and exchanged
a leery glance with Calin. "Do ye not know we've come to
destroy Laird Kinnon and steal the verra title he has secured
for ye?"

"The chieftainship of Clan Kinnon has never been mine to
want. Laird Kinnon has taken every opportunity to tell me I
am but a pawn. I am not of his blood, but the son of a whore
he murdered after my birth."

Darach's words were fact, but Calin was surprised nonetheless to hear the Kinnon's named heir voice them aloud. However, he had no desire to waste time listening to these two
men quibble over a title that didn't belong to either of them.

The chieftainship of Clan Kinnon belonged to his wife. He should have trusted her with the truth long ago.

"I can help ye," Darach said after a long moment of silence.

"And what do ye ask in return for your aid?" Kendrick questioned, obvious distrust riddled his tone.

"Freedom. A cottage, mayhap, on Kinnon soil. My needs are few, but I will fight alongside ye both to rid Dalkirth of that monster."

The warriors in their company didn't hide their amusement. Glances were exchanged and a mockery of quiet snickers circled around them. Kendrick snorted. "Ye are nay bigger than a whelp. Can ye even wield a sword?"

"Nay." Darach cast his haunted eyes downward. "But I am invisible to the laird and can move freely within these walls. The warriors who guard your women pay me nay heed. If it is your wish to deliver a message, then it is done."

"'Tis a fair trade in my way o' thinking. Loyalty for land." Calin decided and already contemplated what words he would send to his wife. "Come. We must make haste."

"Your blood boils, soothsayer, an' I grow weary o' this nigh'," Laird Kinnon slurred, his burr thick with spirits.

He staggered to his feet and threaded his greasy fingers through Akira's long locks, causing her stomach to rebel even more than it already did. When she closed her eyes to stave off another bout of nausea, all she could feel were his repugnant hands. The same hands that raped her mother and Neala, and killed Papa. She would be strong for her family's sake and the child she carried. She had no choice in the matter.

But her time ran thin. Dawn would be upon them soon, and she'd already finagled the night hours from Laird Kinnon. The Beast bought into her ploy about having to prepare Catri-

ona for the offering to her Guardian and sent two maids
shortly before dawn to bathe and dress her. Darach had returned as promised, slipping into the chamber from behind a
wall that yielded no door. When he pressed the MacLeod
brooch into her hand as proof of her husband's presence,
she'd wanted to weep with relief. Knowing Calin was within
the walls of Brycen Castle gave her courage.

She hoped to be back in her husband's arms, and shielded
by his protection soon. But for now, she would abide the company of The Beast and continue to play her ruse. She offered
Laird Kinnon her evilest grin, and stirred her cauldron of
bones, blood, and urine inside the scullery while an old
orange cat slinked around her ankles. Portraying the role of a
witch on the eve of Samhain unnerved her. Silently, she
prayed for God to forgive her acts and hoped He could hear
her thoughts over the blasphemous words she would soon
speak.

Akira peeked over her shoulder at Catriona lying flat atop
a trestle table. Her hair had been trimmed and smoothed with
oils, and the silk of her light-blue gown molded to her curves.
Gray eyes rounded wide and rarely blinked as she held the
pose Akira had instructed of her.

Laird Kinnon circled the table, his eyes mistrusting. "I've
never seen a woman so calm and obedient. Especially one
who awaits death." Laird Kinnon stared at Catriona while a
cat circled his ankles. He retrieved the feline and sat it atop
Catriona's chest.

The cat licked her lips, but Catriona showed no response.

Laird Kinnon ran eager fingers over her body, cupping her
breasts and lewdly rubbing her sex. He was obviously testing
the state of her hypnosis, but Catriona held true to her trance
and never faltered.

A Kinnon warrior entered the chamber. Akira recognized
him and hoped that meant he was a member of the rebellion.

He clasped his hands in front of him. "The vessels travel up the firth just as the witch said. The forerunner flies a flag bearing the MacLeod crest."

"Your magic has served me weel, soothsayer." Laird Kinnon dismissed the warrior with a gesture and then cast her an ugly grin. Before the door closed, he was at her side again, stroking her hair. "Howbeit, I amnae quick to trust a woman with your linaments. Black hair. Cold blue eyes." He pinched her chin between his thumb and forefinger. "Ye remind me o' my late wife."

I have seen her, and ye are her likeness.

Laird Kinnon leaned into her cheek. "I hated my wife. She betrayed me with the MacLeod."

His foul breath reeked worse than the blood Akira boiled, and his words caught her unguarded. Laird Kinnon had murdered Calin's father, but she assumed their feud was over land, not a woman. Akira controlled her expression. She couldn't let Laird Kinnon read her thoughts. Convincing him they were allies was her only option. "Then we share common ground, m'laird. The MacLeod betrayed me with that English whore."

"Ye disapprove of the marriage your brother has chosen for ye?"

"Kendrick is disloyal." She gave Laird Kinnon the words he would want to hear. "He has betrayed the crown as he has ye. He gave me to the MacLeod to further his plight against ye, m'laird. I had planned to escape Cànwyck Castle just before your men brought me here."

Laird Kinnon was so close to her she feared he could hear the blood rushing through her veins.

He wiped perspiration from her top lip and held the glistening drop in front of her face. "'Tis as cold as a year-old corpse in this chamber, lass. Yet, ye sweat. I suspect 'tis because ye lie."

Akira swallowed and felt her nostrils fluctuate with her

rapid breathing. She was failing. She was going to die in this chamber. *Calin, where are ye?* She silently called for him, willing him to her. Her heart felt his presence, but she'd sensed warmth all around her since Darach had claimed the spirit of Laird Kinnon's wife haunted Brycen Castle.

I followed her into the shadows. She reaps fear in Laird Kinnon. Ye must use that fear to gain an advantage. Akira had to trust Darach's words. "I dinnae lie, m'laird. The wall to the Netherworld is thin on this nigh. I sweat because I feel the strength of a hundred souls within this chamber. Your wife is one o' them. Their combined energy has sent my body into a fever. Can ye not feel the heat?"

Laird Kinnon ripped himself away from her so abruptly Akira almost fell. He surveyed the room, his black eyes perusing every stone in the walls and every crack in the ceiling.

Akira watched him in astonishment. Darach had been right. He was afraid of his dead wife. Akira suddenly doubted the woman had died in childbearing. The Beast most likely murdered her and she, too, sought a reckoning.

A chill crawled up her spine, but her toes and fingertips burned.

With his hand on the hilt of his *sgian dubh*, Laird Kinnon shouted orders to his warriors then turned to Akira. "'Tis the witching hour. Make lady English drink your brew. I need to know the MacLeod's next move so I can position my warriors."

Akira panicked. Her heart did a triple beat. She hadn't intended for Catriona to have to drink her potion. The ruse had gone too far, but if she hesitated now they would be dead.

The Beast's threatening presence closed in on her, so she ladled the boiling brew into a pewter cup wrapped in ox hide, then turned to him. "Take us to the highest point of the keep, and I will call upon the Guardian for the vision. Ye—" she pointed to one of the Kinnon warriors, "carry the host."

Laird Kinnon and ten of his warriors led the way up the tower stairwell until they reached the stone walk of the parapet. A yellow haze threatened the eastern horizon and the opaque moon dipped close to the sea. Gray mist curled around the glen, and the breeze of dawn cooled Akira's moist skin.

A Kinnon warrior lowered Catriona to her knees in front of the crenellated wall.

Laird Kinnon pointed at Catriona. "Make her drink it."

Akira's pulse quivered in her neck as she held tight to the cup. The rancid ingredients would make a wild boar ill. Catriona would never be able to keep the concoction down.

To her surprise, Catriona took the cup from Akira's rigid fingers and drank the substance down without batting an eye. Akira's gut gurgled and the coppery taste of bile thickened on her tongue.

Catriona threw the cup at Akira's feet, startling her, then stared Akira down as if commanding her to proceed.

Raising her hands to the Heavens, Akira chanted. She prolonged her mumbling until she sensed Laird Kinnon's anger, then she shifted the language to Gaelic. "Guardian of the Night. Hear me. Bring forth your vision. Speak now through the unholy host, and I will sacrifice the flesh of her flesh unto ye."

The salty wind picked up and blew Akira's hair over her face in a black web. She studied the sky over the sea—calm, clear, only whispers of living stars. But a cloud swirled overhead. A dark, eerie cloud, close enough to touch.

She held her position and continued to pray to her Guardian until a blinding bolt of light erupted out of the cloud's center. An uncanny sensation coiled inside Akira's gut then jarred her innards when the thunder cracked. She did everything within her power to hide her growing fear.

A fear that catapulted when The Beast snarled at her. "Speak the language of your Guardian."

Akira would not deviate to her family language. The cue upon which Catriona would deliver the vision. Once she revealed the final order, the Kinnon warriors had been instructed to toss Catriona over the parapet into the moat as a sacrifice to Akira's false Guardian.

Akira saw the desperation in her gray eyes. Catriona sought peace—an end to her own suffering. But Akira couldn't do it. She couldn't say the words that would end Catriona's life.

Another intimidating bolt of lightning impaled the sky.

Catriona quivered. She was proceeding with the plan on her own.

Nay! Dinnae do it. Akira screamed at Catriona through her eyes and searched her mind for a reprieve. The rolling thunder escalated. Akira turned to Laird Kinnon and shot him a fierce look. "The Guardian of the Night has been angered. We must cease or suffer the Guardian's wrath."

The cloud looming overhead lashed out a web of lightning. Then the sound of suffering crawled up the walls of the keep and over the parapet. Through the square crenel, Akira and Laird Kinnon saw the stable in unison. A mass of belching flames engulfed the structure. The men locked inside cried out for deliverance.

The Beast's evil face twisted into shock. Unsheathing the *sgian dubh* from his stocking, he forced the sharp point into Akira's breastbone. "Ye treacherous witch, ye tricked me. Those are my men inside."

Akira's skin grew clammy and fear strangled the breath in her throat. Her eyes searched the Heavens for help.

The angry black cloud darkening the hour of dawn could not be ignored. From the cloud's center shot another bolt of lightning straight onto the tower. With the thunder came the unsettling hiss of unsheathed swords. The warriors of three

clans emerged onto the garret—all led by the Laird of Clan
MacLeod.

"Calin!" Akira screamed as loud as her dry throat would
allow her.

Laird Kinnon's warriors attacked. The clash of swords and
metal scraping against bone filled the air. Akira watched the
battle in horror. A Kinnon advanced on Kendrick, but Gordon
took off the man's head with a halberd. Jaime drove his claymore through the chest of the warrior who'd taken her from
the healer's cot-house. Men fell to their deaths in groups, and
the blood dripping from their swords made Akira's heart
pound against her ribs.

Where was he? She searched the atrocity.

From the midst of the massacre emerged her knight. Her
husband. Her Calin. With his broadsword drawn, he advanced
on The Beast.

Laird Kinnon swiftly moved in behind Akira, pulled her
head tight against his chest, and then slid the blade up her
neck. Akira held onto his arm with both hands and watched
the band of warriors form a half-circle behind Calin. Her
head filled with images of her husband. Him holding their
newborn babe and smiling sweetly at her as he kissed her
forehead.

Her future.

Their future.

The sharp point of The Beast's blade pierced her skin at the
same moment a dull ache pressed against her abdomen.

The crimson trickling down her neck caused Calin's footing to cease. His fingertips burned. A dull hum deafened his
ears, but his tone remained commanding. "Let her go. 'Tis
over."

"Naught is over. I have men o' two hundred positioned

in the woodland awaiting your warriors," Laird Kinnon hissed back.

"Your army of Lowlanders has been seized. Ye are finished, Beast, as is your reign over Dalkirth." Calin tossed the hilt of his sword from hand to hand. "Let her go and fight me like a mon."

"Think me a fool to release her so your warriors can gut me down. Disband your men."

Calin stood tall. He had to control his emotions. If The Beast saw his fear, Calin would lose the greatest battle he'd ever fought. "Take the wounded into the keep. All of ye, go. Now!"

After much reluctance, Gordon made the first move to obey the order. He lifted Catriona into his arms and the other warriors followed suit. They receded back into the tower, leaving Calin alone with his enemy.

He had awaited this moment for years. His fingers itched with the desire to gut the man who killed his father. But even stronger was the desire to hack off the fingers touching his wife.

Akira's eyes went aflutter, her lips gray and quivering. Calin wanted to pluck her free of The Beast's talons, but he was helpless, just as he'd been the night his father died.

"Do ye love your wife, MacLeod, as much as ye did your father?" Laird Kinnon asked and pushed the blade deeper into Akira's neck causing the skin to dimple further. "Throw down your weapon or I will gut her."

Calin flinched. His heart plunged to his gut the same time his sword fell from his grasp. *Oh God in Heaven help me.* Calin prayed straight to his Maker for aid. "Let her go."

The Beast's laugh was shrill. "'Tis a wicked world is it not, Laird MacLeod? Ye reap this war, kill my loyal men, and for what? To avenge your father's death. But 'twill cost ye your wife's soul. Assuming the witch has one." Laird Kinnon's fingers twisted into her hair and jerked, exposing her throat even further to his blade. He scraped the flat steel up her skin, smearing her blood up the column of her neck.

She clawed at his forearm and cried out.

"The score shall be settled after this, MacLeod. I take your wife as your father took mine."

Calin battled his fears and the coward that awakened the boy inside him. The Beast would not steal another loved one from him. Throwing Laird Kinnon off kilter seemed his only option. If the truth cost him Akira's trust then he'd spend his life rebuilding her faith in him. "Ye cannae kill her. She's the destined chieftain of Clan Kinnon."

Akira's brow wrinkled in confusion, as did The Beast's.

"My son shall reign Laird of Clan Kinnon guided by my hand, and ye will never have your precious alliance."

"Darach cannae claim chieftainship for he is not your blood. Ye only sired daughters. Three of them are in the ground alongside your wife. The fourth I saved the night ye killed my father. I had her fostered by your own kin, then I married her." Calin could only pray he'd catch The Beast unguarded. "Did ye not notice she is the image of your late wife? She has Lena's eyes. Look at her, Beast!"

Laird Kinnon spun Akira around and studied her. Calin knew the bastard would kill her before he drew his next breath. Out of the corner of his eye, Calin caught the movement of a warrior tucked between two thick-stoned merlons. Kendrick stepped from the wall and threw his dagger. The blade sunk into Laird Kinnon's back clean to the hilt.

The Beast howled, twisted Akira around, and flung her into the stone wall. The blow bent her body in two, her chest lay flat atop the wall, her fingers clawed at the edge, her legs dangled. She cried out.

Calin spurred into motion. He flicked a small blade from his leather wristband and grabbed Laird Kinnon by his hair.

In one fluid motion, Calin opened The Beast's throat from ear to ear.

Laird Kinnon's legs buckled beneath him. He sank to his knees then toppled forward, ending his reign as The Beast of Brycen.

Akira slid off the wall into a puddle of plaid. Calin scooped her up behind her back and knees. Her head fell and her eyes pinched tight. Out her open mouth came a bawl of pain.

"Akira!"

White-knuckled fingers clutched her lower abdomen. "I am with child. Calin—" Akira's words ended on another scream, just as her body went limp in his trembling arms.

Oh Saint Aidan, what have I done?

Chapter Twenty-Seven

Akira's mind pushed through a haze of blackness. She was cold.

No, not cold—frozen, like her legs were trapped in ice. Oddly enough, her cheeks were warm, and she felt the pressing weight of down-filled covers. She was abed.

She sensed an emptiness inside her.

"My child . . . Calin . . ." she whispered, more to herself than to the presence beside her.

"Shhh . . . 'tis gonna be alright now. Dinnae worry yourself." A woman consoled her in a gentle voice and brushed her hair at the temple.

"So cold." Akira reached beneath the coverlet and touched the cool, damp towels packed between her legs. Then the devastation of her loss whipped through her like a hundred lashes across her heart.

Her child was gone.

She raised her eyelids and focused on the dimly lit chamber. A wide-rimmed wash bucket beside the bed toppled with discolored towels soaking in water. The gauntly woman bedside pressed a moist cloth against her forehead. Akira recognized

Gunnie. She'd been the only midwife in Dalkirth since she could remember.

Akira managed a question. "How long?"

"Three days, m'lady. I did everything I knew, but the bleeding wouldnae stop. I am verra sorry for your loss. So verra, verra sorry," Gunnie offered and encouraged Akira to drink a bit of honey wine.

Nay! Akira turned away, closed her eyes, and tried to dam the flood of tears falling from beneath her lashes. Why? Why did God take her child from her? As punishment for her acts of heresy?

Her mind, body, and soul washed with confusion. A grief like nothing she had ever known filled her heart and mind. Bits and pieces formed in her mind's eye of the events on the parapet. Laird Kinnon was her father. Blood of The Beast flowed through her veins, sickening her until she felt physically ill.

Calin knew all along.

"Please, leave me. I wish to grieve my loss in solitude," Akira choked out, then pressed the corner of the counterpane against her mouth and sobbed herself into a place she never wanted to leave. A place of darkness and broken dreams. This new place she called home.

The hand brushed her cheekbone then held tight to her fingers. A strong hand, one she wanted to trust. The rich scent of roasted meat curled into her nostrils. Someone supported her neck and pressed a heated cup to her lips. A salty liquid slid down her throat and coated her empty belly.

"Ye must drink. 'Tis been days of five. Please wake and eat, my love. I cannae lose ye, too."

Through the slits of her eyes, she could see Calin. The fire illuminated the golden flecks in his eyes and revealed his sorrow. She didn't want to see his pain. She only wanted to return to her sleep. To the place where she didn't have to come to terms with reality. But it was time to face the truth. The man she loved deceived her and used her as a means to avenge his father's death. What echoed even stronger in her mind was the absence of life in her womb. The life he stole from her.

She eased herself back into the blackness. Willed herself into the peaceful abyss where she didn't have to acknowledge who she was or what she had lost.

Calin pulled her tight to his chest. "Please come back to me, my Akira." His lips brushed her eyelids, his voice sad. "Forgive me, my love. I should have protected ye and the babe. I'll never forgive myself if I lose ye, too."

His heart pounded against her ear, and his words gave her a means of escape from her self-inflicted torment. Part of her wanted to sob against his chest and seek strength and comfort in his arms, but another part wanted to retract from his embrace and blame him.

He was at fault. He should have kept her safe, far away from the evil man who sired her. Now, her child was dead. The child she wanted more than life itself. The child Calin promised her and stole from her in his triumphant moment of vengeance.

Her heart hardened to stone, and her anger fevered her pulse.

Akira stiffened and pushed him away, surprised at how much strength she had physically. She stared into the empty room. "Ye have your alliance, m'laird. I am of no import to ye anymore."

"Akira, please. I have—"

"Nay. I dinnae wish to hear your words. Ye've succeeded in avenging your father's death, but at the cost of your own child. My child. I'll never forgive ye for deceiving me. Ye gave me a family, a life, and then a child, only to steal everything away from me. I am not twin to Isobel, nor sister or daughter to those I hold so dear in my heart. I am no one. I am but a product of your vengeance against The Beast. A part of your skillfully calculated plan to see his blood suffer, as ye did when he stole your father from ye." Her words were delivered with intent—the intent to hurt him as he had hurt her.

"Nay!" His voice cracked with dire emotion. "I never wanted this to happen. I never wanted ye to find out this way." Calin reached for her chin, his hand trembling.

She squeezed her eyes tight and pushed his hand away, not wanting to look at him. Not wanting to witness any grief he may reveal. "Leave me. I am nay longer a pawn for your machinations."

"By the saints, ye are my wife!"

Her head jerked toward him. "And your sister?" She hadn't wanted to give pause to this question, nonetheless, it had to be voiced. "My birth mother was in love with your father. Did ye ever consider the fact that we might share the same blood? Or did your desire to seek vengeance consume ye to the point ye dinnae care?"

"Lena came to my father when she was round with her fourth bairn. I was there the day he met her. She begged him to protect her and her child. My father never knew her before that day. I am not the monster ye accuse me of being. I am your husband. Ye must believe me."

She didn't know what to believe. The facts outweighed her desire to trust his words.

Calin gripped her face and pressed his lips to hers.

Akira refused to return his kiss, refused to allow his touch to weaken her. She fought the emotions rising to the surface—the ones crushing her heart. She wanted to hate him. With every ounce of her being, she wanted rid of the man who caused her so much pain. He deceived her, made her want for things she could never possess—happiness, love, family.

Calin rose from the bed's edge and turned his back to her, but not before she saw the trace of dampness on his roughened cheek. "Please, give me leave to explain."

"There is naught more for ye to say. Ye've nay power over me. As the Laird o' Clan Kinnon, we hold equal status." She had found the flaw in his plan. The reason he never told her the truth. He couldn't own her. She crossed her arms over her chest and prepared for his tirade.

Calin whirled around, his brow stitched together in confusion. "Ye will decree Kendrick as chieftain. He's your half brother and blood of the line."

"I've a responsibility to my clan to rebuild and bring peace amongst the destruction Laird Kinnon has reaped over Dalkirth. Go to your King James and concede to his wishes. Sign the annulment and take Catriona as your wife or choose another and leave her with me. She cannae go back to England, and she has already been punished for her crimes against me."

"Ye cannae mean this." Calin sank to one knee beside the bed and pressed his palm against her heart. "Have ye never felt anything for me at all?"

Akira's chest was hollow. Nothing remained, but an agonizing numbness. "My heart died with the child ye stole from me."

"I cannae go back without ye."

Akira reached for his hand and before he could stop her, she placed her wedding band in his palm. Her lashes swept down to conceal her pain. "Ye can and ye will."

Chapter Twenty-Eight

Akira stared at the lone candle burning in the corner of the empty chapel. Dust filled the beams of colored lights pouring into the place of worship from the stained-glass windows. In a trance, she held tight to her rosary and prayed for guidance the same as she had every morn since her conversation with the midwife. Gunnie had questioned Akira about her menses, and after much discourse, Gunnie explained that the babe had probably been dying before Akira had ever been taken to Brycen Castle.

A tear left a path down her cheek, and she absentmindedly brushed the droplet away. Crying was no longer an emotion she fought. There had been many to console her, offering sympathies and food for her table. She fought the outpouring initially, but found the more she listened to their stories and encouraging words, the easier her loss was to accept. Many had grieved alongside her for the loved ones they'd lost in the battle. Dalkirth had been forever changed. But the kinfolk had begun to rebuild—their homes and their lives, their sense of pride and well-being. Even Darach found peace in a cot-house outside the bailey.

Akira closed her eyes and kissed the crucifix of her rosary.

She wanted to find peace as well. She prayed for it, willed the ache to leave her heart. Though people had surrounded her for weeks, she'd never felt so alone in her life. Images of Calin flashed behind her lids causing her breath to hitch on a sob. She touched her lips and could almost feel his kiss. Her heart screamed at her to accept him back into her life, to forgive him for the secrets he'd hidden from her. Stubbornness made a poor companion.

The sound of shuffling feet brought her out of her misery.

Father Harrald grunted as he genuflected at the edge of the pew, crossed himself, and then knelt alongside her. Every wheezing breath he took sounded like his last as it echoed inside the chapel.

"Would ye like to confess, lass?" he said into his folded hands as he had every morn for more than a month.

"I am in love with my husband," she replied without pause and felt lightheaded from having voiced the words aloud.

Father Harrald chuckled, drew back the hood of his habit, and pushed himself back into the pew. She followed his action and allowed him to hold her hand between his cold callused ones. "'Tis not a sin to love one's husband."

Akira circled the bare finger that once wore Calin's wedding band. "He lied to me."

"He kept a secret to protect ye, lass. Laird Kinnon was a verra disturbed mon. I fear I couldnae reach his soul. Your husband saved ye from the laird's evil intentions when ye were but a babe." Father Harrald's voice was gentle as he tried to explain.

Akira turned to study the priest she had confided in since she was a child. Beneath bushy white brows, his light blue eyes seemed focused and clear, which was unusual. "Calin has confessed this to ye?"

"'Tis nay a sin to protect an innocent child. Your husband was there when ye were born, hidden in the walls of the keep.

What he witnessed would haunt a mon the whole of his life."
Father Harrald trembled. "It has mine."

Akira squeezed his hand, realizing for the first time the
priest had been there as well.

"He was a verra frightened boy then and could have just as
easily left ye," he added. "I would have buried ye alongside
your sisters had he done so."

Akira wiped a tear from her cheek while others quickly
pooled in her eyes. Her anger had died weeks before and had
been replaced with such sadness she felt hollow. She had tried
to push Calin from her heart, but failed miserably. He had
protected the secret of her lineage to protect her, and instead
of thanking him, she had accused him of stealing her life.

"I want to go home," she admitted in confidence.

"Come then. I will walk ye." Father Harrald moved to
stand, but she stopped him with a tug on his arm.

"Nay. I want to go home to Cànwyck Castle." In truth, she
missed the kinfolk and her sister, Isobel. But most of all, she
missed Calin. "'Tis selfish of me. I have a responsibility to
the people of Dalkirth and my defiance of our king's edict
could cost Clan MacLeod everything. But my heart is with
my husband. I am utterly alone without him."

"Ye place too much responsibility on yourself, lass. Kendrick
can lead Clan Kinnon if ye will it, and King James, in all of
his power, cannae prevent ye from loving your husband."

But did he love her in return? He'd never said the words,
nor had he returned to fight for her.

Father Harrald stood and held out his hand to her. "Mayhap
'tis time for ye to go home."

Chapter Twenty-Nine

Calin had lived through three cracked ribs and a broken arm at Glasgow, a sword wound to his back at Drumchatt, and a multitude of injuries from battles too numerous to count, but a broken heart proved to be the most painful wound he'd ever endured in all his twenty-eight years.

He sat in the shadows of his solar rolling the Celtic ring around his fingertip. The ring that belonged to his wife. A wife he hadn't seen in nearly a month, but Akira would come home this day, if only for a visit. She wouldn't miss Isobel's wedding.

The ring had been cold to the touch since the day she'd removed it. However, today the silver felt warm like the blacksmith just finished forging the metal.

He could feel her near, almost smell her sweet scent. Longing for his wife seemed a punishment for the most heinous of crimes. A punishment he rightly deserved. He failed to protect her. He betrayed her trust, betrayed her loyalty to him. His acts of deception had cost him his wife, his family, his soul.

Now an even greater punishment lay before him. He would suffer her presence, knowing how much she hated him. What would he say to her? Ask her how she's faring and offer her some cheese and wine? How could he look at her and not touch her? Calin closed his hand over the ring and gripped it into his palm.

The soft tap against the door startled him.

"Calin, may I enter?" Aunt Wanda pushed the door open without waiting for reply. "Isobel is ready and Jaime is as nervous as a mayfly in a freshly spun web."

Calin nodded, then turned to place the ring back in a rusted strongbox between an old feather and a few colored pebbles for safekeeping. In a rush of embarrassment, he returned the other keepsakes into the box and closed the lid. "Is she here?"

"Aye. Akira arrived not long ago with Father Harrald and her kin. They are with the congregation outside the kirk."

Calin heard the swoosh of Aunt Wanda's skirts just before her hand cupped his elbow. She had been there for him unconditionally. The fortress upon which he bared his soul, his pain, and his grief. Her soothing voice always chased his demons away as a child—today was no different.

"She looks verra weel. 'Twill be good for ye to see her again. The days we see of happiness are too few and 'tis necessary for us to be at peace together . . . necessary for us to heal. Ye should be at her side when Isobel walks through the assembly."

Calin turned around to face his aunt and lose himself in the comfort of her soft green eyes. "And if she does not want me at her side?"

"Then ye will give her more time." Aunt Wanda brushed the lapel of his doublet and straightened the MacLeod brooch pinning his plaid over his shoulder. Stroking his smooth chin, she popped a mint leaf on his tongue and smiled. "Come. Ye look divine. She'll not be able to resist ye."

Calin didn't budge when she tugged on his elbow. Every muscle in his body corded with anxiety. "What will I say to her?"

Aunt Wanda shook her head, rolled her eyes heavenward, and shot him a look as if to call him an ignorant ass. One of her favored accolades she reserved for Uncle Kerk. "'Tis not sacrilege for a mon to tell his wife that he loves her."

"But I've never spoken such words. Not even to ye or Uncle Kerk."

"'Tis because your uncle is an oaf and never allowed me to coddle ye with such sweet words. Said 'twould make ye less of a warrior, less of a mon. I should've fed him hot horse dung and told ye anyway." She swept her cinnamon lashes downward and toyed with the folds of his plaid. "Ye and Jaime are the sons I never had, and I regret not telling both o' ye every day of your lives that I love ye."

Calin stilled her hands. Age only emphasized his aunt's beauty. "Then Uncle Kerk does not say these words to ye?"

She snorted loudly, her dark red locks sprinkled gray bounced with the action. "Of course he does. Every morn and every nigh'. Think ye I'd be married to a mon who does not love me?"

Calin bent and kissed her on the forehead. He'd lived with many regrets in his lifetime. Not speaking soft words was one of them. "Thank ye. I am grateful to have been blessed with ye for a mother." He caught the single tear that escaped her eye. "I love ye, too, Aunt Wanda."

A blush colored her face clear to her ears beneath the words he wished he'd shared with her years ago—words that had not been so difficult to say.

When Calin caught a glimpse of Akira, he wanted to run to her, embrace her and never let her go. Instead, he feared his feet wouldn't carry him the full distance to the kirk. His stomach churned with the same intensity that gripped him when he raised his sword in battle.

Despite the cold, a coral hue touched her cheeks, and her jeweled eyes sparkled like polished sapphires with each heartwarming hug she received. Wearing a deep plum kirtle, she embraced the MacLeod kinswomen and children in overdue greetings.

Calin had not been the only one to miss the Lady o' Cànwyck Castle. The children had been devastated when Akira hadn't appeared for lessons, and the women moped for sennights during her absence.

But she was here now and, coward that he was, Calin couldn't coerce his legs into closing the ten remaining steps between them.

The smell of snow laced the crisp air and swirls of mist danced out his nose with each warm exhale. When the pipes struck up the announcing tune, the rustling crowd stilled in anticipation.

She looked at him.

He looked away.

Aunt Wanda guided him toward Akira then took a place next to Uncle Kerk. Lil' Andrew stood between them, a proud smile wrapped around the thumb in his mouth, and his chubby fingers latched securely in Akira's hand.

By the saints! She's your wife. Have the courage to at least look at her. Calin kept his gaze downcast, ignoring the voice inside his head. He was indeed a pathetic excuse for a leader. He couldn't even look at his own wife for fear he'd shatter into a million pieces.

He could feel her though. Her presence alone somehow gave him a sense of peace. He stood with his hands fisted at his sides and awaited the bride, as did everyone around him.

Visibly distraught, Jaime waited at the chapel entrance with Father Harrald at his right. In an effort to relieve some of his obvious tension, Jaime rolled his head on his neck and grabbed hold of the leg shaking uncontrollably. His twitching came to an abrupt halt when Isobel appeared around the bend of people.

Her pace was slow, and her weight favored one leg while she supported the other with a wooden cane, but she walked.

Isobel had accepted Calin's offer to stay in the keep during Akira's absence. Of course, neither expected Akira to be gone so long. Aileen and Elsbeth graciously offered to aid Isobel with her recovery, knowing she wouldn't marry Jaime until she could walk to the kirk. Today would be the first time Akira would see Isobel walk in more than ten years.

Akira sniffled, as did her sisters at her side.

To his shock, Andrew's small fingers threaded through Calin's. He looked down his nose and watched the lad innocently exchange his hand for Akira's just before Andrew sidestepped around her and back to his mother's side.

It took a great deal of restraint for him not to crush the slender fingers squeezing his hand. He breathed through his mouth to subside the burning in his chest and welcomed the frigid air passing over his teeth to cool his emotions. Trapped by her soft warm touch paralyzing him both inside and out, the pressure of a month's longing came full force to the surface. He closed his eyes and desperately tried to ease his torment.

Father Harrald spoke, but he heard few of the priest's words. What seemed like an eternity was in fact only moments later when a gentle tug encouraged his movement. The congregation followed Jaime and Isobel into the kirk for the second ceremony. Akira held tight to his sweaty palm and drew him up beside her. Only then did he dare a quick glance at her.

She smiled at him and the gates guarding his pain flew wide open.

He didn't dare hope that she might have forgiven him. That was a prayer he was certain had gone unanswered.

The ceremony proved unbearable for him. Hearing the vows he and Akira spoke not long ago and watching Jaime kiss Isobel shattered his already unstable composure. He had to gain control over his emotions before she reduced him to a sniveling twit. When the crowd followed the bride and groom to the Great Hall, he broke his hold with Akira and rushed to the stable. He couldn't escape fast enough.

Once out of earshot, the frightened boy inside him emerged front and center. The one who cried when no one was looking.

Akira watched him flee into a sparse flutter of snowflakes falling from a gray January sky. She hugged herself to ward off a shudder. The sudden cold crawled up her empty hand. The same cold and hollow feeling had dwelled in her heart since losing her child . . . and her husband.

Wiping her cheek, she welcomed Wanda's comforting arm at her waist.

"Calin has not fared as weel as ye." Wanda hugged her. "He still mourns for your child, but even more so for ye. He's just a mon, m'lady. A mon who prays every day for redemption."

Akira had felt his pain through her hand. He'd been hesitant to touch her, and she was responsible for that distance. The last words she'd spoken to him were harsh, but she'd acted out in anger. She knew now he wasn't to blame and, more than anything, she wanted to take away the guilt she'd burdened him with and whatever battles awaited them with King James, they would fight together, as husband and wife.

Akira moved to go to him, but Wanda held tight to her arm. "He wouldnae want ye to see him like this."

"I must speak to him."

"He's a mon in a great deal o' pain. I know ye have suffered a terrible loss, but so has he. Nay one knows his pain more than I. When he's ready, he will come to ye. Listen to his words and dinnae judge him." Wanda paused long enough to give Akira's hand a gentle pat, then diverted the subject.

"Now, your sister is celebrating her marriage, and I think she would be sorely disappointed if ye missed the festivities."

Akira accepted Wanda's wisdom and decided to allow him time to compose himself. She followed Wanda back to the Great Hall where the jovial music of pipes and strings only served as a backdrop to the hum of merriment. Jaime twirled Isobel in a dance and the onslaught of feasting was well underway.

A throng of kinfolk embraced her the moment she entered the Great Hall. For more than an hour, she accepted sympathies from the women and listened patiently to the children reminisce about their Christmastide.

A familiar hand tugged at her skirt. Akira knew who she would find before she ever turned around. "'Tis good to see ye again, Andrew." She squatted to eye level with the sprightly young lad and popped his nose with a kiss. He must have grown two full hands in her absence. Aileen beamed behind him with a new bairn swaddled in her arms, tiny pink fingers escaped the linens and swatted the air.

"I've a new sister, m'lady. I got to pick her name, because I was last born," Andrew said, as if he'd repeated those same words a hundred times.

Akira stood, her knees knocking, and peeled back the linen covering the bairn's face. She was an angel. A perfect pug nose, round cheeks, enormous blue eyes, and heart-shaped lips. It was impossible for Akira not to think of the child she'd lost. Her heart stung for the next two beats before she forged past her sorrow. "And what wonderful name did ye choose for such a beautiful sister?"

Andrew gloated so big his cheeks almost pushed his blue eyes shut. "Akira. I named her Akira. Same as your name, m'lady."

A steady stream of tears curled around Akira's cheeks and

into her smile while she lightly squeezed Aileen. How did this little boy always manage to inch his way into her heart?

When Elsbeth approached her, Akira fanned herself to compose her emotions, and then blew a sigh of relief. Thank Heavens Gordon had escorted Catriona to a private chamber until after the council meeting. Catriona had shown her naught but gratitude and respect over the past month at Brycen Castle, but the MacLeod kin couldn't possibly understand their bond. Akira could only hope Elsbeth might one day forgive her sister.

Seeing Elsbeth plump with child alongside a man Akira assumed was her English husband caught her unguarded. Certainly, she didn't expect Elsbeth to still be mourning Ian's death, but what struck her more odd was the crossbarred plaid pleated to perfection over the Englishman's royal blue doublet.

Only after almost crushing Akira's ribs, did Elsbeth offer a brief introduction. "M'lady, I would like ye to meet my husband, Robert MacLeod."

Akira extended her hand, palm down to receive his kiss, but cocked her head in question. "He took m'laird's name?"

"Aye. Much has happened in your absence, m'lady," Elsbeth explained. "A steward to the King of Scotland arrived just a sennight after ye departed. King James granted my annulment, and m'laird sent a missive to my Robert the following day. Since ye know I could not return to England, my Robert denounced King Henry and pledged fealty to Laird MacLeod."

Seemingly proud of his new attire, Robert exposed a wide grin behind his cropped black beard and kissed Akira's knuckles. "I am eternally indebted to ye, m'lady, for returning me to my wife and son. The information I supplied your husband is a scant beginning to the gratitude I intend to bestow upon your kin."

Akira's smile came slowly, but she only retained two words out of the man's well-spoken mouth—*your husband*.

Where was her husband?

Another hour passed painfully slowly. While trying to entertain idle chatter with the kinswomen, she watched the entrance and waited to see Calin's face.

She needed to speak with him and absolve him of the guilt she had, in her despair, placed on him. When the guests followed Father Harrald into the snow-blanketed bailey for the blessing of the marriage bed, she snuck away in search of Calin.

The stable was empty, as well as the kirk. Akira returned to the keep and climbed the steps of the west tower. A wave of angst stirred low in her stomach as she pieced together the words she would say when she found him.

Standing at his solar door, she questioned whether to knock or just go in. She pushed the door open and whispered his name. Her heart pounded against her vocal cords.

He was not there.

The wind blew snow beneath the tapestry fluttering against the window. Wandering about the room, she welcomed the hearth's warmth to stave off a deep chill settling into her bones. She curled around the bedpost and reminisced the time they shared as husband and wife—lost in each other's arms in the heat of passion. Her whole body flashed at the images those memories evoked.

As she approached the adjoining doors to the lady's solar she was caught curious by the odd-shaped stone painted with a red heart sitting atop the dresser. Picking it up, she studied its design and tried to recall why the trinket jarred her memory. An old piece of parchment poked out from beneath the lid of an unlocked strongbox. The iron coffer looked sturdy enough to protect precious jewels. Carefully, she lifted the lid and examined its contents—her wedding band, a small yellow feather, painted pebbles of various sizes, two twigs fastened by twine to make a cross. Beneath the odd collection were folded pieces of yellowed parchment. When she unfolded the first, she was taken back to her childhood. A drawing of a small girl holding the hand of a boy. The figures were drawn by the hand of a child with only dots for eyes and happy lines for smiles.

Akira retrieved another missive, written in her hand and signed with her name. She couldn't have been more than seven or eight when she wrote it. The note was silly. A memoir about how Papa whipped her for chasing the twins with a spider. Akira chuckled to herself, set it aside, and reached for another. The handwriting had changed. She was older when she wrote the missive, still no more than nine or ten.

Dearest Benefactor,

Ye would be proud of me. Papa took us to the fair at Retterseils. I won a ribbon for my poem. Papa dangled the ribbon in front of my sisters and told them I was his smartest daughter. I am sending ye the ribbon so ye might keep it safe until ye come for me. I worry my sisters may want to ruin it.

I am also sending these magic pebbles. I bought them at the fair from a gypsy who said they would yield me a great fortune. They have not worked for me and I thought ye might know how to use them.

Yours most affectionately,
Akira

Akira smiled as she recalled the fair at Mercat Cross. Mam and Papa took them every year, and every year they bickered over something so trivial it wasn't worth recollecting. Despite the petty badgering among siblings, Akira had been raised by a family who loved her. And they still loved her. They had returned from Clan Donald and were at her side when her world was lost. She condemned Calin for stealing her life from her when, in fact, he was the one who gave her life.

Adrift in her musing, Akira jumped when Calin reached over her shoulder and snatched the missive from her hand.

"What are ye doing here? These are my belongings." Calin's bronze color flushed a brilliant red as he returned everything back to the strongbox and latched it.

"Ye saved every trinket I ever sent ye. All these years Why?"

"Because they were from ye. From the girl I would one day make my bride and cherish for the rest of my life. The gir who once trusted me to protect her most valuable things." He blew an embarrassed breath and tucked the box into the shadows of the anteroom.

If Akira hadn't already loved him, she would after that admission. What grown man keeps such things? She stood dumbfounded in the middle of the chamber. Her jaw open and poised to speak, but her mind could form no words.

"I was a foolish boy then. I protected your magic pebbles and heart of stone, but I wasnae mon enough to protect ye or your child." Calin crossed the room in three strides. "Ye may sleep in either solar. The maids just laundered the linens. I'l have Evie bring ye warm water."

"Wait. Where are ye going?" Akira stopped him just before he stepped over the threshold.

His broad shoulders fell and his head hung low. "I cannae be this close to ye and not touch ye."

Akira ran to him before he disappeared into the darkened corridor. She cupped his hand over her cheek and stole a glimpse into his sorrowful eyes. Knowing she had caused his pain, she wanted to take it away and make it her own. "Then touch me, but dinnae leave."

Chapter Thirty

Calin pulled Akira into his chest. The strength of his embrace frightened her. "I am so verra sorry. I never meant to hurt ye. I never meant to deceive ye or cause the death of our child."

She wept against his chest, and for the first time, she experienced a sense of freedom from her loss. Longing to release him from his guilt, she stepped away and dried her eyes on her sleeve. She cradled his strong jaw in her hands and swallowed. "Ye dinnae cause it. I blamed ye because I had no one else to blame. I was devastated and angry with ye. But I dinnae blame ye, or God or myself anymore."

"I could've prevented it all had I not been such a coward. I should have protected ye."

"Hear me, Calin. I was bleeding before Laird Kinnon's men came for me. I dinnae realize it at the time, but I was already losing the babe. Our midwife explained many things to me. Ye cannae blame yourself, and I was wrong to accuse ye of such."

Calin brought her palm to his lips. "Believe me when I tell ye, I wanted that child. There was never an underlying scheme to see ye suffer. I dinnae marry ye for vengeance. I should've told ye the truth, but I feared losing ye."

Akira tugged on his hand with both of hers, coaxing him back into the chamber enough to close the door. "Then tell me now." She guided him to the cushioned bench beside the peat fire burning in the hearth. "I wish to know of my mother. And of the night of my birth. Father Harrald said ye were there, but he dinnae say more."

Calin squeezed his eyes tight and shook his head. "'Tis too painful. I'll not burden ye with such nightmares. 'Tis enough for ye to know that Laird Kinnon was your father, but only in blood. Naught more."

Akira leaned in and traced his stubborn eyebrow with the tip of her finger. "Please, Calin. I want to know. Dinnae keep the truth from me any longer."

Calin contemplated while he stroked the soft skin between her thumb and forefinger. Then finally, the words came. "Your mother was beautiful. Ye look just like her. Same blue eyes, same silky black hair. Lena gave birth to three other daughters afore ye. They all died shortly after."

"The Beast murdered them because they were girls?" Akira asked, unable to fathom what her mother must have endured.

Calin shrugged. "I cannae say for certain, but Lena believed he did. 'Tis why she came to my father. To ask for his protection." He redirected his gaze to the floor rushes. "I think he fell in love with her almost instantly. They stole away together at the border as often as they could. She was kind to me, and I watched her belly grow until time grew too short for them to meet. I remember the last time she came to Da. A bruise tinted the side of her face and her eyes were swollen from tears. She pleaded with Da to push the alliance between our clans."

"Why?"

"To protect ye. Lena believed she carried another daughter. She had dressed as a peasant and gone into Kilmarck to seek out a soothsayer. The seer drained blood from her belly and performed a ritual, after which she assured Lena she carried a lass. Lena feared Laird Kinnon would kill ye and believed our union was the only way to save ye. She made Da promise to protect ye until we were old enough to wed. I suspect she knew her death was imminent. Either by childbearing or at the hands of her husband."

Calin now stared into the empty room as if watching the scene play out in front of him. "Laird Kinnon was suspicious of Da's relationship with her. Their adulteress acts were probably the reason he agreed to our union. He never intended to follow through. He had Darach bundled in an antechamber awaiting presentation before ye ever came out of the womb." Calin's chin sank lower to his chest with every word. His strong features hardened.

"Think ye the mon would've had the decency to let your mother give birth in a privy chamber, but he paraded her pain in front of Da until she delivered ye on the council table. As soon as ye were born, Laird Kinnon ordered the slaughter of my father and his men then presented Darach as his son to the villagers o' Dalkirth."

Holding her breath, Akira sobbed internally, but she didn't dare stop him. She wanted more than anything to know what happened to her and her mother.

"Laird Kinnon's warriors killed the MacLeod men and then ran my father through with a halberd while Da placed a kiss upon Lena's lips. Ye rested at her breast when they . . ." He paused, a small vein in his temple started to protrude.

She wiped her eyes, sniffled, and inhaled a shaky breath. Holding his hand as comfort, Akira consoled him. "Tell me. I need to know."

"They cut your mother's throat then confessed their sins to Father Harrald before they fled." Calin's voice settled into a husky whisper as if the words he guarded had never once crossed his lips.

"I believe my mother is at peace now. She was there ye know. At Brycen Castle. Her spirit." After Laird Kinnon's death, Darach had searched Brycen Castle for a trace of her mother's warmth. The constant cold that had always been prevalent had dissipated. Father Harrald had accompanied Akira to her mother's grave and blessed the ground her mother and sisters had been buried in.

"Mayhap, she couldnae leave this earth until she knew ye were safe," Calin said.

Offering him a tender smile, Akira saw the young and frightened boy in his eyes. What he'd lived through could have turned his heart to ash, but Calin had chosen to protect her. "Ye have kept me safe. The same as ye did that night. Ye saved me."

He kissed the inside of her wrist. "There is more." Calin folded both her hands together in his as if what he was about to say might cause her to flee. "The mark. The one that has caused ye such grief. 'Tis not the mark of the devil. 'Tis the MacLeod crest. The head of a bull." He pulled off his signet ring and placed it in her hand for her to study.

Holding the gold band beneath her nose, Akira focused on the horned animal. "I dinnae understand."

"My mother died birthing me. Her death caused Da to become obsessed with his possessions. He marked what belonged to him with this symbol." Calin gestured around the solar. "His targe, his claymore, his livestock. When I was but years of seven, I climbed over the curtain wall to follow my father's warriors to the Isle of Mull near Tobermory. When Da found me, he gave me a sound thrashing then branded the bottoms of my feet with this ring.

"I branded ye, because ye were mine. Ye were my betrothed. My father died trying to save ye, and I intended to seek the alliance in his stead. But my triumph has not brought me the great joy I expected. I've lost everything. My child . . . my wife."

And the truth shall set ye free. The verse flashed through Akira's head. She wasn't a witch. A part of her always believed she might be. The part of her that knew she was different from her sisters, yet wanted so very much to belong.

Calin's hand caressed the side of her cheek. "I'd give a thousand lifetimes to return to that night."

Like a seasoned player, her heart directed her and told her to forgive him and bury the past. Reaching for his hand, she returned the signet ring to his finger then brought him to his feet in front of her. She splayed her hands against his—palm to palm. "But we only have this one lifetime, and I want to spend it with ye. I want to come home, Calin." He pressed his brow to hers. Akira felt his hot breath on her face and ached for it. "Ye are my husband and I am your wife."

"Ye are more than my wife." Calin pulled her fingers to his ear. "Ye are my soul mate, and I love ye."

For a timeless moment her heart stilled. A wild energy exploded inside her belly and flitted behind her breast. Akira closed her eyes and drew his bottom lip between hers. She tasted the salt of his tears, or were they hers. They were not tears of sadness, but tears of joy.

Calin loved her.

When she pulled away, she echoed his words. "I love ye, too, my Calin."

Calin wondered if he was trapped inside a dream. Everything seemed so surreal. An intoxicating sense of contentment made him lightheaded and giddy. He could hardly believe he held his wife. A wife who loved him.

He disappeared into the antechamber only to reemerge with her wedding band. He placed the ring on her finger. "Ye are my wife, my love . . . my Akira, and I've been dead inside without ye."

He held her neck and brushed her cheek with the pad of his thumb. He inhaled her air. "Sweet Akira," he whispered into her mouth. "Breathe my soul back into my body."

He kissed her gently. A kiss so filled with love it made his chest burn.

Akira stepped out of his arms and unfastened the brooch at his shoulder, loosening the pleats of his plaid. He removed his thick leather belt holding his sporran and sword. The jacket came next, then his *léine* shirt. She traced the new blue ring that circled his arm, the one that would forever remind him of the loss of his child.

Akira ran her hot hands over his skin, paying heed to every muscle in his torso before she placed her silky lips over his heart.

Her blue eyes glowed with hope as she looked up at him. "I love your heart and I love that ye are gentle with me. I love that ye have magic pebbles in a strongbox instead of gold and rubies."

Calin would have snorted in utter humiliation at that last comment, but he could do little more than breathe with her hands and lips caressing him. She twined her fingers through the sparse hairs dusting his chest then suckled his nipple between her teeth.

He set her back, never once breaking the trance between their eyes. He removed her brooch and *arisaid* in much the same way she had disrobed him. Of course, he was aroused by her nakedness—fully erect, in fact. But the desire to have her seemed somehow different. The urgency was gone and he only wanted to touch her soul—his soul. He believed they were one and the same.

He encircled her waist with both hands and bent to kiss the milky white flesh above her heart. "I love your heart as weel, and I love your strength and your courage."

His lips brushed the valleys of her collarbone and up her

neck until he suckled her tender earlobe. "I love the way ye rub my ear between your fingers, and I love the sweet taste of your skin," he whispered into the whorl of her ear.

Akira sprouted bumps and her nipples hardened against his chest. This could not be ignored. Calin bent and tickled the base of her breast with the tip of his nose. His tongue then swirled the perfect circular nipple, bathing her tight pebble with his saliva. Her upper body gave a shudder when he blew a cool burst of air around her crinkled areola. He showed the other equal attention until they both pointed upright at him. He lingered, taking each one into his mouth repeatedly, sucking and pulling until she squeaked and rubbed her knees together.

Calin moved to stand behind her and brushed her long black tresses over her shoulder. He scraped his teeth over the nape of her neck then kissed his way down the curve of her back, all the while titillating her sensitive breasts. Once he reached the bottom of her spine, he moved back to her ear. Clutching her hipbones, he pressed her backside against him so she could feel his desire for her then raised both her hands to her breasts. He mimicked her fingers over her nipples and whispered seductively in her ear. "I love the way ye touch yourself when I make love to ye."

Her only response—quick heated moans of pleasure.

He left her hands to their own leisure and dipped one, then two fingers into the hot wet silk between her legs letting his thumb stimulate her aroused nub. She pulsed and throbbed all around him and Calin was certain he would explode between the cleft of her shapely backside. Akira had always made love with unabashed freedom. Even now, she arched her hips into his teasing hand and made those sweet mewling noises that set his ears aflame.

"Calin . . . my legs will nay longer hold me."

A shudder rippled her body just before he carried her to his bed. A torch lit the side of her face throwing the other half in shadows. Waves of black hair spilled over the bolster. Her eyes glazed with passion, and her pinked lips were swollen from his kisses. She was beautiful, and she was his wife, and he adored her. He didn't care if that made him less of a man, less of a warrior. He would spoil her with sweet words every day of her life if she let him.

His hands molded to her ankles and followed the curved path over her calves. The pulse behind her knees fluttered in tandem with the beat in his fingertips. He tasted the flesh of her thighs until she rolled her hips against him and whimpered for release.

Akira was certain she would die, or combust into a thousand bits of charred flesh. The hunger intensifying in her loins seemed stronger than ever before. The tension building in her physically, coupled with her heightened emotions, set her pulse to thrumming in her mons.

Threading her fingers through his tousled hair, she yanked him back up her body. "I need ye."

For a flitting moment, they shared each other's breath then her tongue swept through the seam of his lips to possess his.

She moaned and he pulled away. "Is it too soon? I dinnae want to hurt ye." That constant concern riddled his voice.

"'Tis not too soon. I need to be one with ye. I want ye to make love to me because ye love me. I want to hear ye say the words aloud when ye fill my womb with your seed." A frisson of desire pooled in her womb. Their love overcame a lifetime of vengeance. A love that survived a month of grief which nearly destroyed them both. Not even King James could take this love away from them.

She reached between their bodies and guided the smooth tip of his manhood inside her aching core. So much time had passed and he felt so thick and full inside her.

She wrapped her legs around the backs of his muscular thighs and set the pace. He tried to go slow, but she denied him. The walls of her canal flexed and cinched tight around him, begging for release. But he continued the exquisite torture, pulling himself almost completely out before easing his shaft deeper inside her—one succulent inch at a time.

When she could bear the sweet torture no more, she cried out his name then the salvation of his fingers stroked her to a powerful climax. The spasms wracked her body. Waves of ecstasy washed through her, dousing the flames that threatened to incinerate her.

Calin released a fierce growl atop her. His arms shook. Sweat beaded his furrowed brow. He held himself deep inside her and pumped quick tiny draws filling her with a new life.

The weight of his spent body pressed her into the feather tick. They remained connected as one, lingering in the sensuality of their lovemaking. She paced her breathing to the declining beat of their hearts. After extracting her short nails from his arse, she caressed the muscular plain of his back.

Calin raised his head from the crook of her neck and kissed the tip of her nose. He wiped the tears from her eyes—tears she didn't even realize were there—and raised one dark brow.

Akira beguiled him with an impish grin. Her tongue darted out to lick her tingling lips. "*That* was the way I know."

He lightly brushed his lips over her smile then eased himself out of her. When he stepped from the bed, she practically fell off the edge behind him, so intent was her study on his rump. "Crivons! What in all o' Scots have ye done to your arse?"

He grinned a devil's grin and twisted in a way that allowed him to peek over his shoulder at his nicely formed backside. "Ye dinnae like it?" His tone filled with disappointment.

"What is it?" Akira reached out to trace the contours of a blue-black winged serpent tattooed on his left cheek in much the same place as Akira's brand.

"'Tis your mark," he said. "Ye wear the MacLeod crest, and I wear your dragon."

She laughed outright at the sight and rolled back into the bed. "'Tis verra becoming, but I suspect 'tis not where a warrior would typically mark himself."

"'Tis where this warrior did."

Chapter Thirty-One

The sound of trickling water awoke Calin's ears. What smelled like warm mist rising above a fresh spring filled his nostrils. Then came the faint aroma of her sweet scent.

Had he been dreaming? Had Akira even been in his arms, loving him throughout the night? Or did he sleep through the winter only to awaken alone once again? Pushing through the cobwebs of confusion, Calin forced his eyes to slide open and answer those questions.

She was there, her back to him, standing naked beside the hearth. Her hair pinned in loose braids at the nape of her neck with only a few stray wisps to kiss her shoulders. The hues of morning snuck through the narrow window to paint her wet glistening skin in pinks and golds. A pail of steaming water sat atop the cuttie stool at her side. She dipped the sponge and traced the contours of her arm, down her side, and then over her heart-shaped bottom. The path left iridescent bubbles over the perfection of her skin.

Her performance was grace in motion. An erotic dance only she could perform.

She turned slightly.

Calin was rewarded with a view of her perfect breast. He

parted his lips, knowing he should speak, but clamped his mouth shut along with his eyes when she twisted to look at him. He kept the rise and fall of his chest to a steady rhythm and held his face still as stone.

Again, came the bell-like tinkling of water. Barely raising one eye, he peeked through his lashes. The tips of her fingers lathered her neck, her breast, her stomach, then disappeared between her legs. She had to hear his heartbeat as it boomed in his ears like a thousand string-taut drums.

By the saints, she was exquisite. How had he never noticed the sensuality of her movements before?

Akira rinsed herself clean then patted dry with a towel. To his great disappointment, she disappeared into the antechamber only to emerge moments later garbed in a simple linen sark.

The bones in his fingers went rigid when he caught sight of the strongbox in her hands. She would think him weak and foolish for keeping such trinkets. He never should have saved them. If his men knew what was in that box, he'd never live down their badgering.

She curled up with a wool coverlet atop the bench, propped the box in her lap, and inhaled deeply just as she opened the lid. A smile bowed her lips.

Calin watched her read the missives she'd sent him as a young girl. She tickled the skin above her lip with a loose tendril of hair and periodically wiped tears on her sleeve. From time to time, she would hide a giggle behind her hand and roll her eyes as if embarrassed by her own writings. She stole glimpses at him between readings, obviously reassuring herself he still slept.

Just as Calin would have ended his false pretense, she whisked back into motion. Akira replaced the keepsakes, tidied up, and donned a blue kirtle. Hope struck a chord deep inside him when she pinned the blue and green sash over her shoulder.

She would stay. They would have a dozen bairns just as she'd wanted. All she had to do was decree Kendrick at the council meeting and admit she belonged at Cànwyck Castle with him.

The sudden intensity of her frown worried him. "Why would a woman who has been loved so heartily throughout the night wear such a sour face?" he asked with a quirky wit that broke the silence.

Akira's head snapped up at him, then came the wonder of her smile. "Ye are awake. I feared ye may have slipped into the sleep of the dead. Such a lazy mon ye've turned out to be." She held out one hand and arched a wicked brow. "Come to me, husband. I will bathe and dress ye."

"I would prefer ye undress and come back to bed so I can wake ye properly."

"I am already awake, and the elders await us. Think ye I want my husband to smell like a goat at the council meeting?"

He laughed at her, then forced himself to slip from the coverlet and walk to her side. "I have bathed more since I met ye than I have in the past year. 'Tis not manly to always smell of flowers."

She laved him with the water still fragrant with her scent. The aroma, an aphrodisiac to his senses, sent his manhood jutting against his belly.

She smiled and licked her lips. "Your cock doesn't seem to object to a good scrubbing."

His bold little wife had always been forthright and just as he was about to reprimand her for her unladylike candor, she wrapped her strong fingers around him and massaged thick suds into his taut sac. Even if he managed a retort, he doubted his words would make sense.

She bathed his shoulders and arms, then his pectoral muscles until lingering over his abdomen. Her touch ignited his nerve endings and wracked his body with need. Even the cool

water rinsing him couldn't temper the heat rushing beneath
his skin.

He thought she may have brushed her lips over his fevered
flesh, but reality became nothing more than a blurred haze
when her hot mouth slid over his erection.

He sucked in air sharply and fisted his hands in her hair
while she pleasured him. He moaned and opened his eyes to
find her staring up at him. Big blue eyes sparkled with mischief while the scrape of her teeth and swirl of her tongue
nearly caused him to spill his seed then and there. He jerked
her off him with a grunt. "By the saints, wife! Are ye trying
to kill me? Ye are wicked. Verra, verra wicked."

She giggled, wiped her mouth, and handed him a towel,
which felt like a handful of straw compared to the soft silk of
her skin. As soon as his mind functioned properly, he would
try to sort fantasy from reality.

"Mayhap I will let ye punish me later," she said, holding
up his *léine* shirt for him to slip into. "For now 'tis time we
meet with the elders of our clans." She began dressing him,
pleating his plaid to perfection. "Laird Donald has expressed
his desire to return home quickly before the weather forces
him to sojourn here during the winter months. The mon's
sworn oath is sufficient for me, but Kendrick insists on for-
malizing the alliance."

She draped the MacLeod sash over his shoulder then
pinned the ends with a sad smile. "There is also the matter
with Catriona. The charges against her need addressed."
Akira took a subtle step backward. "And as much as the subject may displease ye, our annulment must be discussed with
the MacLeod council. King James' wishes cannae go un-
heeded, and I dinnae wish to bring any trouble to your kinfolk."

"The matter with King James has been resolved."

Her brows stitched together. "What do ye mean has been

resolved? Has our marriage been annulled? When did this happen? I have signed no papers."

Calin pressed his index finger over her lips. "Come, wife. I will let Robert tell ye."

"Robert?" she asked behind his finger. "Elsbeth's husband?"

"Aye."

The council chamber hummed with the talk of peace and resolution. Calin, Kendrick, and Laird Donald sat among the elders of their clans. Goblets of dark wine scattered the stone table along with ripe cheese and a host of steaming barley bread. Father Harrald hovered beneath the colored glass portrait of Saint Aidan awaiting his duty to bless the alliance.

Akira stood at Calin's back, one hand resting on his shoulder, the other clutching two scrolls she had written. He almost felt guilty for making her wait through the formality of aligning the clans before calling Robert to present her with the information he'd only recently supplied Calin.

He brought the meeting to order formally. "Friends. Neighbors. Honored guests. 'Tis my great privilege to pay homage to the Isles' most illustrious leaders. A league bound by fellowship, amity, and trust. With this alliance, our kin will know the rewards of everlasting peace between our clans and the promise of protection for our heirs and successors."

Calin paused only long enough to cover Akira's hand with his own. "If it pleases the members of our council, I would call upon Laird Kinnon to dictate the conditions of the contract whereat a formal vote will be initiated."

A moment passed before Akira realized he was referring to her. She brushed back a damp wisp of hair from her temple, then proceeded to unravel the first of her scrolls. Securing the parchment beneath the weight of four stones, Akira poised herself. "This contract binds our clans together. Its contents state that we, as aligned kin, will protect the borders of the Isles and fight as one entity to protect our people and our land from foreign invasion." Her eyes fixed on the contract. "On this tenth day of January, the year of our Lord, fifteen hundred ought three . . ."

She recited the terms of obligation to be instilled in their clans. By the time she finished, two of the elders were snoring. She cleared her throat and nudged Calin to initiate the vote.

"Those in favor of the alliance respond." His booming voice aroused any man still lost in his thoughts.

"Aye." Their united agreement nearly raised the ceiling.

"Those against."

The chamber fell silent.

Calin moved to dip the quill in the inkhorn and sign the contract, after which he handed Laird Donald the quill, who signed, and then passed it to Akira. As the chieftain of Clan Kinnon, Akira had to sign the contract for the alliance to be finalized. He didn't know what caused her to stop and worry her bottom lip. A tinge of trepidation moved over her sapphire irises.

Calin wanted to comfort her. Instead, he scrutinized her conduct. "M'lady, ye wrote the contract. Do your own terms displease ye?"

Akira shook her head and drew an audible breath then unraveled the second scroll. "Forgive me, m'laird. I should have done this a long time ago." Boasting a proud chin, she spoke directly to the Kinnon elders. "With the blessing of my council, I wish to decree chieftainship over Clan Kinnon unto Kendrick Neish. As blessed blood of the Kinnon line, I bequeath the power of chieftainship unto my half-brother and heir of Baen Kinnon, deceased chieftain of Clan Kinnon."

Akira offered her brother the quill, delaying only long

enough to lovingly brush his hand. "He will undoubtedly make a brave and noble leader."

Kendrick pressed his lips to her forehead. "'Twill be my honor to serve and protect all those residing on Kinnon soil. Given the elders agreement."

The voice of the Kinnon council voted their favor in unison, whereupon Kendrick placed his signature at the bottom of both scrolls.

Her smile radiant, Akira sprinkled sand over the freshly inked signatures. Calin's heart rested and he blew an audible breath, drawing everyone's attention to him.

Father Harrald rushed tableside and blessed both contracts. Calin knew, he too, had waited far too long to see the clans at peace.

It was done. With the alliance formalized and Kendrick ordained as chieftain, nothing could hinder his future with Akira.

So why did she turn to leave the chamber? He had yet to even summon Robert.

"M'lady, ye will take your place at my right as my wife and Lady o' Cànwyck Castle. There is more to discuss that requires your attention." His tone seeped with arrogance. He felt like a falcon in flight. The lift in his lips could no more be prevented than the rise of the sun. Even the barefaced look of hostility puckering Akira's expression couldn't dissuade his good cheer.

"Forgive me, m'laird. I had hoped to discuss the matter of our annulment privately with your council." Akira pinned her fists onto her hips and narrowed her eyes on him.

He would probably regret not taking heed to her stance, but, fool that he was, he couldn't bring himself to care.

Why would he embarrass me like this? He claims to love me, yet flaunts our personal situation before a chamber of men. In a desperate attempt to diminish the council chamber by two-thirds, Akira donned a smile and offered. "Might we bid our guests fareweel first, m'laird? I'm certain Laird Donald and the members of his council, as weel as the Kinnon elders, have no interest in hearing the details of our marriage contract."

Laird Donald perked up, scraping a lock of black hair tipped gray from his brow. "Horseshite. I am verra interested."

"Gordon, fetch Sir Robert. He's in the corridor," Calin ordered.

What did Sir Robert have to do with her marriage? And why did her husband seem so delighted with the Englishman's presence? Akira dragged her feet over the floor rushes until she reached Calin's side. He spun her around, forcing her to face Elsbeth's husband. The weight of Calin's hand resting at the small of her back did little to ease her distress.

"Robert has something to share with ye, wife."

The Englishman bowed in reverence. "When I received missive from Laird MacLeod welcoming me to his clan, I had but three duties to achieve." Robert held up one finger. "Denounce the King of England, which as you know I did." A second finger came up. "Swear fealty to the chieftain of Clan MacLeod, which I have done as well." The third finger rose to join the others. "And finally to bring proof of the bloodline of one Lena Kinnon. 'Tis my privilege to be standing in the same chamber as the great-niece of the sixth Earl of Stafford and granddaughter of the Countess of March. Ye bear many noble titles, m'lady, but most important, ye are English. Well, half anyway, with a smidgen of Irish to boot."

Akira felt her eyes go round and her chin drop, leaving her mouth gaping.

Robert continued to smile, all the while he presented her with a large ruby and diamond-encrusted ring. "You've a great-aunt still living in Queensborough. She is widowed now, but hopes you might find time to pay visit after your King James marries King Henry's daughter. The Treaty of Perpetual Peace has been a year in the making, but soon Scotland and England will be at peace."

"Crivons! I am English?" Akira was once again beside herself with shock. She glared up at Calin. "Ye knew about this, too?"

"I only recently sent queries to England seeking knowledge of your lineage on your mother's side." Calin smiled and shrugged. "King James has been placated. Now quit scowling at me and allow me to revel in my merriment. My conscience is finally free of every secret inside my head. By the saints, have ye any idea how liberating that is?"

"Liberating! Free. I am bluidy English!" Akira pushed him—hard. "Think ye your clan will not have something to say about serving an English lady, with a wee bit o' Irish to boot?"

"If their great King James is pleased, then they will think naught of your lineage at all."

While she experienced yet another devastating moment, all her husband could do was gloat. He thought the discovery of her lineage a reason to be happy, did he? Did he expect the kin of his clan to serve the very blood they had fought so hard to prevent from taking their lands?

She hated the English. As did every Kinnon, MacLeod . . . hell, all o' Scotland hated the English. They were bloodsucking savages. *She* was a bloodsucking savage.

She growled through clenched teeth while her hands curled into tight fists at her sides. She wanted to knock some sense into her husband. How in all o' Scots would the kinfolk of Clan MacLeod treat her with any reverence? They had accepted her as a peasant, but no red-blooded Scot would pay homage to an Englishwoman.

Calin's smile broadened, making her even angrier.

"Ye keep smiling, husband. Mayhap I will travel to England and pay a visit to this aunt of mine. Mayhap I have a tocher. A castle? What say ye, Robert? Have I land on English soil I might be tempted to retreat to?"

"As a matter of fact, m'lady, you—"

"Sir Robert," Calin bit off his words. "Ye have provided enough information for the nonce. Gordon, see him out."

"Nay. I want him to stay. I've much to learn."

"Cool your tongue, wife."

Akira was about to throw another barb when Gordon interrupted the squabble. "M'laird, there is the matter with Catriona still to settle."

The statement caught Akira by surprise and she felt a surge of guilt knowing a fearful Catriona probably stood in the corridor awaiting her sentence.

"Bring her in," Calin ordered.

Akira's already piqued temper exploded when Catriona was escorted into the chamber wearing iron cuffs chained between her wrists. The clanking sound reminded her of the time they'd spent together in the dungeon of Brycen Castle.

Rushing to Catriona's side, Akira glared at Gordon and demanded. "Unchain her."

When Gordon sought his laird's permission, Akira nearly lost control. "Dinnae look at him. I said unchain her. Ye will do as I say or be punished for defiance."

Gordon lowered his gaze and freed Catriona of her confinement.

"Catriona is of noble English blood," Akira said to the MacLeod elders in a defensive tone. "She has been charged with crimes against Scotland. I believe she has already paid for her crimes and would request she be placed in my command until I am able to find her a husband worthy enough to appease both King James and King Henry. Furthermore, I—"

"I'll have her." Laird Donald spoke up before Akira could finish her sentence.

"Laird Donald, your offer is most gracious, but I must inform ye Catriona is barren and wouldnae be able to provide ye with an heir."

"I have all the heirs I need and then some. My lady wife died last spring, leaving me with three sons already married and four daughters who lack the attentions of a lady. My eldest son recently lost his wife in childbearing. My granddaughter is being fostered in my castle and I'd be most willing to have a lady tend to her rearing until my son finds another wife."

Akira glanced at Catriona to gauge her response to this unexpected proposal. Her gray eyes were sheepish, but the upward tilt of her lips told Akira she might be taking to the offer. Still, Akira questioned, "Ye vow not to share her with another?"

Laird Donald's head cocked back like a rooster. "I wouldnae share my wife. Are ye wowf, woman? I'd sooner cut a mon's hand off for touching her than give her to another."

Akira saw the sparkle in Catriona's eyes and agreed. "'Tis done. Ye will wed before ye take your leave."

Calin closed the meeting, after which the horde of clansmen surged to the high table to celebrate the alliance. Akira took advantage of her husband's entrapment and fled the chamber seeking solitude.

She spent the remainder of the morning in the chapel praying for acceptance, after which she walked the distance to the great oak where she'd spent so many days schooling the children of Clan MacLeod. The sodden ground squashed beneath her brogues as the sun melted all traces of the first snow. The air was damp on her face as she looked out over the loch behind Cànwyck Castle. She'd always loved the beauty that was Scotland. Unfortunately, her love for her country didn't make her any less English.

She had lived the majority of her life being shunned by her kin and wasn't certain if she could continue to live a similar life. Would she start to question every whisper, every glance?

Her worries clung to her like Highland mist. The fact that English blood flowed through her veins would change the way the MacLeod kinfolk treated her. Would they whisper about her in secrecy? Would the womenfolk trust her to continue schooling their children? Could she live the remainder of her days questioning their loyalty?

Drawing a deep breath, she nodded her head, answering her own question. Calin loved her. That was all that truly mattered. His love would make her strong enough to cope with any taunts thrown her way.

The tiny hand tugging at her kirtle startled her out of her musing. When she turned to look behind her, she nearly choked on the lump in her throat. She'd been so enveloped in her thoughts she hadn't heard the children walk up behind her. Five young girls dipped a perfect curtsy in unison, their eyes shining with hope.

"'Tis time for lessons, m'lady?" one of the girls posed the question with her hands piously clasped in front of her.

Before Akira could answer, droves of children rushed, skipped, bobbed their way to her side, bringing the knoll to life. A tiny army of warriors ready to fight in her honor. Her lineage wouldn't matter to the children. They were innocent of political strife.

Only moments later, the MacLeod kinswomen emerged over the knoll accompanied by the MacLeod warriors—warriors with clean-shaven jaws. Akira's eyes widened. Her heart slammed against her chest as each man pressed closer into the assembly surrounding her. They had undoubtedly lost their wits. She could do little more than watch them rub their cheeks and make a show of their smooth skin. She hardly recognized some of the kinsmen. The pale color of their skin contrasted with the bronze and red coloring of their upper faces. What had they been thinking?

Shaking her muddled head, she opened her mouth to ask their intent when the crowd parted down the middle. Andrew walked proud and regal through the isle, wooden sword at his hip and a circlet of yellow flowers held out reverently in front of him. Calin towered behind him.

Unable to ignore Andrew's presence, she bent down and allowed him to crown her with the sweet-smelling flowers. Tears pooled in her eyes while the desire to gain their acceptance caused a painful pressure in her chest.

"M'lady, 'tis of nay import if ye are bluidy English. We love ye." Andrew bent to one knee and bowed his head— a sign of his undying loyalty.

Calin stepped to her side, kissed her forehead, and folded her fingers over his own. He spoke no words. A broad toothy smile lifted his lips and pride radiated from his amber eyes as he studied his kin. If Akira's suspicions were correct, she would say he was as stunned as she, but she wasn't yet prepared to find him innocent of their actions. "Did ye organize this?"

"Nay. I just followed them here. I suspect they fear ye may leave them again."

"Would ye have us deface ourselves, then leave us void of your presence?"

Akira sought out the man who spoke, recognizing Gordon's baritone voice. She had never seen him smile and could do little more than laugh at the sight before her. They cared not a wit if she were English or Irish or the blood of The Beast. "How could I leave such foolish people? Have ye nay sense? To remove the warmth from your face with the winter months ahead of ye."

Calin brushed her cheek with the ridge of his knuckles. "This is your home, m'lady, and these are your loyal kinfolk. Ye must never leave us again."

She returned his smile. "All o' Scotland couldnae keep me from ye."

Epilogue

Life couldn't be more perfect, Akira mused.

Settled against the sturdy oak, Calin encircled his arms around her swollen abdomen. Her back rested against his chest, and a breeze whistled through the leaves above them. Their youngest daughter, Coira, slept peacefully on her belly atop a patchwork quilt close enough for Akira to stroke her short black curls. Two kittens napped at Coira's feet, purring a tune that had lulled her to sleep.

"Have I told ye how happy ye make me?" Calin whispered, his warm breath dusting her cheek.

"Not since this morning when ye loved me into a near swoon," Akira teased and held his hand over her belly where a tiny foot was kicking her rib.

Calin turned her in his arms and raised his one wicked brow. "Mayhap tonight I will be successful." He brushed her lips, not once, but twice with a gentle kiss, and her heart fluttered from the simplicity of his touch. Not a day passed that he didn't kiss her and tell her he loved her.

"Mammie! Mammie!"

The familiar squeal of her eldest daughter, Makendra, broke

the peaceful interlude. Akira tensed and checked Coira for movement, but, as was typical, the child didn't flinch.

Kendrick sauntered up the grassy hillside with Makendra clinging to his back, a small hand wrapped around his neck, while the other cupped a new kitten as white as a January snow. Akira blew air through her nose in a quick puff and shook her head. This would be the third cat Makendra brought home in the past fortnight.

The oak leaves tangled in her daughter's auburn hair told Akira that Kendrick probably just retrieved his niece from another tree. Albeit, she felt no pity for Kendrick's task since he'd been the one to teach Makendra how to climb during his last visit.

Akira fully intended to scold her this time, but the sour pout Makendra wore was sure to get her out of any punishment. Pulling herself into a sitting position, Akira waited for Calin to help her to her feet. As soon as she was grounded, her fists found their perch onto her hips, a natural pose she struck regardless of her mood.

"Ye will not scold her for rescuing that kitten she's so proudly bearing," Calin said while he kneaded the small of her back with his fingertips, easing the ache that had become prevalent in her latter months. She didn't recall the tension being so constant with her first two daughters and hoped the difference meant she might give her husband a son. Mayhap a male bairn would possess Calin's gentler nature. Their daughters seemed to have only acquired Akira's rebellion.

"Then Cànwyck Castle will soon be crawling with four-legged creatures if we dinnae put a stop to her heroics," Akira murmured just as Makendra plopped down from Kendrick's back.

"Mammie, dinnae be mad at Uncle Kendrick. Ginny was stuck in a tree and I had to save her." Makendra sidled up to Calin's leg and presented the kitten. Her blue and green checked kirtle dragged the ground and made Akira worry even more about her daughter's safety.

Not even defending his actions, Kendrick snuck away from the scene and propped himself up against the tree trunk. He lifted a sleeping Coira against his chest, saving himself from Akira's tongue-lashing.

Seeing Kendrick with her bairn made Akira's heart hurt. She wished he would find a wife to bear children of his own. That prayer had not yet been answered.

Calin bent to one knee in front of Makendra and stroked the tiny feline's fur. "Ginny?"

"I named her Saint Genevieve. They are sisters and should have matching names. Maggie, I named after Saint Margaret, and Bonnie is named after Saint Boniface. All named after your saints, Da."

"And how do ye know Ginny is sister to the other two ye brought home?" Akira asked, already forgetting to reprimand her daughter for climbing another tree.

"Because she told me so."

"She? Ye must tell me who *she* is so I can ask her to quit giving ye kittens."

"But she is gone now, Mammie." Makendra frowned at Akira as if to suggest she should already know this information. "She had to go away and left with a man that looked just like ye, Da, except he had hair on his chin."

Akira glanced at Calin who shrugged. Makendra had a vivid imagination and conversed more with her pets than she did the other children.

"What did this woman look like, sweetheart?" Calin asked.

"Just like Mammie."

An odd tingle curled around Akira's spine. No one in the clan looked like her. Foolish thoughts exploded in her head. After giving birth to Makendra, Akira had felt her mother's presence, the same as she had years ago at Brycen Castle.

She'd blamed the illness that burdened her after childbearing, but now her heart ached to believe the woman Makendra spoke of was her mother. "Makendra, did this woman tell ye her name?"

Makendra nodded. "Her name was Lena."

Warm tears fell over Akira's face and Calin was at her side brushing them away before they fell.

Calin patted Makendra's bottom. "Stay out of the trees, or I'll make Andrew follow ye around again. Think ye your cousins would like to meet Ginny?"

Makendra nodded again, her crystal blue eyes sparkling.

"Have Uncle Jaime squeeze her some fresh goat's milk."

Makendra skipped off, and Calin's odd gaze washed over Akira. Before she could resist, he pulled her into the privacy of the herb garden. Finding a secluded tree, he pinned her against its trunk and kissed her thoroughly, a demanding kiss she returned with fervor.

He pulled away too soon and stared down at her. "Do ye believe her?"

"I do." Akira smiled and rubbed his earlobe. "The same as I believe that ye are my soul mate, and when our time has come to leave this world, we will be together in the afterlife."

Calin bent his head to suckle the sensitive flesh just below her ear. "And I will love ye for all eternity, my wee fire-breathing dragon."

Romantic Suspense from
Lisa Jackson